ARBITER

THE SENTINEL TRILOGY BOOK 2

JAMIE FOLEY

Copyright © 2017 Fayette Press

10 Digit ISBN: 0692376615
13 Digit ISBN: 978-0692376614
AISN: B01N5WOSX4

Published in Bastrop, Texas

Printed in the United States of America

To the beautiful and hilarious Arden.
Not even state lines can stop our shenanigans.

TABLE OF CONTENTS

Alani
YEAR 4817

SAI

ARISIA

SONG MAI ★

Zerah ★
Ruins

Lorsann •

Aoka •
Flooded

VALINOR

NEW HAELO
& HAEVYN ★

Eremor •

Altair •

JADENVIVE ★

Ceemalao •
Outpost

★ SANCTUARY OF MAQUA

• Roanoke
Outpost

KATROSI

MALAAN

Darkwood •

Jade Glen •
Ruins

TUUMICHI ★

LAKOTA

ILLYRIA

Ironhide •

TERRUTH

SHAILOH ★

ELYON ★

KIOA

Ithiel •

Aeo Suuvah

Grotto •
Flooded

RANSOM ★

1

ACKNOWLEDGMENTS

I remember sitting in my room as a teenager, telling my young cousin one of my stories no one else would listen to. She stared up at me with the biggest, most beautiful green eyes that glistened with awe as she hinged on my every word.

The story was awful, but she insisted that I write it.

Arden, your encouragement to me as we grew up together was more priceless than you know. I dedicate *Arbiter* to you with oodles of high-pitched tweenage love.

My alpha team is literally the best in the world. Mike, you saved me so many re-writes. Becky, you are my soul sister. And Keanan, I have no idea how you're still sane considering what I put you through.

Thanks so much to my wizard cover designer Kirk DouPonce, my awesome editor Frank Redman, and my eagle-eye proofer Abigayle Claire. To Beth Wiseman for being my partner in crime and Janet Murphy for making her home into our writing retreat. To by lightning-fast beta team, Kimberly, Lizzy, Laurie L., Laurie G., and Janet.

And most of all, thanks to Yahweh, who put the passion for storytelling inside me and bashed me on the head until I did it. He spared my daughter and I from a speeding 18-wheeler when I was writing the original draft of *Arbiter,* which inspired a specific event in the book. Ask me about it sometime. :)

1

Darien gaped at the winged lizard that towered over him. Wings like a bluejay's stretched from the suite's kitchenette to the fireplace, with an eagle-like head bent under the ceiling. Eyes of liquid gold fixed on Darien as if he was a rabbit in an open field.

Darien's heart hammered against his ribs, but he didn't move as he clung to the bedspread beneath him. His sister Tera slept peacefully in her coma beside him, as if a beast hadn't just appeared in the underground floor of the Altair Lynx base with a crack of lightning.

"Don't be afraid." The voice was deep and gritty. The creature rolled its eyes as it retracted its wings into scaled black flanks. "I have something for you."

It's a prank. This is an arbiter vision! The last time Darien had seen a beast like this, it had been in a nightmare created by Jet: a bull standing on its hind legs with vast wings of shifting darkness. Darien had just come from Jet's room—obviously his mentor had stuck some sort of aetherial time bomb in his head.

Darien remembered to breathe. He blinked but the beast was still there, watching him as if impatient. *What on Alani is this thing?* His eyes flicked to the VIP suite's security door. It was closed, just as he'd left it. And this room was underground—no one would hear him if he yelled.

The beast's head twitched like a bird's. "Not the right language?" Its talons clacked on the floor, piercing straight through the carpet. "Last time I was in Valinor, they spoke Arisian—"

"What are you?" Darien croaked.

The blue-striped wings twitched. "Humans don't know archangels when they see them anymore?" Something like a growl escaped the creature's throat. "Name's Rigel. And you're called Darien, right?"

Darien swallowed, but his mouth was dry. "Yes..."

"Good." Rigel curled a long, feathered tail around himself and lied on the floor, bringing his head down to a man's standing height. "I'm here to offer you a feather."

It seems so real. Darien's bones creaked as he forced himself up from the awkward position on the bed. He blinked again, but the so-called angel was still there. "Uh... thanks?"

Rigel's bright eyes narrowed. "Do you have any idea how many humans have killed each other for this since Alani's birth?" He looked Darien up and down. "Oh, are you a child? I heard humans have been getting taller over the past century—"

"I'm not a child!" Darien dared a step forward and gawked at the filaments along the creature's feathers. Jet's vision a few months ago had been much less detailed and much more terrifying. *Angels aren't supposed to look like this!*

"They told me you went to a Serran Academy," Rigel said, "but you don't know what a Serran is?"

Serran? Darien gripped the bedpost as his mind whirled. "I thought they were extinct." *But Jet just said...*

"Rare does not mean extinct." Rigel crossed his massive hands in front of him and yanked a claw out of the carpet with an annoyed jerk. "The enemy is handing out feathers like snowballs in Belmora. The human facet has chosen a few in response."

What language is he speaking? Darien stared at the new tear in the carpet. "Human what?"

Rigel's eyelids drooped. "The human facet of the creator—your demigod. Look, I'm needed at the front. Do you want a feather or not?"

Darien felt like his muscles solidified into lead. "I... well... why would I want a feather?"

"To become a Serran!" Rigel groaned. His eyes drifted to the bed, fixated on Tera's still face, and his molten gaze hardened into amber.

I still don't know what that is... Darien followed Rigel's gaze, but the angel turned back to him and waited.

Darien cleared his throat. "Is there some sort of catch?"

"Naturally. All Serrans created the right way make an oath. Yours would be to care for and protect orphans."

Orphans? But I don't know any. Darien blinked. *Aleah? Would she count since she was adopted?*

"We will be watching. If you don't uphold your oath, I will return and retrieve my feather." Rigel's long neck straightened. "And I'll bring your soul back with me."

Darien's jaw slipped open. His eyes flicked to Rigel's knifelike beak, and he stepped back. *Nope, uh, no thanks...*

He glanced back at Tera. *But I'd protect Aleah anyway if I could. Or any orphans I ran across.*

"Do you accept this oath, boy?" Rigel murmured. "Don't make it lightly."

Darien scratched the back of his neck. "Well, so I get just a feather, or a whole pair of wings, or...?"

Rigel snorted and pushed up on his legs, ducking his head under the ceiling fan. "Look, there's already an experienced Serran in your group. Get him to teach you, OK?"

'Him?' Jet! I bleeding knew it! Darien tilted his head. "You know, for an archangel, you're kind of—"

"What?" Rigel's head twitched to the side, and his eyes gleamed.

"Fine! Fine and good. One feather is great. I'll take it. Assuming that you're real, of course." Darien flashed his brightest grin.

A tuft of feathers raised over Rigel's eye. "The oath is made in blood."

His wings spread out and spanned to either wall in a dazzling pattern of black, blue, and white. A clawed hand reached up near his back and plucked a feather free. Blood smeared the dark scales of Rigel's hand as he offered it to Darien. "Cut your hand."

Darien's pulse skyrocketed. *What am I doing?* He slowly reached into his pocket and withdrew the bone-handled pocket knife that Levi had given him. *Jet must have done this, so...* He took a sharp breath, flipped the blade out, and pressed it into his palm until red appeared. He clenched his teeth. *Jet actually did this, right?*

The floor creaked as Rigel stepped forward. He pressed the bloody quill into Darien's cut, then closed his fist around it with cold fingers. "Get some rest for a few days," Rigel said as he moved back.

OK, slightly gross. Darien stared at the blue feather sticking out from his fist. *Is it going to glow or something?*

"All right, so what do I..."

Darien looked up, but the room was as empty and quiet as a tomb.

2

A white-barked twig cracked under Jet's boot. He took a deep breath of cold, cedar-scented air and adjusted the rifle on his shoulder. A sniper rifle like Victoria weighed a good amount, but a deer carcass would have weighed more. *Hopefully Garrett scored something.*

The bright forest parted to reveal a walled city in the mountains and a dead city in the valley below. Altair was hardly recognizable against Jet's memories—the sounds of bustling traffic, the tang of pollution, and Brazen Tower were long gone.

Jet tromped through a thin layer of snow, angling for the closed ancient gate in the wall that had been wide open for the roadway for decades, now closed against wolves and bandits. A guard post of scraggly cedar wood popped up behind it, and a man's figure hunched in the thin window slit. Jet recognized his former unit lead thanks to the black beard and bulk barely contained within a furry winter coat. Diamondback waved and disappeared from view.

The gates whined open as Jet approached. "Thanks, brother," he called.

Diamondback's ice-blue eyes flicked between Jet's shoulders and hands. "No grub, rookie?"

Jet contained a grimace. "Didn't see anything but birds and squirrels. Think the big game might be lying low after that snow last night. Guess winter's coming early."

Diamondback pursed his lips, then grabbed Jet's arm as he passed. "Hey," he whispered, pulling Jet close. "How much longer 'til you can get your people out of the base?"

Jet's breakfast soured in his stomach. "Are the Lynx coming?"

"Haven't heard anything over comms, but you can bet they'll send a team to investigate." Diamondback glanced through the gate, down the abandoned road littered with building debris and snow. "And soon."

Jet summoned his aether and focused it on Diamondback's mind. As a former Lynx—*hopefully* former—Diamondback was on Jet's watch list, even though he'd trust him with his life in a firefight.

But without any mental shields, Diamondback's feelings of unease and genuine concern were as visible to Jet as the distant mountain peaks.

"I haven't heard of any other civilized city left in Valinor besides Haevyn," Jet murmured. "I don't know how less than a dozen people could make it solo in a Valinorian winter with no survival skills."

"Haevyn's crawling with Lynx, and so is Roanoke. I don't know of another city, but trust me that we don't want to be here when—"

A spike of pain itched through Jet's lungs. He coughed into his hand, and his glove came away with a splotch of blood.

Syn.

Diamondback caught a glimpse before Jet could wipe the stain on his pants. A deep frown shifted his beard. "Still dealing with that, brother?"

Jet pulled his coat tighter around his neck. "I'm fine." He swallowed and checked his watch. "I'll talk with Levi about bugging out."

"I already did," Diamondback said. "You should see your sister for that cough. Can she heal it?"

"I got it." Jet pushed past him and marched down the main road.

It's getting harder to hide. Jet cursed, sending out a cloud of warm breath that a frigid gale snatched away. Diamondback was one of the few who knew about the illness, but he still thought it had been caused by breathing in dust at the collapse of Brazen Tower.

If only that were the case.

Snow-speckled grass spread out in a perfect square in the middle of Altair's governmental plaza, framing the memorial for Brazen Tower. Shining silver twisted up from the ground in a double helix, reflected in a placid shallow pool before it. Somewhere inside, a plaque praised the men of Viper Unit, who claimed revenge for the innocents murdered in the attack some six years ago.

Jet's true name was the only one stated publicly, instead of his call sign—a nurse had leaked it to the press. It made him a national hero. An unemployed hero.

Jet glared at the memorial and took a sharp left. *If I'd have known then that I'd be discharged, I wouldn't have let Sorva go.*

His heart twisted. Sorvashti's week-old bullet wound kept her in a mood more sour than his stepmother's attempt at growing grapes. Or maybe it was Aleah's order to remain bedridden for another day.

Or maybe it was because they'd finally told Sorvashti that her husband was dead.

Familiar guilt weighed Jet down. He shrugged it off and pushed through the main door of the Lynx base, whose pockmarked columns declared last week's victory.

The entry and living room put most hotels to shame with plush couches, a fireplace fit for a king, and a TV screen that took up half the wall. Master Eleanor Willow smiled and winked at Jet from the open kitchen's granite bar, where a line of covered bowls and platters smelled like spicy tomato sauce. He waved and ducked into the living quarters before she could ask how the hunting had been.

Maybe I should bring Sorva some lunch. Jet shut the door to his bedroom and leaned Victoria into a corner. *If I could get Master Ellie to make Sorva some bulgogi, her cold shoulder would probably melt.*

Jet rubbed his eyes and glanced in the mirror on the way to the shower. Mud from melted snow smeared his pale skin in the most unexpected places, including a patch of straight black hair that threatened his line of vision. He grumbled and tugged at it. *If the water's any colder because of the snow, we'd better up the ration from those generators. I'll siphon gas from a thousand cars if that's what it takes.*

A knock pounded on the door.

Jet glanced at the shower and considered yanking his clothes off and not answering. He sighed and yelled, "Yeah?"

"Um, hey... can I talk to you for a minute?"

Darien? Jet sighed, crossed back into the bedroom, and opened the door.

There stood his master-assigned disciple, complete with cowlicked brown hair and blue eyes just a tad too bright. But the hue of Darien's tan skin was somehow off, and he dripped sweat as if it was an Illyrian summer day.

Jet frowned. "What's—"

Darien pushed inside and shut the door behind him. He glanced around the room, then focused on Jet with a serious expression. "You're a Serran, right?"

Jet slipped back a step and studied Darien for a moment. "We already had this discussion—"

"No." Darien grabbed Jet's arm. "You have to teach me how to be one."

Darien turned his hand over, revealing a bandage on his palm and a brilliant blue, white, and black feather with crusted blood on the quill. "Please."

Don't tell me... Jet stared at the feather. *There aren't any local birds with that coloring. And it's huge. Not as big as mine, but...*

He focused his energy around the quill. Remnants of aether clung to the filaments, but it wasn't Darien's signature. It flickered bright and pure—too bright to be human.

Jet cursed and reached a hand out to Darien's forehead. He might as well have touched a pan straight out of the oven.

"What was its name?" Jet murmured.

Darien blinked a little too slowly. "What?"

"The demon. What was its name?"

"I… It wasn't a demon." Darien pulled away from Jet's hand. "It was an angel named Rigel."

The archangel? The chief commander of the creator's forces in eastern kai'lani? A laugh burst from Jet. "It lied to you. Break the quill and the bond will be severed. You're more infected than a swamp wound."

Darien stared at him. His eyes glazed. "So you *are* a Serran."

Jet sighed and glanced at the door. "Your perceptive skills are dazzling. Sit down before you fall over."

Darien flopped down on the floor and wiped his forehead with the back of his hand. "The wing I saw when Robinson shot me… it was yours. But where'd it go? And how'd it block a bullet?"

He's even dumber than normal right now—it'd probably be pointless to explain. Jet folded his arms. "Serran form isn't permanent. It can be summoned by placing your aether into the angel's feather, and you revert back when your energy dissipates or you remove it."

Jet watched Darien's chest expand and contract—he was almost panting. "But it looks like you're mid-transformation, so you wouldn't be able to do it for another day or so." He held his hand out. "Give me the feather. Bonding with a demon wasn't your brightest idea."

"No!" Darien pulled the feather close. "It's not a demon 'cause it made me swear to protect orphans. Does that sound like a demon thing to you?"

Jet's eyes widened. *Seriously?* His own oath was similar: to care for widows. But he hadn't paid much heed because he didn't know any—

His heart hiccupped. *Sorva!*

Darien swayed to the side and caught himself. "I dreamed that you were a panda bear. But you were still mean."

"All right." Jet grabbed Darien's arm and hauled him up. "Time to find Aleah."

3

Jet hauled Darien past the long painting of the Malaano jungle, which now featured a bullet hole in the clouds. The hall's rug folded underfoot as Darien dragged his feet and mumbled something. He smelled like he'd sweat in his sleep and hadn't showered that morning.

The door to the medical clinic hung open, revealing a small room with whitewashed cabinets, earth-tone walls, and metal beds bearing thin mattresses. Harsh lights accentuated a woman's figure on one of the beds, curled up under thin sheets.

"Darien!" Aleah shut off the faucet at a small sink and dried her hands. "What's wrong?"

Jet adjusted Darien's arm over his shoulder and led him to an empty bed. "Fever." He glanced at the other woman across the room. Short blond hair fell against the pillow, and pale ink tattoos on her dark skin peeked out from under the covers.

Does Sorva know about Serrans? Jet lowered Darien onto the bed, whose sterile paper crackled under his weight. *Probably not… she's got enough to worry about right now.*

Jet gathered his energy and sent a thought to Aleah: *You're not the rookie Serran anymore.*

Aleah's face brightened. "Oh." Her mental response was nothing but a bundle of glee, but she kept her face straight and put a hand to Darien's forehead. "What else do you feel?"

Darien's red face flushed an even deeper shade. "Uh… I'm fine. Just my ribs hurt a little bit. And my whole chest. And, you know, all of my bones."

"I see." Aleah pulled her hand back and wiped it on her blouse.

Don't say anything about angels or feathers or Serrans, Jet thought to Darien. *Aleah is one, but there were only three of us before you. Keep it on the down-low, understand?*

Darien's head lolled toward Jet. *Why you guys so sneaky?* His thought-voice was slurred and barely audible. *We're all from Jade Glen here—*

No. Students were never told about modern Serrans to keep them from leaking anything to the public. And Altairans each have their own high-caliber pitchfork now. So don't say anything about Serrans to anyone but me, Raydon, or Aleah, got it?

Raydon? Darien squinted into the lights and squeezed his eyes shut. *Mkay. But who even… knows that guy? He's like a… gray blob.*

Jet smirked. *We've been flying together for a couple of months. He's pretty good.*

"By the hearth, you should have come in earlier!" Aleah frowned at her watch and pulled her hand from Darien's wrist. "Jet, get him some water, please."

Jet crossed to the counter and opened one cabinet after the other. *The archangel Rigel… really? How did Darien get chosen?* He found a stack of paper cups and grabbed one. *Wonder if Rigel is half as intense as Kohesh.*

He glanced at Sorvashti as he turned on the faucet. He'd assumed that she was asleep, but her eyes were open. If she glared at the wall any harder, it would catch fire.

Jet handed the water to Darien as Aleah popped a thermometer in his ear. *How's Sorva doing?* Jet asked.

Physically? I just changed her bandage—she's healing well. Aleah turned the thermometer and ignored Darien's protest about poking his brain. *Mentally? I think she wants to murder me for putting her on bedrest for an extra day. Emotionally?* She gave Jet a sidelong glance. *About as good as can be expected.*

Sympathy knotted in Jet's chest. He watched Sorvashti's shoulder rise and fall and marveled at how her aura was so contained. She appeared serene, but if his memories of her from six years ago were still accurate, she was as angry as a trace cat.

She needs time—lots of time. Just leave her be.

Jet turned to leave, but his feet wouldn't move. *My Serran oath... Am I still bound to care for widows since I died?*

A recollection of his bonded angel coalesced from shadows in his mind. *She wouldn't kill me. No, she absolutely would. She'd do it with a smile.*

Jet looked over his shoulder. As terrifying as the thought of talking to Sorvashti was right now, something still pulled him toward her, even after all this time. The illness had depleted him into a thinner, paler version of himself, but Sorvashti was somehow even more beautiful than the memories he'd tried to forget.

OK, just... try to be nice. Just let her know you're here for her.

Jet forced one foot in front of the other until he was at Sorvashti's bedside.

"Hey, Sorva. How're you feeling?"

She didn't move. "Good."

Warning signals flared to life, but Jet held firm. "Can I get you anything?"

Sorvashti said nothing.

Leave her alone or she'll bite your head off! Temptation beckoned to Jet from the door. *Just one more try. You haven't told her you're sorry about Noruntalus.*

Jet cleared his throat and whispered, "Listen, I... I'm really sorry—"

"No."

Jet snapped his mouth shut, but Sorvashti didn't say anything else.

"OK, just know that I'm here for you." Jet put a gentle hand on her shoulder. "If there's anything—"

Sorvashti jerked away and whipped her head around to face him. Eyes like a lioness' seared to his core.

"Thank you," she said through gritted teeth, "but to see you brings much pain now."

Jet grimaced and stepped back. *Of course, you idiot! Why would she want to see an ex-boyfriend after her husband just died? Does she think I'm trying to…?*

He took another step back and dipped his head. "Sorry." He bolted for the door.

Pain cracked through his lungs and forced him to cough. He got his hand up in time to speckle it with blood.

"Hey." Aleah's green gaze held an authoritative glint. *Go to your room. I'll be there in five minutes.*

4

Aleah's fingers prickled against the skin of Jet's back. *It's even worse than usual.*

She siphoned jade aether from her hands to her eyes and squinted. Skin, muscle, and bone seemed to fade, connecting her with the ragged tissue inside her brother's lungs. Her energy glowed against the damaged spots, highlighting them in her vision like dozens of pinpricks across his back.

Aleah frowned and sent wisps of energy lashing across the worst patches. "You should have come to me earlier! I told you it's getting worse over time. And you won't stop running around like—"

"Yeah, yeah." Jet didn't move, but the muscles in his shoulders were as tense as violin strings. He sat in the chair at his plain desk as if she'd tied him there.

He relies on me too much! Aleah clenched her jaw and refocused on healing. *If only we knew what this really was. If it actually was an autoimmune disease, I could probably treat him to a ripe old age, and he could run around playing hero to his heart's content. But this…*

She let out a breath and pulled one hand back. Jet's skin wasn't cold like normal—he steamed like an ember in the snow. His anger was always obvious to everyone, but Aleah could tell that this time was different. Righteous anger fed him strength, but this was volatile. His aether writhed and raged like a wounded beast.

Aleah lowered her voice. "Don't let it bother you. She's been like that to everyone."

"I'm not everyone."

Aleah pursed her lips. *Well what are you, exactly?*

Jet spoke so highly of Sorvashti some six years ago, even after they'd parted. He'd said their break-up was a mutual decision without a burned bridge. Sorvashti was always either at home in LaKota or at art school in Kioa, but the Royal Guard sent Jet all over the world to undisclosed locations for random periods of time.

But when Jet was honorably discharged and returned home, he wasn't the same big brother Aleah got to know over the video calls and breaks between missions. He hated being at home, and he couldn't hold a job. He dated other women—that blonde from the Royal Guard, then the sous chef, and the CIO at Krio Incorporated. But he brushed them all aside, and Aleah had watched the years curdle him into something sour.

"You'd think she'd be a little more…" Jet growled. "After I…"

After you were actually nice to someone other than Mom or me for once? she thought to herself. "You should have heard what she said when I gave her bed rest for a week." Aleah slipped a hand into her pocket and withdrew a small chocolate candy. "She lost everything over the past few months. She doesn't have her family here like we do. Imagine what that must feel like."

"That's why I was trying to be there for her. See if I'll try that again."

Aleah released her aether and tapped into a different power—one that churned in her blood, dark and raw. The Phoera element responded eagerly to her call and warped light around her hand, cloaking it with flawless invisibility.

"Of course you will," Aleah said as she dipped two fingers into Jet's thigh pocket and withdrew his pocketknife. She flipped the chocolate from her palm and left it in the knife's place. "You're still in love with her after six years."

"What?" Jet scoffed and glared over his shoulder. "Wow, I'd actually forgotten that you're a teenage girl for a minute."

Aleah grinned and dropped his knife into her pocket. "So you deny it?"

"Don't mess with me right now." Jet stared at a nail-sized hole in the wall, where he'd torn down some Lynx decoration he didn't want in his bedroom. "You're not one to talk with your not-so-secret boyfriend."

Aleah choked on her own breath. "I—what? I don't have a boyfriend!"

Jet chuckled. "You're so stealthy in every other area, but you act like a schoolgirl around Raydon."

Aleah's pulse thudded into a panicked sprint. "I… I don't…" *By the hearth! How did he find out? How long has he known?*

She stepped back and covered her face. "I kept my shields so strong—"

"I'm your brother, remember?"

Heat flushed Aleah's face at his slick tone of voice. She glanced at the dresser on the opposite side of the room, where she knew he had a pistol stashed. "Does that mean… you're OK with it?" she whispered.

"It's none of my business. It's clear who you really like, anyway."

Aleah snapped her gaze back to Jet's face. He raised a black brow over a humored eye. "But forget about Darien, all right? He might be a year older than you, but he's got the maturity of an eight-year-old."

Shock skittered through Aleah's veins and left her frozen. "I do *not* like him!"

Jet smirked. "Mm-hmm."

No, I really don't! And how does he know, anyway? "Are you suggesting that I'm cheating? Because I would never—"

"No, you're just looking." Jet's dark eyes narrowed. "Right?"

Aleah took a step back and nearly tripped. *Worst nightmare!* "Jet, please! I'm not that serious with Raydon. And Darien's just cute—"

Jet grimaced and held up a hand. "I don't want to know. Just tell me if they try anything. Raydon shouldn't."

Aleah grabbed Jet's arm. "What did you do?"

Jet's smirk returned. "I punished him for trying to keep it a secret from me."

Aleah slammed a fist into his back. "It was my idea! I told him to stay quiet because I didn't want you and Dad murdering him!"

Jet dodged her next strike and slid out of the chair. "He takes responsibility as the man in the relationship."

Aleah's mouth fell open. "That's even more sexist than usual!"

Jet chuckled and strode to a plain dresser under the window. "Of course you're equally guilty, but explain to me how a man taking responsibility is a bad thing." He pulled a white shirt from the perfectly-folded stack in the top drawer.

Unbelievable. Aleah pursed her lips. "I don't know how any woman could ever favor you."

"So well-spoken for a thief." Jet slipped the shirt on and held out a hand toward her. "My knife?"

Aleah sighed. She slipped the pocketknife out and tossed it to him. "I'm sorry; I shouldn't have said that. Maybe Sorvashti would tolerate you since she comes from a traditional culture."

Jet grimaced as he replaced his knife and withdrew the chocolate. "You're going to stop stealing from me whenever you run out of chocolate, right?"

"Oh, don't worry—dark chocolate takes forever to expire." Aleah forced a smile and patted the back of the desk chair.

The candy wrapper crinkled as Jet popped the chocolate in his mouth. He strode forward and kissed her on the forehead. "Be good." He angled toward the door.

"Wait, I'm not done healing you!"

Jet opened the door and paused. "Master Emberhawk."

Aleah bit her lip. *Did he hear me? He must have... but he already knows about Jet's illness, right?*

Jet straightened. "What can I do for you?"

"I'm actually lookin' for Aleah." Levi's signature twang confirmed his presence before his ragged silver-haired head peeked through the doorframe.

Jet raised a welcoming arm and sidestepped to let Levi through.

Aleah glared after her brother as he disappeared down the hall. *He won't last three days if I don't finish. I'll nab him tonight or tomorrow.*

She put on a smile for Levi and bowed. "Master."

"I've got something..." Levi murmured as he glanced back through the open door, "sensitive to talk to you about."

Aleah folded her hands in front of her. "Yes, sir?"

Levi looked from the door to Jet's bathroom to the closet to the sniper rifle leaned into the corner. "You're the only human here with elemental abilities. And your specialty's invisibility, yeah?"

Aleah blinked in surprise. She'd almost forgotten that the Serran Grand Master Council had known that—they'd known everything about everyone. For decades, secrets and blackmail had afforded the Serran Academies their freedom from world governments and prying eyes.

At least, that's what Jet had told her.

Aleah lowered her voice. "You could say that."

"I bet I could." Levi's eyes narrowed. "Can you make objects invisible, too? Or is it just yourself?"

She swallowed and glanced at the door. "I can bend light around moderately-sized objects, but it takes concentration. It's easiest with something I'm holding or something very close to me."

"Good," Levi said. "I need your help smuggling supplies out of the city."

5

Zekk squeezed his eyes shut against the sun's onslaught. A pair of pants crumpled against the curtains, holding them open for a sliver of light from a distant skyscraper.

He groaned and flopped to his other side, then jerked back. Some frazzle-haired girl lay drooling all over his satin bedsheets.

Great. Zekk's head throbbed as he blinked at the glowing blue numbers on the vaulted ceiling. *Well, I didn't have anything to do today, anyway.*

The door flew open and his burly right-hand man, Wul, burst through. The girl beside Zekk jerked awake and frantically pulled the sheets around her.

"Get up!" Wul's glare flicked from Zekk to the girl and back again. "Whitlocke just landed."

The girl fell out of bed with a cry of alarm.

"Oh," Zekk said through a yawn. "I'll see you around, OK, Tiff?"

She paused in mid-scramble. "It's Tina!"

Zekk sat up, smirked, and shrugged. "Maybe not, then."

She snorted, grabbed a pile of laundry, and ran out of the room.

"Unbelievable," Wul muttered. "It's almost noon. I told you he was coming in today!"

"Did you?" Zekk stood and stretched high and wide. "Am I meeting him for lunch or something?"

Wul's eyes darkened under thick brows. "No. He's coming here, and he'll be here any second."

"*What?*" Zekk tripped over his pants and yanked them up as he hopped to the closet. "What's he doing here? Why didn't you tell me?" His mind struggled up to speed. *Syn, the kitchen and living room must be a mess!*

"I had the maid start early today, and Chef has some carbs and electrolytes ready." Wul crossed his arms. "If you'd invited me, this wouldn't be half as bad."

Zekk slipped a shirt on and stuffed his silver handgun in its concealed holster. He bit back a curse at Wul. *Fine, but you don't have to be so smug about it.*

Someone pounded on the exterior door. Wul moved to open it, and Zekk dashed out of his room and slammed its door behind him. He glanced over the three leather couches, the muted projector display, and the kitchen's open marble countertops—all pristine and devoid of last night's bottle collection. The maid stood like a mannequin in the corner, her head bowed.

Zekk tried to pull the wrinkles out of his shirt. *She gets a day off!*

Wul opened the door and bowed his head. "Colonel."

Alon Whitlocke strode into the room with a stern expression on that world-famous handsome mug—handsome enough to be Zekk's father, if he was a tad older. A black flight jacket matched the uniforms of the two bodyguards who followed him in.

Zekk straightened and saluted. "Welcome back to Maqua, sir."

Alon's expression melted. "Aw, that's cold!" He grabbed Zekk in a hug and slapped him on the back.

Zekk released a sigh. "Been too long." He pulled back and inspected

Alon's hairline, which now housed a faint scar instead of the massive bandage from last week. "Feeling OK?"

"Naturally," Alon said with a sly smile. "Apparently the people have taken to calling me 'The Phoenix.'"

Zekk chuckled. "Not dumb or cliché at all."

Alon frowned. "I like it better than 'The Guardian of Civilization' or 'The Peacekeeper.' And this way, you could get a cool title, too— like Talon of the Phoenix. Or Wing, like a wing man? Or would you rather be a beak?"

Zekk rolled his eyes. "I'll keep 'Confidant,' thanks."

"Well then, my fiery feathered Confidant," Alon clapped Zekk's shoulder and turned to the couches, "I've got a mission for you. Did you hear about Altair?"

Zekk slid down into the leather and glanced at Wul. "Just a rumor."

"Somebody busted in and took my most valuable prisoner." Alon held an open hand up over his shoulder. "They say it was raiders, but the data was botched. They lost the video, the reports, everything."

A bodyguard dropped a file folder into Alon's open hand. It slapped onto the coffee table as Alon continued. "The prisoner was Teravyn Aetherswift's kid brother. And now I hear a report about three 'angels' who fly off the cliffs south of Altair every other day." Alon spread the papers with colorful text, photos, and maps across the glass. "But there shouldn't be any Serrans that far south of New Haelo."

"Three wild Serrans?" Zekk stared at one map and noted how small the walled section of Altair was compared to the grayed-out boundary representing the city pre-meteor storm. The next map—blueprints of the standard Lynx base layout—noted issues with elevation and maneuvering materials into the construction site. "You think the attack and the wilders are connected?"

"That's what I need you to find out," Alon said. "Bring the Serrans in and check out the base while you're there. The new guy in command is a former Valinorian special forces unit lead known as Diamondback. After the attack, he took on a war hero who wasn't originally with us. Made the locals happy and replaced our losses from the attack, but…"

Alon turned to a paper clipped stack and handed it to Zekk. A photo of a twenty-something young man stared back at him with sharp black eyes and hair, light skin, and a cut jaw. Zekk flipped past the restricted warnings on the title page and read:

VALINORIAN ROYAL GUARD
SPEC OPS UNIT 14 "VIPER"
NAME: JET VALINOR
DESIGNATION: "KING"
RANK: LIEUTENANT

Zekk flipped through the pages—most of which were blacked-out lines. He whistled. "He's one of ours, right?"

"Good question." Alon flicked the paper at the bottom of the stack.

Zekk turned to the last page. The text listed Jet's birthplace, his known family, every previous address, and every school he'd attended. Under middle school and high school was listed: Haevyn Serran Academy.

Zekk scratched his chin. "So you want me to vet him?"

"I want someone I can trust to go in there and make sure everything's all clear. Find out anything you can about where the Aetherswift kid went, and whoever broke him out."

Zekk studied Alon's face. *Ever since the angel healed him, he's done nothing but hunt Teravyn. Why isn't he going himself?*

He cleared his throat. "So I guess this is over the head of the champion in New Haelo."

"Far over." Alon clasped a hand on the back of Zekk's neck. "You are the only person I trust with this, Confidant. I'd go myself, but I just got a promising lead on the location of the Terruth elemental stone."

"Ah." Zekk looked back down at the papers. *It's probably a dead end. But bringing in three wild Serrans would score me some credits. Not that I need any... but I've been getting bored, anyway.*

He glanced at Wul. "Up for another hunt, bloodhound?"

Wul stood as stiff as Alon's bodyguards. "Yes, sir."

Zekk grinned and dipped his head to Alon. "I'm at your service, Phoenix. I'll assemble my team and head out before nightfall."

*N**o!***

Darien jerked up in bed, sweating and panting. *Wait, where…?*

Aleah and Sorvashti stared at him from across the medical suite.

Just a nightmare. I didn't kill anyone else. Noruntalus was a bad guy. Darien swallowed and sank back down. "Hey… there." He glanced at the clock on the wall. "Um, has Tera happened to wake up yet?"

Sorvashti pushed past Aleah and stormed out of the room.

"Wait!" Aleah stuck her head through the door and yelled, "Check back with me tonight, OK?" She turned back to Darien and closed the door behind her. "Teravyn was still asleep when I checked a couple hours ago."

Darien's heart fell. *Right.*

He took a deep breath and swung his legs over the side of the bed. His muscles felt like he'd run a marathon without training. "Sorry, I didn't mean to interrupt."

"It's fine." Aleah sighed and moved to the thin cabinets over the sink. "How are you feeling?"

"Good," Darien said. Wrinkled sheets hung from Sorvashti's bed. "I don't think she looked at me once that entire time."

"She's… going through a hard time." Aleah pulled a thermometer from the cabinet and slipped a plastic cap on the end.

"Aren't we all?" Darien mumbled. "She never used to be like that."

"She's in a lot of pain." Aleah stuck the thermometer in his ear. "Still having chills?"

"No. If she's in pain, why'd you let her off bed rest?"

Aleah grimaced. "No, she… she lost someone last week."

Darien frowned at the heart rate monitor in the corner. *Did she know Tamara? Or Martin or Cahir?*

The thermometer slipped out of his ear. "Your fever has broken!" Aleah said. "Excellent."

Noruntalus looked like he was from LaKota or Terruth, too… His gut twisted at the thought of the wayward sage. "Was it… Noruntalus?"

Aleah's eyes went wide. "Hey, let's do your first flight training today!"

Darien watched her scurry back to the cabinets. "Huh? Really?"

"If you feel fine, you're all good to go." Aleah cleaned the counter with dizzying speed. "By the hearth, I need to get out of this room. Don't you?"

Darien slid off the bed and breathed in relief when his legs didn't collapse into a gelatinous heap under him like they'd threatened the day before. "Yeah, but didn't you say you needed to do something with Jet tonight?"

"Um, yes. But… I can postpone that until tomorrow." Aleah's childlike smile lit up the room. "Jet loves to get out of the city to go flying, anyway. You don't want to?"

"No, I do—definitely." Darien stretched, keeping his face straight through the aching tension between his ribs. "But what about dinner?"

"I'll pack something up for us." Aleah dashed to the door and threw it open. "The cliffs are a long hike away."

⸻

The mountain air was far too thin for Darien's lungs. He huffed up the trail behind Raydon and wished for the third time that he'd brought a jacket. The wind howled through the cedars as if yelling at him to stop tromping on their ground.

Surely we're far enough from Altair by now. Darien grabbed a piece of slate jutting from under a berry bush and hauled himself up.

Jet chuckled from somewhere along the trail ahead. Darien looked up to see him wiggle his eyebrows at Aleah, who slapped him.

Seems like they've made this hike more than once. Darien skipped a step to catch up with Raydon, who huddled in his coat as if it was ten below. "So, uh… how long have you been a Serran?"

Raydon glanced at Darien and his olive face relaxed. "About a year, I think." He smiled. "Don't worry. Being a Serran can be really profitable."

Darien batted an evergreen branch from his path. "Profitable?"

"Oh, sorry—I think I meant 'useful,'" Raydon said. "Guess I've still got a few kinks with the language to work out."

His accent is hardly noticeable. "Are you Phoeran?"

"Yeah, I grew up in Kioa. That's why I worked for the Lynx as a technical engineer when I was young and stupid enough to not know any better—they originally started in Ransom. They were more like an independent military-for-hire than dominate-the-world overlords at that point." Raydon watched his footing as the path intertwined with tree roots. "But still didn't feel right, so I got out of there as fast as I could. I've lived in a lot of places. Guess we're pretty much stuck in Valinor now, huh?"

"Yeah." Darien tried not to show his discomfort. *I keep forgetting he's former Lynx...* He looked down at the snow-muddied earth. *Calm down; it's a good thing. He hacked the door to the Lynx base for us. Without him, we never could have taken it. And we'd probably all be dead or in prison right now.*

"Oh, hey, by the way," Raydon said. "I know this is odd, but I've been doing some research on the biology of Serrans since we moved into the Lynx base. They've got some nice equipment underground." He fished around in his coat and withdrew a small silver box with a screen and buttons on the side. "Would you mind giving a blood sample?"

That's right—he's the nerdy type. Darien eyed the device. "Needles and I don't exactly get along."

"No needles involved. It's just a prick on the finger." Raydon held up his index finger to show a tiny scab distorting his fingerprint. "But no pressure, of course. We've just noticed a few changes that Aleah and I have been curious about. She doesn't have to wear glasses anymore, for example."

"Oh, really? Cool—that's fine. Here." Darien stopped and held out his hand, and Raydon turned around with the device.

Darien decided to watch Aleah instead—the wind tossed her hair around in silver waves. *Oh yeah, she did used to wear glasses. I kinda miss them.* He winced as something bit his finger.

"Thanks." Raydon withdrew the device, squinted at the screen, and stuffed it in his pocket. "I'll let you know if I find anything interesting."

"'Kay." Darien jogged to catch up with Jet. "Hey! Are we hiking back to Katrosi?"

Jet glanced over his shoulder. "Gotta go out far enough that no one from Altair can see us."

The wind snatched Darien's clouds of breath away as he panted. "I haven't even seen any animals for half an hour!"

"That's because everyone keeps running their mouths." Jet adjusted the pack on his back, letting loose scents of spicy tomato sauce and garlic.

Mr. Sunshine, as usual. Darien jumped over a patch of snow and came alongside him. "Well while we're at it, would you finally tell me how you stopped that bullet from Robinson that should've killed me?"

"Hold up a sec!" Aleah called from Jet's other side. "We should explain the different types of feathers first, because they each have a different ability. There are two kinds of archangels—"

"Three," Jet interrupted.

Aleah blinked at him. "Really?"

Jet ducked under an aspen branch. "I saw a third type in kai'lani. But I haven't seen a Serran of that kind, so never mind."

Kai'lani... that's the spirit realm, right? Apparently Jet visited the spiritual realm when he'd died—until Tera found some way to revive him... which put her in an ethereal coma.

Darien looked down at his feet. *Does he even know what she did for him?*

"Well, we don't know what kind he has," Raydon said behind them. "Darien, may I see your feather?"

"Uh, sure." Darien pulled at Tera's leather necklace, whose carved claw jittered up his shirt. He'd fastened Rigel's feather behind the charm after noticing how Jet had affixed his feather to his dog tags.

Raydon took it with careful hands. "Hmmm... I believe you're a shimmerwing like Aleah. Jet, can I see yours?"

Shimmerwhat? Darien grimaced. *Will I be a butterfly?*

Jet handed his necklace over, and Raydon paused to compare the two feathers side-by-side. Jet's looked dull next to Darien's vibrant bluejay pattern: it was pure black with a white tip.

"Look here—it's thicker to provide more lift." Raydon tapped the quill of Jet's feather. "The ironfeather is designed for soaring long distances, whereas yours has a slimmer cut. Shimmerwings have superior speed and agility. Like the difference between a falcon and a vulture."

"'Ironfeather,'" Darien mused as Raydon returned Rigel's feather. "So is it bulletproof, too?"

"Not now. If you break it, I'll kill you." Jet snatched his feather back.

"Ah, the wind is perfect!" Aleah said.

Darien looked up to see her prance through the treeline ahead, where icy light marked the forest's boundary. He swallowed and stepped out from the cover of the trees. The slate came to an abrupt stop and plummeted to the placid ocean beyond.

The wind blasted in a sudden gale, sending the aspens' jade leaves to dancing. Darien crouched and tore his gaze away from the cliff's edge. *OK, when they said 'cliff,' they really weren't kidding.*

"Are you guys hungry?" Aleah pulled the pack from Jet's back and set it on a smooth stretch of stone.

"Let's see what he's got first," Raydon said. All eyes turned to Darien.

Right now? He took a step back. *Uh, all right. Jet said I could summon wings by putting aether into the feather. Right?*

Rigel's feather tried to escape on the wind. Darien grabbed it and cleared his throat. "How about an example first?"

"Sure!" Aleah shouldered out of her jacket and backed away from the group. "Watch out—it'll be bright."

Darien should have listened. He blinked through the glowing smear in his vision to find another version of Aleah standing at the cliff's edge. Wings of pure white extended ten feet in either direction before she pulled them in from the wind. They attached to her back with thick muscle just above her hips. Her eyes glowed the same jade color he imagined her aether was, wisping out like eyelashes of pure energy.

And her chest was bigger, throwing off her proportions in a way he didn't mind.

No lingering, Jet's voice growled through his mind.

Darien snapped his gaze to the joints in Aleah's wings. *What? I wasn't—*

"What do you think?" Aleah grinned and twirled like a three-year-old in a tutu.

"Beautiful," Darien said, then choked on his own voice. "I mean, the wings. Well, not that you're not—I mean..."

Jet smacked him on the back of the head.

Syn! Darien cowered and looked to Raydon, whose goofy smile seemed only amused.

"Be nice!" Aleah aimed laser eyes at Jet. "Thank you. I want to find more feathers of a similar color to camouflage my Serran feather in my hair. But white is so hard to match with anything." She stumbled a step through a burst of wind, then pulled her wings tight enough around herself as if to replace her coat. "Jet, show him yours!"

Jet frowned. "I'm here to teach him, not to model in a fashion show—"

"Oh, come on! Guys and girls look different in Serran form."

"No, they don't."

"Actually, they do," Raydon said. "I suspect it's because of the difference in our centers of gravity."

Jet rolled his eyes and stepped out from the tree line. A flash of light later, he stood with a pair of massive black wings with white on the edges. Violet energy floated from his bored stare.

His chest is bigger, too… weird. Darien followed the joints to where they connected just below Jet's shoulders.

Raydon hugged his coat tighter around himself in a rustle of fabric. "Why don't you let him feel?"

"No!" Aleah said.

Jet smirked. "Sure." One black wing unfolded and splayed itself before Darien in a wide arc.

Something about Jet's expression sent up a red flag in Darien's mind. He took a step back. "I know what a feather feels like, thanks."

"Not an ironfeather," Jet said.

I'm gonna regret this. Darien cautiously reached a hand out. The instant he touched a stark white feather, its filaments cut through his skin like a dagger through paper. He yanked his hand back and hissed.

"Jet!" Aleah yelled. "You could have cut his fingers off!"

"You asked how I saved your life last week." Jet pulled his wings back and folded them, nearly doubling his height. "You're welcome."

Darien inspected the small slice on his finger and sucked on it. "How do you fly without dicing yourself up?"

"You only gain the ability of your archangel when you place aether into the entire wing," Jet said. "Takes a ton of energy. You only use it when you need it."

And here I thought his special ability was being a grinch. "So you just happened to know the exact moment that Robinson would shoot me?"

"Teravyn sent a thought to me before she arrived," Jet murmured, and Darien barely heard him over the wind. "I guess she foresaw it."

Something clamped over Darien's heart. "She knew you were a Serran?"

Jet shook his head. "I don't know how she knew." He shifted on the cliff's edge. "I assume it's a sage thing."

Darien stared at a tuft of moss held captive in a sliver of ice between cracks in the slate. "Wait, weren't you drugged at the time? Neither of us could use aether."

Light flared across the cliff, and Jet was back to his usual self. He returned to the treeline with an approving eye. "I used Aeo's aether since I couldn't use my own."

The creator god? Darien furrowed his brow. "Is that a joke?"

"No." Jet turned back to watch Aleah play with the wind like a child hanging their hand out a car window. "If you follow him, you can ask for his aether, and sometimes he'll give it."

Is he serious? Darien examined his mentor's face, but Jet was as bland and neutral as usual.

"So… are you seriously telling me that I could ask or pray or whatever to Aeo right now and he could give me the power of a god?"

Jet shrugged. "Sure. If you're lucky. Try asking him to make you rich, too."

Darien's mouth hung open. "Well that worked for you!"

"All right, ready to try?" Raydon said.

"No, hang on a sec!" Darien pointed at Aleah. "What's the shimmerthing special ability?"

Jet squatted beside the pack containing their dinner and pulled out a sliver of dried meat—Darien recognized it as Garrett's attempt at making pemmican. "How about you get the basics first?"

Darien clenched his jaw. *Really?*

"Take your shirt off whenever you're ready," Raydon said.

"What?" Darien whirled on him. "You're hugging that coat like you're a popsicle!"

"I don't want to spend the rest of the day picking cloth fibers out of muscle tissue," Aleah called from the cliff. "We can get a custom shirt made for you back in town."

Darien pursed his lips. *Well, fine. I look like a million units, anyway.* Maybe it was sentinel training with Levi, or Lynx training with Diamondback, or the change in diet, but he was suddenly in the best shape of his life.

He glanced at Aleah to ensure she was watching, reached back between his shoulder blades, and pulled his shirt over his head. The cold bit into his skin and set his hairs on end.

Watch it, window licker, Jet snarled through his head. *And be careful with your aether. If you accidentally sentinel blast your feather, it's all over.*

OK. Get out of my head.

Get your shields up. They're as thin as paper.

Darien sighed and grabbed Rigel's feather. He gazed over the ocean at the few streaking clouds. *Well... here goes nothing.* He closed his eyes and concentrated.

A brilliant landscape flashed across the darkness. It might have been sweeping amber plains or a thrashing yellow sea, but in the next instant, it was gone.

Darien gasped and opened his eyes. He stumbled back and dropped to one knee—he was lighter than he should be. The wind nearly tore him off the mountainside.

If it wasn't for Aleah watching him from the edge, Darien would have thought it was a different cliffside. Colors were brighter, the contrast sharper. He could see the quills on each feather of her wings, the light glinting from each strand of hair, and the creases in her lips.

Bleeding syn! Darien looked down, where he spotted a line of ants marching along the slate toward a cricket's carcass. He could discern the tiny hairs on their backs and the serrations of their maws.

He turned his head to the side. Striking wings of blue, black, and white stretched out from his back—identical to Rigel's.

"How do I turn it off?" Darien whispered.

"Are you all right?" Aleah called.

Raydon took a step back. "If you remove your aether from the feather you'll revert to human form. Or you'll change back automatically whenever your energy dissipates, if you don't maintain it."

OK, breathe. Pull it back—

"Now jump." Jet flicked a hand toward the cliff.

Darien blinked at him. "What?"

Jet ripped off a bite of pemmican. "I'll catch you if you don't get it." He chewed and swallowed. "Go."

"No! Are you crazy?" Wind picked up again, and Darien felt like it was going to fling him into space. He crouched and tried to pull his wings in, but they didn't respond. *How do I...*

"Think of them as a second pair of arms," Aleah said. She moved her arms up and down, and her wings followed suit.

"Just jump off the cliff," Jet said. "You'll get it."

"No!" Darien yelled. "Not now, not over. I mean, ever. Not ever!"

Jet stared at him. "You're afraid of heights."

Darien froze. "I'm not scared. I'm just not stupid. There's plenty of wind! Why can't I just—"

"Because I said so." Jet ripped off a chunk of meat. "You're not a Serran until you grow the guts to jump off that cliff."

"Well, maybe I don't want to be a Serran." Darien jerked his aether out of Rigel's feather and stumbled forward as his wings vanished. He grabbed his shirt, yanked it on, and stormed back to Altair.

7

Jet slung Victoria over his shoulder and frowned at the way her magazine settled against his back—his winter coat distorted the familiar feeling. He glanced outside the window again to confirm that the pre-dawn snow was still falling in gentle waves. *If I don't wear this stupid coat, I'll be buried before any game show up.*

He grabbed a handful of bullets as long as fingers, then crept out of his room and down the dark hallway. Only the hunters of Altair tended to wake up this early, but the door to the room where Darien and Garrett slept room was open.

Jet paused. Garrett always closed that door to assist Darien in his habit of sleeping in as long as possible.

He stuffed the ammo in his pocket and glanced into the room. Both beds were unmade and empty.

Jet frowned. Garrett was probably gone hunting already or re-stringing his bow, but Darien should be more tired than usual after the

Serran flu and their hike out to the cliffs the day before.

Jet closed his eyes and concentrated, searching for Darien's aether signature. Their bond was young and shallow, but considering how vibrant Darien's aether was, Jet should have been able to sense him anywhere within the city walls.

He couldn't detect him.

Jet tried again, but a flare of alarm pried his eyes open. *Calm down, Lieutenant,* he told himself. *He can't be dead. He's just not in the city. He probably went hunting with Garrett.*

Jet continued down the hall, out of the Lynx base, and past the Brazen Tower memorial, but an unplaced sense of dread shadowed him. *A bond with Garrett would be nice right about now.*

He trudged through a new snow drift on the street and blinked at a white fleck that landed on his eyelashes. *Wait, is that him?* A figure in a thick coat stood in the wall's open gate, wrestling with a quiver on its thigh.

"Garrett?" Jet called, and the figure turned. A dark face grinned at him from inside a ring of fluffy blond fur—Garrett had tied the hood of his coat up far too tight.

"Mornin', mate!" Garrett said with a wave. "Finally realized that hunting isn't sniping, huh? Want some tips?"

Jet jogged up to him, crunching snow under his boots. "Is Darien with you?"

"No." Garrett struggled with the quiver's strap around his leg. "He's at the lake."

What? Jet squinted through the flurries into the bleak forest. "What's he doing there?"

"I dunno. But I can sense him over there."

Jet paused. "You can sense him at the lake all the way from here?"

Garrett grabbed his bow from its usual resting spot near the gate. "Yeah. Can't you?" He eyed Jet through a cloud of breath. "You wanna zip up that coat?"

Wow, I knew they were roommates, but... can anyone sense that far? "Are you sure?"

"I could sense his whale aether if he was halfway across the planet, mate." Garrett pointed east with a thick gloved finger. "LaKotan babe's out there, too. Sor... Soriah?"

Jet stared at him. "Sorvashti's with Darien?"

Garrett nodded. "Yeah. Hey, I'm going to head south today. Maybe try north, past the—"

"How can you sense her so far out if you don't even know her name?"

Garrett shrugged. "You can't? I thought there was something between you two."

The thorn in Jet's heart twisted and ached anew. "No, I... I can only sense my own family within a few hundred yards. What's your aether gift, again?"

"I don't have one," Garrett said.

Yeah, right. "I'd bet a hundred units you've got a rare gift." Jet peered through the treetops at the newborn sun. "Talk to Aleah."

Garrett's eyes widened. "Seriously? How is sensing a rare gift? Everyone can do it!"

A dark feeling sloshed in Jet's gut. "Can you tell how Darien and Sorva are feeling? Are they injured?"

"I'm not a valnah, mate." Garrett shook a chunk of mud from his boot. "Is something wrong?"

God, I hope not. Jet marched into the aspen forest, avoiding Altair's ice-slicked road.

If he can sense them both, they're still alive. Calm down. But Jet's feet moved faster and faster until he was tromping through the brush at a dangerous pace.

"To see you brings much pain now." Sorvashti's voice flitted through his head, along with her glare... and those timeless eyes. The amber gaze of a lioness that held honor and tradition above all else. Eyes that had witnessed death and inflicted it upon the unjust.

"Ko'herz."

Jet skidded to a stop as a memory from six years ago slammed into him.

Sorvashti was in his arms, curled up with a bowl of bulgogi on the couch. She pointed at the TV in the wall, which played the latest LaKotan shoot-'em-up movie. "The tall one kills his niece, so he is bound of the *ko'herz* to revenge her. All of the family is."

Jet pieced together the meaning of the word in the Terruthian language. "Blood-oath?"

She grinned and kissed him on the cheek. "Ah! Maybe you can truly be the translate of the Vipers now, yes?"

She's going to kill him.

Branches clawed Jet's face as he ran. "Sorva!"

The land sloped downward as he neared the lake. He slipped on a patch of ice under the snow, slid, and jumped right back up. "Sorva!"

Ice stretched out over the lake's edges. Jet stopped and panted as the frigid air soothed the itching fire in his lungs. His gaze flicked around the shore. Only a white-tailed deer stared back from the other side.

Jet cursed and closed his eyes. *Come on, come on...*

He couldn't sense any blue aether, but a golden spot appeared to the east. It flickered with rage and sorrow and terror.

Jet dropped Victoria and tore his coat off. Wings flashed to life, and he jumped and slammed them down. Snow exploded outward as he soared over the lake's edge.

Let me get there. Let me make it!

The lake's water gave way to ice, then a new patch of forest. Treetops slashed at Jet's legs until he released his wings and crashed through the canopy.

Pain arched from his ankles as he landed. He hissed through his teeth and looked up.

Darien knelt in the snow twenty paces to the left. His eyes were wide and his arms bound behind his back.

Jet jumped to his feet. "Where is she?"

A tear slipped down Darien's cheek. "Run."

Something popped at Jet's feet. Orange clouds spewed upward, and Jet jerked back. He covered his face and dashed away.

The earth warbled and the trees swayed. Jet tripped, landed on all fours, and coughed. The tingling sensation along his nerves was familiar—the Royal Guard had trained him to resist it.

Fadeleaf!

A feminine figure appeared from behind an aspen. Glistening

streaks ran down either side of Sorvashti's face, but her expression was carved from ice.

"I am sorry, *shlanga*."

Jet stumbled farther from the gas and gulped in fresh air. His vision darkened and warped. "Don't do this, Sorva!"

"He kills my husband," Sorvashti whispered. "His blood is mine by honor."

Jet gritted his teeth, shot to his feet, and charged toward her.

He didn't see her fist coming before he felt it in his gut. His breath fled, the horizon flipped, and suddenly he was gazing up at swimming snow clouds.

A dark blur moved from his side and drifted in Darien's direction.

Jet flipped over and pushed onto his feet, but his legs buckled and sent him right back to the chilled mud. He coughed and gasped. "Sorva, wait!"

Something clinked along the ground beside him. A canister rolled to a stop and belched smears of orange… then gray… then black.

8

*H*e's alive. She wouldn't kill him. She wants me.

The pounding of Darien's pulse boomed through his ears as Jet's body relaxed in the snow. Flurries sifted through the trees and lighted on his clothing—the only movement in the still forest.

Sorvashti stood just out of arm's reach. Fiery eyes stared down from an expressionless face.

Darien squeezed his eyes shut. "I'm sorry."

Wrath poured from Sorvashti in waves—he could feel it melting the snow around them. A long moment passed, and he heard her pull something from her clothing.

Darien opened his eyes and caught the glint of a dagger.

God, no! Darien's legs burned to run. If he moved a quarter-inch, panic would fly him back to Altair. He could do it—she'd only bound his wrists.

But he refused to move. He'd killed Noruntalus and made his friend a widow—a friend who had gone into the lion's den to save him. A friend who'd taken a bullet for him.

And he hadn't even realized it until she'd just told him.

Maybe if he let her kill him, he'd be forgiven. The nightmares and guilt would stop.

Darien heard Sorvashti take a step forward, quiet as a snow leopard. Horror lanced through his heart and lit his bones.

"Wait," he whispered.

He didn't hear anything else. He swallowed hard and forced his eyes open.

Sorvashti was close enough now that he could see the tears streaming down her dark skin. Her knuckles lightened around the dagger's ornately-carved hilt.

Her lips barely moved as she spoke. "You may speak the last words."

Darien took a shuddering breath. "Do you know why he shot Jet?"

Sorvashti blinked and a new fire sparked in her eyes. "You do not say that Noraluntus does evil."

She... doesn't know? Darien's gaze landed on her dagger. "I'm not calling him evil, I—"

"No matter what it is you say, you will die today for killing the innocent." Sorvashti's eyes darkened. "Speak the last words."

"Noruntalus wasn't innocent." Darien's pulse redoubled, but he stared up at her with any remaining strength. "He shot Jet and killed him—Aleah and Tera did some miracle to bring him back. Did no one tell—"

Sorvashti's lip curled up in a snarl, and she charged at him. "*Sem itash nicht*, you lying—"

"He has scars!" Darien jerked back as she grabbed him by the throat. The dagger reared back.

Creator, help me!

A memory flashed through Darien's terror. Sorvashti and Jet sat in his old blue beater over a bridge in Roanoke—the border between Katrosi and Valinor. Jet had combined the sentinel and arbiter gifts to breach the guard's mind.

Then he'd said the technique was forbidden.

Darien gathered every wisp of aether and shot it into Sorvashti's eyes.

The forest vanished into black. All around him, aether swirled like flecks of molten gold—a maelstrom of anguish.

Darien reeled back, but he couldn't feel his body anymore. He was a severed spirit, and he was fading.

Sorvashti screamed at him in an unintelligible cry of rage. *Get out!*

Darien ignored her and recalled his memories from a week ago— the ones that haunted him every night. The scene painted itself across the landscape of his mind: a dark bedroom with bleeding, glassy-eyed bodies crumpled on the floor. A broken window with Tera blocking the moonlight, as eager to leave as abruptly as she'd arrived. Noruntalus stepping through the shattered glass and pulling the trigger.

The amber aether stilled, but Sorvashti's thoughts murmured around him in a cacophony of whispers:

His last moments!

This isn't real.

What is that look on his face?

No, Jet!

He must have had a reason.

Darien made this up!

Does Jet really have scars?

Noruntalus would never do this!

Why?

Darien's consciousness faded, and his memories evaporated into Sorvashti's mind.

*P*op.

Hiss.

Crack.

Darien awoke to a blazing heat at his front and winter's bite at his back. His body was curled toward the campfire that sizzled at every snowflake. Deep treads of combat boots lay at his head, and a bundled figure sat at his feet.

I'm alive?

His heart stumbled into a sprint. *Where… This looks like the same forest.*

Darien's eyes fixed on the sitting figure. Sorvashti's breath clouded in the air despite the fire's heat. Her puffy eyes glanced at him, then back to the fire.

Darien swallowed and mentally checked through the sensations in his skin, searching for pain. He found nothing.

"It is the OK." Sorvashti pulled a heavy coat tighter around her shoulders.

Darien stared at her. *She must need me awake for some ceremony before she can kill me.*

"The *ko'herz* is broken," Sorvashti whispered. "Noruntalus gives up his avenge when he kills the innocent."

Darien froze. *Wait. Does that mean she won't kill me?*

Sorvashti slowly blinked at the embers.

Darien shifted away from a rock that jutted into his hip. "So you won't—" His voice failed and restarted. "So you won't avenge him?"

"It is not my honor." Sorvashti nodded at Jet, who lay sleeping on the other side of the fire. "Noruntalus kills your mentor, so you have the *ko'herz* to kill him. The family of the evil one cannot also…" She took a shuddering breath and clenched her jaw.

Darien pushed up from the ground, careful with every movement.

A flare of joy at being alive was smothered as he watched her face.

He sat quietly and turned his wet shoulder to the heat. "I can't tell you how sorry I am, Sorv," he whispered. "I would still understand… if…"

Yellow eyes met his. "If you wish to die, I will help you."

Darien grimaced and looked away. "I wish none of that would have happened."

"I wish you know why he does this." Sorvashti wiped her cheek on her shoulder. "Noruntalus is a good man. But Jet is also a good man. Jet will not do the evil to demand his death."

Darien peered through the fire at Jet's face. Even in sleep he wore a stern expression. "I'm sure Tera knows why."

Sorvashti furrowed her brow at Darien. "Why does she sleep?"

His ragged heart twisted in a different direction. "I don't know."

The fire popped and lapped at an aspen branch overhead. *So my dad is dead. Mom is god knows where. Tera is in a coma. My mentor is the world's biggest jackwagon. Life as we knew it is over, and I'm a killer.* He took a deep breath, but the weight on his shoulders made it shallow. *And the creator is supposed to be good.*

"Darien." A sudden breeze tossed Sorvashti's short blonde hair in her eyes. "It is true I hate what happens." Her voice constricted, as if she was fighting to prevent her own voice from slipping out. "And I hate you, and I will kill you if you want. But the enemy kills us both."

Darien clenched his fists until they hurt. "Sorv, I…" His breath shuddered. "I will not let anyone kill you."

Jet jerked upright with a gasp. His wild gaze darted to Sorvashti, then Darien, then back again, tossing snow from his black hair. A hand went to a pocket on his thigh, and his expression darkened to something more dangerous than Darien had ever seen.

9

"**G**et away from him!"

Jet's vision reeled, either from his sudden movement or the sloshing in his head. Every nerve tingled and his brain felt like slush.

"Jet, I'm fine!"

Darien? There he was, across the fire—apparently alive.

Jet blinked. *What...?*

Sorvashti stared at Jet with dull and distant eyes. The hilt of a LaKotan ceremonial dagger peeked out of her tunic. She glanced at his hand that hovered over the knife in his thigh pocket.

Either that, or she was looking into the fire, or somewhere behind him—the world wouldn't stop spinning long enough for him to tell.

"She's not going to hurt us," Darien said. "I think."

Jet's vision began to stabilize, and he searched Darien's clothes for bloodstains or bandages. He appeared healthy besides his expression—

like a cornered mouse. *How is he alive?*

"You used military-grade fadeleaf on me so you two could have a fireside chat? Where in the bleeding..." Jet paused and willed the horizon to still.

"I am very much sorry." Sorvashti shifted under her bundled coat. "I get it from the Lynx place underground. I think you will come to Darien, so—"

"Swell." Jet pushed to his feet as quickly as he dared, demanding that his body not sway. Lightning skittered through his system, but it felt like a tickle compared to the anger that seared beneath.

I've been trying to forget this woman for years. This is it. I'm done.

"I think you should sit down," Darien murmured. "You don't look so—"

"Why did you stop?" Jet forced the words through gritted teeth.

Sorvashti watched him for a long moment. "Darien shows me truth. The *ko'herz* is not my honor."

Bleed her and all her traditions that ruined everything in the first place. Jet shifted a step back to keep his balance and turned his gaze on Darien. "Really?"

Darien shrank. "I've been getting good at arbiter. I've got a really good mentor."

Jet pointed at him. "You lying—"

"I just combined it with sentinel a bit. She had shields—"

"You *what?* I told you that was forbidden! You could have killed her!"

Darien grimaced. "So you can use it on a border guard but I can't use it to save my own life? I prayed and—"

"You think a novice sentinel has the same chance to use it successfully as a master-level arbiter?" Jet swayed, caught himself, and turned on his heel. *Son of a bleeding stupid d'hakka. Why on beautiful Alani did I drop Victoria to come after him?* He staggered toward the frozen lake.

"Jet, wait!" Something blurred beside him, and Sorvashti stopped directly in his path.

Jet barely caught himself in time. He glared down at her with all the fury he could infuse into his stature. "Get out of my way."

She stared right back. "I am not afraid of you, King. I need you to know my apology."

"You made your choice," Jet murmured, "and I've accepted it. Now leave me alone." He shouldered past her.

Snow flew as Sorvashti rounded on him again. He stumbled, and she caught him. "Please, sit—"

Jet snarled and threw her hands off as a blaze of electricity spiked through his nerves. "I'm done with you, understand?" He sneered down at her. "Done."

Sorvashti looked as if he'd backhanded her. She dropped her eyes and sank to her knees in the snow.

"I understand," she said. "But I must tell you. I take the old traditions to save Darien, because I see his heart in my mind. In the old traditions, *la'avod* is not paid when I save you. It is the life-long."

Jet blinked down at her, barely able to process her meaning through the smog in his head. *Is she saying... she's re-activating the la'avod from when we saved her from Ari Qua'set?*

He closed his eyes through a sudden wave of nausea. He released a breath, and his anger cooled into a glacier. "No. I've had enough of your traditions."

"I am the sorry," Sorvashti whispered. "I will make it paid."

"Hey, there!"

Jet whirled around at the call of an unfamiliar voice.

A pair of men approached from the deep forest. One was tall and thick as an ox, and the other young and unnaturally handsome. Both wore variants of dark Lynx armor.

What the...

The young one swished wavy umber hair from his eyes and grinned. "Are we interrupting something?"

Adrenaline poured through Jet's veins, silencing everything else. He slid between the newcomers and Sorvashti, then gauged the distance between them and Darien, who sat frozen at the campfire.

What on Alani are they doing out here?

"No," Jet called back. "Can I help you?"

"We're sort of lost," the young one said. He tromped through the snow and gave a disgusted look at the mud on his otherwise perfect boots. "Looking for the Lynx base of Altair."

"We are the Lynx of Altair." Jet sensed Sorvashti shift at his back, and he sidestepped to block her. "Where did you come from?"

"Oh, a ways off. I'm Zekk Sorrowsong." The young one hooked a thumb at the ox behind him. "And this is my buddy, Wul Canyon."

'Buddy?' Jet furrowed his brow. *Diamondback reported that I was joining the Lynx with my real name.* "Jet Valinor."

"I'd recognize that mug anywhere." Zekk strode up to Jet and offered his hand with a charming smile. Aqua eyes beamed from smooth medium skin—telltale signs of Malaano heritage. "It's an honor, Lieutenant."

They can't be from Maqua. Can anyone get a heli-jet off the ground anymore? Jet hesitantly shook his hand. *It's OK. They think everything's legit.* He tried to return Zekk's grin.

"You OK back there, beautiful?" Zekk leaned around Jet's shoulder. "Was he yelling at you?"

Guilt slammed into Jet, chased by shame, then a different flavor of anger. His fake smile vanished as he sidestepped again to cut Zekk off from Sorvashti. "What are you after?"

Zekk stuffed his hands in his pockets and glanced at the campfire, where Darien sat with eyes as wide as a lemur's. "We got a report of three... angels... in this area." Zekk lifted an eyebrow. "See anything like that around here?"

Jet's pulse slammed against his frayed nerves. *How could anyone have reported us? There's satellite internet at The Plug, but we went miles out so townsfolk wouldn't see.*

"Angel?" Sorvashti repeated. "This is a creature of the heaven, yes? Do you make the joke?"

Humor lit Zekk's face. "No, beautiful. What's your name?"

"We haven't seen anything strange around here," Jet said. "And I'm afraid Altair isn't accepting new citizens right now due to winter."

"Hmm..." Zekk's leather glove tapped his clean-shaven chin. "That's strange. Because Wul here sensed your signature last night at like a thousand feet in the air. You're sure it was him, right?"

Wul nodded. "A hundred percent."

They're aethryn? Jet froze. "Well… obviously that's not possible."

"Not for you or me, maybe." Zekk reached up and patted Wul's shoulder. "But Wul here's a sifter. He could smell a goldfish halfway across the planet. Isn't that right, Wul?"

Wul's face fell flat. "Moderately."

Garrett's a sifter. Jet straightened his stature. "All right, I'm a Serran. What of it?"

Darien stood, and Zekk's gaze snapped back to him. "Interesting. Got any other secrets laying around here?"

"No." Jet lowered his voice. "You can be on your way."

Zekk smirked. "Actually, I'm gonna need you all to come with me."

10

Jet weighed his words carefully. His eyes flicked from Wul's empty hands to his belt and jacket. *He could hide a tank in all that bulk.*

He looked down on Zekk. "Where are we going?"

"You're being transferred to the Sanctuary of Maqua. You're all Lynx, yes?" Zekk glanced over his shoulder at Darien and gave a charming smile. "The world isn't at its best right now, but you'd never know it in Maqua. Think of it as a promotion." He wrinkled his nose at the lake shore, where scraggly twigs and dead grass stuck out from the ice. "A big promotion."

Jet glanced at Darien and felt Sorvashti's warmth at his back. *We might have to defend ourselves,* he thought to them.

Vanguard will protect us.

I'll blast pretty boy back to his frilly Sanctuary.

Jet smirked and examined Zekk. He was probably in his early twenties, but Darien was taller and thicker at seventeen. *Aethryn or not,*

*I could take him easy even with my head full of mush. The other guy...
we'll manage.*

He kept his voice pleasant. "Thanks, but we'll have to decline."

Zekk frowned as if genuinely hurt. "Well, that's unfortunate." He
tugged off his right glove one finger at a time. "You see, I'm a collector of
sorts, and the boss man pays very well." He glanced back at Darien with
a smooth, confident grin. "And I just hit the jackpot."

Wul slid a handgun from a side pocket in his coat and aimed it at
Darien.

Jet grabbed his sidearm, but it wasn't there. He cursed, snatched his
knife, and flipped it open in the same motion. He lunged at Zekk and
collided with an invisible barrier.

A sound like warring thunderheads boomed through the forest. Jet
blinked and stumbled back just as Zekk did.

What the...

Jet focused on the air in front of him. Aether gleamed like a desert
sun, spilling from Sorvashti's hands into a perfectly flat shield between
them and Zekk. Energy radiated back toward her like streams of light
shifting under water.

And beyond the other side, colorless aether seeped from Zekk's
hand like wisps of smoke.

Heh. Vanguard beats sentinel.

A screech like a firework exploded through the trees, and Wul flew
backward and crashed into the lake with an icy splash. Darien stood
beside the campfire in a perfect replica of Levi's sentinel stance.

Nice. Jet reclaimed his grip on his knife and gave Sorvashti a sidelong
glance. *Thanks, but let your wall down so I can handle this.*

You're weak from the fadeleaf, Sorvashti thought back. She nodded
to indicate her side. *Your gun is in my inside coat pocket.*

Jet clenched his jaw as Zekk stood and dusted himself off. *Did you
think I'd shoot you?* He fished where she'd indicated, ignoring the close
proximity to her stomach. His fingers found carbon steel.

Sorvashti's hands didn't move from her wall. *I'm sorry.*

Zekk slapped an open palm on the ethereal surface. He grinned in
awe, like a child before an aquarium's glass. "So compact! Very nice."

Jet pulled his pistol's slide and found a copper bullet in the chamber. He slipped his knife back and looked for the edge to Sorvashti's wall, but it seemed to fade out as his concentration swayed with his vision. *Syn, not again!*

Amber light streamed from Sorvashti's wall and swirled around Zekk's arm. She grimaced as her aether absorbed into Zekk's skin.

How is he...?

"Ah." A surreal fire lit in Zekk's aqua eyes. "Nutmeg."

Sorvashti hissed as her wall flicked out of existence, and Jet raised his gun.

A gloved hand caught his wrist. Something rammed into his gut, and the forest sloshed like an ocean storm. His shoulder slammed into cold earth.

Jet blinked up at swirling aspens. *My gun... where's my gun?* Electricity danced along his nerves.

Sorvashti snarled beside him. Shapes blurred together, flinging splashes of snow.

Jet flipped over and pushed onto his knees as Darien ran toward them. A war cry warped with a sentinel strike, and a gray blur flew off of Sorvashti and thudded into the snow several yards back.

Creator, let me see straight! Jet gritted his teeth and stumbled between Sorvashti and the pile he assumed was Zekk. A quick glance didn't reveal any injuries on Sorvashti, but her golden eyes stared up at the sky as if in shock.

Rage focused Jet's vision. He gathered energy between his hands in a mass of aether wild enough to tear bone from joint—something between a sentinel blast and chaotic valnah wrath. *The Masters won't mind.*

Zekk stood and removed his coat, revealing dark-skinned arms and a flawless physique. He struck a hand out toward Darien. Flurries in the air distorted, and Darien flew as if he'd been hit by a truck. He hit an aspen with a crunch, and when he fell, the shuddering branches' snow fell and buried him.

Jet roared and shot the screaming energy at Zekk's chest.

Zekk held a hand up and caught the blast as if it was a ball. "That's...

creative. I'll bet you're better with a gun, huh?" His palm absorbed the aether in a flash, then pointed right back at Jet.

Jet called his wings to shield him, but whatever hit him in the chest was twice as fast as his creation had been.

Time warped and his wings vanished. Jet blinked and realized he was on the ground with blood on his tongue and a high-pitched whine in his ears. He coughed and rolled onto his side. Pain lanced through his ribs, and his vision winked out.

Sorvashti whimpered somewhere to his right. Jet gritted his teeth and demanded that his shaking arms hold his weight.

His vision cleared to reveal Zekk kneeling over Sorvashti, lifting his arm upward as if pulling a thread of golden aether from her coat. The thread snapped, and she sighed and collapsed in the snow.

Don't touch her!

Jet lurched toward Zekk. Something cracked against his jaw, and he fell into a mouthful of muddy snow.

"If you're going to experiment with crossing gifts, aim for something a little more stable." Zekk's voice sounded muffled, as if he was speaking from another room. A knee planted into the small of Jet's back. "Not that any aether attack would work on an exorcist. Guess special forces doesn't mean you're a decent aethryn."

Energy skittered up from the bare skin of Jet's neck and into Zekk's fingers. It was as if his blood siphoned out with his aether... and his strength... and his soul.

Jet writhed but his body hardly responded. Shadows drooped into the forest. *No, move! Move!*

Another voice mumbled through the haze, and the transfer of aether stopped. Jet gasped and coughed. The white blur in front of him speckled with red.

"He looked thick enough to take it." Zekk's weight lifted from Jet's back. "He hit like a train. You OK?"

Jet commanded his arms to move, but his hand only skittered across the chilled mud. *Bleeding...!*

"Freezing," muttered another voice—Wul. "Better get Heals to make sure you didn't snap his back. Can we bring the Caracal any closer? I don't want to drag all three of them a mile through the—"

"Did you see a closer landing spot?" Zekk asked.

Jet gritted his teeth, closed his eyes, and drowned them out along with his agony and rage. *Focus.*

He sensed Wul approaching from the direction of the lake. The sifter didn't hum with excess energy like Zekk did—and his shields weren't as thick, either.

Jet flipped through his false memory collections and selected one in which he, Sorvashti, and Darien were family—the same one he'd used on the Roanoke border guard. He gathered the last of his energy, craned his neck toward Wul, and shot it straight through his shields.

Wul stopped mid-complaint and looked down. Jet couldn't discern his expression, but he marched forward and grabbed Zekk by the throat. Zekk gasped as he was lifted up until his feet left the ground.

Jet urged his body forward, clawing through the mud until he could see Sorvashti's still face. Soft clouds flitted from her lips.

They're both alive. Jet calmed his panting and coughed blood into the snow. He closed his eyes and extended his senses back toward Altair. *Aleah!*

But the distance was too great—he couldn't even sense her.

Jet looked back at Wul. *Maybe I can make him contact—*

Zekk pulled a sliver of Jet's violet aether from Wul's head, and the sifter dropped him with a thud. Wul stumbled back and put a hand to his forehead.

"Wow, he… got you good." Zekk rubbed his throat and eyed Jet with a smirk. "Arbiter, eh?"

Jet cursed and willed his feet under him, but they felt like sludge.

"Come here." Zekk grabbed a handful of Jet's hair and yanked upward.

"If we kill him, there will only be two of them to haul," Wul growled, "and we won't have to make a second trip."

"You can kill him after I get paid for him."

The last of Jet's aether escaped through his skin, and his pain evaporated into darkness.

11

Zekk hauled Jet's body onto the ramp with one final yank. *Note to self: don't take contracts for Arisians, LaKotans, or Valinorians anymore. They weigh a thousand pounds each.*

He straightened his back and stretched, paying close attention to the tension between his ribs. Darien's sentinel strike must have bruised them, but the pain was just the right amount to feel good. He hadn't felt so alive since the last idiot challenged him in the arena.

Zekk strode into his Caracal's cargo bay, where the heat from idling jet engines beat back the early winter chill. His pair of all-terrain vehicles lined up in the middle, reminding him of how worthless they were in cold climates. Snowmobiles would be a good use of this job's reward.

Zekk grabbed the overhead bar and slid along the thin bench seat until he reached the back wall, where Doctor Fadahari curled over the second most wanted person on the planet. Darien Aetherswift apparently had some internal damage from his waltz with an aspen, but his sleep seemed peaceful.

"Did I break him?"

Fadahari gave him an evil eye—the one he'd learned to love. "You should be a little more careful with the people you bring in if you want to get paid for them."

Zekk put on his most charming grin. "Well, I've got the best healer on the planet, so I don't worry too much."

Something about the creases around Fadahari's eyes made her deadpan look all the more chastising. "I can't heal dead," she said in a voice more gravelly than usual. She straightened to look over the ATVs at his latest catch. "And that one looks more dead than—" Her eyes went wide.

"What? He's alive." Zekk shimmied back across the bench and squatted beside Jet's mess of black hair. A pair of fingers pressed into his neck felt a strong pulse. "Just a little blood from a love-pat to the face."

"No, it's from an incurable autoimmune disorder." Fadahari stood and hurried to the loading ramp. "How did you catch Jet Valinor?"

"You know him?" Zekk stood and nudged Jet's arm with his boot. "He seemed pretty out of it... but are you implying that he might have given me trouble?" He raised an eyebrow.

"If he didn't, there's something wrong." Fadahari knelt at Jet's side and pressed a stethoscope to his chest. Her expression darkened. "You'd better be glad I'm here. Put him on the bench."

Zekk leaned back. *Since when do slaves order me around?* He glanced down at Jet. *He is really pale, even for a Valinorian.* "How do you know him?"

"He's from Jade Glen. His little sister was one of my apprentices." Fadahari pointed to the bench. "I taught her how to combat this illness to prolong his life. And if you don't help me out, he'll drown in his own blood within the day."

This must be why he was discharged from the Royal Guard. Zekk released a sigh. *A new pair of snowmobiles had better be worth it.*

He slipped his arms under Jet's shoulders and hauled him onto the cargo bay's right bench. "His file... didn't say anything... about Jade Glen."

"We were off the grid." Fadahari peered under Jet's bloodstained shirt. "That kid was there, too. I saw him once when I healed his sister's arm."

Darien's sister...? Zekk stared at her. "You healed Teravyn Aetherswift's arm?"

Fadahari pulled an antiseptic wipe from a medical kit in the wall, then used it to wipe the crusting blood from Jet's skin. "Guess so."

Zekk rounded on her. "And you didn't think this was important enough to tell me?"

Fadahari didn't look at him. "Why would it be?"

"She shot Alon in the head, Heals." Zekk caught her arm and waited until she looked up at him with blank eyes. "Tell me everything you know about her."

Fadahari sighed. "I know she sliced her arm in a car wreck the first day of the meteor shower. I know she's Arisian with dirty blonde hair and blue eyes. I know she's got an attitude. I know that's her little brother, and I know she was in sage training at Jade Glen." Her face looked even more tired than usual. "Now do you want me to save this one or not?"

Zekk released her arm and stepped back. "I want a full report before we get back to Maqua."

Fadahari rolled her eyes. "And I want a top sirloin and a glass of wine."

"Deal. Don't leave any details out, got it?" Zekk stomped to the back hatch and leaned against the hydraulics. *These Jade Glen aethryn are nothing but trouble.*

He peered out through the white haze—the morning's gentle snow had thickened into a wooly gale. A dark figure emerged from the tree line and into the clearing, where the Caracal's engines had tossed the snow back to reveal lichen-covered earth.

"Took you long enough!" Zekk yelled. "My pinky toes are getting cold!"

He heard Wul's growl over the distance and chuckled. The sifter held a bundled body close to his chest as he stomped closer and finally huffed up the ramp.

"Hey," Zekk called to Fadahari. "Do you know this one, too?" He pointed at the sleeping woman in Wul's arms.

Fadahari looked up from Jet and squinted. "No."

Well, that would have been just too convenient. Zekk moved to the bench across from Jet and tugged at cloth straps that hung from the overhead bar. "Here." He stepped aside as Wul squeezed into the small space and balanced the woman upright on the bench. "Does she need healing?"

Wul lifted one of the woman's arms up to the straps and wrapped them around her wrist. "She's got a bandage on her side. Might have re-opened a prior wound."

"Well then don't hang her there!" Fadahari waved at the bench. "Lay her down and give me half an hour—"

"She's dangerous, Heals. You should have seen her vanguard wall." Zekk took the woman's other wrist and bound it tight. "Made steel look like putty."

Fadahari rolled her eyes. "Well, I wonder who'll be on the team next."

Zekk grinned. "What? Just 'cause she's gorgeous doesn't mean—"

"Yeah, right. If you find a blonde healer half as good as me, I'll be out on my butt."

Zekk chuckled and sidestepped toward the cabin door. "You know that's not true, Doc. I'll have the finest bottle of wine sent to your room as soon as we land."

Fadahari smirked. "Make it two. I'm one of two people in the world who can heal this one." She tapped on Jet's chest.

Zekk bowed and flourished imaginary coat tails. "A full case and a night on the town for you, my dear."

"What about me?" Wul grumbled as he lumbered to the back wall and began binding Darien. "I just hauled two of the three through the snowpocalypse—"

"You get to bask in the glory of my presence." Zekk waited just long enough to catch Wul's sneer before he slipped through the door and snickered. *After we finish up in Altair, I'll give him a week off.*

The Caracal's midsection had been customized from a military transport to a luxury liner, complete with all of Zekk's requests—

including the mini bar, couches, and fold-out bed. He pulled his jacket off and slumped into his white leather sofa, propping his feet up over the armrest. *Darien Aetherswift. Could I be any luckier?*

Zekk ran a hand through his hair and flicked off a clump of snow. *Guess he's luckier—to be a sentinel with so much aether! Tasted so weird, though. Like some artificial berry flavoring. Well, I guess that makes sense, considering his history with the Titan Project.*

He glanced at the far door to the cockpit. *So back to Maqua real quick to drop off the priority-one prisoner. Then back to Altair to figure out what happened to our base there.*

Zekk leaned over and pulled a bottle of sparkling water from the mini fridge. *Or I could find out before we get there... and where Teravyn is. If anyone knows, it's Darien.* The bottle's lid snapped along its serration as he twisted it open. *He shouldn't be too hard to crack.*

The door to the cockpit swished open, and his pilot's head popped out. "Sir, we're ready when you are."

Zekk downed the drink in a single go. "Fire her up."

12

Wind nipped at Aleah's wings with cold despite the clear azure sky. She ducked her chin into her gale-whipped scarf and stared down at the ocean's assault against rocky shale cliffs.

I should turn back.

Aleah's stomach clenched—and not just because she'd been holding herself in flying position for so long. Her core and the muscles that rooted her wings into her back felt shredded.

Jet, where are you?

He hadn't returned from his regular morning hunt. He missed lunch, and Aleah had never seen him be late once in the four years she'd known him. If she'd ever changed plans on him at the last minute, even if he agreed, he'd be grumpy just because his schedule changed.

And when she'd tried to sense him hours later, she couldn't detect him inside the city. Or in the outskirts. Or the nature preserves, parks, and forests where she'd thought the hunters frequented.

Something felt very wrong.

Aleah's wings shuddered against an updraft. The wind along the cliffs where they flew was always strong, but today it churned violently, ripping one way and then the other.

OK, calm down. It's Jet—of course he's fine. There's some explanation. Maybe he just used all of his aether and fell asleep or something, so his energy is too faint for me to sense. There's no way he'll miss dinner, too.

She veered east, and the ocean's gale backed her wings and blasted her back over the land. *I should focus harder on learning the other aether gifts. Maybe if I was closer to becoming a Grand Master, I could sense them or help somehow...*

Aleah sighed. *Well, while I'm out here, I might as well keep looking for our home away from home.*

Fence lines in the drooping valley below separated one rural plot from another. Pure snow stretched across still plains in a flawless sheet, undisturbed.

That's a good sign. Aleah swooped down, searching for buildings. A blackened husk of a home sat in one field, but its neighbor had a house beside a patch of trees and a barn nearby.

Please let me not get shot... Invisibility was so difficult to maintain around her huge wings, especially when they moved in flight. *Gotta work on that.*

She landed in knee-deep snow near a rustic wooden door. Red-shuttered windows were closed and sealed, and she didn't see any lights on inside. No surprise there.

"Hello?" Aleah called.

Only a bird squawked from nearby cedars.

Aleah released her wings in a flash and pulled her coat tight around herself. The two massive holes she'd cut in the back for her wings made the coat halfway worthless.

She trudged through the snow and approached the door. An ice hornet nest hung from the light sconce. She leaned away from it and knocked below the peephole.

"Hello!"

Silence.

Aleah swallowed. She tried the door handle. Locked.

Well, if someone lives here, sorry about this. She squatted and inspected the lock, then smirked. *Cracked this kind enough times. If only I still had my tools.* But the Valinors frowned on such things. Thracian had thrown her lock picks away a long time ago.

But she didn't need to have any tools to use the Phoera element. It simmered in her blood, eager to be released. *Felix must have given me too much last time.*

Aleah's fingers brushed the keyhole. *Cylinder lock's there... the latch bolt's here, and the spindle should be right... there.*

A spark ignited inside the lock with a screech. She honed in on the energy and increased the temperature until metal hissed and writhed and wilted. Smoke sputtered from the lock, and the surrounding wood burst into flame.

Oops. Aleah commanded the energy in the door to still, and the flames winked out in an instant.

She closed her eyes and summoned her aether. Switching between the two was like putting a car in reverse and gunning it in the opposite direction, but the whiplash was familiar. If her element was a roar, aether was a whisper. Phoera flared like the sun while aether emitted light as softly as the moon.

Aleah's aether slipped into the lock and tapped the deadbolt out of the doorframe. She smirked. Felix would have yelled at her for using aether instead of just burning down the door, but he wasn't here to spout his elemental prejudice.

Hope he's doing all right with the other group of survivors, wherever they are.

Aleah slowly pushed the door open and slipped inside.

The wind from her entrance stirred up dust from a bookshelf, overdressed lamp shade, and dated TV. The air settled and laid stale, and the only light filtered in from heavily draped windows.

Aleah pulled her scarf down from her neck. "Anyone home?"

Her footsteps clacked on wood floors as she passed through the living room and into a kitchen with dated appliances. *Gas stove!* She dashed up to it and turned the knob.

Click, click, click. Blue fire sprang to life.

Aleah grinned. *Excellent.*

She tried the water from the sink. It trickled with hardly any pressure.

Hmm. Probably well water with a gas-powered pump. With the tens of thousands of abandoned cars scattered about old Altair and its suburbs, gasoline was one of their most abundant resources.

Aleah turned into the hallway and counted the doors. Three bedrooms, two baths, a dining room, and an office that branched off from a breakfast area. *Let's see: me, Dad, Mom, Jet, Raydon, Darien, Master Ellie, Master Levi, Garrett, Cassie, Sorvashti... and Teravyn, but she's still asleep. That's essentially seven or so rooms we need.*

She sneezed and rubbed her nose, then turned to head back out. *But this is a start. Maybe there's a ranch hand's loft in the barn—*

A gut-wrenching smell halted her thoughts as she reached a closed door. She grimaced and backed away. *By the hearth, what is that?*

A slip of paper with scribbled ink tucked under the door. Aleah held her nose and crouched to snatch it. The handwriting made Doctor Fadahari's look like calligraphy.

> Sera,
>
> Sure hope Katrosi is doing better than Valinor. I wish like anything I... find you.
>
> If you find... note, I'm sorry I couldn't hang on for you. Only had a month of my meds... cabinet, and pretty sure the pharmacy is overrun... thugs like the rest of the big stores.
>
> Don't cry for me, baby. I'm well past my time, and I've... a good run. Just wish I could kiss... freckles one last time.
>
> Just do one thing for me and forgive... brother. Love you.
>
> Be safe.
>
> Rex

Aleah frowned and slipped the note back under the door. *How awful...*

She stood, bowed toward the door, and whispered, "We will respect your home, Rex. I promise."

Aleah hurried back to the living room and out the front door. *So that room will have to be cleaned. Or we could just... never open that door. But everything else looks good.* She squinted against the wind and looked across the sun-glinted snow to a red-paneled barn. *And it's the perfect distance from Altair. Just gotta check—*

A figure with a massive wingspan descended from the sky, headed straight for her.

Aleah's heart leaped. *Jet!*

But the wings weren't dark enough to be his. She contained a disappointed look as Raydon swooped closer. He carried something big—was that a person?

Aleah's jaw dropped as Raydon landed close by and placed a coat-bundled Garrett Yager beside him. *He told Garrett we're Serrans?*

Raydon stomped toward her with an emotional blaze in his ethereal brown eyes. He grabbed her in a hug and pulled her in tight. Wings with elegant pattern of white, brown, and soft orange curled around them and sheltered her from the wind.

"Where have you been?" Raydon muffled into her scarf. "Did you know people are missing? I was worried sick!"

People? Aleah pulled back. "I was looking for Jet—is someone else missing?"

Come to think of it, Sorvashti hadn't checked in that morning to get her bullet wound tended to, but Aleah would have been shocked if she'd actually shown up.

Snow crunched behind Raydon's wing. "Darien's gone too, babe," came Garrett's voice. "And Sorvashti. I can't sense any of them."

Oh, no. Aleah's former worry tripled and seeped into her bones. *Darien, too? What could...*

She leaned over to look around Raydon's wing, and he retracted it. Garrett looked like a giant marshmallow with a thick coat pulled up to his dark eyes and furrowed brow.

"Not for a few dozen miles, at least," Garrett added.

Aleah frowned. "A *dozen*?"

"A *few* dozen, *at least.*" Garrett huddled his shoulders up to his ears as another gale blasted them. "Why am I the only one who can sense people?"

Aleah stared at him. "I can sense people, just not from that far away! I don't think this is a time to joke—"

"I'm not!" Garrett huffed and kicked at the snow. "Yeesh. It's not hard, babe."

The look in his eyes was serious for once. *No way...* "What's your aether gift?" Aleah asked.

"Don't have one," Garrett muttered. "Jet was giving me some lip about it earlier and told me to talk to you, but I've been through all this before at Jade Glen. I just don't have a gift, and that's fine. I'm getting tired of being picked on, yeah?"

Aleah grinned. "You're a sifter."

Garrett's eyes snapped up to hers. "A who what now?"

"It's a rare gift that can sense aether from great distances, and even thought-speak with training. There was a book in the Haevyn Academy library written by a master-level sifter who could even sense animals."

Garrett blinked at her. "Are you serious?"

"Of course!"

Raydon slapped a hand on Garrett's shoulder. "Congratulations."

Garrett turned on him. "You must have already known—is that why you came to me asking where Darien was? And why you dragged me everywhere looking for him and told me about this crazy angel stuff and brought me out here?"

Raydon chuckled. "Well, I just asked you first because I knew you were Darien's best friend, so you had the best chance of sensing him. When you told me you couldn't sense him at the lake anymore, I knew something was up." Raydon's gentle gaze lighted on Aleah, spilling whispers of umber fire. "And I knew Miss Bookworm could explain it so much better."

"Well, bonza, but..." Garrett looked back down at the snow. "Doesn't do much good if I can't find anyone now. Either they're hundreds of miles away, or…"

Or they're dead. Aleah grimaced and mentally reprimanded herself. *Don't think like that. Jet would find a way to survive on a volcanic island with nothing but a spoon.*

She ran her fingers through the frills on her scarf. *Did they leave? They could have flown off somewhere. No, Darien doesn't know how to fly yet, and Jet said his ironfeather wings can only carry one other person.*

She chewed on the inside of her cheek. *Was it bandits?*

"What were you doing here?" Raydon asked. "Do you know this place?"

Aleah cleared her throat. "No, I was just checking it out." She glanced back at the ice hornet nest by the door. "Needs a little cleaning up, but what do you think?"

"Uh, bit of a downgrade," Garrett said. "Why?"

Aleah glanced at Raydon, who returned her worried expression. "The Lynx will come to check up on their base eventually," she murmured, "and we don't think they'll like what they find."

13

The world blurred from hazy dream to dim detail—dark lines, hard angles, and the gleam of artificial light on metal.

Jet blinked and shifted, but his hands didn't move with him. He squinted up at them—his wrists were bound to a horizontal pole welded into the wall above his head. He slouched on some sort of hard bench, which his feet were apparently stuck to.

Another dream... It had to be, because the familiar, ever-present pain in his lungs was gone, leaving only a whisper of discomfort in its place.

Jet jolted awake and felt the smog of fadeleaf still clinging to the shadows of his mind. He recognized the standard cargo bay of a heli-jet model he knew well—the K-290 Caracal.

And across the hold, Sorvashti and Darien slept while sitting on a bench with their arms cuffed to a pole above their heads.

No.

Despair settled over him like a hunter's net. An engine rumbled the wall at his back. *Are we airborne? Where are we?*

Jet stared at the door to the Caracal's midsection. *Zekk. He said we were being transferred to Maqua. No, the Sanctuary of Maqua. Is that a Lynx base?*

He calmed his breathing and willed his mind to clear. *The original Maqua is half-way around the world, across the Sea of Bones... Does a Caracal have enough fuel capacity for that trip?*

He pulled against his restraints. If they'd been zip-ties, he might have been able to tear free at the right angle, but whatever was around his wrists was some kind of skin-hugging metal design he'd never seen before.

Jet cursed at a pair of all-terrain vehicles between him and Sorvashti. *Why don't my lungs hurt?* The lack of pain was a luxury, but its absence rang ominous. *Only Aleah could have—did they go to Altair and take her? No, she's not here. But they could be holding more prisoners in the midsection.*

He closed his eyes and searched for Aleah's aether signature. He didn't find her, but there was another faint familiar presence... *Fadahari?*

Jet's eyes flew open. *She's alive? No wonder I feel so bleedin' good!*

He tested the bonds on his ankles and growled when they didn't budge. *How am I going to...?* He wracked his mind for solutions and came up empty-handed. *That Zekk is some kind of vampire, but I could beat him now that the fadeleaf's wearing off.*

Jet glared across the cabin at Sorvashti's still face, which was the picture of calm despite the smears of dirt and blood on her tribal-patterned tunic and beige pants. *If she hadn't—*

No. If someone hadn't reported us!

Jet gritted his teeth. *Raydon... he's always in that Lynx server room. And we were so careful to make sure the townsfolk wouldn't see!*

But Raydon had been with Levi and Ellie's group since Jade Glen. And he'd hacked the door to the Lynx base so they could rescue Darien after his idiot-of-the-year display.

This doesn't make any sense...

The door to the midsection clicked and opened, and Jet steeled himself.

A middle-aged woman with careless eyes and a sloppy bun of graying blond hair stepped through the rounded door frame. Doctor Fadahari's proud LaKotan stature was hunched, and her dark skin creased in her signature frown.

Jet gaped at her, unsure of whether to be happy or not.

"Oh, hey." Fadahari's lips twitched into a slight smirk. "Sorry, guess I was late. Long time, no see."

Late? Jet stared at her for a long moment. "You healed me."

"Yeah, what else is new?" Fadahari shambled over to Sorvashti and blocked Jet's view of her.

Jet craned his neck. "Is she OK?"

"Now she is. She'd ripped open an old bullet wound. Looked like it'd been healed, but it was a pretty big deal to begin with." Fadahari peered over her shoulder at him. "Been having lots of fun in Altair, huh?"

Jet studied her blank expression for intentions and came up empty. "What are you doing here?"

Fadahari turned back to Sorvashti. "I was taken like the rest of the high-skilled in Jade Glen. Except for you guys, apparently."

A faint wisp of aether brushed across Jet's mental shields. Fadahari's voice sounded just as scratchy in his head as it did audibly: *Don't tell me anything.*

Jet frowned. "So you're working for him now?"

"Don't really have a choice." A knobby finger pulled Fadahari's jacket collar down from her neck, revealing a slim gray collar. "They'll hurt my leverage if I disobey."

The sight of that collar sent Jet's pulse into a sprint. "Leverage?"

"One of my nurses from Jade Glen." Fabric shuffled as Fadahari tugged on Sorvashti's clothing. "But I'm not going to sit by and refuse to heal people, anyhow—wild or civilized. You'd better be glad of that."

'Wild'? Jet wished he could see whatever Fadahari was doing. *So she's a slave.*

"How many others from Jade Glen are still alive? Are they all slaves?"

"Mmm, a few dozen I know of," Fadahari muttered as she worked. "I wouldn't really call it slavery. They just don't really have a better word for it. We're not paid, so we're not employees or servants. But we're generally treated well, since we're valuable." She pulled white gauze from her jacket pocket with an annoyed jerk. "Actually, I take that back. It depends. But Zekk pampers his people like you wouldn't believe. I'm living better under him than I ever had before, and I was a knee surgeon."

I find that hard to believe. Jet shifted on the hard bench. The cuffs were oddly comfortable around his wrists, but his arms felt like they'd run out of blood hours ago. "So they're hunting aethryn to enslave us."

"Eh, they've got better things to do at the moment—reestablishing civilization and all. This was a special occasion."

Jet snorted. "Slavery is the new civilization?"

The snipping of fabric was the only sound besides the engines' rumble for a few moments. "Not all of us are slaves. Some swear loyalty to become independent agents, who can fight in the arenas and win people and equipment to make their own team. Then they can take contracts—missions gathering supplies, rescuing people, founding new outposts, et cetera. The harder the job, the better the reward. The competition works well." Fadahari stuffed something in her pocket and turned to raise an eyebrow at him. "Except I don't think they'd let you do that. You're in trouble."

So Zekk is one of these agents, and he's getting paid to hunt us like wild game? Dark anger boiled in Jet's blood. "You mean rescuing people like you *rescued* us?"

"Keep your shirt on, kid." Fadahari rounded the vehicles until she stood in front of Jet. "Normal people get rescued. Aethryn get collars until we prove loyalty." She leaned back on one of the four-wheeler's seats and folded her arms. "It's not so bad. Just the way the world is now."

Jet wrinkled his nose—she smelled like cigarette smoke and antiseptic, like she always had. "So the Lynx are in control of the entire world?"

"Of course not," she chuckled. "Most of the world is an uncivilized ruin. There are plenty of raiders, barbarians, militias. And Terruth is doing its own thing—apparently their original government survived the meteors. But yeah, the only organization with modern tech left is the Lynx, far as I know."

Jet glared. "You keep using this word, 'civilized.' I'm not sure you know what it means."

Fadahari rolled her eyes. "Look, what do you want me to do? All the Grand Masters are enslaved or dead or missing. And even if they weren't, they couldn't dream of overthrowing the Lynx. They were a private collection of the world's top military contractors before the meteors, and now they're ten times bigger. How many masters were there from all of the Serran Academies combined? Six dozen, maybe, with like seven of those being Grand Masters?"

She pointed a finger straight at Jet's nose. "You'll lose that snooty attitude. But until then, you'd better come and see me every few days, or that illness will kill you before you can blink. I told you it would only get worse with time. Didn't you say it killed your mother when she was twenty-three? How old are you, twenty-nine?"

Jet grimaced. He looked down at his mud-stained cargo pants. "I appreciate your help."

The cabin shuddered with turbulence. "No prob, kid." Fadahari's tattered voice softened. "You know what happened to Aleah?"

"She's safe." Jet looked back up at her with a flare of strength. *And it had better stay that way, or creator help you and everyone who's ever thought anything good about the Lynx.*

"I'm glad." A weary smile lit Fadahari's face. "Anything I can get you? You thirsty?"

Jet's gaze slipped behind her to Darien, who snored like a clogged drain. "Are you keeping them asleep?"

"Valnah's magic, ain't it?" Fadahari glanced over her shoulder and smirked. "Let me guess: you want me to wake the girl up."

Jet felt his face flush and really hoped it didn't show. "I just want to make sure she's all right."

"Mmhmm." Fadahari pushed off the four-wheeler and shuffled back to Sorvashti. She ran a thumb across Sorvashti's forehead. "Wake up, lucky girl."

Sorvashti sighed, blinked, and shifted. She lifted her head and furrowed her brow at Fadahari. A slurred question in another language tumbled from her mouth.

"Sorry, my Terruthian's rusty," Fadahari said. "Feeling all right?"

"But you look of the LaKota..." Sorvashti's eyes grew wide and frantic as she glanced around. "Where is this?"

"It's OK," Jet said. "How do you feel?"

"I am the fine." Sorvashti pulled at her wrists and feet, then met Jet's gaze with terrified eyes. "But this is..."

"Don't stress," Fadahari said. "You're not in trouble like the boys are—at least, I don't think so."

Sorvashti furrowed her brow at Fadahari. "What will happen of us?"

"You'll be an arena prize, I bet." Fadahari scratched the back of her neck, where stray strands of gray hair met her collar. "Don't worry—you'll have plenty of guys fighting for you, gorgeous. You'll have a wealthy owner, I'm sure."

Jet's heart clenched as Sorvashti's face lightened a shade. "I belong to no man except the one I choose the oath to serve," she whispered.

Fadahari maneuvered around the four-wheeler's handlebars and moved toward the door. "I'm sorry, sweetheart. It's always rough at first. But if you're not a virgin, it's not as bad as it could be."

Jet forgot to breathe. His mouth fell open, but no thoughts or words formed.

Sorvashti let out a strangled breath. She stared at Fadahari with glistening eyes. "How can you say this?" she whispered.

"Ah, I shouldn't have said anything." Fadahari turned back around to face them but didn't meet their eyes. "Just don't want you to be unprepared or it'll be harder. But hey, maybe if you swear the loyalty oath, the Phoenix will let you become an agent yourself. Well... Zekk said you're a good vanguard, but normally only people with offensive aether gifts become agents... and there aren't many women..." Fadahari cleared her throat. "But if you're tough as nails, you could probably swing it in the lower ranks."

Sorvashti's cuffs clanked against the bar. She looked down and bit her lip. A tear slipped through closed eyes.

"I think you've done enough, thanks," Jet growled at Fadahari.

"I'm sorry, sweetheart. The world's not what it used to be." Fadahari pressed a button beside the door, which slid open. *Aeo leywa ai shea.*

Classical music drifted through the door before she shut it behind her.

Sorvashti choked on a sob. She hissed in a breath and clenched her teeth.

Jet felt like his blood had been replaced with used oil. *This... this is... what can I say?*

"This is my fault," Sorvashti sputtered.

"No, it's not," Jet whispered.

"I brought Darien out." She pressed her eyes into her shoulder's tunic sleeve. "I drug you, and I take your weapon—"

"Listen to me." Jet sent a wisp of aether to caress her cheek. She opened watery eyes and blinked at him.

"I will not let that happen to you."

"Maybe this is good." Sorvashti looked down at the shackles around her ankles. "Maybe the creator punishes me. Yes—he is good, and I do evil. This is justice."

"You were just following the traditions of your people," Jet said. "You didn't know what... what Noruntalus had done." Mentioning his own death burned on his tongue—after all his years spent in combat, he never thought he'd be murdered in cold blood.

"Yes, this is good." Sorvashti sniffed and sat up straight. "I cannot go back to the masters and say what I do of shame. My family is gone. I hurt you and I have no one. So I can start this new life of the agent and protect me." She blinked and looked up at him with hard eyes. "But I do not let them hurt you."

Is she listening at all? "You're flying way off the tracks, Sorva. You do have family left."

Her eyes brightened. "You are true! Maybe they live in LaKota, and I can become the agent and fly to find them! The Lynx have this air boat, yes?"

Jet shifted. "No, I mean, you have me."

Sorvashti paused and seemed to actually look at him for the first time. "You hate me. You say we are done. How is this the family?"

He winced. "I don't hate you. You swore *la'avod* to me. Doesn't that make a sort of family, according to tradition?"

Sorvashti's golden eyes thinned. "You do know the traditions, then, *shlanga.* But you say no to my *la'avod.*"

"The original *la'avod* cannot be declined; it is given freely by one's own choice. Are you abandoning the traditions after all this time? I thought you were reverting to the old LaKotan ways."

Sorvashti's eyes filled again, and a tear spilled over. "The traditions destroy everything to me," she whispered. "The *fortlaben* takes me to a school where evil ones steal me. The no foreigners takes me away from you. The honor of my father marries me to a man I do not want. And now *ko'herz* kills my friends and makes you hate me."

A sob mangled her words. "I think this is wrong, and I go back to the old ways, when traditions are different. But this is not good either." She looked up at him. "The world is different, yes?"

Something in her expression skewered straight through Jet's chest. "I don't hate you," he said firmly. "You're very… important to me."

Sorvashti furrowed her brow at him. "You speak in the past of tense, that you teach me, yes?"

A chuckle escaped him. *Yeah, the past tense that you're learning so well.*

"No. I… never really stopped."

"Stop what?" Sorvashti sniffed and wiped her face with her other shoulder. "We do the break up years past."

Jet swallowed hard and glanced at Darien—he'd stopped snoring, but now a dark spot of drool splotched his shirt. *If that leech Zekk hadn't stolen all my aether, thought-speaking would be a lot easier.*

"I know, and we both thought breaking up was a good idea," Jet murmured. "You made your family happy by breaking it off with a foreigner and going home, and I got to keep my job—for a while, anyway." He looked down at the rubber grating between his boots. "But I missed you… I just couldn't stop. So I tried to hate you, but it didn't work."

Jet sighed and looked up at her. "I'm sorry. I know this is a really hard time for you."

Sorvashti's eyes sharpened. "Tell me what you say, Jet."

His pulse thudded against his lungs, but it didn't hurt like it should. "I'm saying it's always been you." He steeled himself and didn't look away. "I still love you."

Sorvashti stared at him, motionless. A fresh tear slipped down her cheek.

Syn! "No, don't—I'm sorry. Never mind—"

"Do not lie to me, *shlanga.*" A slow smirk tugged at her dark lips. "This is the most truth I ever hear to come from your mouth."

Heat flushed Jet's face. "OK, well, I know nothing can ever happen, so just ignore it. I'm sorry—I just wanted you to feel like you still have some kind of family." He lowered his voice and wished he could send her a portion of his strength. "Please don't give in. Fight with me. We have to make it back home."

Sorvashti took a shuddering breath and released it. "Why do you say this can never happen?"

Jet blinked. "B-because you're married. Or you were, or—" He bit his tongue to stop it.

She looked down at the four-wheeler's wide seat. "I do need the time. I never love Noruntalus like I love you, when we are together in the past of tense. I marry him for my family, for honor—for my *oba.* But he is a good man and much good to me. I am happy with him."

Her eyes darkened. "But when we come to Jade Glen to learn the sage, he… changes. He does not care for me or look at me. Then he runs away with another woman and leaves me."

Sorvashti's face twisted with something between pain and disgust. "Much dishonor. But I think maybe he knows—maybe the gift of sage tells him what I do not know, and he is still good. But when I see Darien's heart…" She glanced at the Caracal's angled back hatch. "I see that I lose Noruntalus much time past."

Jet searched her expression as a weight lifted from his shoulders. Finally, he knew… but now he felt guilty for knowing. "I'm sorry."

"Do not be sorry." Sorvashti looked up at him and smiled faintly. "Maybe the creator sees us. Maybe he gives us the next chance."

A second chance? She can't really mean… does she?

Joy like Jet hadn't felt in years spilled through his veins without permission, but he didn't stop it. A wide grin claimed his face. "Let's get out of here first."

A mischievous spark flickered in Sorvashti's eye. "The Zekk is just human. Together we can do this—we will be like the past tense." She smirked. "But now my walls stop the bullets."

Jet blinked. "Your vanguard walls are bulletproof? How could you know that?"

"I thank Darien." Sorvashti tipped her head at the sleeping body beside her. "I lay in the healing bed for the week, and my hate of him presses my walls like diamond. Funny to see his heart and have the love and hate together." She looked up and examined the metal around her wrists. "How do we get back to home?"

"I've got an idea." Jet glanced at the door to the midsection. "But I haven't been completely honest with you."

Sorvashti chuckled. "I have very much surprise."

After all this time, she still knows me better than anyone else.

Jet allowed his eyes to drink her in for the first time in years. The curve of her hips, the flawless chocolate skin, and the single freckle hidden under full lips. She hadn't changed at all.

As soon as you're ready, Sorvashti of the Ironhide clan, you'll be mine again. And this time, I will never let you go.

He swallowed and cleared his throat. "Do you know what a Serran is?"

14

Zekk frowned at his options in the mini fridge. The bar in his suite had a more diverse selection, including that new grapefruit soju. He grumbled and grabbed a bottle of red wine.

A scuffle sounded from the cargo bay—a series of thumps and grunts. *I thought I told him to be gentle!* Zekk sighed as he flopped back onto his white leather sofa. *No respect.*

The cargo bay door slid open and one of the prisoners stumbled through—the Valinorian. Zekk figured he might as well get the hardest one out of the way first.

Wul shoved Jet into the midsection and pushed him down onto the thin couch opposite Zekk. Then he stood behind Jet with an enormous scowl and a bleeding lip.

"Sorry about my brutish associate." Zekk's eyes flicked from the cuffs around Jet's wrists to the dangerous glint in his black eyes. A fresh shiner spread from one of his cheekbones. "You guys doing OK back there?"

Jet's glare might have lit him on fire.

"Ah, things will be better in Maqua." Zekk glanced out the rounded window behind Wul. Clouds flitted past the Caracal's angled wing. "But I wanted to have a friendly chat with you before we get there." He screwed the bottle opener into the wine's cork and popped it out. "Wine?"

Jet said nothing and didn't move an inch.

"Yeah, you look like a whiskey kind of guy." Zekk poured a few ounces into his flute glass, grateful for smooth flying. The deep scent of fermented fruits soothed his impatience.

He took a sip and smiled at Jet, then snuggled back into the sofa. "So, how's the Lynx base in Altair doing? Completely overrun by wilders, I assume?"

A long moment passed, filled with nothing but engine noise. Then Jet sprang forward.

Wul grabbed Jet's collar from behind and threw him to the rug. A metallic burst of electricity tore through the air, and Jet gasped and twitched. A strangled sound wrenched from his throat.

"That's enough," Zekk said. "He gets the picture."

Wul reached down and hauled Jet back into his seat. The Valinorian slumped and panted, eyes wide and hair disheveled.

"Now that that's out of the way..." Zekk swirled the wine in his glass and smirked up at Wul. "I rather like these new cuffs, don't you?"

Wul frowned down at him with a look that said, *Get on with it.*

Zekk watched Jet recover and replace his stone-skinned visage. "Ready to chat now?"

No response.

"Was it you who broke Aetherswift out of the Altair base?"

Silence.

Zekk sighed. *Well, I knew he wasn't going to talk.* He lifted his wrist, and the small screen on his watch flicked on. Zekk thumbed through the options. *Of course Wul forgot to label them. Which one is Darien?* He tapped the button labeled 'CUFF01 - ACTIVE.'

A scream ripped through the wall shared with the cargo bay—a young man's.

Zekk watched Jet's face as Darien's cries continued. Jet sat there like an ivory carving.

OK, maybe they don't get along. Zekk tapped the button again and the screaming stopped.

"What the bleeding syn was that?" Darien yelled through the wall. He followed that up with an unintelligible stream of curses.

Zekk chuckled and put his arm down. "Who's the girl?" he asked Jet. There was no reaction.

"Why didn't she have a Serran feather on her? Where is it?"

Jet stared at something behind Zekk's head—probably the opposite window. He looked like he'd vacated his own body.

"What's her name?"

More silence.

Zekk pulled up the screen on his wrist. *Which one is she—two or three? We brought her in last, so maybe...* He hit the third option.

A woman's cry spiked through the wall, high and agonized.

A muscle in Jet's cheek twitched, but otherwise, he remained perfectly still.

It's almost like he's done this before. Zekk tapped the button again, and the screaming ceased.

Zekk pushed off the sofa and made his way to the cockpit door, keeping his hand on the glass half-wall that separated the computer station and its wide screen from the walkway. He rapped his knuckles on the cockpit door. "Hey, Heals."

The door slid open and Fadahari's wrinkled face blinked up at him. Behind her, his pilot put his phone's colorful game down on the dashboard of about a thousand controls. Blue ocean beyond the thick glass stretched out for miles and met a thin line of yellow and green on the distant horizon.

Zekk's heart swelled at the sight. No matter how many times he left, coming home to Malaan Island always felt just as warm.

"Yes, sir?" Fadahari asked, her eyes actually open instead of their normal drooping nonchalance. She tended to be alert whenever he interacted with wilders—maybe trying to anticipate how complicated her job would be when he was done. Or maybe the reminder of his authority made her a little more respectful.

"Did you find out what the girl's name is?" Zekk asked.

Fadahari looked down. "No, sir."

Zekk tapped his fingers on the doorframe. "What did you talk to them about?"

Fadahari glanced back into the cockpit, at the controls, at the window, the sloped ceiling—anything but him or the open door to the midsection. "I… was just explaining how things are in the Sanctuary. How the Lynx agents operate."

"Drop your shields for me."

Fadahari bowed her head and closed her eyes. After a moment, she looked back up and met his gaze.

Zekk gathered his aether and entered her mind unhindered. Immediately he sensed her fear of him, but it was only a whisper against a foundation of trust. Fadahari felt contentment, curiosity, and worry for the prisoners. She wanted that sirloin steak and crate of wine he'd promised, to get home to her room in Zekk's suite and take a warm salt bath, and to snuggle up with that steamy romance novel.

What? Fadahari, for shame! Where did you get that?

He didn't feel a smidgen of embarrassment from her mind, only a dash of humor at his reaction. *You gave me an allowance after I healed your tibia fracture from that arena fight with a sentinel, remember? You wouldn't believe what they have at the bookstore.*

Zekk shuddered. *You're right—I wouldn't. Recall your chat with the prisoners for me.*

Memory blossomed across Fadahari's mind like living watercolor. She was in the cargo bay, cleaning a nasty wound in the otherwise smooth flesh of the young woman's side. She'd positioned herself so the prisoner on the other side of the bay couldn't see.

Even though Fadahari didn't know the girl, she looked pure-blood LaKotan, just like Fadahari's father had been. Even though Fadahari didn't follow the old ways herself, the odds that this young woman did were high, judging by the light-ink tattoos on her shoulders, which swirled in the *fortlaben* pattern. And honoring that meant protecting the girl's modesty.

Fadahari had glanced over her shoulder at the young soldier whose arms hung from the cuffs above his head. She peered through his skin and examined his lungs, noting the rate of deterioration since she'd last healed them. The healer's gift notified her of several points of scar tissue that lanced into his torso—two of which seemed new.

"Been having lots of fun in Altair, huh?" she'd asked.

Jet had watched her for a long moment. "What are you doing here?"

Fadahari had turned back to the woman. "I was taken like the rest of the high-skilled in Jade Glen. Except for you guys, apparently."

She'd crafted a faint thought and sent it to Jet: *Don't tell me anything.*

Annoyance flared through Zekk. He held back from reprimanding Fadahari as he flipped through the rest of the scene.

Ah, she asked Jet about a girl named Aleah. She assumed that he knew her location, and she didn't want me to find out.

Zekk let out a frustrated sigh. He could easily delve deeper into Fadahari's memories and discover anything he wanted to know. But he had no reason to go after some random wilder—especially someone special to Fadahari.

He'd decided a long time ago not to take his slaves' private memories like most agents did. It just felt... dehumanizing. That was one of the many reasons that every slave in Maqua wished they were his—or so he'd heard.

Besides, he simply preferred people to like him, especially *his* people. It made his job easier and life more fun. And it allowed him not to worry about his maid slitting his throat in his sleep.

"Thanks." Zekk retreated from Fadahari's mind and returned his senses to the cockpit. Relief flooded her mind as he left.

Fadahari bowed her head deeply. "Anything for you, Confidant."

"Eh, drop the title." Zekk turned back into the midsection and slid the door closed behind him.

Jet watched him, but as their gazes met, the black eyes flicked back to the Caracal's window.

Zekk tilted his head. "You favor the LaKotan?"

Jet had once again solidified into stone.

Great. Zekk strode to the couch and looked down on him. "It's in your best interest to answer me."

Jet glared up at Zekk and spat in his eyes.

Zekk cried out and reeled back, wiping his eyes with his sleeve. He snarled and grabbed Jet's throat, yanking him close.

"I could take her right here, right now, while you watch," Zekk whispered. "Would you like that?"

Jet's eyes widened, then thinned and erupted into black fire. "I will kill you for those words."

Words? Zekk hit him across the jaw. *Bleeding arbiter. Just because I don't prefer it doesn't mean I can't do it.*

Zekk grabbed a fistful of Jet's hair and ripped aether from his mind. Olive-flavored energy surged up his arm, lost its taste, and joined his own.

Jet grimaced and pulled back as his mental shields disintegrated one layer at a time. Wul grabbed his arms and held him in place.

Zekk absorbed the last of Jet's shields and shook his hand out. Excess energy tickled along his skin, itching to be released.

Jet looked down and squeezed his eyes shut.

Zekk harrumphed and smirked. "You will listen to her cries until you look at me."

Jet didn't move.

Zekk lifted his wrist, but Jet's head snapped up with a black stare. "Go ahead and try."

Arrogant son of a d'hakka. Zekk grabbed Jet's face and bored into his mind.

Inside, a dark void rippled with rage—the typical space Zekk had seen in other wild prisoners, but this one had less fear and far more control. The faint network of flickering memories beyond seemed organized and precise, like a well-oiled machine.

What do you know about the Altair Lynx base? Zekk demanded.

Memory of a modern-designed building capped with snow and a blueprint-like layout flashed through Jet's mind. Then it vanished and was replaced by an image of a cantaloupe.

Zekk stared in bewilderment for a moment. *The Altair base.*

The blueprints reappeared, then switched back to the orange fruit and its large melon seeds. The beige texture on the outside. The huge knife needed to cut through it.

What the... Annoyance pricked him. *How do you know Darien Aetherswift?*

A visage of a quaint cafeteria flared to life. A wild-haired, blue-eyed boy sat across the table with an overstuffed sandwich and two cartons of chocolate milk.

The scene abruptly swapped to an image of a watermelon.

He's dodging me? Zekk called information on the LaKotan girl, Jet's angel feather, and Jade Glen, but was interrupted by details of grapefruits and joyberries and kumquats at every turn.

Is he a master-level arbiter?

You're Alon Whitlocke's right-hand man? Jet's voice murmured. *But you're so soft. How'd you get that position?*

Zekk jerked back and yanked himself from Jet's mind. He blinked and stared down at Jet.

Jet smirked. "Need anything else?"

Zekk growled and took a step back, straightening his shirt. He turned and stormed back to the table beside his sofa. "The interrogators will have fun with you." He grabbed his wine glass and took a long drink. "Put him back and bring me Darien."

Wul yanked Jet up and hauled him back to the cargo hold.

What a waste of time. Zekk's glass clanked back onto the table. *I knew it would be.* He grabbed his tablet from its charging dock and scrolled through the report he'd started writing.

The cargo bay door slammed shut. Zekk glanced over his shoulder to find Wul empty-handed.

"I thought I said to bring Darien—"

"Why did you do that?"

Zekk noted Wul's reddened face. "Do what?"

"Why'd you let him go?"

Zekk turned back to his tablet. "He's former special ops and a master arbiter. It would take weeks to break him, and I've got better things to do."

"You threatened the girl but didn't go through with it," Wul said. "He'll think you're weak."

"I don't care what he thinks, and I don't sleep with women unless they're willing." Zekk lifted his wine and relished its deep sweetness.

"Let me do it."

Zekk frowned. "We've been over this. There are plenty of women in the Sanctuary. Land one the right way. If it's so hard, I'll introduce you to a few."

"I don't want your leftovers," Wul growled. "Just let me start and he'll break—"

"I said no."

"She's just a prisoner!" Wul pointed through the wall. "And you know she'll be a prize, anyway!"

"Yeah, just like you were," Zekk said, "but I didn't rape you, did I?"

Wul's mouth snapped shut. His lips pursed as he glared.

Zekk lowered the tablet and glared right back. "As long as she's my property, you will not touch her without my permission. If you want to do that, become an agent yourself."

Wul's bear-sized hands balled into fists. "Maybe I will."

Zekk concealed his surprise. Wul had stood up to him plenty of times before, but he'd never suggested that he actually wanted to leave. *Well... I suppose I don't want someone like that on my team, anyway.*

"Fine. But for now, you're still mine." Zekk flicked his wrist at the cargo bay door. "Bring me Darien. And if you mouth off to me like that again, I'll put you up on the prize block before you get a chance to take the proving trials."

Wul turned and disappeared through the door.

Zekk sighed and returned to his report. *I can win a new sifter. Maybe not one who was original Lynx, but it's not like they're as rare as sages.*

He glanced at the screen mounted in the wall beside the cockpit door. An illustration of a Caracal touched the border of the Sea of Bones and Malaan Island on an illuminated map. A dotted line arced toward a dot labeled 'MAQUA' further inland.

An hour left. Plenty of time to get through Darien and the LaKotan.

15

Jet shifted as Wul reattached his cuffs to the bar above his head. He could feel Darien and Sorvashti's stares, but his eyes didn't leave Wul's scowl as his mind whirled.

If he takes Darien, it's all over! Wul's between us now—we can use aether to at least knock him out. But that shock from the cuffs! And then Zekk would come in here and—

Wul turned and stormed back through the midsection door. Without Darien.

Jet released a breath. *Make it count! The number one problem is these cuffs.*

"Are you the OK?" Sorvashti whispered.

"What happened?" Darien's voice cracked as he looked Jet up and down.

Jet squirmed in his cuffs and pressed the lower bone of his thumb against the metal. "We have to get out of here. *Now.*"

Darien exchanged a glance with Sorvashti. "I mean, sure, but aren't we like way up in the air?"

"I don't care where we are. We're getting off." Jet pushed his thumb against the metal until pain lanced down his arm. He clenched his jaw and applied more pressure.

Darien paled to a shade of green. "What are you doing?"

"Just don't look," Jet hissed through his teeth. *Don't think breaking it will let me slip through, but maybe if I broke my wrist—*

"Do not do this," Sorvashti said. "I practice and I have it when you are there!"

Does she mean... Jet glanced at her cuffs, whose smooth lines looked warped. *Her vanguard is strong enough to break metal?*

Sorvashti slipped a hand out of her cuffs and waved at him, wiggling her fingers beside a mischievous grin.

Jet grew his own smile. *Yes!* Something brushed between the thin space between his skin and the cuffs, and he held still.

"She almost had mine done," Darien whispered, looking like a puppy during a thunderstorm. "But how can we get out of here? Can you fly this high up?"

Pressure built up beside Jet's wrist. "Yes, but I can't carry both of you. You'll have to fly yourself, if it comes to that."

Darien's eyes widened even more. "What? But I don't know how to fly!"

"I know—that's why we're going to fight and take over the plane."

"Be the still," Sorvashti murmured. The hair on Jet's arm prickled as energy amassed and metal groaned.

"We couldn't beat them before!" Darien whispered. "You think we can do it now that we're all half-drained and electrocuted? And do you have any weapons?"

"Would you rather wait until we land and all have shiny new collars?"

Darien glanced at the slanted cargo bay door as a deep voice shouted something incoherent from the other side. "Well, even if we won, would we have enough fuel to fly back home?"

"I don't know—probably not," Jet said. "We'll capture the pilot and ask him."

Darien paused. "You can't fly it?"

Jet glared at him. "Of course not, idiot!"

"What? Aren't you supposed to be special forces or something?"

"That doesn't mean I can fly a plane. Do I look like a pilot to you?"

"Well yeah, actually, your name is 'Jet' and you were hiding magic wings for months—"

"Be the quiet!" Sorvashti snapped.

Jet closed his mouth and waited. The cuff around his left hand cracked, and Sorvashti's energy vanished and reemerged on his right.

Jet pulled his left hand through with just enough clearance. *Yes!*

The midsection door slid open, and Jet shoved his hand back into the cuff.

Wul stepped through with an expression even more foul than before. He turned sideways to squeeze his bulk between Darien and Sorvashti's bench and the foremost ATV. His back turned to Jet as he inched toward Darien.

Jet spotted a combat knife on Wul's hip. His muscles coiled like adrenaline-fueled springs. He pulled at his right hand. *Come on, Sorva...*

Wul grabbed Darien's cuffs. They clicked away from the overhead bar, and Wul shoved Darien down with unnecessary force. Then he looked at Sorvashti and paused—her eyes were closed.

Jet's pulse pounded as his right cuff yawned open.

Wul's other hand reached for Sorvashti.

Jet ripped his hands free and leaped onto the ATV. He yanked Wul's knife from its sheath, and as the sifter turned, Jet grabbed his chin and drove the knife into his throat. Blood sputtered onto Darien.

Jet withdrew the knife and released Wul, who gurgled, hit the bench, and twitched on the floor.

Sorvashti scrambled away with her hand over her mouth, and Darien hunched over and vomited.

"Sorry, Sorva." Jet stared down at Wul with knife raised, watching his movements slow. "You OK?"

She didn't answer. Her wide eyes glazed over.

No, no! Don't go into shock! Jet climbed over the ATV, blocked Sorvashti's view of Wul, and tucked the knife behind his back. He put a hand on her shoulder and tried to meet her glassy gaze. "Sorva."

Darien coughed and gasped behind him.

Jet glanced back at Wul and concentrated for a second. The sifter's aether faded away and disappeared.

"Sorva!" Jet shook her gently. *She's seen death before. Though maybe not like this.*

Sorvashti stared right back at him, but with no focus.

Jet cursed. *She has to set Darien free. What can I...?*

He leaned in and kissed her on the cheek.

Sorvashti blinked and seemed to snap back into her body. Golden eyes frantically looked around until settling on him.

"Hey, Sorva, I'm sorry about that. But I need you to break Darien's cuffs now. Can you do that?"

She swallowed and pressed her lips into a thin line. "Yes. Move of the way."

Jet watched the midsection door as he crawled back over the ATV. He flipped the bloody knife inverse in his hand. *Could Zekk sense it?*

"Be the still." Sorvashti grabbed Darien's cuffs and splayed her fingers over one wrist. Darien trembled and wiped his mouth on his shoulder. Blood speckled one side of his face like freckles.

Jet pawed at Wul's body, patting in all the regular places for a gun. He found none—only a radio that he stashed in his own pocket.

The midsection door slid open to a horror-stricken Zekk. As the exorcist stared down at Wul, his face contorted in rage.

Syn!

Darien thrust his hands forward, and an eagle's cry sent Zekk flying back into the midsection.

Jet's boots hit the floor's rubber mesh and he sprinted to the door. As soon as he reached it, an invisible force slammed into his chest. His back hit something hard, and the knife escaped his grip.

Zekk sprinted back in and absorbed Darien's second strike with an open palm. He struck out at Darien and Sorvashti with an ear-splitting boom.

Sorvashti's hand shot out in front of Darien, who kept his feet as she flew backward and smacked into the angled back hatch. The ATVs bounced on their shocks.

Jet regained his feet and charged Zekk, tackling him. He strained for an arm lock, smearing Wul's blood across gray silk. Zekk slipped his arm free, but Jet got an arm around his neck and pulled tight.

A sensation like fire swept across Jet's skin, but he gritted his teeth and held tight. *I can blood choke him before he can... drain...*

Zekk pulled against Jet's elbow and coughed. His fingers clawed into Jet's arm, and the blaze doubled.

The cargo bay faded and slurred. *Syn!*

Darien staggered forward, one hand dangling cuffs. He grabbed Wul's knife from the floor.

"Kill him!" Jet gasped.

Darien raised the knife over Zekk and froze.

"Kill him!"

Darien's arms trembled, but he just stood there with terror-filled eyes.

Zekk let go of Jet's arm and reached a hand toward the hatch control. The door lowered under Sorvashti like a ramp, opening to a blue maelstrom beyond. She cried out as wind tore her from the Caracal and flung her into open sky.

16

Darien stared out the open hatch in horror. Sorvashti's form disappeared under the cargo ramp, and violent wind drowned out her scream.

Jet released Zekk and dashed forward, scrambling over Wul's body. Darien's instinct demanded he follow, but his body was carved from ice. The bloody knife nearly slipped from his hand.

Zekk gasped and stumbled around Darien's other side. He pushed off the ATVs and tackled Jet, bringing them both down on the ramp with a thud more felt than heard.

Darien snarled and threw a hand out toward Zekk, willing his energy to fly with it. Aether struck out and hit Zekk in the ribs, shoving him sideways and toward the ramp's edge. Zekk grunted and held tight onto Jet, dragging them both into the angry wind.

No! Darien rushed to the ramp and dropped the knife to grab Jet's arms with both hands. He pulled with all of his strength and reared back with gritted teeth.

Jet yelled something, but Darien didn't register it. He glared at Zekk, who clawed into Jet's leg as he slipped off the ramp and waved on the wind.

"Let me go!" Jet screamed. "She's falling!"

Darien blinked. *He's a Serran!*

His bones ached as he let go.

Jet tumbled out into open sky, and Zekk with him.

The wind smothered Zekk's cry. He thrust his hands forward, and Jet flew back toward the loading ramp. Jet hit something below the ramp with a sickening crack.

And then they were gone.

Darien panted and clutched the loading ramp. He dared to grab the hydraulics and lean out.

A belt of sand below separated azure ocean from lush green jungle. Maybe that spot was Sorvashti, or... Zekk? Darien fixated on a light-colored smudge that had to be Jet—he'd been wearing a white shirt and khakis.

Where're his wings?

Darien's gut churned as he watched the figures fall. "Jet!"

The spots shrank smaller and smaller. No light flashed, and no wings appeared.

He must've been knocked out when he hit the plane! Darien blinked back hot tears. *I can't—what do I...?* His heart threatened to burst. *Even if I could fly, I couldn't carry both of them!*

Bloody fingers grabbed at Tera's necklace under his shirt. He found Rigel's feather.

I can't leave them. I won't! Icy fear paralyzed Darien as he stared at the earth so far below. *Creator, help me!*

He clenched his eyes shut and ran off the back of the ramp.

Wind claimed Darien and tore at him like a wildcat. He found his aether and begged it to go into his feather, but his focus was as chaotic as his mind.

Light flickered behind his eyelids, and he hit something soft. The gale ceased, and everything was still.

What? Darien panted until his head felt light, refusing to open his eyes. He had the sensation of lying on his back in a bed of grass.

I couldn't have hit the ground yet. I must have passed out. Am I dead?

"You're right, but if we move the archers here..." A nearby voice trailed off.

Who...? Terror sealed Darien's eyes shut.

"Uh, sir... did you just pull a live human here?"

That voice was familiar. *Rigel?*

Darien opened his eyes.

He *was* lying on grass, but it looked more like purple sponge-moss than grass. Wide sheets of leather stretched upward in a circle around him, as if he was in a tent or teepee of some kind. At his feet, massive spears, swords, and bows hung from a rack, and arrows the size of walking sticks stuck out of a crate. Something at his head smelled like sulfur. Darien craned his neck back and found barrels oozing with black tar.

What... the...

"The timing was rather delicate," another voice said. "Sorry, just a moment."

Darien sat upright and peered around the barrels. A table stood in the center of the tent, but it was so tall that he could barely see the papers strewn across it. On the far side stood a massive winged lizard with the colors of a bluejay—Rigel.

A young man's smiling face appeared around a barrel, and Darien nearly leaped out of his skin. The man's skin was like bronze and his eyes like fire.

"It's OK," the man said. "You're safe now."

Darien's mouth fell open. *Zekk drugged me. He must have. Or I'm dead. I have to be dead.*

"I'm Joshua." The strange man held out a hand, clanking a suit of gleaming silver plate and chainmail. "It's Darien, right?" He glanced over his shoulder at Rigel. "Didn't I assign him to you?"

Rigel's birdlike neck straightened. "Yes, sir. He's my newest Serran bond."

Joshua drew his hand back when Darien was too baffled to take it.

His fiery eyes thinned at the angel across the table. "Did you know I just pulled him from certain death because he doesn't know how to fly?"

Rigel's eyes went wide, and he bowed. "Sorry, sir. I left him with Kohesh's Serran, thinking he would train him."

"Um, excuse me." Darien's voice cracked as if he was five years younger. His throat was as dry as Illyria. "Where am I?"

Joshua and Rigel both looked at him, then back at each other.

"With all due, respect, sir," Rigel murmured, "we don't have time for this. The southern flank is bare. We have to move—"

"I need the facet! Where is he?" The tent flap burst open and the face of a white lioness burst through. Her frenzied expression calmed when her green eyes landed on Joshua. "Oh, I'm sorry to interrupt, Facet. But the northern citadel has been overrun!"

A low growl uttered from Rigel's throat, and Joshua stroked the thin beard on his chin. Both of them looked down on the papers on the table.

What in the bleeding, burning skies is going on here? Darien poked his arm—it felt like flesh. He pinched himself and winced. Dreams didn't normally feel so real.

He stared at his feet. *Sorv... Jet...* His gut clenched as his eyes watered. *This is my fault. If I'd killed Zekk, this wouldn't have...* A tear fell. *What happened?*

"Is there a human regiment here?"

Darien looked up to find the lioness examining him with crystal blue eyes.

"No, he's a special case." Joshua glanced over his silver pauldron at Darien. "Rigel, I want you to take him and teach him how to fly—no shortcuts. He's part of my efforts on Alani."

Rigel huffed a breath. "But sir, the citadel—"

"I'll take care of the citadel. Ezrel, take the southern flank. If they take the pass, Sidkha will fall."

"Yes, sir!" The lioness's huge maw disappeared back through the tent flap.

Joshua turned to Darien and smirked. "Do your best, OK?"

Darien just stared as Joshua turned and left in a flurry of violet cloak. *This isn't... that's not the guy I saw in Jet's head as he died. Right?*

Those memories were like the murk on a lake's bottom.

"Sir!" Rigel took a step forward with a clawed foot, bumping into the table and rattling it.

Joshua paused in the entrance and turned back. Beyond, Darien saw armored beasts dashing down a trampled path and between tents that flew banners of shimmering white.

"Ezrel is a healer," Rigel said. "You know I can do a better job of holding the south. And if we lose the best healer in the realm—"

"Ezrel is an archangel just like you," Joshua interrupted. "She's more than capable. You wouldn't be in this situation if you'd trained your new Serran properly in the first place. Do I need to ask Kohesh to show you how it's done?"

Rigel winced. "No, sir." He dipped his sleek blue-feathered head in a low bow. "Forgive me, Facet. I will do as you say."

Joshua left, and the tent fell still and quiet. Rigel stood there with clenched fists and wings drawn tightly to his scaled back.

Darien swallowed but his throat was too dry. "Um… am I dead?"

Rigel released a sigh. "No. He pulled your spirit here while your body still lives. Not many living humans ever get to see this realm."

Darien blinked. "'Realm'?"

Rigel looked over a muscular shoulder at him. "The spirit realm, kai'lani."

Darien's tired pulse kicked up again. "You mean Alani?"

"No, that's human slang for your planet's name. They derived it from ma'lani, the Ancient word for the physical realm, which means 'sky of water.'" Rigel pointed upward. "We're in kai'lani—the sky of fire."

Nausea swirled in Darien's gut. "But my friends—"

"Are frozen in time, just like your mortal body." Rigel threw the tent flap open and extended his wings as far as the exit would allow. "Hop on, boy."

Darien just stared at him. "You… you want me to—"

"Get on my back and hang on tight." Rigel glared back at him with the eyes of an eagle.

I'm crazy. I'm absolutely insane.

Darien's legs shook as he pushed onto his feet. He hesitantly approached Rigel, who snorted and looked outside.

Please don't eat me.

Darien swung his leg over Rigel's tail and heaved himself onto the sleek blue feathers that began at his neck. His foot hit the bone of a thick wing. "S-sorry—"

"Hang on."

Rigel burst out of the tent and pumped his wings, taking to the air in an instant. Darien choked on a scream and held onto Rigel's neck with all of his strength. He squeezed his eyes shut.

I'm not afraid of heights. I'm not afraid of heights. I just jumped out of an airplane. I'm not afraid of heights.

"You're definitely afraid of heights." Rigel's chuckle rumbled under Darien. "Your thoughts are loud for a human. Why do you have so much aether?"

Darien pried his eyes open out of sheer defiance. "How should I… know…?"

They were already high enough in the air that trees below looked like tufts of moss. But these trees were tall and thin like spikes, jutting up from a hill with violet grass and an encampment with gleaming white flags. Beyond the forest, amber plains stretched as far as the eye could see. Legions upon legions of beasts—some with wings and others with armor—scattered across the landscape like swarms of insects.

And above, the sky danced with auroras like lavender-colored fire.

Darien's mouth hung open. "What… where are we going?" Turbulence shuddered through Rigel's body, and Darien clung to his feathers and forced his eyes to stay open. "I have to save my friends! They're—"

"Calm down, hero boy. You're gonna be here a *long* time." Rigel banked left, angling away from the encampment and soaring higher. "When we get to Quetil'zar, I'll hear your story and see what we can do."

17

*C*abbage, potatoes, radishes... no. Who likes radishes?

Aleah grabbed a handful of carrots and set them gently in a cardboard box, then tested its weight. The gardens of Valinor Manor had produced more vegetables than she'd imagined possible from a few acres, but fruits were scarce. Thankfully their walk-in freezer and pantry were wide enough to park a car in.

If only we had another gatherer to find more wild joyberries. Any bucket of the juicy black berries would vanish within the day. I hope they're still producing in this cold.

Worry spiked through Aleah's chest at the thought of the weather. It'd been an extra level of frigid last night, and still no sign of Jet, Darien, or Sorvashti.

Aleah folded the box shut with more force than was necessary. *They're fine. It's Jet—he's not a lost puppy. Maybe he made up with*

Sorvashti and they're off smooching somewhere. She almost laughed out loud at the nonexistent likelihood of that one. *And Darien's just... being Darien.*

Her stomach disagreed with an awkward twist of nausea and hunger. She hadn't been able to eat dinner last night or breakfast that morning.

A knock rapped on the pantry door, jolting Aleah from her personal web of doubt. She jumped away from the cardboard box and stuffed her hand into a jar of mixed nuts.

Raydon chuckled from the doorway. "You're not fooling anyone." He glanced over his shoulder, then warped his voice into that of a crusty old man. "Where're you takin' my radishes, missy?"

Aleah deflated with relief and pulled her hand from the jar. "Nowhere. You can have all the radishes you want." She craned her neck to look behind Raydon's slim figure. No one was in sight, but it probably didn't matter. If anyone asked where she was taking a crate of veggies, she'd just tell them she was going to make a big dinner at the Lynx base.

Most of the townsfolk probably wouldn't be too happy if they knew where she was actually smuggling their food supply, even if it was only a few boxes.

"You OK?" Raydon touched her arm and tried to catch her gaze. "You don't look well."

Aleah sighed and pried her last empty cardboard box open. "I'm just so worried about them. What if something happened?"

"Not sure what else we can do. I'm sure they're fine, though." Raydon grabbed a handful of nuts and popped one in his mouth. "To be honest, I'm kinda glad to get a break from Jet being as mad and mean as a hornet. If he argued with Diamondback one more time, I was gonna lose it."

Aleah frowned at him. "Jet's not mean."

"*Really?*" Raydon raised an eyebrow. "Well, I guess you don't get it as bad as everyone else. But I almost slugged him when he called you ugly last week."

Aleah's mouth fell open. "He's never called me ugly, nor would he ever!"

"What, did you forget?" Raydon crunched on another nut.

"No, of course..." Aleah's lips parted as she searched her memory.

Sure enough, last week, she'd fussed with her hair as they'd moved clothing and personal belongings into the Lynx base. A snow-speckled gale had whipped her wavy silver locks into a rare mess.

"Ugh!" she'd mumbled on the road, still hating the morning sunlight. "I'm so hideous today!"

Jet had hefted a bag over his shoulder. "Just like every other day."

He couldn't have meant it. Still, hurt throbbed in Aleah's chest. *He must've been kidding. I didn't even remember it.*

"Well." She grabbed a bag of salt and dropped it in her box with a *thunk.* "He's got a lot going on right now."

"Think he's the biggest bully I've ever met." Raydon took an extra flask of olive oil and offered it to her. "He treats Darien like a wad of trash on the street. Maybe he has PTSD or something."

Aleah glared at him and yanked the oil away. "Come on, now. That's not fair."

"Sorry, I just mean he's been through a lot. It's understandable." Raydon popped another nut in his mouth. "He just always has that *look,* you know? Like he's still stuck in some war."

"That's just the way he is." Aleah crinkled a newspaper around the oil flask. "Jet's a good man. He's just going through a lot right now… I told you he's sick. If I was in constant pain, I'd probably be pretty grumpy, too." She carefully set the oil next to the salt and murmured, "He'd better get back here, because if I don't heal him again soon, he'll be in trouble."

Raydon shifted on his heel. "Have you ever thought it's funny that Thracian and Marie adopted you, who just so happens to have the rare gift of healing, when their son needs to be healed all the time?"

Aleah's mouth dropped open, and she rounded on Raydon with clenched fists. "How could you say that? It's just a happy coincidence!"

Raydon's hands raised in a gesture of surrender. "I'm sorry! It was just an observation." He lowered his voice. "It's just that I love you, and I don't want you to be used."

He what? Aleah looked away. He'd never said *that* before. They'd only been dating for a couple of months. And he was great, but, well… he was just kind of… bland. This was by far the most extreme conversation he'd ever started.

Aleah stared at a glass jar of minced garlic as her mind whirled. *I can't say I love him back. I shouldn't lie—*

"I mean, if Jet's nice to you, that's great," Raydon said. "But it wouldn't be hard to be nice to the person who's literally keeping you alive."

"That's enough." Aleah forced herself to meet his gaze and did her best to seem firm. "Yes, Jet's rough around the edges, but he's my brother. Where is this coming from all of a sudden? I thought you two were friends!"

Raydon looked at his shoes. "Ah, I'm sorry, baby. I was out of line." He slipped a hand around her neck, tickling her hair as he pulled her close and kissed her forehead. "Guess I'm too protective. I won't mention it again." He leaned back, grinned, and considered her boxes. "Let me help you with these. Which one's heaviest?"

Aleah forced a smile in return as she released her frustration. *Well, I can sure see why someone wouldn't like Jet. But he apologized, so just let it go.*

She cleared her throat. "Um, if you could take the big bag of sugar, that'd be great."

"Sure thing." Raydon hefted the crinkling bag over his shoulder and lumbered out of the pantry, maneuvering around the containers of dog food that blocked the door.

Aleah's heart lifted as she watched him go. *At least he's always helpful and kind.* It was times like these that she felt like an idiot for looking twice at Darien. That guy wouldn't know thoughtfulness if it ran him over.

"Aleah, honey?" Grand Master Eleanor Willow's voice sang from the kitchen. "Are you around?"

"Yes, Master!" Aleah tugged at a wrinkle in her green blouse. She dashed into the kitchen and found Ellie's plump form emerging behind a stack of black ovens. Aleah dipped her head in a quick bow.

Ellie's smile lit up the kitchen. "I've got a question for you, sweetheart." She set a head of cabbage on the wood-topped island between them. "You've got a green thumb, right?"

"I know a bit." Aleah moved closer and noticed a pair of mud-smeared gloves hanging from Ellie's belt. Her long gray hair had speckles of dirt stuck in it, and dirt stained the knees of her pants—she hadn't worn her Grand Master robes since she'd joined the harvesters of Valinor Manor.

"I'm learning, but this looks like frost damage to me." Ellie pulled at a cabbage leaf that flopped on the table, much thinner and a darker shade of green than it should have been. "But I thought this type was supposed to be cold-tolerant."

Aleah's eyes widened. "Master, where was that one planted?"

"The front garden." Ellie's aqua eyes flickered with uncharacteristic concern. "They're all like this."

Aleah's blood slowed into sludge. *No... that hard frost last night! We normally don't get temperatures like that until mid-winter.* She picked through the outer leaves and breathed in relief when she found the cabbage's core intact. "We'll have to harvest early—now. We have to preserve them, or we'll lose the whole crop." She met Ellie's gaze. "Would you please take this to Mom? She'll know what to do."

Ellie nodded, took her cabbage, and turned away. "Chin up, buttercup. It'll be all right."

No, it won't. Aleah looked out the window at the western garden, to rows of broccoli and kale. *We weren't sure we'd have enough food for winter for the whole city in the first place. With this loss...*

She glanced back at her boxes in the closet. *I can't take any more food. But it's ours, after all. Everyone else could have grown their own...*

Aleah's stomach clenched. *Well, maybe not, but we can't responsible for the whole city!* She bit her lip. *We can't just turn our back on hungry people, though.*

Another thought suddenly shattered her musings. *Wait, I've been meaning to ask Ellie about becoming a Grand Master!*

She ran after Ellie. "Master Willow!"

Ellie turned in the hallway and smiled. "Yes?"

Trepidation lodged in Aleah's throat. *No, I'm just a girl... she's trained for years to master all of the common gifts, and I'm not even that good at healing!*

Ellie tilted her head. "What is it, sweetheart?"

Aleah swallowed hard. "I want to become a Grand Master," she blurted.

Ellie's gray eyebrows raised. "Oh! Why do you want to do that? Becoming a master healer alone would take quite a while!"

"Um…" Aleah squirmed as her mind grasped for a coherent answer. "I want to be more than just a healer. I love learning, and I've always wanted to be a teacher. I want to preserve the history of the Serran Academies." She looked down and nudged the rug fibers with her shoe. "So maybe we can rebuild one day."

"Aren't you already more than just a healer?" Ellie bent down until she caught Aleah's gaze. Her voice dropped to a whisper. "You're the only human elementalist I know."

Aleah's breath hitched. *How does she know that?*

She cleared her throat and looked back down into the intricate ruby design on the rug between them. "Well, yes, I know how to use the Phoera element. But I prefer aether. It's gentle and constant, whereas Phoera feels volatile and raw. Like a bonfire that has to be constantly monitored, lest it spread."

Aleah sank to her knees and bowed her head. "Please take me as your disciple."

She heard nothing for a long moment. Then Ellie chuckled. "Well, now, you want me to teach you valnah, arbiter, vanguard, *and* sentinel? You know how long that'll take?"

"I'll ask Master Emberhawk to teach me sentinel if you like." Aleah looked up at her with a sheepish grin. "But aren't you a master of all four, since you're a Grand Master?"

Ellie lifted an eyebrow and smirked. "That may be."

"I forget…" Aleah furrowed her brow. "What's your natural gift, Master?"

Ellie gazed at a floral bouquet on an end table for a long moment. "I'm sorry, but I cannot become your mentor, sugar bun."

Aleah's heart plummeted. Shame hit her like high tide, and she dropped her head.

She honestly hadn't imagined being rejected. She was a model student, and did her best to love everyone, and always—

Smooth fingers slipped under Aleah's chin and raised her head.

Ellie's wrinkles creased into a smile. "But I can teach you everything these old bones know."

"Oh." Aleah grew a hesitant smile. *What's the difference?*

Ellie straightened and pursed her lips. "My last disciple... didn't do so well." She nodded to herself and patted her cabbage. "Maybe one day I'll take another, but at the moment I'm thinking of retirement." Aqua eyes sparkled as she winked. "I'm already tired of all this fighting. That better not be what you're after—aether wasn't meant for combat, and I never knew the first thing about how to fight anyhow."

"I've seen enough death." Aleah squeezed her eyes shut against an image of Noruntalus pulling the trigger. She took a deep breath and slowly released it. "I grew up in a war-torn country, and Altair is looking more and more like it. I lost my birth parents, my friends at Jade Glen, and I almost lost my brother."

Aleah lifted her head and set her jaw. "I don't want to learn how to fight, Master. I want to learn how to prevent them."

18

Darien pulled his wings in close and shot through a break in the branches with inches to spare. He threw his wings open again and curved around the trunk of a red oak, closer to the thick bark than he'd ever come before.

Nailed it.

He smirked and broke into a wide clearing, only pumping his wings once to brake before slamming down on wind-flattened grass.

"Ha!" Darien yelled through his panting. "How's that?"

A blue-striped gryphon rolled over in the grass and blinked heavy black eyelids. "Eh?"

Seriously? Darien almost blasted him with aether. "You weren't looking *again?* How many times do I have to—"

Rigel waved a white-feathered, clawed hand. "Just kidding. It was great." His beak stretched open in a yawn. "Why don't you catch the falling weight now?"

Darien clenched his fists. "I've mastered that! I'm ready!"

Rigel grunted. "I'll find a bigger water-pear then."

The sweat on Darien's shoulders nearly boiled off. "Why?"

"Do you know exactly how much your friend weighs? Do you think the atmosphere is the same there as it is here in kai'lani?" Rigel stretched muscular arms under his head. "And do you realize that my wings can't hold much more weight than your own body, so you'll probably shatter bone by landing while carrying twice your own weight?"

Darien took a deep breath of humid air and wiped his forehead, clearing the sweat-plastered hair that hung into his line of vision. "I'll be fine. What I should be doing is more speed training. I'll have to grab Sorv first, then go and catch Jet."

"Ah, right; you're trying to save two." Rigel stared up into the canopy created by the hundred-foot red oaks surrounding them. "You do realize that if you can't do anything but fall gracefully while holding another human's weight, there's no way you'll be able to fly with two. Maybe you could get to them both as they're falling, but you'd all three die on impact."

Darien released his wings in a flash of light and flopped on his back on the silk-soft grass. "I know that. I'll set Sorv down first, then take off again and grab Jet real quick."

"You won't have enough time for that, according to how you first described it to me. You'll be lucky to dive fast enough to catch one of them." Rigel glanced back at him with solemn golden eyes. "I'm sorry, but you'll only be able to save one. I'd recommend choosing whoever fell last, so you'll have a better chance of diving to them on time and get enough updraft so you don't splat on impact. I can almost guarantee that you'll be injured upon landing, regardless."

Darien clenched his jaw. "I'm going to save both of them." His stomach rumbled, and he yanked a thick jelly-leaf from his belt. His knife—formerly an angelic arrowhead—sliced a new layer into the leaf's orange flesh. Clear liquid oozed out.

Darien slurped it up and reveled in the sweet citrusy taste. "If I have infinity to train here, I'm going to find a way."

"No, you won't," Rigel growled. "Get it through your head—it's a matter of simple physics. I'm a shimmerwing; my wings are designed for speed and agility, not hauling weight like an ironfeather."

The bluejay-patterned wings pulled into Rigel's scaled flanks as he rolled over and pushed onto all fours. "You shouldn't even be able to save one of them, so be grateful. And you don't have infinity. You're pretty much at the limit of what I can teach you."

A drop of sweet juice dripped into the new thin whiskers on Darien's chin, and he jerked upright and wiped furiously at the sticky substance. *No, no! I'll be slime-beard for two cycles!*

He dropped the leaf and scrubbed his face against his tunic. "Well, what's the point of learning all this if I can't save them?"

"My point was to teach you to fly, as Joshua ordered." Rigel grinned at Darien's plight. "And, miraculously, I believe I've held up my end of the bargain."

Darien pulled his face away from his shirt before the two could stick together. He growled and felt his precious first beard—the sparse young hairs felt like he'd slathered them in super glue. At least it was tasty super glue.

"Looks fantastic. You're definitely a man now."

Darien glared at Rigel. "Wow, wouldn't it have been nice if you'd have brought those kiwis like you promised?"

"You shouldn't just eat sweets all the time." Rigel stretched up on his hind legs to his full height—nearly twice Darien's—and crossed his arms. "Did you make that guacamole?"

"Men don't eat green slop." Darien stood and licked sap from the edge of his knife. "You poofed into Alani before to give me my feather. Can't you do it again to catch one of them?"

"It's more complicated than that. I won't transfer to Alani without orders. Everything there is so... fragile." Rigel glanced up at the auroras through the maze of branches. "Look, I'm sorry about your friends. But all mortals die at some point or another. And then they'll get to come here, see? It's not so bad." He scratched his neck with a long talon. "Well, as long as you're on the right side."

Fantastic. Sure, just let them die. No problem. Darien stuffed his knife back into his handmade sheath. He sighed, put his hands on his hips, and stared into the forest.

His memories of Alani had faded in the strangest way—as if he'd lived them in another life. They were stripped of emotion, and recalling them was like watching a video with no sound. But he couldn't forget his friends' faces, even if it felt like he hadn't seen them in two years.

Or maybe it was more like five years. The cycles of kai'lani were from a wildly complex calendar that he didn't care to understand, and Rigel had said that their time had no bearing on Alani's timeline, anyway.

If only I had ironfeather wings instead. Darien wiped cold sweat from his eyes. "So if I'd been the one knocked out and Jet was the one saving us, he might have been able to carry us all?" he murmured. "Well, no, because then he wouldn't have my speed to make the dive." He blew out a breath. *If it's impossible, then what was the point of all this? I can't choose to save one of them and let the other one die. No matter who I chose, I'd feel guilty for the rest of my life.*

"One of the ones falling is a Serran?" Rigel asked.

Darien shifted his weight to one leg, and his boot squeaked. "Yeah, but he's hurt. I didn't see him pull his wings out as he fell."

"Who's his angel?"

Darien gave him a sidelong glance. "How should I know?"

Rigel tilted his head. "Is he a chosen one of Aeo, or is he a dark Serran?"

Uh... dark Serrans are a thing? "I don't know. He's good, I guess?"

"What do his wings look like?"

Darien furrowed his brow as he recalled the faded memory at the ocean cliffs. "Black with white tips, I think."

"Oh, he's Kohesh's Serran? Why didn't you say so?" Rigel's feathery eyebrows raised. "Glory. If he dies, Kohesh will be even more of a mess than usual," he muttered. "You could catch him first, use her wings instead, and then land while carrying him so you won't break your legs. But then you'd lose the speed necessary to catch the other one, if that's even possible."

Darien blinked at him. "I can use Jet's feather?"

"You can use any Serran feather," Rigel said. "Do you know where he keeps Kohesh's?"

"I…" Darien racked his brain. "I think he kept it on a necklace. But how can I use his angel's wings? Isn't my bond with you?"

"That just means I'm responsible for you. Unfortunately." Rigel smirked and unfurled his wings. "I'll go grab Kohesh, then, so you can ask her really nicely for a feather that you can train with while you're here. Just get her a gift of something shiny or orange or pink. And compliment whatever she's wearing, no matter how ridiculous it is."

Is this really Jet's angel he's talking about? "Wait, where are you going?"

Rigel stretched his wings to their full extent—a span of something like thirty feet. "Kohesh is one of us seven archangels—she's the Guardian of the City of Peace. She maintains the barrier around it, so odds are that she's there."

Darien's heart leaped. "Can I go?"

"We've been over this." Rigel glanced over his shoulder with the piercing gaze of an eagle. "No."

Darien felt himself slump. *But I want to try and find my family and friends while I'm here… like my sentinel trainer from Jade Glen… Tamara.* The memory of her death in his arms nipped at him. *If I could just see her here, happy…*

"You know the drill. Stay here and keep your head down." Rigel crouched and readied his wings. "Do one more circuit and have that guacamole made before I get back."

He took off in a burst of wind and disappeared between the trees.

Darien sighed. Alone again.

Their hollowed-out red oak seemed normal from its exterior—the door just looked like a squirrel's hole. If the squirrel was the size of an elephant.

Darien landed on the welcome mat woven of the plush grass, whose blades never died. The dim space in the carved-out walls wouldn't have been big enough for two angels to live in, but thankfully, he only needed half as much space. Aether particles slipped up and down wooden filaments along the walls like crystalline fireflies, delivering energy and nutrients from the roots to the branches and back again. The ethereal light was just enough to illuminate Darien's cramped loft above the main living space, where his rickety hand-carved furniture looked like a doll's next to Rigel's enormous bed, table, chest, and standing pantry.

Darien slouched on his couch of piled grass, ignoring the squeak of wood against wood. Maybe later he'd build a new one with the knowledge he'd gleaned last time around, but at the moment, his stomach demanded more tribute.

Stupid guacamole. I'm too tired. He gazed into the wall, watching a fleck of glimmering aether float lazily into the ceiling. *What should I make for Kohesh? Aether crystals are too common. Maybe—*

Something shimmered in the corner, catching his eye. Darien whirled toward it and grabbed the hilt of his knife.

"Who's there?"

A warp in space flickered behind his dresser, then smoothed into a blonde young woman with ice-blue eyes and a crooked smile.

"I finally found you," she said.

"Tera!"

Darien leaped to his sister and grabbed her in a crippling hug. "Glory, I've missed you!" Joy-filled tears watered his eyes.

His pulse hiccupped in the next moment. "But if you're here, that means... you're dead?"

"Well, yeah." Tera squeezed him back. "It means I finally beat my own game. Why is your aether scattered all over the Honeylands?"

It is? Darien blinked. "But you're not dead. You're in a coma... sleep... thing."

Tera pulled back and tilted her head. "Oh... I must be brain dead, then. Sorry." Her lips twisted into an awkward expression. "Hope your death wasn't too bad."

The words hit him like a punch to the gut. "I'm not dead. I was brought here to learn to fly."

"Oh." Tera's eyes brightened like aquamarine as she poked at his beard, which crackled with drying sap. "Can't believe you have a beard... you look so much like Dad!"

Darien grinned. "How long have you been here? Have you seen Dad or Mom?"

Tera's smile faltered. "No. You need access to the Archangel of Lore in the City to find anyone whose aether you can't track. And I don't know Dad's signature, because obviously I wasn't an aethryn before he died."

She stepped around his thin table and sat in its chair, which creaked and dropped her an inch. She clung to the table with wide eyes. "Uh... sorry."

Embarrassment flushed Darien's cheeks. "It always does that. I'm not very good—just started learning so I could have furniture the right size." He scratched the back of his neck. "So you haven't been to the City?"

"Unfortunately, no." Tera cautiously leaned back in the chair. "Turns out Joshua lied about that."

Darien watched her lips thin and eyes tighten. "Really?" He hadn't seen the facet since he'd first arrived in kai'lani, but he'd never forget those fiery eyes. "He didn't seem like a liar."

"Well then, that bull-witch Kohesh should let me into the City." Tera crossed her arms. "It's only for those allied with the creator, but I'm pretty sure I sacrificed everything to do the right thing when I was still alive—including my own life." She glared at a jar of ink on the table, next to the sketches of a recliner he'd probably scrap. "I swear the creator's power went through me right before I died, but then I got here and they wouldn't let me in."

Darien stared at her cloak of woven feathers as he processed her meaning. "That doesn't sound right..."

"No, it doesn't." Tera crossed her legs, rustling the dark fabric of her pants. "Only Joshua's favorites can enter the City. The rest of us have to fight over our scrap of the war-scarred Honeylands."

Unease churned in Darien's gut. "There must be some misunderstanding." He forced a smile and took a step toward the basket of black fruit on the cutting board. "Are you hungry? I need to make some guacamole."

A smile broke through the lines of tension on Tera's face. "You cook now? I'm impressed."

"I know. I'm awesome." Darien hopped down from the loft. He snatched an avocado from the basket and a kitchen knife long enough to be a short sword. "I'm sure if you talked to Rigel, he could—"

"He would kill me, or he would try."

The knife stalled halfway through the avocado's bumpy black skin.

"You can't tell him I was here," Tera said behind him.

Darien put the knife down and turned to face her. "Tera, what's going on?"

"Has he let you in?"

Darien stared up at her. "What?"

"Has Rigel let you into the City of Peace?" Tera asked.

Darien swallowed the lump in his throat. "No. But Joshua is the facet of the creator. He wouldn't—"

"He's *a* facet. There's one for every race. And not all of them are good." Tera stood up from the squeaky chair and hopped down from the loft.

Rigel never told me that. Darien's pulse accelerated. "That doesn't make sense. I thought the facets have the creator's power, or they were part of him, or something like that. Why would they turn against him?"

"The facets have free will. Have you been sitting in this tree the entire time you've been here?" Tera's playful smile sliced through Darien's discomfort. She pulled another kitchen knife from the rack, grabbed another avocado, and sliced it open.

"The elemental facet sacrificed her life to imprison the four primary elementals into stones. That's where we got the keystone—it *is* the elemental facet. Or used to be." An avocado seed rolled across the cutting board, and Tera ignored it as she carved through the green flesh. "And I hear Orso spends his days off in Alani, apparently saving the human race, even though he's the angelic facet."

Orso? Wasn't he the god of another religion on Alani? Darien's mind whirled as Tera grabbed another fruit from the basket.

"Tera, what are you implying?" he whispered. "Are you allied with Orso?"

She snorted and cut through the avocado so hard that her knife embedded in the seed. "Of course not. I'm independent." She wrenched her knife free and bumped him with her hip. "But hey, who cares about politics? I've got an awesome place in Belmora. No offense, but it's kind of an upgrade from this place. A big upgrade." Humor danced in her eyes.

She wants me to live with her? Darien resumed the slow cut into his avocado. *She seems... different. Am I not remembering her right?*

Tera abruptly straightened and cursed. She glanced over her shoulder at the exit, and pale hair whipped around three colorful feathers stuck in her messy bun. "Your blue friend's coming back."

"I'm sure he won't mind—"

Tera's kitchen knife clattered onto the cutting board. She stuffed her hand in her pocket, then slapped a folded piece of paper onto the table. "Don't show this to him." She gripped Darien's shoulder and stared into his eyes with unmasked affection. "I've missed you so much." She pulled him into a tight hug. "Come and find me as soon as you can get away from him."

Darien hugged her back loosely, confusion staggering his movements. "Wait, where—"

"I love you." Brilliant light flashed through the room, and wings of ruby and gold emerged from under Tera's cloak. They folded around her, and in the next instant, she vanished.

Darien's jaw fell open as he stared at the empty space. "Tera!"

The only sound heard was a distant gaggle-bird cooing for its mate.

What in the creator's radiant glory just happened?

Darien grabbed the paper she'd left on the cutting board and unfolded it. A hand-drawn map crinkled along the worn paper, displaying the provinces of kai'lani and a dot inside the section labeled 'BELMORA.'

Is this where she lives? Slippery unease gripped his heart. *Why's she so scared of Rigel? He would never...*

He looked up at the light streaming from the entrance, then moved to it and stared out. A thin blue line flitted through the trees beyond. *Wow, he's going fast.*

Darien stepped back from the entryway just in time for Rigel to burst through. The archangel's nostrils flared as his eyes flicked around the living space.

"Where is she?"

Darien's pulse thudded against his ribs. "Who?"

Rigel looked down on him with keen eyes. "Your sister."

"Is there a problem?"

Rigel dipped his head and rubbed a hand over his eyelids and beak. "Darien, you have to tell me where she is."

Glory. Darien's gut sank. *What does he want with her?*

"Why?"

Rigel turned to face Darien, took each of his arms in a thick hand, and stared him straight in the eye. "I need you to trust me and tell me everything you know about her."

Darien clenched his jaw. "You first."

Rigel sighed. "You already know too much. I should have sent you back last cycle." He released Darien and reared back to his full height. "Your flight training is complete. Ready to go back?"

Darien's mouth fell open. "What? No! What's going on?"

"I'm trying to protect you," Rigel said. "You'll forget about your mortal life if you stay here too long. I'm sending you back."

"What is this?" Darien took a step back. "Why won't you let me or Tera into the City?"

Rigel grimaced. "Listen to me. You have to forget everything she told you. Do you know where she is?"

Darien snorted. "Like I'll tell you. She said you'd kill her, and then you come back here sniffing like a bloodhound!"

"You have no idea." Rigel's eyes softened, and he put a hand on Darien's shoulder. "You've done very well, Serran. You're one of the most skilled fliers I've ever trained. That fear of heights was a good thing, after all; your form is solid—perfect. I'm proud of you."

Pride swelled against the fear in Darien's chest. "Thank you, but I need to learn the ironfeather—"

"You'll be fine. Grab Kohesh's Serran, take her feather, and switch wings. Her wingspan has more power and will let you land with the added weight without breaking your legs."

Darien clenched his fists. "OK, but I still have to figure out how to save the other one."

"I know you'll do your best." Rigel closed his eyes, and his hand weighed heavy on Darien's shoulder.

Darien pulled back. "No, wait—"

Darkness swallowed his vision, and in the next instant, Darien was enveloped by a gale-force wind. He opened his eyes to clear azure sky— the auroras were gone.

And he was falling.

19

Darien gasped in shock, but the air was thin and empty. The roar of engines faded above him, and green earth spun with white-capped ocean below.

Rigel's wings quivered in the wind on either side of him—the only things that felt familiar. Darien thrust them outward, and his wild spiral evened out.

An unmoving figure fell beneath him, closer to the ocean. Darien squinted and his vision identified a man with light skin and black hair. *Jet!*

Darien pumped his wings to increase his speed, then tucked them close and dove. *Sorv fell first, so she must be...*

He searched the air over the distant trees, the beach, and the ocean. He didn't see another body.

Panic blasted through his veins. *Where is she?*

Wind howled in Darien's ears as he plummeted toward Jet, his search becoming frantic. *I should be able to see her!*

Unless she already hit the ground. Jet would hit the tree canopy in seconds. *How much time passed between her fall and his?*

Adrenaline surged as Darien perfected his dive. He collided with Jet harder than he should have and pushed his wings out to hard brake.

Too fast! Branches with wide, spiked leaves rushed up at him.

Darien found Jet's necklace fluttering out of his shirt, caught on his jaw. A black and white feather shuddered wildly on the string—Darien grabbed it and shoved his aether into it while yanking energy from his own.

The flash blinded him, and suddenly his wings were bigger and thicker. Darien pushed them down and grunted at the force of gravity that crushed him from both directions.

Jet slipped from his grip, and Darien grabbed his arm. Blood slicked his fingers and slid his grip to Jet's wrist. Jet's body whiplashed back up to him, revealing a long gash along the side of his head. Blood slicked his black hair and streamed down his face.

Darien cursed and beat the black wings again, but they felt so different. His feet cracked against a branch, and he clenched his eyes shut as they crashed through the canopy.

The world spun, and pain sliced from his wings and back. He curled around Jet and hit the earth with a thud.

Darien panted for a moment, then dared to open his eyes. Warm mud embraced him like a soft, wet blanket. Agony throbbed from his right wing, which was bent at an incorrect angle with scattered black feathers above him. He gritted his teeth and pulled his energy from the feather, and the wings vanished along with the pain.

He groaned and pushed himself up. Jet's body was sprawled across his middle, splattered with mud. The gash oozed bright red blood.

Darien's stomach flipped. *Is he dead?*

He clambered out from under Jet and pulled him onto a maze of thick roots that dove into the waterlogged ground. Darien pressed his hand into Jet's neck and watched his chest rise and fall. *Still alive.*

He looked up into the tree canopy, where their fall had just cleared a path for rays of sunlight. Vines tumbled from a myriad of red-barked trees, each bearing fruit of yellow and orange. *Not enough space to take off again...* There was hardly enough room to breathe. Trunks and barbed foliage clustered around patches of mud and stagnant water.

Sorv! Despair coursed through Darien's veins. *No!*

Jet stirred at his feet, and a strangled moan escaped him. His brow creased, then smoothed again as his body relaxed back into sleep.

So much blood. Darien blinked to clear his vision and searched his pockets—he'd forgotten that he was wearing dark Lynx armor with a bulletproof vest and black cargo pants. A sleek cuff clung to one of his wrists with mangled metal twisting outward from its other empty binding. But his belt was gone, and with it, any gear that he thought should have been there.

Darien patted Jet's pockets and found nothing. He cursed and tore at Jet's sleeves, struggling with the seam. The fabric ripped free to reveal a tattoo of a snake coiled around a sword on Jet's upper arm.

Darien pressed the cloth over Jet's wound and gave up the fight against the tears. *I have to find her...* He choked on his own breath. *No, she must be dead. Do you really want to see it?*

His stomach grumbled and churned with a level of hunger he'd rarely felt before. His arms and wrists ached as he kept pressure on the gash. Something was wrong with his thigh.

Darien squeezed his eyes shut. He felt like a foreigner in his own body, which felt smaller and weaker than it had been. His hair wasn't in his eyes any longer, and the mud felt smooth along his jaw. The colors of the jungle were gray compared to the foliage in Quetil'zar, and the air smelled of mold and rot.

What if he dies too and leaves me here alone?

Darien swallowed bile. *I never should have left kai'lani.*

20

Zekk pushed his wings to their limit, straining after the Caracal as it roared into the distance. *No!*

He switched his aether into the second feather in the case in his breast pocket. A thinner pair of gray wings flashed onto his back, and he flew after the Caracal at top speed.

It wasn't nearly fast enough.

Zekk cursed and slowed as his heli-jet flew on toward the distant viridian hills. Its back hatch hung open as if it had intended to dump his precious cargo without a care in the world.

Bleed that pilot! Shouldn't there be a light or alarm or something? If he's playing that bubble game on his phone again, I'll put him on the arena prize block!

Zekk panted for empty air. He grabbed for his phone, but only his tablet was in its place. The slim device had no communication abilities—

only offline files for reference while away from internet access.

Syn!

A lightheaded feeling threatened Zekk's balance. He slowed his breathing, but apparently even Serran lungs weren't meant for this altitude.

He gave one last longing look at the Caracal's outline before diving toward the jungle canopy below.

How did they get out? Zekk padded down his pockets and took a mental inventory—only his tablet, pocketknife, wallet, watch, and the smooth Malo elemental stone that he'd been given as champion of the Maqua arena. *I'd bet my suite that Jet is the one who killed Wul.*

He carefully opened his wallet, peeking at slips of paper desperate to escape on the wind. *Bleed the units. I'll kill him. I'll get triple for Darien, anyway.*

Zekk leveled off and turned back the direction he'd come from, insides lurching with the tug of gravity. At least all of his prisoners were Serrans, and he hadn't taken their feathers yet, so they should survive the fall. He just had to collect them.

Unless the kiss with the Caracal had already killed Jet. That would be convenient.

A figure hovered in the distant sky, but it didn't look like a bird. Zekk squinted. *Is that a woman?*

His female prisoner stood in the middle of the open sky as if she was standing on floating glass. Her toned arms tensed with a proud stance as wind tossed pale hair around her face. She stared back at him with eyes carved of gold.

Well, that's one use for vanguard. Zekk glanced along the horizon and down at the trees and ocean below, but saw no other figures. *But why isn't she using her wings?*

He looked back to his former prisoner. Her hands and wrists were free, and she twirled her fingers as if playing with fire as she watched him approach.

She must have broken the cuffs off! Anger flared through Zekk's blood. *It was her!*

His enhanced vision caught the smallest smirk on her lips as he flew toward her. One of her feet slipped behind her.

She's waiting for me... why—

Zekk inhaled sharply in a flash of panic, and he banked hard to the left. *She wants me to come within range—she'll put a wall right in front of me, and I'll break my neck!*

He veered far away and circled, watching the woman examine him with a tiger's glare. *Yeesh. I'll have to get her on the ground... with surprise... in close-range.* Maybe Fadahari was right—someone that dangerous would serve well on his team. If only she was a sifter.

Zekk's heart sank as the image of Wul's body returned fresh to his mind. Yes, they'd had their differences, but Wul had been a man on his team—one he'd failed to protect.

Zekk shoved the shock and sorrow aside as he dipped lower. It wasn't the first time he'd lost a friend on a mission, but this time, revenge was opportune.

The canopy of leaves, branches, and vines concealed everything below them. Darien and Jet weren't in the sky, and Zekk didn't spot them in the ocean or on the beach, so they must have already landed, one way or another.

"Bring the Serrans in," Alon had said. He hadn't necessarily said 'alive,' had he?

Zekk growled deep in his throat. It went without saying—his captures always had to be alive. That was the whole point, and it was why he was the best. The hit contracts generally paid much less—not worth his time.

He breathed in salty air and looked up to where he'd last seen the dark-skinned woman—she was closer to the ground now. As he watched, she held an open palm to her feet, closed her other hand, and fell to another invisible surface several feet below.

Smart. Zekk looked below her and estimated that she'd reach the earth either in the clear waters or on the stretch of pure white sand. *Why doesn't she just fly, though?*

His eyes widened and felt cool against the wind. *Because she's not a Serran; that's why I couldn't find her feather. Either that, or she doesn't have it with her. But what Serran doesn't keep their feather on them?*

Zekk kept an eye on her as he landed on the beach a safe distance away. Soft sand enveloped his boots. *Then who was the third Serran in the report?*

He dismissed his wings and slipped under the shadow of a swaying palm tree. *I'll bring my whole team to Altair and root out every bleeding one of them.*

Zekk looked back up at the vanguard. *She'll find Darien for me. I'll be sitting pretty by the time the Caracal comes back.*

21

Blaring pain echoed through Jet's head. He opened his eyes and squinted at the light that filtered through a hole in the canopy of spike-fingered leaves above. A groan rumbled through his chest, agitating a deep ache in his lungs.

What the... Jet shifted and found that he was lying on waterlogged earth. Insects and birds chirped from thick jungle surrounding a small clearing. Twigs and broken branches piled up beside him.

Where am I?

Jet's hand went to the holster on his hip. But his military issue sidearm wasn't there, nor was the holster itself.

He blinked and looked down at himself. Dried mud cracked along a torn white shirt and khaki cargo pants with his movements—definitely not part of his Royal Guard desert, mountain, or forest gear. *What is this?*

His pulse pounded through his head as he searched for his knife holster, the concealed blade in his boot, and his ammunition. All of them were gone, but his boots were familiar. He found a cut in the rubber sole and eased a thin concealed blade out.

A purple bruise on his wrist caught his eye. *I was taken prisoner?*

Jet pushed himself up, bursting pollen from a cluster of tropical flowers on his right. He hissed through the pain in his head and stared into the jungle in every direction. Nothing but greenery and a curious rainbow bird stared back at him.

This looks more like Malaan than the Kioan desert. His mind strained to recover his last memories. He'd been on a mission with Viper Unit, hunting the terrorist network that had bombed Brazen Tower. He was supposed to be on overwatch, guarding Diamondback's six through Victoria's scope.

But his rifle was nowhere in sight.

There was some kind of explosion…

Jet grimaced as his skull screamed for attention. He raised a hand to the left side of his head. Some sort of bandage stuck to his hair, which was matted with what felt like dried blood.

Swollen pretty bad. Wait—why is my hair so long? He'd never let it grow out so far; Diamondback would write him up. *How long was I out? Was I drugged?*

Jet stared into the jungle. *If they captured me, why in the bleeding skies did they drop me here?*

A branch cracked to his right.

Jet ducked and dashed into the brush. He crouched behind a thick red-trunked tree and peered through a maze of vines.

A young man tromped through the forest, heading straight toward where Jet had been laying. Maybe sixteen or seventeen, by the look of it—light skin, wild brown hair, and a muscular build. A bundle of sticks and dried vines tangled in his arms.

Since when do the Revoth terrorists employ Arisian teenagers? Jet willed his pulse to slow, calming his breathing into silence.

The teen arrived at the small clearing and furrowed his brow at the spot where Jet had been. He grumbled, looked around, and dropped his sticks on top of the existing pile. "Jet?" he yelled.

Jet cringed. *He knows my real name? How could he possibly...* His head throbbed. *What on beautiful Alani is going on here?*

"Great." The young man blew out a breath and cupped his hands on either side of his mouth. "Jet!" he hollered, louder this time.

Jet remained perfectly still, squinting at the teen's dark cloth getup. *Wait. Is that some variant of Lynx armor? But this guy's too young to be Lynx!*

The teen sighed and pulled a yellow pear-shaped fruit from his pocket. He turned it over in his hand and sniffed it.

Whoever he is, he knows more than I do. Jet watched the young man turn his back and stare at the fruit suspiciously. *Decent mental shields— he's an aethryn. Interesting.*

Jet rocked back on his haunches and took a steadying breath. *Now!*

He dashed around the vines, leaped over roots, and crashed through the brush. The young man barely had time to turn before Jet slammed into him. He smashed him into the mud with an arm lock in a half-second.

"Jet! What the—" The teen choked as Jet put pressure on his throat.

"Where are we?" Jet murmured.

"What? I don't... how should I know?" The young man struggled and coughed. "That hurts!"

"It'll hurt a lot more if you resist." Jet twisted the teen's arm up until he gasped and stopped moving. "Who are you?"

"This isn't funny!" The teen panted into the mud. "I'm the guy who's gonna kick your butt if you don't cut it out!"

"Am I laughing?" Jet brought his concealed blade around and held it in front of the young man's face.

The Arisian's blue eyes went wide. "OK... Jet... listen. Listen to me. You hit your head, OK? But I'm your friend." His gaze snapped up from the mud, trying to look back at him. "Friend!"

Doubt it. Jet remained perfectly still and stared down at the teen for a long moment. He summoned his aether to his mind, willing the arbiter gift to filter truth from lie.

"What's your name?"

"Darien. Darien Aetherswift." The teen stared at the knife in front of his eyes. "We're friends."

Jet's aether warped in his mind, indicating a half-truth. Jet leaned into the twist in his victim's arm.

The teen screamed. "Taylor! My last name might be Taylor. Maybe, I don't know! But I'm Darien. And you're my mentor. Person. Thing." His eyes glinted with fear. "Are you in special forces mode? Please don't kill me."

Truth. OK... Jet pursed his lips and loosened his grip. "How did we get here?"

"Th-there was a bad guy and a plane. Zekk. He took us from Altair. But we escaped and fell. There's a beach over there." Darien swallowed and blinked a drop of sweat from his eye.

Truth. What the...? We fell out of a plane? Jet leaned behind Darien's view to block the astonishment on his face. *I don't see any parachutes. And how could we land in the middle of a jungle?*

"How do you know my name?"

"We met at Jade Glen," Darien said, "in the year forty-eight sixteen."

Truth? Jet's pulse skipped a beat. *He must be insane for that not to register as a lie. The year is forty-eight ten!*

Darien slowly twisted back to catch Jet's gaze, ignoring the knife. "Jet... I think you've lost your memory."

22

Jet's knife dove into the wood, creating an uneven divot in the spear's tip.

The chunk flopped onto the pile between Jet's boots, where the waterlogged earth softened the shavings into something that smelled like mildew and rain.

Great. Now do I just leave the divot, or should I carve the entire thing smaller to fix it?

Black hair fell into Jet's eyes for the dozenth time, and he swatted it away. *Can't focus without food. When was the last time I ate?* He was pretty sure the fruit Darien had found was inedible, but at this rate, he just might try it.

Hours had passed since he'd woken, but his head still throbbed—especially the swollen knot on the side that felt like he'd smashed it into a wall. Or a plane, apparently.

Jet glanced across the small campsite at Darien. The teen was cracking yet another coconut on a rock, peeking into the green flesh after every few impacts. He looked like Jet felt, with mosquito-gnawed skin, wild hair plastered to his neck with sweat, and mud splattered on the few pieces of sleek armor that hadn't been discarded in the heat.

I swear I've never seen him before in my life. Jet squinted through the throbbing in his head. *How could he possibly know everything he does about me? But he said I'm not in the Royal Guard anymore—obviously that can't be right.*

"What?" Darien paused the coconut torture to tilt his head at Jet. "Did you remember everything yet?"

Jet snapped his gaze back to his spear. "The sun's setting. We'll need more firewood to keep it going through the night." After the hours they'd spent finally getting a flame going, losing it was a worst-case scenario. "Can you find some that isn't wet this time?"

Darien snorted and dropped the coconut next to its plump brethren, across the camp from the ant-covered discard pile. "Is there anything dry on this swamp island?"

"Good question," Jet muttered. "Why don't you fly around with those fancy wings and check?" Apparently waking up in the middle of a jungle wasn't insane enough, so the teen had sprouted wings like a sunburned pubescent angel to search for resources.

I'm definitely drugged. Creator, let me be drugged.

Darien sighed and glanced up through the hole in the treetops. The sky blazed orange on one side and darkened on the other. "Won't have much time, but I can check to the north. There's gotta be some houses nearby." He wiped his hands on his mud-smeared shirt. "You know, it's really weird that you make fun of my wings when you just taught me about them a few days ago."

Jet harrumphed. "A few days ago, I was with my unit in Illyria. And that bleeding desert was heaven compared to this."

The fire popped as Darien rolled his eyes. "Maybe if your head gets bashed again, you'll remember everything."

"Maybe if you touch me, I'll kill you." Jet stood and slipped the knife into his belt. His legs ached in protest. "Go find some fresh water— maybe a spring that feeds the river. I'll get something for dinner."

"With *that?*" Darien pointed at Jet's hand-carved spear. "Is that a pencil?"

Jet tossed his spear to his other hand. *OK, maybe it is a little thin.* "Well, not all of us can be sentinels."

"You know how to use sentinel, too!" Darien growled and rustled his dirty-blonde hair. "Ugh. Forget dinner. Just lay down or something. If you get your memory back, you'll figure us a way out of this in no time."

Light flashed through the jungle, and a pair of bluejay-patterned wings appeared from Darien's shoulders. He jumped and beat them in a flurry of wind, scattering their campsite with a gust.

"Hey!" Jet lurched forward to cover the campfire, whose flame sputtered and revived. He glared at Darien's figure as it disappeared into the sky over the tree line. *Idiot!*

Jet retrieved his spear with a sigh and set off toward the beach. *This is insane. How in the bleeding skies did I end up here?*

He pulled at the chain around his neck. Dog tags jingled up his back and over his shoulder, then fell into his hand alongside a black feather with a stark white tip. *I'm supposed to have wings, too?* His thumb pressed into his tags, feeling the nicks and scuffs that hadn't been in the metal just days before. *It doesn't feel like six years have passed. It feels like I'm in a different world.*

Memories of Illyria flooded Jet's aching mind, wracking him with nostalgia. *If we're so far in the future, then where's my unit?* A golden-eyed woman grinned in his mind's eye, contrasting bright teeth with dark, flawless skin. *What happened to Sorvashti?*

The brush and trees gave way, and the mud submitted to white sand. Jet gazed over the serene ocean and took a breath of humid, salty air. *Just survive for now.* Rapids from a thin river churned into the ocean nearby, clashing with the waves in a soothing rhythm. *Guess there are worse places to be stranded.*

Something scuttled across the sand, catching his eye. Jet paused and found another on the rocks, then another. *Crabs—of course! They come out at dusk!*

He slunk forward and jabbed at a crusty-shelled crab with his spear.

It was faster. They were all faster.

Worthless pencil. Panting, Jet plopped down on the sand and tossed his spear aside. He tore his boots off. The sand was cool and smooth between his toes. *I'll catch you with my bare hands—*

A coughing fit erupted from his lungs. Jet leaned over and hacked until red spots appeared on the perfect sand.

He steadied his breathing and stared. *Did I just cough up blood?* He ran his fingers over the stained sand. *What the... Is future me sick?*

A branch cracked from the tree line. Jet whirled around.

Slitted red eyes glinted in the dying sunlight. A reptile as tall as a man hunkered in the riverbank's trees, standing on its hind legs with dagger-like claws. A brilliant array of feathers stuck out from its skull like a crown.

Jet's heart stuttered. *Is that a xavi?*

The blood on his fingers suddenly felt cold. *I smell like weakness.*

The xavi lurched at him, fast as a snake. Jet cursed and scrambled for his spear.

A high-pitched screech split the twilight as the xavi jumped, bearing its claws. Jet rolled out of the way in a spew of sand. Slices of pain raked across his back.

Jet shot to his feet and held his spear out. *Too fast!*

The xavi turned and snapped its jaws, catching the spear in its fangs like a toothpick. Jet wrenched it free and the creature leaped again, aiming its claws for Jet's neck.

Jet twisted the spear, changing its trajectory as the beast's weight came down. A sickening squelch sounded as the breath was knocked from his lungs.

I'm dead.

Jet clenched his eyes shut as a gurgling noise spilled out with rancid breath above him. A scaled leg twitched in the sand, and the xavi teetered and flopped to the beach beside him.

Jet scrambled away. He gasped for breath and stared down at the convulsing creature. His spear stuck out from its back like a victory flag.

Son of a d'hakka! Jet looked himself over for wounds. Besides the stinging scratches in his back, he was whole. *The elemental of luck loves me!*

He watched the xavi still on the sand. Light behind the serpentine eyes dimmed and went out.

That didn't just happen. Wait—how much meat is that? It must weigh as much as me. Can we eat a carnivore?

A smile spread wide across his face. "Yes!"

"Jet!" Darien yelled from the jungle.

Jet took off in a sprint, reveling in his triumph. Brush cracked underfoot as he called back, "You'd better apologize to my pencil! You'll never guess what—"

"I found food!" Darien interrupted. "And something better!"

Jet stopped up short in a slosh of wet earth. There, beside their measly campfire, was the most stunning woman he'd ever seen. Light ink tattoos flowed across her shoulders in a graceful design, unhindered by the filth that clung to her skin. Pale hair framed the golden eyes he remembered—perhaps a few years older, but still harboring an ageless quality.

Sorvashti grinned. "Hello, *shlanga.* Apology—I am here."

23

Jet knew his mouth was hanging open, but he didn't care to shut it. Sorvashti's smile beamed despite her water-soaked tunic and shorts. Ragged edges had been torn from her pants, leaving the smooth dark skin of her legs revealed to glow in the jungle's strangled sunlight.

What is she doing here?

Sorvashti leaped forward with a cry of joy and crushed Jet in a hug. "Thank the creator you are the OK!" she said into his chest.

This is not a side-hug. Jet's arms slowly curled around her as he felt his ears warm. *Is she my girl? She must be—why else would she be here with me, if we're several years in the future?*

He glanced at Darien for a clue, but a tear slipped down the teen's smiling face. He swiped it away and grinned at Sorvashti like she was the most wonderful thing he'd ever seen.

She barely looks any older. How old am I supposed to be, again?

"Careful," Darien said. "He's not as OK as he looks."

Jet glared at him as Sorvashti pulled back.

Darien blinked, and his voice drifted through Jet's mind. *What, you think you can keep it a secret? Why are you so obsessed with secrets?*

Jet didn't let the surprise show on his face—Darien's voice rang clear for a non-arbiter. He must have had some decent cross-gift training.

It's my business, so I'll handle it, Jet thought back.

Darien raised an eyebrow at him.

"Darien, do you do this?" Sorvashti raised a hand to Jet's jaw and turned his head to the side so she could see what must have been a mess on the left side of his head. Her face contorted with disgust. "Does the cloth monster spit on his head?"

"Sorry, I was just trying to stop the bleeding. Those used to be his sleeves—figured he wouldn't need 'em in the heat anyway." Darien sniffed, rubbed his eyes, and slipped his hands in his pockets. "I don't know anything about first aid."

"Truly." Sorvashti pulled at something near Jet's wound, and he suppressed a wince. "It will be of the infect."

Jet clenched his jaw. *Awesome. An infection in the middle of a rainforest would be just lovely. Although...* He let his eyes drift down for a half-second. *Being stranded on a deserted island doesn't seem quite so bad anymore.*

Darien cleared his throat quite loudly. His voice blared through Jet's head. *I thought there was something between you two, but turn it down, man! If you've got a bond with her, she could hear you!*

Jet choked on his own breath as Sorvashti tugged at his hair. *I'm an arbiter, OK? Get your nose out of—*

Oh, no. Nuh uh. Darien crossed his arms like a disapproving middle school teacher. *Your shields used to be way stronger—they're weakening every hour. I've never been able to hear you like that through our bond before.*

Jet glanced at Sorvashti's thin-lipped expression before glaring back at Darien. *I don't have a bond with you, angel-boy.*

I wish that were the case right now. 'Cause if I hear something like that again, I'll throw up. On you.

"It needs the medicine now," Sorvashti murmured. "It has the..."

Her mouth scrunched to the side, and her voice brushed across his shields: *It's angry, and swollen pretty bad.*

"I'm not surprised." Jet found his voice was warped, and he swallowed.

Sorvashti turned and pushed through a mass of vines, then tromped in the direction of the beach. "Come! I will show you this place I find. Maybe it has the medicine."

"Did you hit the water beside it?" Darien crashed after her. "Is that how you landed safely? I thought you were dead!"

Sorvashti shot a condescending look over his shoulder. "No, *perrunt.* The water would kills me. The vanguard is full of use." She winked.

So she doesn't have wings like we apparently do? Jet tested the barrier of aether around his mind as he followed. It felt plenty thick. He wasn't accustomed to having to maintain shields at all—not since he'd left Haevyn Serran Academy. On Viper Unit, he wasn't around any other aethryn who might hear his thoughts. Well, aside from Coral, but it wasn't worth the effort of maintaining shields just to keep his thoughts from her.

Hothra's quiet-thought technique should work. Jet strained to recall his arbiter training, and his head throbbed. *Yeesh, that'd be annoying to maintain. Why do I have a bond with this idiot, anyway?*

"Well, I'm so glad you're OK," Darien said. "I thought we'd lost you."

"I am of the Ironhide." Sorvashti brushed a spiked branch away from their path. "It is not much easy for us to die." She glanced back at Darien. "Or the Valinor, yes? Thank you for saving of him."

Darien smiled back. "Of course."

He saved me? Really? Jet frowned at the mud as he stepped over a tree root. *Could this get any more convoluted?* Somehow he felt like the lesser of the group—which made about as much sense as him waking up in Malaan missing years of memory.

Jet straightened his back. "So I killed a xavi." He pointed south, where the sound of distant rushing water gurgled as they stepped into muddy sand. "Think it's that way, by the river."

Darien stopped and looked back at him with eyes as wide as the setting sun. "A xavi? Like, the velociraptor thing behind two layers of bars at the zoo?"

Jet glanced over the ocean's horizon and shrugged. *That's right, wonder-boy.*

"Does this hurt you?" Sorvashti looked Jet up and down, peering through the holes in his shirt.

"Just a scratch on my back," Jet admitted, knowing it would probably be impossible to hide. The pang of sweat falling into the broken skin beneath his shoulder blades was tame in comparison to the throbbing in his head.

Sand flicked up around Sorvashti's feet as she ran to Jet and whirled around his back. *"Shlanga!* This is two! And it is bleeding!"

Guess she still calls me 'snake,' then. Jet kept his spine straight and looked over his shoulder. "No biggie."

Sorvashti snorted, grabbed his wrist, and stomped closer to the ocean waves. She muttered something under her breath that sounded like Terruthian—he caught something about 'men.'

"Uh, can we eat a xavi?" Darien called from the tree line. "Or is there any food at the new place? I'm starving!"

"Get the meat!" Sorvashti yelled back without stopping.

"OK." Darien jogged over. "Can I have your knife?"

Jet fished his blade from his pocket and tossed it to him. "Don't lose it."

"Do I look like a two-year-old?" Darien gave him a blank look as he caught the knife. "Maybe you aren't so different after all."

Jet glanced at Sorvashti as she waded into the surf, then narrowed his eyes at Darien. *Watch it.*

Don't have too much fun, lovebird. Darien's wings burst to life behind him, and sand exploded as he leaped into the sky.

Jet harrumphed and turned back to the scarlet sun, which lightly kissed the glare-streaked ocean below. Sorvashti looked back at him from the waves like a sea nymph.

"I forget," she said. "You have the wings to carry one, yes?" Something sparkled in her golden gaze.

Uh... syn. Do I? Jet forced a smile. "Where are we going?"

Sorvashti pointed out over the water.

Jet squinted where she indicated. A portion of the sunlit glare refracted in a different direction—apparently from the gleaming roof of a tiny building on what must have been a very small island.

"Is that a house?" he asked.

"Yes, it is very good," Sorvashti said. "I see this in the sky. Darien says he sees it, too, and he finds me there." She flicked her wrist at the jungle's edge. "A good place to sleep, but if you like the trees—"

"Oh, no," Jet chuckled. "That's fantastic! The owners will let us stay there?"

Sorvashti tilted her head. "There is no one there."

So... Jet studied her puzzled face. "Did you just... break in?"

"I have to push the window with vanguard." Sorvashti splayed her hands out and pushed them forward to illustrate. "Of course if someone is there, I do not do this."

"Right." Jet couldn't shake the feeling that something was off. Certainly they were in some sort of emergency scenario, but since when could someone break and enter another's property with so little care? *I haven't known her very long, but she didn't strike me as the criminal type.*

"So..." Sorvashti looked at him expectantly.

"Hmm?"

"Will you carry me with the wings you say me of? I wish to see them."

Oh. Jet scratched the back of his neck. "Actually, you know, I think I'd rather swim out there. I'm covered in creator knows what." He pulled his shirt over his head.

"But the water will be in your..." Sorvashti gestured at his forehead. Her eyes flicked to his bare chest, widened, then dashed away.

"I'll keep above water." Jet bundled his stained shirt into a wad and stuffed it in a large pocket on his thigh. *Heh, she definitely thinks I'm—*

His thought fell flat as he looked down at himself. His muscles weren't as prominent nor as toned as they had been a few hours ago. *Son of a d'hakka. I didn't keep up with high-intensity training?*

Scars Jet didn't recognize marred his chest and stomach. He grimaced at the one that indicated he'd been gut-shot. It and another on his pectoral looked like former bullet wounds, but maybe the jagged line on his side was from a knife.

And his skin looked lighter than it should be, now that he could see a portion that wasn't sunburned. *I look... too pale. Sickly.*

A splash interrupted his thoughts. Sorvashti dove under an oncoming wave, then bobbed up above the surface with her short hair flattened and shining. She grinned back at him.

Jet waded in after her, relishing the cool surf. He'd never been one to enjoy beaches, but this felt heavenly. Until the salt water stung like blazes on the cuts in his back.

The waves calmed a short ways out, and Jet fell into the swimming form that the Royal Guard had drilled into him. The exercise had just started to feel good when they arrived at a rocky sandbar that curled in a circular barrier around a strip of land.

A thin island sprawled through the water, barely large enough to uphold the tiny house and collection of palm trees beside it. Solar panels formed the entire roof while glass and white metal composed the walls.

Jet let out a low whistle as they floated around to a break in the rocks, where a boat dock and ladder dipped into the ocean. *How much did it cost to build out here?*

Water sloshed from Sorvashti's clothes as she climbed the ladder. Jet followed and straightened on the creaking dock, deciding not to put his ragged shirt back on. *Doesn't look like anyone's home.* He glanced from the empty boat tether to a small clearing with a symbol on the ground. *Helicopter landing pad. Nice.*

"Good evening, Lady Ironhide," said a speaker on a light post in a smooth feminine voice, and Jet nearly jumped off the dock. "Did you enjoy your swim?"

"Yes, thank you," Sorvashti replied as she strode toward the arched front door.

Jet's mouth hung open. "I thought you said no one was here!"

"Oh, this is the house." Sorvashti pointed at the door. "My father has this in the Governor's mansion also."

That's right; she's the daughter of a LaKotan Governor. Jet stared at the light post. *The house has an AI? And I thought Thracian was loaded!*

"So this is *your* house? I thought you said you broke in—"

"No!" Sorvashti laughed. "The house sees that the world destroys months ago, and loses the connection. She does not see her master. But the sun keeps her awake." She pointed at the roof, which glinted with solar panels. "I tell her I am the guest."

Something dark slurried through Jet's veins. *'The world destroys?' Does that mean... she can't be saying what I think she's saying. What idiot has been teaching her Arisian?*

Sorvashti waved for him to follow and smiled. "Come! I find the medicine." She opened the front door, and the lights warmed to a soft glow of their own accord.

Jet cautiously stepped onto the welcome mat, feeling like a drowned rat in a five-star hotel. The living room and kitchen were compact displays of modern amenities and appliances, as if it were a model home display at a ritzy furniture store. Two thick leather couches faced a wall-sized television that flicked on as Sorvashti passed.

"Would you like to watch a movie this evening?" the AI asked.

Jet's hand drifted to where his handgun should have been as he found small cameras in every other corner. *This is creepy as syn!*

"No, thank you," Sorvashti said as she turned down a hall. "Why do you say the Arisian again? I ask you to say the Terruthian."

The AI responded in an apologetic tone of the harsh Terruthian dialect.

"*Cimaluth ter shootz,*" Sorvashti said to a camera in the ceiling. "Yes, he stays here too. His name is Jet. He knows some of the Terruthian." She ducked into a bathroom and opened a decorative cabinet on the wall, examining the bottles and boxes inside.

I guess I learned more Terruthian, then? But I have no idea what she said. Jet felt like he should stand in the walk-in shower so his clothes would continue to drip dirty water onto its embedded river stones rather than the carpet. He watched Sorvashti work through the wide mirror. *I can't figure this out. Are we together or not?*

The more time passed, the more he grew uneasy. *Everything is wrong somehow. I should just be straight with her and find out what in the bleeding skies happened. Seems like she'll be helpful either way.*

He cleared his throat. "I, uh... I should tell you something."

Sorvashti furrowed her brow at a pill bottle. "Hmm?"

Jet swallowed. "I don't think I remember you as well as I wish I did."

Sorvashti raised her voice and said something in Terruthian, then turned to him with a confused expression. "What do you say?"

He looked down at his waterlogged boots. "I don't... really... know how I got here."

She stepped closer and leaned down until she caught his gaze. "Your memory is hurt?" She frowned at the side of his head. "What do you know?"

Jet pulled his shirt out of his pocket and squeezed it over the drain. "I said goodbye to you at the Valinorian Embassy in Shailoh, then my unit went after Qua'set." Brown water slipped between his fingers. "I went upstairs for overwatch, then woke up in the jungle a couple hours ago."

Sorvashti's eyes went huge. "You... do not know anything from then?"

"Well... no."

She stared at him for a long moment. "Truly?"

Jet squirmed under her scrutiny. "Sorry." He slung his shirt over the shower's pane of glass. "Would you mind, uh, filling me in?"

Pain, fear, and a dozen masked emotions flitted behind Sorvashti's eyes. She lowered her voice. "Jet, you have much hurt at this time." She reached out a hand and gently touched his side.

Jet looked down. Her fingers brushed across the jagged scar beside his abs.

He pursed his lips. "What happened to my unit?"

Sorvashti's frown deepened, and she shook her head. "Great evil." She raised her hand to his forehead. "Your mind goes back to this?"

Jet took her hand in his. "Why are we here, together?" He lowered his voice to a whisper. "Are we married or something?"

Sorvashti's skin flushed even darker. "N-no. It is... a long story, yes?" She pulled her hand back, looked down at the pill bottle, and said something in Terruthian.

Jet felt relief as the AI responded in kind. As long as he wasn't married to someone he barely knew, relying on his father for money, or a hippie, everything would be all right.

"This will work." Sorvashti jogged into the bedroom, grabbed a chair, and pushed it into the middle of the wood floor. "Please, sit."

Jet obeyed and took the pair of pills she offered. He glanced at the bottle to confirm they were antibiotics before swallowing them whole.

"I am sorry this happens of you," Sorvashti said as she set a roll of cloth bandages, tape, and medical scissors on the bed. She pursed her lips as she stared at his head. "This will not be good. I do not know the medicine good." She dashed back into the bathroom.

"It's fine—I can do it myself. Is there a needle and thread in there?"

"No." Sorvashti's cringe was apparent through her voice before she returned with another bottle of pills. "Is this of the pain?"

Jet glanced at the text on the bottle. "Yeah, but I don't need—"

"I know you do not need of this, *shlanga*." Sorvashti struggled with the cap until it cracked open, and she shoved another pill into his hand. She smirked down at him. "You do not need to impress of me."

Jet felt his cheeks flush. He cleared his throat, took the pill, and downed it. "So we're just friends, then."

Sorvashti sighed and tossed the bottle onto the bed. "There is a hole the large of Elyon in your head, and you ask of this." She grabbed the roll of bandages, then raised an eyebrow at him. "Is this of your bad memory, or do you truly stop the love of me?"

So we were together at some point, then. Jet flashed her his best smile. "Would it be possible to stop?"

Sorvashti laughed and snipped off a long stretch of cloth. "Oh, Jet. You are so bad at this. It is good I do not like you for this reason." She draped the bandage over her shoulder and crouched beside him with the scissors.

"So you do like me."

She rolled her eyes. "You are definitely the young again." Hair gently tugged in her grip before the scissors sliced shut.

"Oh, hey." Jet did his best to remain still and not wince as she worked. "Don't worry about my hair too much. I'm going to cut it down to the right length anyway."

"Oh, but I like it." Sorvashti frowned in his peripheral vision. "If your memory comes back in the hour, you will be angry of me for letting you do the cut."

"I promise I won't." He grinned. "Does it matter what you think of it if we're not together?"

She chuckled. "Yes, because you want me."

A sudden burst of pain lit through Jet's chest. He coughed and tasted blood.

Sorvashti released his hair and stepped back. "Are you the OK?"

"Yeah, I'm—"

An unbearable itching crawled through Jet's lungs. He bent over and coughed until dark spots speckled the floor.

They both stared for a moment of chilled silence.

"Jet," Sorvashti whispered. "What is this?"

I felt this a few times before, but never this bad. It was just from breathing in dust at the Brazen Tower collapse. Right? Jet swallowed the coppery taste on his tongue and grimaced at a sensation of a knife sliding down his throat. *Six years...*

He wiped his lips and stared at the blood on his fingers. "I don't know."

24

Frigid wind chilled Aleah's wings to the bone. Her soft white feathers camouflaged her in a maelstrom of flurries so thick she could hardly see the ground.

She breathed into her scarf and clung to the box in her hands. *I'll catch my death like this!*

An old barn of tin and wood emerged through the blizzard. Aleah swooped low and landed in front of the door. Snow swallowed her legs up to her knees.

"Get in, quick!" a voice yelled from the darkness beyond the sliding door. A familiar hand reached out, grabbed Aleah's coat, and pulled her into the barn.

Raydon's warm smile lit the barn as Aleah's eyes adjusted. She shivered and pulled her hood back, scattering snowflakes on the dry dirt. Hay bales stacked up to the ceiling, where a glow-eyed cat stared down from the rafters.

"I was getting worried." Raydon brushed snow from Aleah's hair and took the box from her exhausted arms. "If I'd have known it'd get this bad, I wouldn't let you go back for another trip!"

"There's still so much to do." Aleah released her wings and breathed in dusty scents of corn feed and fertilizer. Anything was better than the wind in her freezing nose and throat.

"Well, we're doing the best we can. It's not like we can load up a truck and have no one notice." Raydon stepped up onto a wooden platform and opened a creaking wooden door. Stacks of boxes lined one side, and the shelves on the other held glass jars and canned foods of every color.

Raydon looked over his shoulder with a spark in his eye. "You sure you're totally invisible when you sneak stuff out?"

Aleah grinned. "Would you like another demonstration?"

Raydon's eyes narrowed as the set the box down with a *thunk* and a plume of dust. He patted his pockets and looked down at himself. "What're you going to steal next time? My ears?"

"'Steal' is such a negative word. I prefer 'borrow.'" Aleah slipped past him and examined his work—the jars were arranged by macronutrient, just as she'd requested. Potatoes, corn, and carrots lined one side while broccoli, vidali, and greens stacked on the other. *We're short on protein. Well, hopefully there'll be something left to hunt in the winter.*

Her heart panged like an old bruise. Still they'd heard nothing of those who'd gone missing, including her brother.

"Well, you might not want to *borrow* anything from that one room."

Raydon's words jolted Aleah from her thoughts. She turned back to find him rifling through the contents of the new box. "Oh?"

"I don't think we'll ever be able to clean up the mess from the body," Raydon said. "We might just want to never open that door again after we bury him. I think people might rather sleep in here than... yeah."

The smell assaulted Aleah even from her memory, and she wrinkled her nose. "Agreed." *I really need to find us a better place. If only we weren't so rushed.*

She walked out of the storage closet and squinted at the light shining through the barn's sliding door. Wind clacked tin against tin, and the wooden rafters groaned above her. *Guess I'd better sit tight till the storm dies down.*

"It's a real shame," Raydon said from the pantry. "I guess the body is Rex. Found his note; it reminds me of my old man. I hope they're OK somewhere." Glass clinked over the moaning wind. "What were your real parents like?"

Aleah pulled her coat tighter around her chest. "I think you mean my biological parents. Thracian and Marie are my real parents now."

"Oh, of course. I didn't mean that—I'm sorry." Raydon's head poked around the door with an apologetic look. "If it's hard for you to talk about, I don't want to—"

"No, it's fine." Aleah found the brown-striped cat in the rafters. It lounged on a thick beam of wood and licked its leg, claws extended.

"My mom had silver hair like mine—wavy and so bright it was almost white. She never stopped smiling. But Dad was always grumpy about something." *Except for that one birthday when we bought him that prank necktie.* A smile tugged at Aleah's lips. "Well, he just wanted everyone to think he was grumpy. He always wanted more for us—I don't think he ever understood that Mom and I were happy, even though we were poor. I didn't know what I was missing, and I didn't care."

Raydon paused to listen. "Sounds like a good man who just wanted more for his family."

"Yeah, but I never wanted anything more than what we already had." Aleah sighed and glanced at him with heavy eyelids. "It's been a long time, but I still miss them so much."

"I'm so sorry." Raydon hopped down from the platform and took her in a gentle but firm hug. "I can't believe anyone would want to hurt them."

"Hmm?" Aleah breathed in his scent. "No one did, of course. It was an accident." Old memories of fire and sirens and colored lights reared up, and Aleah forced them back down. "Illyria and Kioa were at war—there was so much tension and violence in the streets." She swallowed the lump in her throat. "No one looked twice at a house fire."

"I can't imagine." Raydon hugged her tighter. "Maybe it's better that there wasn't any foul play suspected."

Maybe so. Wait... Aleah stilled as another memory flared from the corner of her mind that she'd suppressed for so long. A face—a color photo paper-clipped to a police report. Gray hair, tanned skin, silver eyes.

Her blood slowed to an icy slush. *That man looked just like a young Levi. Like his son, Brailey.*

"There was someone," Aleah murmured. "The police approached me a year or so later. Said they had a suspect."

"Oh? Did they catch him?"

Wow, they look exactly alike. Aleah's coat suddenly felt too warm. *I must've never realized it before.*

"Aleah?" Raydon said.

She pulled back and rubbed her temples. "I... sorry." Her day-old migraine throbbed with new ferocity. "I just... realized something. But it's stupid."

Raydon furrowed his dark brow at her. "What?"

"Never mind. It's just a coincidence. A bad one." Aleah shrugged out of her coat. The barn definitely wasn't warm, but for some reason, she was sweating.

"Babe, are you OK?" Raydon caught her gaze with deep brown eyes swirling with concern. "You look like you don't feel well."

"I'm fine." Aleah glanced around for a clean place to drop her coat, then decided to let the fuzzy hood tickle her nose instead. "It's just that the suspect looked like Master Emberhawk for some reason."

Raydon's face contorted in confusion. "Master Levi?"

"Yeah, like I said, it's stupid." Wind howled and rattled the tin door, and Aleah clutched her coat tighter.

Raydon lowered his head until their eyes were on the level. "You don't think Levi had anything to do with... well..." He tilted his head and squinted one eye. "That's a little crazy, babe."

"No, I—of course it's crazy. I'm not saying that." Aleah took a step back and looked down at strands of hay trampled in the dust. "But it looked like him. A lot like him. It just... scared me. I've never realized it till now." Her eyes watered, and she blinked them rapidly. *Just forget about it. Why would Levi be a suspect? It couldn't have been his son Brailey, either—it was years ago, so he would have just been a child.*

"Strange that the suspect didn't look Kioan or Illyrian," Raydon mused. "Levi looks like he's from Sai, which is across the world from Illyria. He didn't have any connection to you back then. And it's not like he knew you'd become one of his students."

"Of course," Aleah said. "Let's go back…"

Another memory bubbled to life. Noruntalus, just before his death, gloating that he'd seen the future and told the Serran Grand Master Council about Darien and Teravyn. He'd implied that Darien owed him his life for sending Levi out to retrieve them during the meteor storm.

Aleah's pulse raced even as her muscles solidified. *That's not true. The masters wouldn't…*

"You're doing that thing again." Raydon waved a hand in front of her face.

Aleah snapped back into the barn. "Sorry." She cleared her throat. "You don't think…" She glanced up at him and lowered her voice. "You don't think the masters use the sage gift to identify their students, do you? And then they alter the future by choosing the most powerful students?"

Raydon's eyebrows lifted. "Where'd you come up with that?"

"Noruntalus implied it," Aleah murmured. "You don't think…"

"No, I don't." Raydon took her by the shoulders. "Listen: Levi didn't kill your parents. They didn't target you, and—"

"They targeted Teravyn and Darien. She's a sage and he's got a huge amount of aether." Aleah raised her hand and snapped, and fire burst to life an inch above her fingernails. "I'm a healer and a Phoeran elementalist."

Raydon took a step back. "And a Serran. OK, I see your point."

Aleah snuffed the flame out and pursed her lips. "But that's ridiculous. I'm sure Noruntalus was lying. He didn't seem completely sane." She slipped back into her jacket and tried to suppress the other memories from that night—the ones that seeped into her nightmares. "I'll ask Master Willow about this. Surely she'll just laugh."

"Surely." Raydon smirked.

Aleah narrowed her eyes at him. "What?"

"Oh, nothing." Raydon lifted his hand. A veridian ribbon dangled from his fingers.

Aleah's jaw dropped, and she grabbed at it. "Hey! Did you pickpocket that from my coat?"

Raydon jerked his hand away and wiggled the ribbon above her head. "'Pickpocket' is such a negative word. I prefer 'pilfer.'"

Aleah chuckled and swiped the ribbon back. "Jackwagon." She glanced outside—the blizzard had calmed to a steady drift. "Let's get back home before we freeze to death."

25

Jet's finger tapped the digital map on the TV screen. *Judging from the vegetation, I'd bet we're in Malaan...* He recalled the sun's position. *West side.*

He furrowed his brow at a divot in the Sea of Bones. "AI, where is this house located?"

"Twenty-three miles south of Ceemalao, on the western coast of the Malaano Empire," the feminine voice chimed.

"You miss a spot of the back of your head."

Jet glanced over his shoulder to find Sorvashti clipping her toenails on the leather sofa. "Do you have the memory yet? Remember you promise not to be angry of me."

He blew out a frustrated breath and ran a hand through his hair, trying to find the spot she spoke of. His hand came away with severed black strands. "Why are you so insistent that I'll be mad at you? Was I a jerk or something?"

Sorvashti choked on a laugh as she concentrated with the clippers. "Something."

An awkward knock sounded from the back door of sliding glass. Darien hunched outside, holding a severed scaled leg—the xavi's thigh.

Jet jogged over and opened the door. Darien stumbled in, panting and sweating.

"No!" Sorvashti scrambled over the side of the couch. "Do not bring—"

The leg landed on the kitchen island with a wet thump. Blood oozed onto the granite countertop.

"Cut this outside!" Sorvashti pointed back out the door. "You are cleaning of this!"

"Cleaning? It's not like we're moving in." The sink hiccupped brown water before running clean. Darien washed his hands and scowled down at his scarlet-smeared shirt. "You have no idea how hard that was to get off."

Jet examined the jagged cuts along the striations of thick red muscle. *No fat on this… I wonder how it'll taste.* "My knife?"

Darien slung water from his hands and handed the blade over. "I'll take a real knife, thank you." He grabbed a kitchen knife from a magnetic strip on the wall.

"Can't ask too much from a concealed blade." Jet slipped the thin knife back into its hidden sheath in his boot. "You're welcome."

"I can try to make the bulgogi and japchae of this," Sorvashti murmured. She opened the pantry door and pulled out a box of noodles—one of the few non-perishable food items they'd found in the entire house. "Jet, can you cook the *damoon?*" The noodle box clacked on the counter.

"Uh, sure." Jet picked up the box and squinted at the Malaano script. *Well… maybe not.*

"Oh, sweet!" Darien stared at the map on the TV as he dried his hands with a green towel. "Did you find out where we are?"

"Twenty-three miles south of Ceemalao," Jet said into a scarce cabinet. He grabbed a silver pot.

Darien tossed the towel on the counter. "Great." He stomped up to the screen and glared at the illustration of the Sea of Bones—the vast blue expanse that separated the western coast of Katrosi from the island of Malaan. "How're we ever gonna get home?"

Jet turned the sink's water dial to red. "Where is home, exactly?"

Darien gave him an incredulous look. "Did you forget where your house is, too?"

"I don't have a house," Jet said. *If he says Valinor Manor, I'll—*

"Your parents do, in Altair."

Jet gritted his teeth. *Future me is a real winner!* He kept his expression bland. "So we all live there with my parents?"

"More or less," Darien said.

Jet tested the water's heat and dipped the pot under the stream. "I'm fine to stay here."

Darien snorted. "No, no, brainpan. You're coming back home so Aleah can fix you. As much as I'm enjoying this, you're freaking me out."

"You think the healer can fix this?" Sorvashti asked as she carved scales from meat. "I think they make the skin come together. This does not seem the same."

Darien's mouth twisted as he glanced at the bandage on Jet's head. "Well, what else could we do?"

"Maybe the sleep can fix this," Sorvashti said as she focused on the meat, "and maybe the staying here is not so bad."

Darien looked as if he'd been backhanded. "You... you just don't want to have to tell the masters what you did!"

Sorvashti grimaced. "Things are bad in the Altair. And it is much hard to get back."

What did she do? Water spilled over the side of the pot, and Jet shut off the faucet and poured some back out. He lifted it to the flat obsidian cooktop. "You have an aircraft, angel-boy? Are you a pilot?" He studied the heat controls.

"Zekk has a heli-plane thing." Darien returned to the kitchen and rested his hands on the countertop across from Sorvashti. "Have you seen any sign of him?"

"Yes." Sorvashti cut a thick steak from the bone. "He is a Serran—he is not dead. I see him fly to the trees."

The cooktop beeped as Jet set the burner heat to high. "Who?"

"Long story. Real bad guy who took us from Altair." Darien pointed at Jet's bandage. "The one who gave you that."

Not a friendly, then. Jet watched Darien pull a collection of feathers from a pocket—he recognized them from the xavi's crown. "What does he want?"

Sorvashti visibly stiffened. "To bring us of the Maqua."

Silence grew thick in the small house. Jet stared at the bubbles on the bottom of the pot. "What's wrong with Maqua?"

"Murderers. Slavery. Zekk." Darien sat at a barstool and carefully pulled flecks of tissue from the xavi feather quills.

Slavery? Is he serious? Jet stared at Darien. "Making a keychain for your purse, fashionista?"

"They're for your sis—" Darien swallowed his words and slowly looked up at Jet. "Do you know a girl named Aleah?"

Jet couldn't decrypt his expression. "The Illyrian actress?"

Sorvashti's knife halted. They both stared at him with eyes as round as the xavi's femur.

Jet blinked back as a bubble in the pot floated to the top. "What?"

"Uh, yep, they're for my purse." Darien returned his attention to the feathers. "We don't need a plane, anyway—we're Serrans. We can fly back ourselves."

Jet glanced at Sorvashti. "You have wings, too?"

"No." She squatted under the counter and came back up with a skillet. "But you can carry of me with yours."

The throbbing in Jet's head pounded dully against the pain meds. He rubbed his temple. "Yeah, minor problem with that: I'm not crazy and I'm not a bird-man."

"The water is much far." The skillet clanked next to the pot as Sorvashti pointed at the map. "Can you fly this far?"

"I dunno. I could fly forever in kai'lani." Darien looked at Jet. "I'd need your wings for a test flight. Ironfeathers fly further."

Ironwhat? Jet's headache doubled. "I said I don't have any wings."

"Give me your necklace."

Jet sighed and pulled the jingling metal chain over his head. His dog tags, scuffed and dirty, were the only familiar thing he'd seen since he'd woken in the jungle. Well, aside from Sorvashti, but he barely knew her.

His heart dropped as he ran his thumb over the metal. *Where is Viper Unit?*

"Just the feather," Darien said in a quieter tone.

Doesn't belong here anyway. Jet snapped the clasp open, slid the long black feather from the chain, and handed it over.

"Thanks. I'll be careful with it." Darien pulled his leather necklace off and struggled with untying its knot. "I'm beat, and it's getting dark. I'll leave first thing in the morning."

Xavi steak tasted like sandpaper, and the overcooked noodles didn't help. Sorvashti complained at the lack of vegetables, but none of them knew enough about wild Malaano plants to risk eating random vegetation. The yellow fruit Darien had tried earlier had turned his face green for an hour.

Jet ate without complaint—he'd endured much worse cuisine in combat situations—but he'd have bet that the expired can of soup in the pantry would have tasted better. At least they'd found some salt.

They kept all the lights off as the sun fell—apparently the 'Zekk' boogeyman might see them otherwise. Darien volunteered for the first watch with some mumbling about sleep bringing Jet's memories back.

The biggest problem was that the small house had only one bedroom with a queen-sized bed. Sorvashti claimed it before Darien could finish offering to sleep on one of the couches. She shut the door behind her, squashing Jet's feeble hope.

None of the blankets they'd scrounged were long enough to stretch from Jet's feet to his chin. He laid on his back and stared at the ceiling while Darien gazed out the glass back door.

Well, I'll take this over sleeping in the jungle any day. He closed his eyes and hoped the pains in his head and lungs would allow him to sleep. *Maybe Darien's right. Maybe I'll just wake up in the morning and magically remember how I landed in Crazyville.*

A soft purring coaxed Jet from sleep. He frowned against the morning light and opened his eyes. Dormant can lighting looked down on him from a recessed ceiling.

Jet blinked crystallized sleep from his eyes. His headache had subsided, but the fiery itch in his lungs was somehow worse. *Well, so much for remembering everything in my sleep.*

Purring sounded again, and Jet realized it was soft snoring. He looked down and found Sorvashti curled beside his couch, huddled in a poofy striped blanket.

A smile tugged at his lips. *What's she doing here? We give up the bed for her and she lays on the floor?*

Snoring of a different sort sounded from across the room. Darien was slumped in his chair by the back door, arms crossed, head lolled back and mouth gaping open.

Jet suppressed a chuckle. *Some night watchman. And he's supposedly a 'sentinel.'*

His stomach rumbled, apparently unsatisfied with last night's offering. He sat up slowly, preventing his blanket from disturbing Sorvashti.

The couch creaked under him.

Sorvashti jolted awake in an eruption of pillows. She swiped locks of blond hair from her face, met Jet's gaze, and turned a shade of raspberry dark chocolate.

Jet raised an eyebrow. "Sleep well?"

"I… there was… a *vamir.* Creature." She sat up straight and cleared her throat. "Apology. There is something of the noise in my room."

Jet couldn't keep the grin off his face. "I'm glad you came to me; I run an extermination service in my sleep."

Sorvashti clutched her blanket to herself, jumped to her feet, and nearly tripped over a corner of the blanket she stood on. "I do not know this word." She ran to the bedroom in a flurry of pillows and cloth. The door slammed shut behind her.

A loud snort sounded from the back door as Darien jerked awake. He glanced around in a frenzy, wiped drool from his cheek, and mumbled something unintelligible.

"Hey, *sentinel*," Jet called. "See any baddies last night?"

"Sorry," Darien muttered. He staggered out of the chair. "Everyone OK?"

"Apparently." Jet stretched his back and winced at the resulting pang in his chest. He coughed, then held his breath, willing another fit not to claim him. The urge slowly subsided. *Ah, I can control it.*

"Remember anything?" Darien popped his neck and gave Jet a curious look.

"Only trivial stuff. Like my special forces training and how not to fall asleep in the middle of a watch."

Darien grimaced. "I'm really sorry. That was my first night in… well… a really long time. Sleep is different in kai'lani."

Jet stared at him. *He's completely insane.*

"Yeah, never mind." Darien strode to the refrigerator and grabbed a leftover slice of pan-seared xavi. "I'm gonna take off, then. You'll be OK to keep a lookout for Zekk?"

"Mm, yeah, Zekk. Scary dude." Jet strode to the pantry and frowned at the lone can of soup. "Really good at attacking random people at inopportune moments, like when the night watch snores on the job."

"You have no idea." Darien slammed the fridge door shut. "He can suck your aether dry in half a second, and he probably wants to kill you for what you did to his friend. He's Malaano—kinda short with medium skin, blueish eyes, brown hair. Looks like he just walked off the set of a teen girls' movie."

A laugh burst from Jet. "Terrifying." *So he's some kind of energy vampire? I rarely use aether, anyway.*

"Fine, then ask Sorv to keep watch." Darien took a bite of cold meat and made a face as he headed for the door. "Wish me luck."

Jet waved him off. "Luck."

Maybe the soup wasn't such a good idea. If Sorvashti saw him eating expired artificial food instead of her home cooking, she might not be thrilled.

A shower would be nice. Jet ignored his hunger and checked the small guest bathroom beside the kitchen to ensure that there wasn't a bath or shower in it. No such luck.

The bedroom door opened, and Sorvashti appeared with a fresh smile. "Does Darien already leave?" She drifted to the back door and slid it open.

"Yeah." Jet observed the same torn clothes she'd worn yesterday and assumed that there weren't any spare outfits in the closet.

"I do not like this xavi food. Maybe it is not meant to be eat, or maybe I am the bad cook." Sorvashti grinned over her shoulder at him. "Let us go to the fishing."

Relief melted Jet's tension as he recalled a fishing net that hung on the wall of a small shed on the boat dock. "Great idea."

The fishing poles he'd learned with at survival training weren't a tenth as complicated as the rods in the shed. Jet had only used such a complex pole once, on a lake trip with his uncle.

Sorvashti selected two poles and threaded the lines with ease. She snatched a canister of bait, squinted at it, and shrugged. Sticky globs squished onto each of their hooks.

"You look like you know what you're doing," Jet said.

She handed him a pole and strode out onto the dock. "I fish with my *oba*."

Oba...? Jet took the pole and strained to remember the meaning of the Terruthian word. He found what he thought was the line release and cast his lure into the ocean. *"Oba?"*

"The lead of my clan." Sorvashti cast her own hook out just as far. "My father."

"Ah." *Must be nice to fish with your dad as a kid.* Thracian detested the smell of raw fish. And time spent with his dead wife's child in general.

Waves lapped at the barnacles encrusted around the dock's supports. Jet took a deep breath of ocean air and felt the hitch in his lungs relax. *Well, obviously things could be better, but…* He gazed out over the azure horizon. *Not sure I really want to remember anything.*

Sorvashti sat and swung her bare feet over the side of the dock, dipping her toes in the water. A slight smile toyed with her lips as the wind tossed her hair.

She doesn't talk much. Jet sat beside her and admired the flowing designs on her shoulders when she wasn't looking. *She must have been a model at some point.*

One of the bobbers dunked under the water, and Sorvashti shouted and yanked her line back. *"Ayah!"*

"Already?" Jet stared as Sorvashti reeled her line in with a competitive glint in her eye. A flat fish a few inches long splashed out of the water and flopped onto the dock.

"Oh, you are little," Sorvashti said with a disappointed tone. She grabbed the fish behind its bright orange gills, avoiding the spines along its back.

Jet took Sorvashti's rod as she maneuvered the hook from the fish's mouth. "Hey, I'd rather eat him than the xavi."

Sorvashti stuck her tongue out at him.

He grinned. "I just meant… I don't think people eat carnivores in general. And it's not like Darien would know the best slab of meat to cut."

"I am glad you know much of this, because you will cook the next food." Sorvashti plopped the fish into a net attached to the dock.

Syn! Jet kept the smile plastered on his face. "I don't know how to cook. I thought you—"

"You think I will do all the cook because I am the woman?" Sorvashti's smile was dangerously sweet. "This is the good time to learn the cook, *shlanga*."

He swallowed. "As long as I can learn from you instead of Darien."

"Ha! I think Darien's cook will kill us dead." Sorvashti took her rod back from him and walked straight off the dock. Her foot landed in midair, as if on an invisible surface the same height as the dock.

Jet stared as she strode out over the water. *That's right—she said she was a vanguard! But skies... can all vanguards do that? She must be a master!*

"I think the big fish are there." Sorvashti pointed out over the ocean, where the cerulean waves deepened to dark blue. She smirked over her shoulder. "Do you wish to come with?"

Jet looked at her sideways. "You'll drop me."

Sorvashti's white teeth shone through her smile. "Maybe."

Jet chuckled and set his fishing rod down on the dock. "I think you've got fishing covered." He picked up the container of bait and tossed it to her. "I'm going to have a look around the island. See if there's anything else useful nearby."

Sorvashti caught the bait and gave him a slight bow, then turned and walked out over the water.

Jet scanned the landscape. The house's unkempt landscaping and the helicopter pad's tattered windsock swayed lazily on the breeze. All seemed peaceful and quiet.

Except the feeling in his gut that told him he was being watched.

26

Zekk stared at Jet through the waving palm trees, confident that the zwoshii root paste and mud on his face camouflaged him flawlessly. Jet scanned the island and strode down the path toward him like a bluefin tuna on a silver platter.

Unbelievable.

Watching his prisoners had been as entertaining as it was confusing. They'd talked like they actually believed Jet had some sort of amnesia. But maybe it was true if Jet was suddenly stupid enough to let the group split up. Attacking them while they were all together last night would have probably been the end of Zekk, but single targets were a vampire's bread and butter.

Apparently, the idiots didn't realize that. His cash cow flying off to try and cross the Sea of Bones made him uneasy, but Darien was sure to return, exhausted, within a few hours. Zekk couldn't have planned it better himself—so perfect it felt like a trap.

But he didn't want to spend one more day missing in action. Wul's radio might still be in Jet's pocket—his ticket home.

Zekk shifted and swayed on his knees, mimicking the thorned aloe that shrouded him. His pulse ignited as Jet strode closer. It didn't matter if he could recall killing Wul or not. He'd still pay full price for it.

Zekk crept backward and into the sand-covered metal hatch in the ground. He didn't blame the woman they called 'Sorv' or 'Sorva' for missing it—he'd also thought it was some sort of plumbing and almost ignored it. If Jet was out hunting for resources, though, there was a good chance he'd take a closer look.

Perfect.

Stairs descended into a dimly-lit stairwell painted with swirling blues and greens. Zekk closed the grate behind him, careful not to let it clang. Pairs of lights embedded in each step illuminated from the ground up, just like all of the lighting in the underground suite.

Zekk skipped every other step and glanced up at a fat-bellied shark that drifted over the glass dome set in the ocean floor. Morning sunlight trickled down through the water above and through the thick glass, shimmering off the small hot tub's pool of water that lay flush in the azure tile, which in turn lay flush with the ocean floor. The irony of it was stunningly beautiful—almost like the suite was an inverse aquarium display for the vibrant coral reef outside to observe human life.

The kitchenette on Zekk's left was short one knife, but surely Jet wouldn't notice that in time. His tablet on the reading chair didn't look out of place. *I probably should have made the bed.* No time now, and Zekk didn't really remember how to do that, anyway.

He slipped into the closet and left the door slightly ajar behind him. A pair of bath robes hung pristine from their hangers. Zekk ripped one of their belts out and pulled it between his hands with all of his strength. The sash stretched under the tension but didn't snap. *It'll do.*

Zekk flipped off the closet light and waited.

Only the hum of the atmosphere transfer unit and the air conditioner sounded through the suite. Zekk closed his eyes and concentrated. He'd familiarized himself with all three of his target's aether signatures. Jet's olive-flavored energy was just at the edge of his limited range.

And it was coming closer.

The hatch opened, spilling light onto the floor through the cracked closet door's slim view. After a moment's pause, a footstep landed on the stairs.

Zekk took a silent breath, dampening his wild adrenaline as the Lynx had trained him. He wrapped the belt tight around each hand, leaving a foot or so between his fists.

"Hello?" Jet's voice called.

Zekk breathed out. *Hello, snake.*

A long silence passed. Then footsteps slowly padded down the stairs.

Energy coiled in Zekk's muscles, enough to make him twitch. He waited as Jet whistled and let out an awed curse. Kitchen cabinets clacked open and shut. Metal slid against metal with a *shick.*

He took a knife. Sweat trickled down Zekk's temple. He stared at the sliver of tile just outside the closet, daring a shadow to pass. *Come here.*

A tall, dark figure strode past his field of view.

Zekk burst from the closet, flipped the belt over Jet's head, and reared back.

Jet's shout strangled in his throat. He teetered back and grabbed at the belt. Zekk cinched it tight around his neck.

A kitchen knife flashed back at Zekk, and he dodged behind Jet's back.

Jet reared forward to throw Zekk off. The knife stabbed from his other side.

Zekk twisted away and moved with Jet's momentum, flipping over his back without releasing any pressure from the belt.

Jet contorted awkwardly, hitting the floor on his side rather than breaking his neck. His cough gurgled.

Zekk kicked at the knife in Jet's grip, but Jet struck back at him and sliced through his pant leg.

White-hot pain shot up Zekk's shin. He hissed and jerked away, dropping the belt. He jumped to his feet and retreated to the edge of the hot tub.

Jet gulped in a huge breath, but it sounded like his lungs didn't fill. He lurched forward and coughed, hacking blood onto the tile.

A smirk played on Zekk's lips. *Ah, yes.* He dashed forward and kicked at the bandage on Jet's head.

Jet dodged and charged him. His shoulder plowed into Zekk's gut, driving out his breath before they hit the glass wall with a warped *thud*.

Zekk grabbed Jet's arm before the knife could fillet him. He bent it back, wrenching Jet's hand and forcing the joints to release it.

But Jet abruptly released the knife and twisted in a similar direction, using Zekk's own strength to bend his arm into a crippling lock.

Jet shifted his weight and slammed Zekk into the tile.

Syn! Zekk's cheek smashed against the cold floor as he pushed against it and wriggled away from Jet's grip. His shoulder wrenched, and flecks of light exploded through his vision. He heard himself cry out.

"Oh, look," Jet said in a broken voice above him. He coughed, and something hot splashed on Zekk's ear. "I've caught the boogeyman."

Zekk breathed through the pain, willing his mind not to snap into darkness. If he could endure it in the arena, he could survive it here. But no one in the arena was dumb enough to fall for his lure anymore.

Zekk concentrated and felt his aether lash up at Jet like tendrils of shadow. It latched onto him and swallowed royal violet energy.

Jet's grip twitched and faltered. He grunted and reached for the knife on the floor.

Zekk flipped over and struck out at Jet's jaw. Jet lurched back but not in time to fully dodge, and he blinked in shock for a half-second.

Zekk drove an uppercut into Jet's stomach. Jet's breath spilled out in a choked gush.

The hot tub glowed blue behind Jet—Zekk leveraged his weight and shoved him into the water. Dark liquid enveloped Jet with a splash.

Zekk jumped on top of him, grabbed his throat, and held him beneath the surface. Water sloshed onto the tile as Jet writhed and kicked.

Purple aether arced up and bounced off Zekk's shields. *From master to amateur.* He huffed a laugh and clutched Jet's neck tighter.

Water slowed Jet's strikes and sloppied his attempts to break free. He grabbed Zekk's arm, clawing into his skin. The upward flow of bubbles stopped, revealing wide black eyes below the water's calming surface.

Zekk closed his eyes and steeled himself as Jet's thrashing weakened. The lurch in his heart at sights like this was the primary reason why he didn't take hit contracts. This death was justified because of Wul, but Zekk's victims prowled his nightmares regardless.

Jet's grip on his arm loosened, and his hand slipped into the water.

Zekk opened his eyes. Jet's eyelids had closed, and his expression had blanked. Scarlet ribbons slipped from his mouth and darkened the water around Zekk's arms.

Maybe I could get info on Teravyn or Altair from him before he dies. Zekk slowly released Jet's neck. *Assuming he conveniently remembers those details but forgot that annoying fruit technique.*

He straightened his back and watched Jet float unhindered. *That info would be valuable enough to make it worth a shot.*

Zekk sloshed out of the tub, grabbed Jet's arm, and hauled his limp body onto the tile. He laid there in an awkward position, with short hair plastered to his waterlogged bandage.

Zekk fished around in Jet's pockets, found Wul's radio, and released a tense breath when the red light clicked on. *Thank Lillian for waterproof gear.*

He glanced down at his shin. The knife cut stung like wildfire, but it looked shallow.

Zekk kicked Jet in the ribs.

Jet's eyes flew open. He sputtered and heaved bloody water onto the tile. His arms shook beneath him, and he collapsed back to the floor, retching and gasping.

Zekk bent down and scooped the knife up. His boot turned Jet over onto his back, and Zekk crouched over him and pushed the blade tip into his neck.

"Look here if you want to live a little longer."

Jet stilled under the knife, taking ragged, desperate breaths that sounded oddly shallow. His gaze flicked to Zekk's.

The arbiter's mental shields had all but evaporated—or maybe he just hadn't rebuilt them since Zekk had last drained them. If he did have any memories of Teravyn or Altair left, they could be plucked like cherries from a tree.

Zekk bored into his mind.

Terror and agony swirled like a hurricane. Zekk tried to shield himself from feeling Jet's pain as he sifted through the maelstrom.

The colorful network of memories wasn't where it should have been—the flickering maze of connections normally sat in the back of one's mind. But Jet's mind was like a dirty lake; everything was muddled except for the faint flickers of blurred memories at the bottom.

Zekk felt his own surprise be drowned out by Jet's flare of anger.

What... do you... want?

Zekk drew more of his own aether around himself as the pain crept closer. *Tell me what you know about Teravyn Aetherswift.*

Never heard of... him.

Him? Zekk watched Jet's memories, but only one was brought forward into clarity—a snot-nosed boy named Terruvyn whom Jet had known in elementary school.

What about Altair?

Hundreds of memories blossomed outward. Jet's childhood house— apparently called Valinor Manor—an image of his father's disapproving face, and the overwhelming combination of homesickness and anger-scarred grudge. Every recollection was several years old.

Another memory flicker below the haze, too blurred for Zekk to make out. But it looked like the face of a bearded Valinorian.

Is that his unit lead? Zekk recalled the leader of Viper Unit—call sign Diamondback—from the paperwork Alon had shown him. The man currently in charge of the Altair base.

Zekk reached his energy out toward the memory and willed his gift into Jet's mind. *Maybe since memories are related to aether, I could pull it free...* He latched onto the haze and pulled.

Jet gasped and coughed under him. Zekk snapped back into his own body a moment to see that his knife had drawn blood from Jet's neck. It dripped in a matching trail from his mouth.

Zekk withdrew the knife's pressure a fraction.

Is that... what DB... looks like now? Jet's internal thought was weak. *Ugly jackwagon.*

Zekk peered harder into the muck of Jet's mind. *Teravyn Aetherswift.*

Memories moved under the surface. Zekk lashed out his aether, grabbed them, and ripped them forward.

Jet screamed.

There she was—blue eyes sharp as icicles, golden hair half-wrangled into a careless bun, and a freckled nose mocking the strength she strove to portray. The photos and surveillance footage didn't do her justice.

She lay in a coma, hidden away in Altair's Lynx base VIP suite. Maybe she was brain dead, but she was breathing.

And the keystone itself was lodged in her core—the primary reason that Zekk had been sent to lead the raid on Jade Glen. The two bundled together to make the biggest prize he'd ever score.

So that's how she eluded us.

Zekk smiled as Jet groaned through shallow breathing. "Well, now." He turned back to the haze of memories and grabbed another handful. "What other delightful things do you know?"

27

Aleah's breath clouded as she stared at the smoke plume belching from Altair's walls. The dark column twisted in the northern sky, listing away from the mountains like a dark flag.

Please don't let it be my house!

Aleah nearly slipped on the icy main road in her haste to push through Altair's open gates. Throngs of people and noise choked the street and open-air market, scurrying around her in a multi-colored frenzy, but she couldn't tear her eyes from the sky. She shoved her way down the main street.

The closer she got, the more the thick plume appeared to be originating from Valinor Manor. Flames peeked above the distant neighbors' rooftops.

Tears stung Aleah's eyes. *Please, creator, no!*

A hand gripped her arm, hard. Aleah jerked to a stop and pulled against the hooded figure who'd grabbed her. The dark man stood still in the roiling crowd.

"Come with me!" a familiar voice whispered.

Aleah peeked under the hood. *Garrett?*

"What's going on?" Raydon jogged up behind her.

"Open your eyes, mate! The city went to Zoth as soon as you left for the ranch this morning!" Garrett released Aleah and swung an arm out to indicate the chaos surrounding them. Aleah noticed then that many Altairans carried impromptu weapons—a snapped broom handle, a machete, a shotgun.

Her heart pounded against her ribs. *What—*

"We have to get to the Lynx base." Garrett pointed toward the gray building near the government plaza and limped toward it. *"Now."*

Aleah stumbled as she felt herself getting pulled along. She found her voice and forced it out. "Is my house on fire?"

"Can you cover your hair?" Garrett stopped and slipped in front of Aleah, cutting off her view of the smoke. He grabbed the fluffy white rim of her hood and pulled it over her head. "Yes," he whispered. "I'm sorry."

Aleah's blood turned to ice. Hot tears welled up and blurred the smoke. *How? Why?*

"What happened?" Raydon demanded.

Garrett charged behind the market stalls as fast as his limp would allow. "I'll explain when—"

"It's her!" someone screamed.

Aleah blinked and found a woman pointing at her from a candle stand. Her eyes were lit with rage.

"She's their adopted daughter!"

Garrett cursed and pulled a compound bow from his cloak. In an instant, a green-feathered arrow was nocked and aimed straight at the woman. "Stand down!"

The nearby crowd slowed and stilled. Dozens of eyes fixed on Aleah.

"She's one of them!"

"Get her!"

A cry strangled in Aleah's throat as Raydon yanked her away from Garrett.

"Run!" Garrett yelled.

Firm hands dragged Aleah toward the government plaza, straight through the crowd. Her legs felt like sludge and her hands trembled. *What's happening?*

A man blocked their path, and Raydon shouldered around him. "Make us invisible," Raydon said in her ear.

In the middle of…? Lightheadedness slurred Aleah's thoughts. *People are watching…* Like that overweight man coming at her with a shovel.

Aleah closed her eyes and felt light's caress on her skin. She rejected it, and the sun's rays warped away and flowed around her. She pushed the light out toward Raydon, and impenetrable darkness swallowed them.

Aleah hugged Raydon tight, stood perfectly still, and listened.

Heavy footsteps stomped up to them and stopped. "Where'd they go?"

"Did you see that?"

"She's a witch!"

Raydon's breath was hot in her hair. *Can you see anything?* his thought-voice asked.

Aleah swallowed hard. Using Phoera to bend energy was as instinctive as the beat of her heart, but manipulating light to touch only her eyes was a matter of skill. She took a deep breath to calm her panicked mind.

If I let light reach my eyes, people will be able to see them. But we have to see to get out of here. She looked down and willed the flow of light to reach her pupils. *Creator, help me!*

Wet asphalt snapped into view beneath Aleah. Her legs were missing, as were Raydon's. She was an invisible spirit in a terrified crowd that looked every which way except at her. Their livid eyes glanced straight through her.

"That's how they were sneaking food out!" the fat man yelled beside her.

A chill slid down Aleah's neck. *Is that what this is about?*

I'm blind. Raydon's thought was laced with fear. *Where—*

It's OK, she thought back. *Stay very close to me.*

She grabbed his hand and looked up, hoping no one would notice a floating pair of green eyes amidst the panic. The government plaza was mostly empty only a few dozen paces away. She charged toward it, weaving through the crowd. A child ran head-first into her side and fell back on his rump, dazed.

Incredible, Raydon said. *You're amazing!*

Aleah released the tension in her jaw as the crowd dispersed and the Lynx base loomed over them. Diamondback stood in the open doorway with an automatic rifle shouldered. He snarled at a half-circle of Altairans who hovered several paces away, jeering at him and yelling obscenities.

"Thieves!"

"We know you're hiding it here!"

"Just give us the Valinors and we'll let you live!"

Tears blotted Aleah's vision as she dragged Raydon through the crowd's edge and made a beeline for Diamondback. *This can't be happening!*

One man rushed Diamondback, who shot him in the knee. The man collapsed on the snowy lawn as the crowd roared and pulsed back and forth.

A sob broke free as Aleah slipped behind Diamondback and dragged Raydon into the open door with her.

Inside, shadows hung from huddled bodies in the living room. Her father cradled her crying mother near the dim fireplace. Ellie huddled on a couch with a redheaded girl named Cassie who'd come with them from Jade Glen, and Levi paced between bullet-pocked columns in the hallway.

Aleah released the flows of light and ran toward her parents. She collapsed in Thracian's surprised arms.

"Leah!"

Marie clawed onto her and pulled her tight. "Oh, thank you, Aeo!"

Aleah hugged her back and felt her body tremble with relief. "Are you OK?" Her voice fractured. "Did Jet come back?"

The joy in Thracian's eyes darkened. "Not yet."

Aleah's throat closed. *I haven't healed him in days—he must be dying!* Shock numbed her bones. "What… happened?"

Thracian glanced at Levi, who hadn't stopped pacing. "We were accused of stealing and hiding food just after you left this morning," he whispered. "Several of our workers noticed the stores being depleted. They decided to blame it on us."

Marie sniffled and wiped her eyes. "The hard frost wiped out a good portion of the young winter gardens, and everyone knew we wouldn't have enough food for the winter. They wanted to disperse our stock evenly, but I doubt that's happened." She ran a hand through Aleah's silver locks and smiled faintly. "But none of that matters, my baby. You're safe now, and Aeo will provide."

Aeo? Nausea contorted in Aleah's gut. *First he took Jade Glen, then my brother, and now my home?*

"Don't blame the creator, sweetheart," Ellie whispered from the couch. "He showed me this would happen. I just didn't know when."

"Eleanor!" Levi snapped.

"Oh, hush." Ellie tucked a beige blanket under her feet. "It's my secret to tell."

Aleah swallowed and wiped her cheeks with her coat sleeve. "He *showed* you?"

"You asked me what my gift was before, and I didn't answer." Ellie's eyelids drooped over her tired aqua gaze. "I am called a prophet."

Aleah stared at her for a long moment. "You're a sage?"

Ellie nodded. "One who does not use the sage gift of her own accord," she whispered. "I only receive visions from Aeo. These are the only glimpses of the future that are absolutely true."

"Raydon," Levi barked.

Raydon straightened his back. "Sir?"

"Wipe all the computers. Everything on them. Now."

"Yes, sir." Raydon ran down the hall and jumped down the stairs to the bottom level.

Aleah's throat went dry as she stared at Ellie. "Did you know about the attack on Jade Glen?"

Ellie looked into the glowing fireplace. "I was told of that, yes. That was how Felix escaped with so many, and how our group made it out safely as well."

"I thought Noruntalus was the sage," Aleah whispered.

"He was my disciple." A frown pulled on Ellie's wrinkled lips. "But he used the sage gift himself instead of letting the creator work through him." She pulled the blanket up under her chin. "For sages, that path always leads to madness."

How many secrets? Aleah's numb stare drifted between Ellie and Levi. *How many lies?*

"Master," Aleah whispered, "were you the one foreseeing the Serran Academy's future students?"

"When Aeo showed them to me," Ellie said. She shifted and patted the redhead's knee, who smiled weakly back at her. "Sometimes kids needed a little help getting there."

Aleah's heart lurched. *Like me?*

"Noruntalus said he foresaw Darien and Teravyn, and that the Grand Master Council ordered Master Levi to go and get them."

"Yes—they were in danger." Ellie's gentle gaze lighted on her. "Don't be afraid, sugar. We always help people when we can, but it's Aeo's turn to get us out of this mess now." She offered a faint smile. "You did a good job preparing the ranch for us."

It's not ready yet. Aleah swallowed the lump in her throat. *And there are hundreds of people out there wanting to kill us. How can we—*

A gunshot rang out, and she flinched. Garrett ran inside as Diamondback backed into the door and slammed it shut. The lock clicked home, and seconds later, banging thumped on the door.

Levi cursed. "Will the lock hold long enough for them to calm down?"

"This city will never be safe for you again." Diamondback adjusted the rifle in his arms. "We have to bug out to that ranch."

"It's not ready yet." Aleah's voice sounded too quiet even in her own ears. "There's not enough—"

"We don't have a choice. Even if we could hunker down here from the townsfolk, the Lynx could be back any day," Diamondback said. "Surprised they haven't shown up yet."

"Bleeding rich d'hakka!" a man's yell muffled through the door. "You can't hide in there forever! Come out and leave the food and we'll let you go with your lives!"

Marie started crying again.

"There's an escape route in the bottom level." Diamondback pointed at the stairs. "Tunnel connects to the government buildings' old underground network."

"Then we'd have to walk through the crowd to get to the gates," Thracian murmured.

"Aleah." Levi moved to crouch in front of her with a piercing silver gaze. "Can you make us all invisible?"

She shook her head. "Just myself and something I'm holding. Or one person close to me."

Levi shifted his jaw. "Then you can do one at a time?"

Aleah gathered her strength and nodded. "I'd need help with Teravyn, though. Is she still asleep?"

"I'll carry her." Levi stood and strode toward the stairs. "Everyone up!"

"I'll hold the rear," Diamondback said.

Levi paused and furrowed his brow at him. "You don't think the door will hold?"

"I'll make sure it will."

28

Zekk watched in awe as Jet's memory replayed the first time he'd entered the City of Peace in kai'lani. Gleaming gates guarded streets that shimmered like diamonds, and the towers inside looked to have been carved from onyx, crafted with mother of pearl, or forged of molten bronze. Winged beasts like gryphons and minotaurs flew overhead, tended shops, or chatted on balconies and porches.

Jet knew more than any human should know. He knew everything.

Zekk tore through Jet's memories of the afterlife, straining for every last detail. But the recollections of kai'lani were strangely blurred, as if Jet remembered them from a dream.

But still they glimmered there, unfabricated. And Zekk couldn't deny that they were true.

Somehow the creator Aeo was alive, and Orso wasn't a god but the angelic facet of the creator. The elementals weren't gods, either; they were just another sentient race like angels and humans.

And according to Jet's knowledge, Lillian, the primary elemental of water whom Zekk had prayed to for years, was actually asleep. She was encapsulated in the Malo stone Alon had entrusted Zekk with as the champion of Maqua.

And so his goddess was literally just a rock sitting in his pocket.

Like a sick joke.

Hours ago it'd made Zekk's stomach sour. Now he was just numb.

He flipped through Jet's memories of kai'lani, following the connections from one memory to the next. Although Jet had only been dead for a minute or so on the physical plane, he had enough memories of kai'lani to have lasted years.

You done yet? Jet's thought-voice was deep with annoyance. *Yeah, everything you've ever known is a lie. Wow, shocking. Now get out of my head before you start believing we're the same person.*

You'll sit there and shut up and be patient. It'll take longer if you keep interrupting.

Zekk withdrew from Jet's mind and gasped as the dark underwater suite swayed into view. Dizziness blurred the colors of fish on the other side of the glass as they darted in and out of wiggling anemones.

OK... maybe I did stay too long that time. Zekk had never imagined that delving into Jet's mind would take a dangerous length of time. But it was worth it—now he also knew secrets of the Valinorian Royal Guard, an awakened Phoeran elemental named Felix Kael Tae who'd trained Jet's sister, the inner workings of the Serran Grand Master council, how they'd evaded Zekk at Jade Glen, how they'd taken down the Altair Lynx, and—most importantly—detailed intelligence on Teravyn Aetherswift.

Zekk had ripped every single one of Jet's damaged memories free, but still he wasn't satisfied. He did feel slightly better about Wul's death, though, now that he knew the lecher had disobeyed his order regarding Sorvashti. Or tried to.

Zekk looked down as his eyes adjusted and found Jet lying on the bloodstained, waterlogged rug beside him. The Valinorian's breathing was shallow and ragged, even worse than the last time Zekk had checked. Blood stained Jet's lips and trailed in streams down his face. His skin was as pale as the tile under the hot tub's pink water.

He won't last much longer.

Jet cracked an eye half open and glared at Zekk. *Did you forget you were going to kill me?*

Zekk stretched his back and shoulders. "Oh, now you want me to?"

It'd be better than dying from this. Jet's breathing hitched, and he coughed. *Just promise me you won't let anything bad happen to Sorva.*

Zekk scoffed. "And why would I do that?"

Because it's my last request, and you've sat in my head for so long that you've bonded to me.

Zekk froze mid-stretch. "What? No, I haven't."

A faint smirk tugged on Jet's lips. *Don't pretend it's not true. You know me better than I knew myself a few hours ago.*

"Yeah, well, you're welcome for fixing your jacked-up brain." Zekk rubbed his eyes. "We're a lot alike, you and I."

Jet frowned and closed his eye. *You wish.*

Zekk chuckled. "Really? We're both in the same line of work. Where I come from, there's mutual respect between soldiers of our caliber."

No. I fought for my country and to protect the innocent. Jet swallowed and grimaced. *You enslave innocents for money.*

The words pricked Zekk's heart. "We rescue people from the wilderness. The Lynx are my country—they took me in and trained me." He straightened. "The money is just a bonus."

Do you really believe that? Jet opened a black eye and stared at him. *You think you* rescued *all those aethryn from Jade Glen?*

"To some degree, yes. Did you think your food stores would last forever?"

You think you can lie to an arbiter? Black fire simmered in Jet's eye. *You're a slaver, plain and simple.*

Zekk winced and glanced away. "Look, think whatever you want, but I'm not a slaver."

Oh, good. Then you'll let Sorva go.

Zekk sighed. "Nothing bad will happen to her in Maqua."

Really? Jet's thought-voice dripped with sarcasm.

"OK, fine! I've been considering keeping her on my own team, anyway." Zekk gave Jet a sidelong glance. "I'll keep her for your final request. She'll be safe and well provided for. No one will touch her. Happy?"

Jet glared at him. *She'd kill you in your sleep.*

Zekk snorted, but he knew from Jet's memories of Sorvashti that he was probably right. Still, he wasn't about to back down.

"Why would she? I treat my team like family."

Why?

Zekk paused and looked down at Jet. "What?"

Why do you treat your slaves like family?

Something knotted in Zekk's throat. "Because they work better that way."

Jet's faint chuckle turned into a coughing fit. Blood dribbled down his cheek, and he gritted his teeth as he recovered, gasping shallow, awkward breaths. *Liar. You treat them well because you know the Lynx system is wrong. You pretend they're your employees.*

"The system's fine," Zekk snapped. "If everyone's respectful and does their part, everyone's happy."

Jet wheezed and looked up at him again. *You don't know the meaning of freedom, do you?*

Zekk clenched his jaw. "I have all the freedom in the world."

Really? Then could you leave the Lynx if you wanted to?

Annoyance flared in Zekk's chest. "What are you getting at? You think I'd ever want to leave? And live in a deserted city ruin with no hot water like you?"

No. It's just amusing to prod a brainwashed lab rat like you. Jet spat to the side. *You just tolerate this syn because it's all you've ever known. Waking up in a Lynx med center with no memories at sixteen—I can understand a teenager going along with it. But you're twenty-three now, even if you look like an eight-year-old girl. There's no excuse for a grown man to do what you do.*

Adrenaline surged through Zekk's veins. "That's enough preaching. You don't know anything about my past."

Neither do you.

Zekk hissed a breath through his teeth and resisted the urge to end Jet right there. He still had more memories of kai'lani floating around in there, and Zekk wasn't about to miss the opportunity to gaze deeper into the spirit realm.

One more dive, then he'd put him out of his misery. Jet knew too much about him now—far too much.

But no more than he knew about himself. No one had ever been able to fix Zekk's memory as he'd just done for Jet. There was no suppressed network in the back of his mind, no murky lake—his earliest memory was waking up in the Maqua med bay, as if he'd been born there at age sixteen. Anything that happened before had been wiped clean, like chemicals on a white eraser board.

Zekk grabbed Jet's jaw and forced their eyes to meet. Delving back inside Jet's mind was even more difficult now—pain crashed in wave after wave and consciousness waned.

Kai'lani, Zekk called, and thousands of memories bubbled to the surface. He'd seen most of them, but that one with an old woman was new. He summoned it forward.

A plump woman smiled up at Jet with aqua eyes and long gray hair. "Hey, sugar pie!" She grabbed him in a hug.

Jet stood awkwardly in a bakery, feeling a strange combination of surprise, happiness, and sorrow. "Master Willow!" He pulled back from her embrace and inspected her healthy wrinkled skin. "What are you doing in kai'lani? Did you pass away?"

"How rude!" The woman—Jet's mind identified her as Eleanor 'Ellie' Willow—folded her arms across her breast and harrumphed. A mischievous sparkle in her eye matched her grin. "Just how old do you think I am?"

Jet's voice strangled in his throat. He glanced at the winged leopard at the counter, who rapped her fingers against a glass case filled with sweetcakes. "I didn't mean—"

"You're not dead either, you know," Ellie said.

Jet stepped out of line and moved to an empty table. "Uh, I'm pretty sure I am."

"Nuance." Ellie flicked her wrist, jingling her bracelets. "Listen, I have a message for you. Well, actually, it's not for you. But I just need you to listen for a minute." She slipped into a chair and patted the table.

Jet just stared at her. "Master, what are you doing here?"

Ellie sighed. "I might be a Serran. I like to visit my angel sometimes." She grinned ruefully. "Don't tattle."

Jet slid into the chair across from her and thought she was nuts. Who was he going to tell when he was dead? "OK."

"Now just hush up and listen for a minute, and I'll buy you a sweetcake." Ellie looked deep into Jet's eyes, took a deep breath, and smiled. "Zack, listen to me, wherever you are. You might not remember me, but I am your grandmother, and I miss you so much."

Her aqua eyes watered. "You disappeared from my house so long ago, a few years after your parents died. I thought you ran away, but I know now that you were stolen from me."

Zekk's pulse accelerated as a tear slipped from the woman's eye. *This is weird. Who's Zack?* Jet didn't know anyone by that name.

"Aeo told me to connect with you now, but I don't know what to say." Ellie's voice trembled. "Just know that I love you. So, so much. Please come home."

Oh... my... Jet's voice echoed with disbelief. *You're her grandkid?*

Zekk shoved the memory away. *Me? Of course not. She's a Grand Master? She's crazy.*

She sent you that message through... Jet's words stumbled on his disbelief. *Through time and bleeding space!*

Zekk looked for new memories, but focus eluded him. *Last time I checked, my name's not Zack.*

Close enough!

If she was my grandmother, she'd know my name.

You don't think the Lynx would change your name if they kidnapped you and wiped your memory? Jet's voice was livid. *Your eyes are exactly like hers!*

Zekk yanked himself out of Jet's mind. The suite tilted as he pushed to his feet and blinked.

She wasn't talking to me. What, could she see the future and somehow know I'd be inside Jet's mind, watching his memories one day? That's insane.

Zekk staggered around the hot tub and slumped into a chair. *Fine,*

I'm done with him. He pulled Wul's radio out of his pocket and tuned it to the emergency frequency.

What a disappointment, Jet thought at him from the floor. *Ellie deserves better than you.*

"Shut up," Zekk muttered as he flicked through static. "I'll deal with you in a sec."

The Titan Project.

Zekk glanced up at Jet. "What?"

Jet's bloodshot eyes were wide. *The Titan Project—I saw it in your memory. The Lynx take promising kids—those with better-than-average abilities or rare aether gifts or strong elemental blood—and try to make super soldiers.* Jet met his gaze. *You were the grandson of a Grand Master with the rare exorcist gift. That's why they took you.*

Zekk huffed a laugh. "I think I would know if I was a part of that messed-up project."

Would you?

Zekk's finger paused on the dial. *Of course I would.* He glanced at his datapad on the couch's armrest.

His heartbeat wouldn't still.

Ugh, this is stupid. He grabbed the datapad and powered it on.

The screen glowed with a background photo of the blue ice-cliffs of Sai. Zekk thumbed to the search feature. He didn't have internet access, but the purpose of these data pads was to provide offline intel to agents in the field. Maybe the Titan files were in the directory somewhere.

Zekk searched for them, and a result came up with a red warning triangle.

PROJECT: TITAN
RESTRICTED: A-3

Zekk tapped the override button and entered his personal code.

DENIED. SEE YOUR SUPERIOR TO REQUEST ACCESS.

Zekk blinked at the screen. He'd never been denied access to any files as the Confidant—his only superior was Alon Whitlocke himself.

Sweat dripped into Zekk's eye, and he rubbed it away. He smashed in Wul's code, which he'd personally given access to up to level A-2.

WELCOME, WUL CANYON.

A file system hierarchy unfolded on the screen with a gentle animation. Folders labeled as time logs, sub-projects, and employees displayed before him. Zekk tapped on the one labeled 'CANDIDATES.'

Dozens of names listed across the screen: Brandon Law, Mae Shallowater, Michael Taylor... Zekk flicked down the list. The last name was Zackary Willow.

Zekk slowly tapped the name.

ZACKARY WILLOW
SPECIALIST: EXORCIST
STATUS: APPROVED, ACTIVE

SELECTION: Third-generation aethryn. Grandmother is Grand Master Eleanor Willow, and parents are Slate and Kia Willow, both Masters of Maqua Serran Academy. Child shows exceptional skill in use of rare gift. Recommend clariol wipe for fresh training start to account for older age.

ACQUISITION: Clariol wipe successful. Subject is cognizant and non-aggressive. No notable side effects. Retained instinctual exorcist skills and hand-to-hand combat.

Recommend advanced training immediately.

Zekk felt lightheaded. *This can't be me.* He scrolled down and found a note in red text:

> *You've all done very well on Zekk—*
> *Titan's first true success. Although it's unclear*
> *if his third-gen heritage is the root of his skill,*
> *I want you to stop all observation and testing*
> *on him. I see the potential for my Confidant*
> *in Zekk, and I won't risk him discovering*
> *his role in this project. He is not, under any*
> *circumstances, to be told any details of his*
> *acquisition.*
>
> *Instead, focus on the Taylors and*
> *replicate your work there. Again, job well*
> *done. You'll all find a humble bonus among*
> *your next wages.*
>
> *Alon*

Zekk stared at the screen, unable to move or breathe or think. The datapad's screen timed out and powered off.

I'm an experiment?

A shark drifted above him, and a school of cerulean fish ducked into a coral formation. Zekk stared at them as the datapad slipped out of his hand and clattered onto the floor.

Alon... how could you?

Jet coughed from the other side of the suite. *It's true, isn't it?*

Zekk slowly turned to him. His entire body felt numb.

Something flicked behind Jet's eyes. *What did they do to you?*

The hatch door clanged open above the stairwell.

Zekk looked up as a blast of aether screamed down the stairs. It slammed into his chair, toppling it over and flinging Zekk to the floor. He pushed himself up and recognized Darien and Sorvashti rushing down the stairs.

"Wait—"

Another sentinel strike hit Zekk square in the chest and rammed him into the glass barrier. He bounced off it and put out his hands to catch himself.

Darien caught Zekk instead and shoved something at his stomach.

Crippling agony branched like lightning from Zekk's gut. He looked down—a kitchen knife was buried in him up to its hilt.

29

No! Jet tried to yell, but his voice wouldn't work.

Zekk looked down at his stomach as Darien pulled his foot-long knife free in a smear of blood. Zekk's breath poured out in a strangled whimper, and he fell to his knees.

Sorvashti ran down the stairs as Darien lifted the shaking knife over Zekk's head.

Stop! Jet sent his thought with enough force to send Darien staggering backward.

Darien blinked and stared back at Jet. His normally tanned face was stark white.

"What does he do to you?" Sorvashti's voice broke over Jet.

Jet didn't look at her—he stared at Darien with all the strength he had left. *Don't kill him.*

Zekk slumped to his side, but Darien's blade didn't move besides its violent shaking.

Darien's wide eyes filled with horror. "Jet..."

Zekk didn't do this—well, this isn't his fault, Jet thought to both of them, guessing from their expressions how he must look. *Stop his bleeding!*

Sorvashti snarled something in Terruthian and knelt at Jet's side. Her hands slid over him in a gentle search.

"You told me to kill him before," Darien croaked, "and if I would have, we wouldn't have—"

That was when we were on a heli-jet! We need him now to get back home!

Darien looked down and took a step back as Zekk moaned. "You honestly think he'd help us get back?"

"Maybe he does now," Sorvashti said. "Make him call of the Fadahari!"

Darien white-knuckled his knife in one hand and yanked a radio from Zekk with the other.

"Yes," Zekk gasped, and Jet barely heard him. Zekk reached a bloody hand up to Darien.

"So you can order them to kill us or haul us to Maqua?" Darien slipped his blade down to Zekk's throat.

He's Ellie's grandson!

Sorvashti and Darien both froze and stared at Jet.

"Help me," Zekk murmured, "and I'll call... Heals."

Only the atmosphere transfer unit could be heard for a still moment. Darien's knife didn't move. "If you betray us—"

"Swear." Zekk's reaching hand trembled.

Darien pursed his lips and looked at Jet.

Jet breathed as deeply and evenly as the liquid in his lungs would allow. *Give him the radio and put pressure on that wound right now.*

Darien slowly relinquished the radio to Zekk.

Zekk dropped the radio, gasped, and picked it up again. A button clicked and static crackled through the suite.

"The raven watches," Zekk said.

Silence.

Static clicked again. "The raven… watches."

A voice garbled through the radio's speaker: "Access code."

"Four Lorsann nine"—Zekk paused to breathe—"Malo two six Rothari."

"Zekk! Oh, thank Orso!" the radio voice cried. "Where are you? We've been searching for hours!"

Jet's stomach knotted with tension as Zekk panted.

"Twenty miles… south… Ceemalao. Island… house."

"Copy." There was a pause. "We're twenty minutes out. Are you injured, sir?"

Zekk blinked at the glass bubble above them as if there was something in his eye. "Yes."

"OK, hang in there. I've got the doc in the back with full supply, and your whole team's on my six."

A spike of panic shot through Jet as Darien pressed the knife into Zekk's skin.

"Negative," Zekk gasped. "Send team… back. Just need… you and Heals."

Static flickered through a long pause. Then the voice continued in a different tone: "The raven flies at dusk."

A distress query? Jet's lungs roiled with the urge to cough. He resisted and turned his head to the side to let a fresh stream of blood drain out. *Syn! He could—*

"And straight on… 'til dawn," Zekk's voice slurred.

Jet's pulse pounded like a war drum, sending new agony through him with every beat. *What does that mean?*

"Three… friendlies," Zekk said. "Do not… engage."

Thank you, Aeo!

Another pause. "Copy. Hang tight, sir. We've got you."

Zekk's hand dropped, and the blood-smeared radio clattered across the floor. Darien removed the knife's point from his neck.

"I can find no *lascent*." Sorvashti touched Jet's face and gently turned it toward her. He noticed the wet trails down her cheeks then, and the warring fear and strength in her golden eyes. "Where is the hurt?"

Something else flickered in her gaze—something he hadn't seen in years.

No, Jet thought. *Don't look at me like that, or you'll hurt so much more.* He swallowed and took as deep a breath as he dared without triggering a coughing fit.

I'm not injured, he told her.

A tear escaped from her dark lashes. "What is this lies? Tell me!"

Zekk's head lolled to the side. His eyes opened disturbingly wide, and they didn't quite focus on Jet. *Do you think she'd really love me?* Numb, detached confusion drowned his thought-voice.

Jet realized he was going into shock and cursed. *Clamp that wound, now,* he yelled at Darien, *or he'll bleed out before they get here. Then glory knows what they'd do to us!*

Darien grimaced and set his knife down a safe distance away from Zekk. He stood over the exorcist, pursed his lips, and pressed his hands over the wound.

Zekk's scream raked against Jet's heart. His weak struggle didn't deter Darien.

"Why can you not speak?" Sorvashti gripped Jet's face with both hands, smearing the warm blood on his cheeks. "What is wrong? How do I help you?" Her eyes smothered him with love—which kind, he couldn't tell.

Creator, no. Don't let her love me. Don't make her go through this again.

Jet tried to raise his hand, but only his fingers twitched. Fear mired around him as if he were lying in a swamp. Darkness floated at the edges of his vision.

He closed his eyes. *I'm sorry.*

"Do not say me this! You fight!" Sorvashti grabbed his hand in an iron grip. "What is this?"

Zekk moaned under Darien's weight. "I can't stop it," Darien murmured.

Jet swallowed, then panted from the break in his shallow breathing. *It's a genetic disorder. It killed my mother when she was twenty-three, during my birth.* He couldn't bear to open his eyes and meet her gaze. *Something's wrong with my lungs—doctors don't know what. I've only lived this long because of Aleah.*

The next moments filled with tense quiet. Jet cracked an eye open.

Sorvashti's face contorted with shock and pain. "Why do you not tell me of this?" she whispered.

Jet regretted telling her, but maybe this way she wouldn't carry a fatal grudge for the rest of her life. *I didn't know about it until I was discharged for it.* He sucked in a breath. *I'm so sorry. I never should have told you how I felt.*

She gripped his hand tighter. "Do not say this." Her face steeled under her tears. "You are the strongest of men that I know. You must not die."

I've been fighting... for a long time. The darkness snaked closer, and Jet willed a gentle brush of energy to caress her cheek. *Whatever you do, don't go back... to what we had.*

"It is too late." Sorvashti leaned over and kissed him, sending a wave of warmth through his pain. She pulled back with blood on her lips. "Do not leave me again!"

Jet's heart swelled and burst. *I'm sorry.*

Darkness consumed him.

30

Jet awoke to the rumble of engines and the taste of chemicals. Fog bloomed and receded on clear plastic as he breathed. Every inhalation felt like muted fire in his chest.

This... doesn't seem like kai'lani.

He blinked and squinted over the intrusive breath mask. Embedded lights in a curved ceiling glowed down at him, and sunlight from round windows lit a leather couch across from him and a mini-bar behind it.

The Caracal?

Clouds flitted outside the window like cotton being whisked into thread—not above the window, but directly outside.

A monitor beside Jet beeped as his heart rate increased. *We're flying!*

Jet turned his head and found a female figure hunched over a fold-out bed. Zekk lay there, motionless with closed eyes, with an IV in his arm and an oxygen mask identical to Jet's. His smooth medium skin had paled to an ashen beige, and his own heart rate monitor zig-zagged its colored lines in a silent dance.

He's alive?

Jet's gaze flicked to a digital screen on the wall with a zoomed-in map of the world. An arc crested through Katrosi and approached a dot labeled 'ALTAIR.'

Jet blinked and squinted at the letters, certain he'd read them wrong. *How...?*

"Rise and shine, sleeping zombie." Fadahari smirked at Jet over her shoulder. "Calm down or that monitor will explode."

Jet lifted his hand to remove the mask and found that his arm felt as heavy as a sandbag. He swallowed and grimaced as pain slid down his throat.

Fadahari stood from her chair. "How do you feel?"

Jet set the mask on the bed beside him—no, it must have been a couch. His feet were propped up over the far armrest.

"Like syn."

"Better than nothing." Fadahari skirted around another couch to approach him, and Jet realized that the blankets piled on the cushions concealed a human. Sorvashti's sleeping face and tousled blond hair poked out from a swath of blue linen.

"Thanks for the save," Jet whispered, tearing his eyes from Sorvashti to the bandage covering Zekk's middle. "Did you heal both of us at once? I didn't think that was possible."

Fadahari blew a short breath through her teeth. "Please. I was a doctor before I was a healer. I worked in an emergency room after med school, before I started my own practice." She arrived at his side and silenced the heart rate monitor. "Who do you think I am? Your bushy-tailed little sister?"

A grin tugged at Jet's lips. *Aleah... I've been gone so long now she must think I'm dead.* Excitement flared at the thought of the look on her face if he ever got to see her again. He glanced at the map again. Surely it was wrong.

"You might've noticed that I'm not done with you yet." Fadahari's brown eyes seemed to pierce right through Jet's chest as she stared down at him. "Sorry, but the boss takes priority. That wound was nasty—he's lucky to be alive." Those strange eyes flicked to his throat. "Even more lucky than you."

Jet pushed up on his elbows and felt soreness in places he didn't know he had. The room listed and reoriented itself.

"Easy, there," Fadahari murmured.

Jet nodded to indicate the map. "That right?"

Fadahari glanced at it. "I dunno. Probably. Been several hours since we left." She folded her arms, wrinkling the crisp fabric of her bloodstained coat. "Any idea why he was so adamant about flying to Altair instead of Maqua?"

Jet glanced at Zekk. "A faint one." *But why would he help us at all after Darien gutted him?*

"You must have brainwashed him or something," Fadahari said. "He said he 'released' the pilot and me, as if we're not slaves anymore, then *asked* him to fly us to Altair." She tilted her head back and gave Jet a sidelong glance. "Which drug was it?"

Jet chuckled, then regretted it. "I'm just as surprised as you, I swear." He watched Zekk's bandaged torso rise and fall. "Why'd you call him 'boss' if he set you free?"

"He couldn't have been serious; he was in shock. Pilot wanted to obey orders anyway." Fadahari turned and maneuvered her way back to Zekk. "Even if he meant it, my loyalty runs deeper than title. Kid's always been good to me."

So 'slave' is just a title to her? The thought boiled in Jet's gut. *Or is that just how good Zekk treats his slaves?*

Jet shifted on his elbows. "Does your loyalty run back to Jade Glen?"

Fadahari paused. She glanced at the cockpit door. "Please tell me you aren't going to lead him to the survivors," she said under her breath.

"Did you know one of the survivors is his grandmother?"

Fadahari's eyes widened. "His grandmother was from Jade Glen? Are you serious?"

Jet watched Sorvashti's still face. "Did you know he doesn't remember anything before he was sixteen?"

"I'd heard the rumors..." Fadahari paled. "You aren't suggesting he'll..." She stared at Zekk's still face.

"No idea what he'll do." Jet looked back up at her. "Unfortunately, he already knows everything I do about the survivors. And everything else I've ever known."

Fadahari's mouth dropped open. "I thought he couldn't break you!"

"Long story." Jet carefully pushed himself up to a sitting position, ignoring Fadahari's warning glare. "Doesn't matter what he knows. If he does anything against us, I'll undo all your fine work there."

Fadahari frowned and glanced back between Zekk's vitals monitor and the cockpit door. "You should all find a new place to hide—some place you don't know about so he can't trace it. He's too close to Whitlocke. He'll want Zekk to finish what he started at Jade Glen, and get revenge for all the mess with the Aetherswifts and whatever happened to the Altair base." She smirked. "You blew it up, didn't you?"

Jet grinned and took a deep breath, analyzing the sensations in his lungs. She definitely hadn't finished healing him, but it was enough that he could manage. "Don't worry about us."

Thracian might have some bug out location he never told me about. Maybe they'll just drop us off and leave... wouldn't that be swell? He stared at Zekk, wishing that he was in his mind again so he could hear his genuine thoughts. *He wouldn't be taking us to Altair without his team unless he's got good intentions, right? Unless he was just in shock when he ordered that.*

Jet realized what he'd just wished, shuddered, and shoved the thought away. *That idiot did form a bond between us! I told him not to stay in my head so long!*

Grumbling, he searched the cabin for another pile of blankets. "Where's Darien?"

"In the cargo hold." Fadahari sat in her chair and laid her hands gently over Zekk's stomach.

Jet narrowed his eyes at her. "Did you hog-tie him?"

"No! He just went in there when we took off and hasn't come back out."

Strange. You'd think that's the last place he'd want to be.

Jet looked at Sorvashti's wild hair and smiled. *Did she kiss me, or did I dream that? I might have been in shock, too.*

The ache in his heart rivaled the throbbing in his lungs. *Stop it, King. Don't consider it.* He looked down at his hands. *So I got lucky this time, but how much longer can I live like this?*

Jet swallowed. "Is there a bathroom?"

"Mm-hmm." Fadahari pointed to a thin door and a bulge in the wall beside the map screen.

Jet pushed himself up to stand and it felt like the aircraft did a somersault. He gripped the armrest.

"Careful, idiot! You've got severe blood loss!"

"I'm OK." Jet spread his feet to steady himself, and the horizon righted. *As long as there's no turbulence.* He started toward the bathroom.

"Hey, no more foolin' around." The look in Fadahari's eye could have cut steel. "You come see me every six hours. Or Aleah, creator willing."

Jet's insides sank. "For the rest of my life?"

"Until you get back on your feet, at least. Without wobbling like pudding." Fadahari's thinned eyes looked him up and down. "Your illness, whatever it is, is not to be underestimated. If we'd shown up an hour later, even I couldn't have saved you. Understand?"

Jet nodded and put a hand out to the wall. "Guess there's still no hope for a cure."

He knew there wasn't, but he had to ask. If the Lynx were hiding things like the Titan Project, who knew what else they were cooking up.

Fadahari tilted her head. "If you were a Lynx, Research & Development would probably try something. You'd probably be high-ranking enough for them to look into it—humans are becoming scarce. Skilled ones, aethryn, and elementalists even more so. But as it is..." Her shoulders lifted. "I just don't have the resources for such an endeavor by myself. Zekk might be able to pull some strings. But we know it responds well to aetherial healing, if it's *consistent.*" She jabbed at him but didn't actually touch him.

Jet opened the thin door and clutched its frame for support. "Yeah, I'll try not to get kidnapped by our glorious overlords next time."

Fadahari snorted but couldn't hide a smirk. "Shut up and let me concentrate."

The mirror showed Jet what he would have looked like as a ghost.

His skin was so blanched that it had an almost bluish tint. Someone must have cleaned him up, but a speck of dried blood still sat on his lip. The bandage on his head had been changed—it was much smaller than it had been.

He gripped the sink and turned the water on. *Idiot. Why did you offer Sorva a relationship when you knew this would happen?* He glared at his reflection and rubbed at the old blood. *Even with a healer, you can't last forever. How long until it wins out or suffocates you in your sleep? A few days? A couple months?*

Jet rinsed his hands and watched the pink water swirl down the drain. *Maybe it would've been better if I'd died on the island. The closer she gets to me, the more she'll hurt.*

Black eyes glared back at him. *I don't care how much you want it. You're a soldier; you protect the innocent. And you're a Serran—your oath is to protect widows.*

He closed his eyes, let out a deep breath, and resolved not to let anything else happen between them.

He'd scared off plenty of women before. An ex-girlfriend would be easy. He knew what made the Ironhide tick and what buttons to push. She'd loathe him by tomorrow morning.

Jet buried his resistance as he squeezed out of the cramped bathroom. He didn't look at Sorvashti as he walked past her, but the room warbled and he half-collapsed onto the back of her wide sofa.

Sorvashti jumped awake like a startled kitten. She blinked up at him through a fold in her blanket.

Jet cleared his throat and made sure his hands weren't in any wrong places—one had landed next to her side as the other clutched the top of the couch. "Sorry." He tried to straighten, then realized he had about half the strength he needed to do so.

Sorvashti's eyes gleamed with joy, and she reached up and hugged his neck. "You are the awake!"

It took all of Jet's concentration not to collapse on her. "I can't… balance—"

"This is OK! Come do the snuggle with me!" Sorvashti pulled down and pushed her body into the cushions, and Jet fell over her in an awkward flop to the other side of the wide couch.

"You are the alive! Does she fix you good?"

The world spun like a demented carnival ride. "I'm gonna fall—"

"Then come closer." Soft, strong hands slipped around Jet's shoulders and waist, then pulled him against Sorvashti's body.

Jet was certain that if he had any blood left, it was coloring his face. *Don't think about it. Don't think about it!*

"Can you believe this?" Sorvashti's bright gaze was the only thing he could focus on. "We are all alive, and your mind is back, and we go to the home!"

Jet tried to wriggle out of her grip. "Yeah, uh, great." *Ignore her. She hates being ignored.* He looked into the thick threads of the leather cushion below them.

Sorvashti's head tilted to scoop up his gaze. "Do you hurt?"

"No." Jet pushed away from her with all of his remaining strength, but she kept him from falling off the couch as if she hadn't even noticed his attempt.

"I thought you leave me again." Sorvashti leaned in and planted a kiss on his forehead, then pulled back with a chastising smile. "You must stop this getting of the hurt."

Heat raced through Jet and provided a sudden reserve of energy from nowhere. He stared into those mischievous gold eyes—he knew that look. He hadn't seen it in years, but he'd never forget it. Oh, the things he could do... His mind went wild.

Jet clenched his eyes shut. *No!*

"You two keep quiet or get a room," Fadahari said behind him. "Trying to heal a fatal wound here."

Son of a d'hakka. Jet wished he could shrink into himself and evaporate.

Sorvashti touched his chin and whispered, "Speak of the thoughts to me. What is wrong?"

He swallowed hard. *I can't thought-speak with her right now— emotions would stick to my thoughts. She'd know!*

"Listen, I'm sorry," Jet whispered back. "I can't do this."

Sorvashti tilted her head. "Do what?"

"You. I mean…" Jet cursed himself and blinked sweat from his eye. "I can't be with you again. Not like that."

She frowned. "What? Why?"

He grasped for an excuse—anything. "Because you were with another man."

Hurt flashed behind Sorvashti's eyes. She scooted back a bit into the cushions. "I tell you not to lie of me, *shlanga*."

"I'm not lying." Jet looked away, into the blue blanket wrinkled over his shoulder. "I don't want to be with you."

A long moment of silence passed.

"I am not good at the arbiter, but this is a very big lie." Sorvashti reached out and slid dark fingers through his hair. "Tell me what is wrong."

Unbelievable. Jet took in and let out a deep breath, then noticed that his pain was somehow less. *This is pointless.*

He sent her a stream of thoughts: *OK, listen. I got lucky this time, but I've got a fatal illness. I should never have started things with you. I didn't think it'd go anywhere because… of what you were going through.*

He met her gaze again. *I'm sorry.*

Sorvashti furrowed her brow at him. *People with your illness cannot love?*

I'm going to die! And probably sooner rather than later, Jet thought back. *So it would be wrong of me to be with you. Understand?*

Sorvashti's face flattened. *Everyone dies. I could choke on bulgogi and die tomorrow.*

No, that… This is different.

Is it?

Yes! Jet set his jaw. *I've sworn to protect you. Even if that means protecting you from myself.*

Sorvashti snickered under her breath and covered her mouth with the blanket.

Jet pursed his lips. *What?*

She raised an eyebrow at him. *Do you love me?*

His throat tightened. *That's not fair.*

Sorvashti grinned. *I couldn't stop loving you either, no matter how* much I tried. *You never left my dreams, and Noruntalus hated you for it.* Her humored expression sobered. *I was always loyal and stayed with him through everything, even when he abandoned me, but he lost me the moment he committed murder.*

Jet considered his words carefully. *I know it feels like forever ago, but that was just a few weeks ago, Sorva.* Surely she needed more time to process or grieve or something. If he had the chance to be with her again, he'd do it right this time. And the right way probably didn't start with him being her rebound.

I didn't say it's not hard. Sorvashti smiled faintly. *I'll need a long time to heal. But I feel like this is right.*

The word 'feel' made his skin crawl. *Do you think we can just pick up where we left off six years ago?*

No, I think we're better than where we left off. You're even more handsome, and you think I'm irresistible. A mischievous sparkle glimmered in her eye.

Jet jerked back and nearly fell off the couch.

Sorvashti caught him and laughed, then smiled apologetically at Fadahari's death glare.

She's playing me! Jet made an effort to calm his breathing and organize his thoughts. He scrubbed a thought clean of emotion before sending it to her: *Tell me what you want.*

Sorvashti's eyes picked him apart, but her smile softened. *I want us to heal together from all that we've been through. I want to be free and strong and carve out any joy this world has left to offer. For as long as either of us live.*

Jet placed himself squarely in analytical mode. *Are you proposing?*

Sorvashti's eyebrows lifted. *Oh, you think you're marriage material?*

He grimaced. *Well, I guess not—*

Do you remember what you were like the past few days? She struggled to contain a giggle. *You wouldn't have blinked at my teasing back then!*

Jet felt his face flush—again. *I'm so... so sorry.*

Sorvashti shook her head vigorously. *You can flip back any time!*

A growl rumbled in Jet's throat as he looked over his shoulder. *Am I ever going to live it down?*

Nope. Her fingers stroked his hair, avoiding the bandage. *Will you grow it back out for me?*

Yeah, I'll have to cover the scar. Hopefully it'll look more awesome than gross. Jet looked back at her, resisting the feeling that her touch sent electricity through his nerves. Either she was simply trying to make him feel good, or she was enjoying the power it gave her over him—he wouldn't allow either at the moment.

Are you sure you realize what you're getting into?

It's the end of the world. Sorvashti shrugged. *There's no one I'd rather spend it with.*

Tension unraveled and dissolved inside him. *Then are we official?*

On one condition. A dark finger popped up from under her blanket. *Never lie to me again.*

Jet bit his lip. *Fine.*

Sorvashti grinned. *You seem really tired. Why don't you get some more rest?*

I'm all right. Jet glanced at the door to the cargo bay. *I need to find Darien and make sure he's OK.*

You can't even walk. I'm sure Darien's fine—seems like he grew up overnight. She tickled his hair with a light touch. *Sleep now.*

A valnah suggestion of fatigue brushed across Jet's mind, but he didn't need it to feel exhausted.

I can't believe it, Jet thought to himself. Joy welled up inside him, afraid to flow out. *Well... I tried. She's made her own choice.*

He closed his eyes and surrendered, and his spirit sang.

She chose me.

Jet released his tension with a breath and relished in her affection. Sleep came swift and deep.

31

Darien rested his elbows on his knees and watched cloth straps on the ceiling sway with turbulence. *He fell asleep, didn't he?* He could sense Jet's violet aether through the wall behind him—it hadn't moved in several minutes. *Didn't even check on me.*

He sighed. What felt like years of training in kai'lani, babysitting Jet when he was brain dead, and even being willing to kill someone to protect him, and not a single thank you—or even an acknowledgement of his existence.

Come on, Darien. Don't be a child. Jet's really sick—he'll say 'hi' when he's feeling better.

But then again, when had Jet ever checked on him? He'd loathed Darien from the moment the council had assigned him as his disciple—and he'd made that abundantly clear.

Wait, he did check on me when Sorv dragged me out in the forest to kill me. Even if he failed to stop her. Darien shifted on the hard bench and stared at one of the ATV's tire treads. *He doesn't even know what I did for them in kai'lani. His brain was fried when I mentioned it; maybe he doesn't remember.*

Darien rubbed his forehead. Sleep was probably a good idea, but it eluded him. The cargo bay was cold and rigid and full of fogged memories, but something else gnawed at his spirit. A foreign emotion similar to loneliness hollowed him out. He felt adrift from this planet... his own body... and even time itself. Memories of kai'lani and the time before he'd left blurred together like mirages in a sandstorm.

But kai'lani had placed elements of his life—or what remained of it—into a clearer perspective. He'd lived with a group of people he'd only known for a few months, without half of the luxuries he'd grown up with or one tenth of those in kai'lani, under the constant threat of death.

One of their own group had tried to kill him. His mentor didn't want him. The girl of his dreams was with another man.

And his sister was dead.

Tension coiled tighter inside Darien, sucking his energy away. *I should never have left kai'lani. Why do we fight so hard to survive in this syn-hole when paradise is on the other side?*

He took a shuddering breath and released it. *Man up. You're not a kid anymore, even if you look like it.*

The door to the midsection slid open, making Darien jump. He whirled and blinked at the hunched figure in the doorway.

Zekk looked like a mummy with a blanket draped over sagging shoulders, huge straps of bandages covering his abs, and strands of tubing trailing up to the IV stand he pulled behind him.

The bags under Zekk's eyes shifted when he smiled weakly. "Uh, hey."

Darien steeled. He used to be terrified of this man, but now he knew he could blast the vampire into the wall hard enough to fracture bone.

"What do you want?" nearly slipped out of Darien's mouth. *He's bringing us back to Altair. The pilot listens to him. Don't make him mad.*

Darien bit his tongue and struggled for words that didn't sound quite so rude, but that made his stance perfectly clear. "What can I do for you?" he muttered through gritted teeth.

Zekk raised a hand. "I come in peace." He blinked slowly. "Can I come in?"

Darien huffed a laugh. "It's your plane."

The IV stand clattered as Zekk tugged it behind him. Fadahari grumbled something from the midsection, and Zekk made an indignant noise back at her as he shut the door. He shuffled to the bench opposite Darien and sat down with pain etched across his face.

Darien analyzed his every movement. *What's he doing?*

"I owe you… an apology." Zekk seemed to focus on his breathing. "For the, uh… unrequested airlift."

Darien blinked at him in shock. *He can't be serious.*

But Zekk just looked back at him expectantly with heavy eyelids and that creepy half-smile.

Darien clenched his jaw. *Does he expect me to apologize, too?* He wouldn't say he was sorry for stabbing him, because he wasn't. When they found that underwater suite, it was clear that there had been a fight, and Jet had looked like he'd been drowned in his own blood. Darien was certain Zekk had murdered him, no matter what Jet said.

"You hungry? There's shrimp something-or-other in the mini fridge. And sushi." Zekk squinted at the ceiling. "Actually, sushi's probably gone bad."

"Why are you here?" Darien murmured.

"To annoy Heals." Zekk chuckled, then grimaced. "I have something… to chat about." He pulled a silver object from under his blanket. It looked like some sort of digital tablet.

"I'm not in a talkative mood right now." Darien tried to keep the contempt out of his voice.

"OK." Zekk put the tablet on the bench beside him and leaned back until the lines of pain in his face smoothed out. "Why don't we clear the air, then?"

Darien stared at him in disbelief. *This is some kind of trick or trap or game he's playing.* He shifted to look for anything else Zekk might have hidden under his blanket. "Why are you bringing us to Altair?"

"There's someone there I'd like to meet," Zekk said.

Darien narrowed his eyes. "Ah, like the rest of the survivors of Jade

Glen, huh? The three of us weren't enough slaves for you?"

Zekk frowned. "Did Jet tell you about my grandmother?"

A derisive laugh burst from Darien. "How'd you convince him of that syn?"

"He convinced me, actually." Zekk rested his head back against the curved metal wall. "The Lynx kidnapped me and wiped my memory when I was sixteen. Seems they thought I'd make a good soldier because my grandmother and parents were all master level."

Darien felt his brow crease. "Does it also *seem* like they give you a gold star sticker for every aethryn you enslave?"

"As much as I don't want to believe it, it's true." Zekk tapped the tablet beside him. "There's stuff in here about you, too."

The room suddenly felt hotter. Darien clenched his fists. "What? Stuff about my sister?"

"About your parents. Did you know they're Lynx?"

"They *are?*" Darien gritted his teeth. "Don't pretend you know anything. My father's dead, and my mother's—"

"Active duty."

Darien stopped up short. "What?"

"Your mother is active duty Lynx."

Horror kindled in Darien's gut. "I'll kill you—"

"Here." Zekk held out the tablet with a weak hand.

Darien glared for a second, then snatched the device. A photo of a younger version of his mother stared back at him from the screen.

KERRI TAYLOR
SPECIALIST: WEAVER
STATION: N/A
ASSIGNMENT: N/A
STATUS: ACTIVE

Darien's mouth went dry. *What? The Altair base computer said she was missing when I looked last week!*

"I can try and find her location if the Altair base is still online, if you want," Zekk said. "This data is a few days old."

Darien's voice cracked through his throat. "Why would you do that?"

"I haven't had parents for as long as I can remember." Zekk shrugged. "It's not a feeling I want to spread around."

Darien stared at him, aghast. "Did you forget that I stabbed you?"

"I'm trying not to think about it." Zekk took a deep breath and closed his eyes. "I know you were just trying to protect your mentor."

Darien lost count of the red flags that'd popped up during the conversation. "Do you think I'm a fool?" he murmured. "What do you want from us? What are you after?"

Zekk pursed his lips. His eyes opened, and discomfort swam in his aqua gaze. "Can you keep a secret?"

Darien snorted. "If I want to."

Zekk turned his head to look at the slanted cargo bay door. When he spoke, his voice was hesitant and quiet. "I have... almost everything I've ever wanted. My title, my suite, my credits. I have so much that I've grown bored with it."

Darien analyzed him. *Is that even possible?*

"I built a solid team under me. The best of the best—Fadahari, an ace pilot, three sentinels, two vanguards, two valnah, a weaver, a sifter, a maid, a chef..." Zekk's gaze went distant. "We all live together in my suite, and I treat them like family, but they know they're slaves. I can have any woman I want, and I'm surrounded by allies, but I've never felt..." He trailed off.

Darien waited a long moment. "Am I supposed to feel sorry for you?"

"No. You asked what I'm after, so I'm trying to explain." Zekk released a deep breath. "Jet's memories showed the strangest thing. Many of you don't get along, but you constantly risk your lives for each other. Not for money or advancement or yourselves. You just do it, just because." He glanced back at Darien. "You're family."

Discomfort made Darien squirm. "Doesn't feel that way to me," he muttered.

"I know I sound like a kid's show." Zekk swallowed and grimaced. "Let's just say I admire what you all have, and I don't want to ruin it. The Lynx act like their way is the only way, and sometimes they're right, since most of the world is in chaos. You wouldn't believe the evil I've seen—what people can do to each other when there is no law." A muscle twitched in Zekk's cheek. "But you've found another way to be civilized. It would be wrong to force you to live as we do." His voice quieted. "Like they did to me."

You're just now realizing that, you idiot? Anger flared through Darien's mind even as the knot in his chest unraveled. Zekk looked like the definition of brokenness.

Don't fall for it. He manipulates and captures people for a living. There must be some reason he's trying to win me over.

"I just want to meet my grandmother, then I'll go," Zekk said as he stared at the ceiling. "I'll report that the three of you died on the beach, and I won't tell them what I know. I'll work something out with my doc and pilot to keep them quiet."

Darien barely prevented himself from scoffing. *If he took Jet's memories, we can't let him go back to the Lynx—they'd know everything. And even on the one percent chance that he's actually being honest, couldn't they just search his memories and we'd be jacked?*

He couldn't decide how to respond. Should he just tell Zekk where to shove it? Or pretend that he'd fallen for his obvious swill? Or become a blank slate until they arrived in Altair?

Zekk didn't say anything or meet Darien's gaze. His sickly skin color had reddened to a strange hue.

I don't get him. Darien looked down at the forgotten tablet in his hands. "You said you had something to show me."

Zekk cleared his throat. "Uh, yeah. But it has to do with your parents, so…"

Darien powered the tablet's screen on and scrolled through his mother's file. Text that had been blacked out in the Altair base was now clear, but he wasn't sure he wanted to read it. "What?"

"You, me, and Teravyn were all part of a Lynx project called Titan. I'm listed there as Zackary Willow." Zekk pointed at the data pad. "And you're under the name Michael Taylor."

Michael? Darien tapped on the tab labeled 'TITAN' at the top. A list of names lined the screen, including the ones Zekk mentioned.

Darien's pulse fluttered. He slowly touched Michael's name.

MICHAEL TAYLOR
COMMON CRAFT: SENTINEL
STATUS: MISSING

SELECTION: Offspring of weaver specialist Kerri Taylor and TITAN researcher Jacob Taylor, volunteered at conception to TITAN. Selected to further the study of live tissue aether-weaving after initial testing proved promising on older sister, Kathryn Taylor.

Kathryn—is that Tera? Darien didn't breathe as he scrolled down.

INITIAL FINDINGS: Kerri refuses to allow any other weavers to perform the aether binding to the fetus' tissues but herself. She notes that the process is slow and difficult, as the bones are only partially formed, but the potential for future increased aether capacity is great.

She was... weaving aether into me in her womb? As an experiment? The page blurred as he flicked down to the very bottom.

G-17: Child cries at every weaving session. My proposal to remove Jacob and Kerri from the sessions was declined. They stopped the process mid-way through today. Progress is a quarter what it could be.

G-18: Jacob refused to bring Michael in today. Requesting approval for order A21.

A red notice interrupted the notes:

My team is working around the clock to retrieve the Taylors. I will take personal responsibility for not foreseeing their betrayal, so don't worry about your own necks. Yes, we've lost the subjects, but not the data. We know what works now, and that's more important.

Continue your work on the other aether-woven subjects. We will recover our property— it's just a matter of time.

Good work, everyone.

Alon

Darien felt like his stomach dropped out of him. *Dad... this is why they killed him. He wouldn't let them test on us anymore.* Nausea swayed over him. *But how could they do this in the first place?*

The word 'property' glared back at him. *Is this why they're so adamant about capturing Tera?*

"The reports can be hard to understand," Zekk said quietly. "Do you want me to explain?"

"I understand enough." Darien swiped his eyes and shoved the tablet toward Zekk. "You know where my... where Kerri is?"

"No, but I can request that information when I get back online." Zekk's eyes were as deep as a clear pond. "I'm sorry. I wish I could say I know how it feels, but... well, my case is a little more cut and dry."

Darien swallowed bile in his throat. He looked down at his hand and opened and closed his fist, seeing it as he never had before. "Did they... weave aether into you, too?"

Zekk shook his head. "From what I can tell from their notes, that only really works on children as they grow. You were the youngest..." The IV stand clacked as he shifted. "Now I understand why you have such a large aether pool. Does Teravyn have as much?"

"Almost." Darien's voice fractured. *She must remember this. Or did Mom weave over her memories, too?*

He braced his hands on the bench and struggled to keep the xavi meat down. "What were they trying to accomplish?"

"Rumor in Maqua says Titan is super-soldier experiments, and that's exactly what the files read like." Zekk slipped the tablet back inside his blanket. "I don't recommend reading too far in."

"And you didn't know any of this until now?" Darien furrowed his brow at him. "You don't remember anything?"

Zekk shook his head. "Just the training from the deepest pit of Zoth. I never knew I was a part of the project." He smiled weakly. "Maybe if they'd never taken me from my grandmother, we'd have been friends."

Don't think so. Darien looked down at his dirty boots. He inhaled and released a shuddering breath. "I'm sorry. For what they did." He gave Zekk a sidelong glance. "Not for what I did. Try to hurt us again, and I won't hold back."

Zekk tipped his head in a slight nod. "I wouldn't have it any other way."

He makes literally no sense. A sense of weariness weighed down on Darien's shoulders. *I should probably thank him for telling me...* But the last thing he felt was thankfulness. His nausea rotted into disgust.

"Altair in sight," crackled an electronic voice.

Darien sat up straight and found a speaker in a corner of the ceiling. *Was that the pilot?*

"We've got a problem," the voice said.

Adrenaline washed everything else from Darien's muscles. He jumped up and slid the door to the midsection open.

Sorvashti and Jet huddled together under a blue blanket on a wide couch. She sat up with concern etched into her dark face as Jet groaned beside her.

Darien crossed to a rounded window where Doctor Fadahari stared out with wide eyes at a snow-covered landscape.

A familiar walled city nestled in the mountains, surrounded by modern ruins and aspen forests. A thick plume of smoke rose from the northern side—right where the acreage of Valinor Manor should have been.

32

Aleah carefully poured yellow liquid into the generator's fuel port as wind scattered her hair in her eyes. Nausea rose in her stomach at the smell of gasoline—both at the strength of the fumes and the latent fear of flammable substances. One spark from the Phoera element would be her end.

She let the last few drops slide off, then peered into the dark hole. *How much more do we need?*

Without this generator, the heater in Rex's house wouldn't have power. And only the creator knew how cold it was going to get tonight.

She was grateful for the distraction—the task at hand. Thoughts of her home burning prowled at the edge of her mind like snow leopards in the forest beyond the barbed-wire fence.

Aleah squeezed her eyes shut in an attempt to hold her stunned grief at bay. *It's OK. Mom and Dad are safe. We'll be fine.*

Footfalls crunched in the snow behind her. Aleah looked over her shoulder and swatted her fuzzy-rimmed hood out of the way.

Raydon approached with a dirty gas canister. He had his face and arms tucked into his coat like a turtle in its shell. His nose shone a rosy pink and his breath fogged on the wind.

"Found some in one of his tractors." He handed her the canister.

Would that mean it's diesel? Does that make a difference? Aleah twisted the cap off and began pouring. "OK, let's see if we can get it to work after this."

Raydon stood quietly beside her for a long moment. "I found something on the Lynx computers."

Aleah didn't look at him as she focused on not wasting a single drop. "Oh?"

"Someone was communicating with the Lynx."

Gasoline spilled over the lip, and Aleah yanked the canister back up. She whirled on Raydon. "What?"

His expression was grim as he glanced at the ranch house behind them, then down the fence line to the barn across a snowy field. "Levi."

Aleah sniffed and tipped the canister's spout back to the generator. "That's not funny."

"I agree," Raydon said. "I was wiping the computers when I saw the communication logs." He paused, and she heard a zipping sound and rustling of fabric. "Looked suspicious, so I made a backup to my tablet."

He can't be serious. "Master Emberhawk told you to wipe the data, not to make backups."

"Yeah, and now I know why." Raydon held something out to her in her peripheral vision.

Aleah frowned as the last drops of gasoline slipped out. She set the canister down, wiped her hand on her coat, and took the silver tablet he offered.

Crisp lines of text ran across the screen.

… primary food source. Altair is no longer safe. They want to bug out to a nearby abandoned ranch.

Negative. Stay on-base and lockdown.

We can't. The whole city blames us. They'll starve us out.

You will obey, Emberhawk, or there will be consequences.

If we all die, you'll never find the other group of survivors.

Accompany them and remain in contact...

Aleah stared at the name 'Emberhawk.' Her brain went as numb as her fingers.

"I think this is why your brother disappeared," Raydon said under his breath. "Maybe he found out, and Levi fed them intel to capture him."

Aleah winced and shoved the tablet back at him. "There's some mistake. Master Emberhawk would never—"

"They have leverage on him." Raydon swiped his finger over the screen. "His son, Brailey, was captured at Jade Glen." He flipped the tablet around so she could see. "They sent proof of life."

A young man resembling Levi stared back at her from a photo, bound and bleeding in a whitewashed room. He glared at the camera from his knees while two men in Lynx armor held him on either side.

Numbness spread into Aleah's bones. She'd never known Brailey personally, but she recognized him as one of the sentinel trainers from Jade Glen.

And he looked just like the suspect from her parents' murder case. *This can't be...*

But her gut wasn't so sure. What parent wouldn't do anything to save their child?

Aleah tried to swallow a lump in her throat but couldn't. "Did he tell them where this ranch is?" she whispered.

Raydon studied the tablet and shook his head. "Looks like it's just a matter of time."

Then we'll settle this now. Aleah twisted the cap on the generator and ignored the spilled gasoline. She pulled her gloves on and marched toward the barn.

"Where are you going?" Raydon called behind her. "Didn't you want to turn this on?"

"I saw him go into the barn a few minutes ago."

Raydon grabbed her arm. "Are you crazy? He's a Grand Master consorting with the Lynx! He could—"

"He's not evil even if he is." Aleah shrugged his arm off. "I'm going to ask him to his face if this is true."

"What more proof do you need? Don't—"

"Then give me the tablet if you're scared." Aleah stopped and held out her hand.

Something Aleah couldn't identify flashed behind Raydon's brown eyes. He pursed his lips. "I won't let him hurt you."

As if he would. Regardless of the nausea swimming in her stomach, she refused to even consider it until she heard Levi's side. Her mind couldn't handle any more unknowns.

So much had gone wrong in the past few days that nothing made sense anymore. She desperately wanted things to go back to the way they were just a few days ago—when Altair was safe, the Serran Grand Master Council was blameless, and her birth parents were at peace in their graves.

If only Jet was here. He'd know what to make of all of this.

Ache for her brother flared, but Aleah shoved it back down. She trudged back down the fence line where the snow level was lowest, careful not to let her coat snag on the barbed wire. Trepidation and fear pounded stronger with every step, and her migraine reemerged.

The barn door screeched open as Aleah shoved it aside. She blinked into the cavernous interior. A set of green cat eyes watched her from the dusty rafters, and a dim firelight flickered from an old-fashioned lantern near the open pantry door.

"Master?"

"Here." Levi's wild gray hair popped out from the pantry. "Did you get the generator running?"

Aleah stared into his tired silver gaze. He looked as tired as she felt. "Have you been communicating with the Lynx?"

Levi's face blanched. His eyes shifted to Raydon behind her, then lit with rage. "What are you doing?"

"So it's true?" Raydon demanded.

Levi exited the pantry and glanced at the door. His voice dropped low. "They have my son."

His words lanced through Aleah. Her lips parted, but no words came.

Levi pointed at Raydon. "He was my handler."

Raydon snorted. "Really? We just caught you red-handed communicating with them directly!"

"I should have killed you from the start!" Levi's face reddened. "What have you done? Are you poisoning her?"

"Master." Aleah's voice fractured. "Why?"

Levi stepped forward as his expression snapped from rage to pleading. "Listen to me, Aleah. Raydon is the Lynx. You can't listen to anything he says."

"I just listened to what you said." Aleah swallowed hard. "Was my brother taken because of you?"

Levi's eyes widened. "No, I don't know what happened—"

"How much have you told them?" Aleah shouted. "Is this why you wanted me to prepare? What's the point if you tell them where we are?"

Levi's duster rustled as he shifted. "Yes, this is why I asked you to prepare a backup place for us. But you weren't supposed to tell anyone." His gaze flicked to Raydon.

I can't believe this!

Aleah's tears fell. "How could you—"

"They'll kill my son. They did... things to him when I tried to subvert them." Levi clenched his fists. "I've done everything in my power to protect everyone."

"Traitor," Aleah whispered.

Pain sliced across Levi's face. He pointed at Raydon again. "He's the enemy here. He was a Lynx spy in Jade Glen from the beginning—he was after Darien and Tera."

What? Aleah blinked to clear her eyes. "He's *former* Lynx, and that's a good thing! He let us into the Lynx base so we could rescue Jet and Sorva!"

A harsh laugh huffed from Levi's throat. "He did that because he never dreamed we'd win. He thought we'd all be captured, and then he could use their equipment to prove Darien and Tera's identities and bring them in for a reward." He gave Raydon a vindictive smirk. "Tera ruined your plans, didn't she?"

Raydon said nothing. Aleah looked over her shoulder at him, and he glanced at her before looking back at Levi with a cool expression. "You're pretty good at making up stories on the spot." He lifted his tablet into the air and wiggled it. "Let me guess: you don't have a single shred of proof."

Levi spat on the dirt floor. "Have you told them about this location yet?"

A reflection of a smile crossed Raydon's face. "You're not convincing anyone."

Levi's hand shot out at Raydon. An earsplitting boom rattled the barn, and the shockwave cleared the dust on the floor. Raydon flew back and hit a stack of hay bales in an explosion of straw.

Aleah ducked away and cried out. She stared up at Levi as he marched toward Raydon. His eyes were like cold steel.

Aleah grabbed Levi's arm. "No!"

Levi yanked his arm back. "You just sit tight for a sec."

Raydon grunted as he got to his feet and looked up at Levi with terror-filled eyes. He thrust a hand toward Levi, and the collision of aether blew straw out of Raydon's hair.

Levi punched him in the jaw, and he collapsed.

"Stop it!" Aleah grabbed Levi from behind. "Please!"

Levi ignored her as he grabbed a length of thick rope from a post. He stuck a knee in the small of Raydon's back, wrenched his arms together, and began to tie them.

A sob choked Aleah. She pulled against Levi, but she might as well have been tugging on an elephant's leg.

Master Willow. I have to get Master Willow!

She let go of Levi and dashed for the door.

"Hold up!" Levi hollered, but Aleah didn't stop until she ran straight into the soft positive side of a vanguard wall. It bounced her away from itself like an air mattress.

Panic skittered up Aleah's spine as she dashed to the right, but the invisible wall was there, too. She ran left and stopped up short. The entire barn door was blocked.

"Aleah, I need you to calm down and listen to me," Levi said. Raydon struggled under him, and Levi hit him again.

Lightheadedness made Aleah sway. Some part of her recognized the symptoms of hyperventilation, but she couldn't calm her breathing.

"Raydon's an arbiter—he probably stuffed your head full of false memories and lies. Now that I look, I can sense some of his slime in your head right now."

What? Aleah glanced down at Raydon. He glared up at Levi through an eye that was swelling shut. *I think I'd notice if he was planting false memories! And why would he?*

"With Raydon taken care of, they can't control me anymore." Levi's voice softened. "You're right that I should never have worked with them, and I'm sorry. I'll find out where they're keeping Brailey and rescue him myself. I just need to make sure you're all safe before I leave."

Aleah pressed against the vanguard wall beside her. "What are you going to do with him?" she whispered.

Levi looked down on Raydon and yanked a knot tight. "I'm gonna find out if he's already told them about this location or not."

Raydon cursed, and Levi backhanded him.

"Stop." Aleah's eyes filled again. "Please don't hurt him."

"Put your shields down for me." Levi hauled Raydon up and wound the other end of the rope around the rafters. "I'll do the same, and everything will clear up real quick."

Fear tickled the back of Aleah's neck. She'd never been ordered to lower her shields before—nothing made a person more vulnerable. Only troublesome students or aspirants for master training had to do so at the Serran Academies.

He wants to silence me! If I refuse, will he attack me and tie me up, too?

Levi looked at her and the hard lines of his face smoothed. He took a step toward her, and she took a step back and bumped into the vanguard wall.

Aleah squeezed her eyes shut as a sob escaped. *Please, creator, help me!*

"I'm sorry," Levi whispered. "I didn't mean to scare ya. You don't have to lower your shields if you don't want to."

Aleah steadied her breathing and dared to open her eyes.

Levi wore a plastered smile. "I'll tell Eleanor everything, OK?"

"Don't you touch her," Raydon growled. "You can let me freeze to death in here, you traitor, but if you—"

Levi cut him off with a laugh. "Oh no, you won't freeze. I'll make it much more appropriate for your crimes."

"Master!" Aleah croaked. "If you're as upright as you claim, then promise me you'll never hurt him again!"

Levi's face fell into a conflicted expression. "Look, I'll let him be for tonight, and tell everyone everything."

He took a step forward and placed a hand on her shoulder. She shrank under it.

"I'll help you sort through the false memories tomorrow. For now we need to get that generator running." Levi glanced over his shoulder at Raydon. "I don't want you in here or talking to him at all until Eleanor and I can talk." Silver eyes looked down at her. "Understand?"

Aleah pursed her lips and looked down at his mud-encrusted boots. "Yes, Mast—" The word stuck in her throat and refused to come out. "Levi."

33

A cid sludged through Jet's veins as he watched his childhood home smolder—a black scar on the otherwise snow-white landscape. The Caracal was still a half-mile from Altair, but after he'd become a Serran, his eyesight had sharpened tremendously. He was certain that the charred ruin that fed a column of withering smoke was Valinor Manor.

Sorvashti touched Jet's arm, snapping him from his shock. *Mom, Dad, Aleah!* His heart kick started. *Where are they?*

"Altair, this is Coriander-two-eight-Rothari," the pilot's voice crackled over the speakers. "Requesting permission to land."

"What happened?" Darien's voice warped as he moved away from the crowded window.

"Is that what I think it is?" Zekk whispered. He stared out the window beside Jet with a furrowed brow.

Jet fought against a panic that threatened to overpower him. *He has all of my memories—he knows what it is.*

"Two-eight, your code checks out," said a different voice over the intercom. "What's your directive?"

That doesn't sound like Raydon. Jet glanced at the open cockpit door to the hundreds of buttons and switches. The pilot looked over his shoulder at Zekk, bobbing an antenna on his headset.

"Original contract details," Zekk said.

The pilot turned back to his instruments and pressed a red button. "Personal directive from the Phoenix. Orders are to investigate and secure the base after the raid."

Jet tensed. *They'll think we're hostile—they could open fire!* His mind raced. *How can we tell them we're friendly?*

"Copy, two-eight. You're clear for landing."

That voice was definitely not Raydon.

Jet turned to Zekk. "Where are my weapons?"

Zekk hesitated. "Think we're in trouble?"

"I don't know." Jet stared down at Zekk, daring him to argue.

Zekk appeared oblivious to the threat. He waved his hand at a drawer in a thin desk below the digital map display. "Key's there for a locker in the cargo bay."

"Neither of you are in a position to stand, much less fight," Fadahari's scratchy voice warned. "Sit down and let us handle this."

Jet got the key and marched to the cargo bay. He found the locker and opened it, then stuffed his switchblade in his belt and chambered a round in his sidearm. *Is Victoria still laying on that lake's edge?* He grumbled as he grabbed the knife Levi had given to Darien and Sorvashti's ceremonial dagger, then slammed the locker shut.

The landscape was much closer to the window when Jet reentered the midsection. Sorvashti sat on a couch with concern etched on her face, and Zekk sat across from her with closed eyes. Fadahari pulled the IV out and pressed a clean cloth over the bend of Zekk's arm. Zekk clenched his elbow shut as Jet handed Darien his knife.

"Hang on," the pilot said, and Jet leaned against the window.

Maybe I'm just not recognizing Raydon's voice over the comms. Or maybe they picked up some new guy, or got someone from the Manor to handle the comms.

Antennas on the Lynx base roof slowly raised into the window's view, then the trapdoor whose stairs led down to the first level. Snow swirled and fled in every direction as the Caracal hovered lower, revealing white heli-pad marks on the wet rooftop.

They'll be freaked out with a Lynx heli-jet landing on top of them.

"Let me handle this," Jet said as the Caracal rocked and touched down with barely a disturbance in the cabin. Jet glanced at Zekk and noted his sickly complexion.

"'K," Zekk muttered without opening his eyes.

The hum of the engines whirred down and the lock on the exterior door disengaged. Jet stared out the window as the trapdoor in the roof swung open. A man in Lynx armor climbed out, then another, and another, each with a bone-streaked mask complete with glowing blue visor. One of them was slim enough to be female, but they all held assault rifles loosely in front of them.

Five? Trepidation roiled in Jet's gut. "I don't think... they're our people."

Zekk frowned. "Then they're probably mine." He let out a long breath as he stood, and Fadahari snarled at him. He grumbled and waved as if to shoo her off.

Darien looked out the window. "Where is everyone?"

"Get your face out of the window." Jet pointed to the couch as he put his back to the wall. "Sit down. Don't let them see you."

Darien silently sat on the couch next to Sorvashti, who was watching Jet with warm, concerned eyes. "Are we the OK?"

"Don't worry," Zekk said through a groan. He shuffled to the door, and as he yanked the hatch and pulled it open, his back straightened and his shoulders broadened. The appearance of weakness molted from him like a lizard's skin.

Jet's hand went to his sidearm as he listened.

"Welcome to Altair—oh, Confidant! We didn't expect you, sir!"

Fabric rustled and boots clacked.

"At ease," Zekk said. "What's the situation here?"

"Locals panicked over the food shortage and early onset of winter," a man's voice said. "They raided and looted the city's primary food source."

Pain and fear wrestled in Jet's chest, but the familiarity of that voice struck him. He hadn't heard it in years.

I have a fake Lynx ID and Diamondback's support—I can show my face.

Jet slipped behind Zekk and stared down at the five Lynx masks looking up at him. *Which one—*

"King?" one of them called.

"Bleeding Zoth, it's King!" Another Lynx ripped his helmet off, revealing a mess of black hair, joy-filled eyes, and a lopsided grin.

Copperhead! Jet's tension melted as another Lynx removed his helmet. The man who'd forged him into one of the best snipers in the Royal Guard, Moccasin, wore a rare smile and relief in his sharp obsidian eyes.

Jet pushed past Zekk and jumped down to the helipad, then steadied himself against the Caracal's hull. His long-lost brothers rushed forward and embraced him in a clamor of thick armor.

Copperhead slapped Jet on the back and gripped his shoulder. "So glad to see you, rookie. Feared the worst!"

Jet noticed that Copperhead's eyes were rimmed with red, and his brief happiness faltered. "What are you two doing here?"

Moccasin glanced at Copperhead. "Report said there was some trouble out here, and that DB took command and you joined up. We didn't even know you'd made it through the meteors." Moccasin ran a hand through black helmet-hair. "We joined the backup squad to get the team back together. Where've you been frolicking off to? You look like syn."

Why won't he look me in the eye? Moccasin was notorious for his patented glare—the deadly one Jet had gleaned from him. But now his former mentor's eyes hovered downward... like the time he'd broken Jet's wrist.

Something's wrong.

"The Vipers!" Sorvashti's voice rang out behind him. Jet turned to see her jump out of the Caracal and run over. She greeted them with a bow and a Terruthian saying that meant 'creator smile on you.'

Copperhead and Moccasin both bowed and attempted to repeat the

Terruthian phrase with varying degrees of success.

Dread soured on Jet's tongue. "Where's Diamondback?"

Copperhead grimaced as Moccasin finally looked at Jet. "We buried him by the Brazen Tower memorial."

The words hit Jet in the chest. He stared at Moccasin, speechless, and saw the truth of it in his eyes. Sorvashti whimpered and put a hand over her mouth.

"I'm sorry, brother," Moccasin whispered. "We couldn't find you. Thought you'd suffered the same fate."

Jet's throat closed. "What fate?" The column of smoke listed in the corner of his vision. "Were there any survivors?"

"We'd like to know, but the records have been wiped clean," Moccasin murmured.

Copperhead's light Valinorian skin flushed red. "When we got here, the place was overrun with squatters. Questioned one of them who said DB was guarding this whole base by himself."

What? Jet clenched his fists. *Levi, you left him here alone? If you're alive, I'll—*

"We drove them out and reclaimed the base, not that it's worth anything now." Moccasin glanced up at Zekk, who turned and disappeared back into the Caracal. "Place is trashed and the armory's empty."

"Did you find any other bodies?" Jet demanded. They should have met General Thracian Lance Valinor before—at another soldier's funeral, six years ago. "My father?"

Copperhead shook his head.

Jet struggled to think through the shock. He'd lost brothers in arms before, but Viper Actual...

He squeezed his eyes shut. *Everyone else is alive. They have to be. Diamondback wouldn't have died for anything less.* He let out a steadying breath and looked at the smoke plume curling away from the mountains. *But where are they?*

Footsteps approached from behind. "Old buddies?" Darien asked.

"Darien!"

A Lynx helmet clattered on the rooftop. Jet blinked at a middle-aged woman with short dirty-blonde hair and dark blue eyes—she bore a noticeable similarity to Teravyn Aetherswift.

The woman burst forward and crashed into Darien, crushing him in a hug.

Darien's eyes bulged as he looked down at her. "Mom?"

34

*I*s this really her?

The woman in Darien's arms clutched him as if he were her heart, and she was trying to squeeze him back into her chest.

This is the woman who volunteered me for experiments as an unborn child. Darien's arms held her tightly, but his hands were limp. *And then sacrificed everything to stop it.*

Kerri pulled back and put a hand on his cheek. Her eyes watered as they stared into his. "Look at you," she breathed.

Darien's throat closed up. Her eyes were clear and intelligent—like Teravyn's had been. The film that had covered them for years was gone. *Is she sober?*

One of the men who'd greeted Jet—the mean-looking one—had a stare so intense that Darien could feel it boring into him. "Is this who I think it is, King?" he muttered.

"If you think he's under my protection, then yes." Jet's look could have fried and scrambled a perfect continental breakfast.

"He's my son, sir." Kerri blinked back tears and released Darien.

The man's eyebrows raised. He lifted a hand to the two masked Lynx behind him. "Back to your posts."

The masked ones turned and went back down the stairs.

Darien stared at Kerri's wild short hair. "Mom," he said through a fractured voice, "what are you doing here?"

Kerri took Darien's arm and guided him away from Jet, Sorvashti, and the two Lynx Jet apparently knew. She rounded the Caracal, then backed up until the wind's fury was blocked by the steel-gray aircraft tail.

"I've been searching desperately for you ever since the collapse of civilization." Kerri's eyes flicked over his mud-smeared Lynx armor, but he doubted she recognized it since he'd torn off the sleeves and some pieces of kevlar in the Malaano jungle's heat. "I heard that Teravyn was wanted, so I joined the Lynx for their resources, but they couldn't find her."

Kerri's dark blue eyes flicked to the other men. "Then a few days ago, a report came through that you were in Altair—confirmed by a blood sample. So I begged to join this squad, but when we got here..." She looked back up at him, then clenched her eyes shut and buried her face in his chest.

Darien didn't stretch his arms around her. "You mean you *rejoined* the Lynx."

Kerri stilled.

"So they took you back after you deserted the Titan project?" Darien's voice deepened. "After they executed Dad?"

Kerri slowly pulled away and looked up at him. "You know about Titan?"

Darien's anger lashed at her like a solar flare. "You experimented on me! You altered my memories." He remained perfectly still, lest he do something he'd regret. "What kind of mother—"

"Two of the single greatest regrets in my life," Kerri rushed. "Your father and I hated what they made us do. That's why we left."

Darien snorted. "They *made* you? The file said you volunteered me at conception!"

Kerri grimaced and looked away. "They made us… after we decided to stop. We didn't know how much it would hurt you." She placed a hand on his chest. "But it was all for you—to make you powerful. And look at you now!"

Darien felt like he might vomit. "I don't care about power. All I wanted was a family. I needed Dad and a sober mother!"

Anguish flashed across Kerri's eyes. She turned away from him and hugged herself. The wind sifted through her dirty-blonde hair.

"I know, and I'm sorry," she whispered. "I couldn't handle it when they took Jacob." Her jaw clenched as a tear slipped down her cheek. "But I sobered after the meteors, and I'm here for you now. I'll do anything to make it up to you, and I'll never go back to the way I was. I swear it."

Resolve hardened her gaze. "Tera was right, and now I finally see— she did the right thing in taking me to court and gaining custody of you. So strong and brave. Just like Jacob."

Kerri swiped the tear off her cheek in apparent annoyance. She stood up straight. "Where is she?"

Darien's heart wrenched as if she'd reached through his skin and grabbed it. His lips parted, but no words came.

Kerri glanced sidelong at him. "Do you know?"

"She's gone," Darien whispered.

Kerri's face blanched. "What do you mean?"

Hot tears stung Darien's eyes. He squeezed them shut as a sob wracked him.

"Gone. Everything's gone."

He felt Kerri's arms slip back around him and pull him tight. She cried against him, and his dam broke. He clutched his mother and wept.

35

The setting sun draped the mountains with orange silhouettes, casting Altair's shattered skyscrapers in shadow. Jet leaned his elbows on the roof railing and stared out over the skyline. The column of smoke faded as it rose, blotting out a swath of young stars.

I should just go as soon as it gets dark enough. I'd have a better chance of not being recognized and pitchforked.

But fear rooted him firmly to the Lynx base, where Moccasin assured them they were safe for the time being. Creator only knew what he would find if he went. Nothing useful, to be sure. He'd sifted through plenty of wreckage before, but never his own home.

Any burned body I found could be them. How would I identify...?

Jet squeezed his eyes shut and took a deep breath as numb shock warred with grief. *Don't mourn them until you know for sure. You always hated that house, anyway.*

"Shlanga?"

Jet glanced over his shoulder at the cold, dark form of the Caracal's wings. "Here."

Sorvashti rounded the Caracal's tail fin with that same blue blanket scrunched up to her eyes. She waddled toward him and squealed as a night wind blasted over the edge of the railing. *"Aeo stutsch mich!* It is so cold!" She snuggled up to him and wrapped her blanket-covered hands around his bare arm. "How are you not the bicycle?"

Icicle? Jet grinned. He slipped an arm around her and pulled her tight. "I'll take this over the jungle any day."

"No!" Sorvashti shook her head, nuzzling into his side. "It was more like home."

"Ugh, yeah." Jet wrinkled his nose. "I went to Elyon on assignment once. Nearly melted in the humidity."

"Oh, no. In Ironhide, it is not like the city. The air is dry and hot."

Jet glanced down at her. "Is it closer to the desert?"

"It is not the desert, but the summers feel like the desert," Sorvashti said. "The winters are so good. We do not have the snow or the mountains. We have the hills and the short trees and the water-caves under the ground." Her breath clouded as she sighed. "Many people do not say LaKota is beautiful, but to me, it is many much more beautiful than this."

Well, if the land is anything like its people, I believe it. Jet brushed a lock of straight pale hair from her eyes. "If Zekk could fly us there, would you want to go?"

"No," Sorvashti said with a snort. "I do not trust him. And I do not know what is there now. Maybe the comet hits the land. Maybe no one is..." She tugged the blanket tighter around herself.

I'm afraid of what I might find. Sorvashti's thought warmed Jet's shields like a ray of sunlight. *In my mind, my family is alive and living well off the land. Disaster preparedness was a custom in LaKotan culture, and my parents were very traditional. Our house ran on solar energy, was heated by warmth from deep in the earth, and drew water from a modern well.*

Jet's eyebrows rose as he wondered how much wealthier the Ironhide clan was compared to the average LaKotan family. He recalled that her father was a governor and assumed that had something to do with it. *For a girl from a rich family, she sure doesn't act like it.*

Sorvashti shivered, and Jet hugged her tighter. "Sounds like a smart setup," he said.

Yes, but I would think the real danger would have come from other people. Her thought softened with pity. *I'm so sorry about your home. Do you want me to go with you?*

Jet frowned. "I... don't know."

Her golden eyes peeked up at him. "Will the smoke be bad of your...?" She patted a blanket-covered fist on his chest.

Right. "Uh, yeah, probably. I'll wait till the smoke clears."

Sorvashti still looked up at him, but Jet resisted the urge to meet her gaze. She radiated solace, warmth, comfort... and if he took it, he knew he'd break.

"I am sure they are the OK," she whispered.

"Yeah. Of course." Jet swallowed hard. "Diamondback wouldn't have sacrificed his life for nothing. He must have had a way out and covered their escape."

Diamondback. The pain in his chest doubled and throbbed.

Sorvashti shifted under his arm. "Do you know where they go?"

"No," Jet murmured. "Thracian has a lake house in Lorsann, but it's too far away. And even colder."

A blanket-covered hand reached up and pulled down on Jet's jaw until he met her gaze. Molten gold enraptured him. "We will find them," Sorvashti whispered.

Longing welled up and overflowed even as Jet fought to hold it back. Everything about her was intoxicating—he could drown in her, losing himself and forgetting everything.

No, she's still healing. I shouldn't...

But his body leaned over her without permission, and she tilted her head up to meet him.

Her lips sent a wave of heat crashing through him. He breathed in her honey-sweet scent and slipped a hand behind her neck, pulling her closer.

His protests shriveled and flitted away on the mountain breeze.

A voice cracked against his shields: *Turning Lynx and smooching a widow. Bonza.*

Jet jerked away. *Garrett?* He kept Sorvashti close as he pushed through the blissful haze back to reality.

No one hid behind the Caracal's frame. No one watched from the ice-covered road below. No one sat on Altair's nearby wall—only the forests observed from afar.

Dunno why I thought you were better, mate. Has Darien turned traitor, too, or have you got him locked up in there?

"What's wrong?" Sorvashti's voice quivered as she blinked up at him.

"N-nothing. It's Garrett..." Jet desperately looked for the young Terruthian so he could shred him for interrupting the moment he'd been daydreaming about for years. "He's talking to me."

Just put your thoughts outside your shields and I can hear them, Garrett thought. *I'm curious to hear your excuses.*

Jet stared into the shadows of the snow-laden evergreen forest and gritted his teeth. *Where are you?* He sent the thought just outside his shields and let it hang awkwardly in the air.

Lovely little aspect of sifter—I can hide my signature. Sorry, but I'm not gonna tell ya where I am, Lynx.

Jet held Sorvashti tight against a burst of wind. *I'd like to know where everyone* is. *And I'm not a Lynx.*

So you disappear for a few days, make buddy-buddy with the pretty boy on the Lynx recruitment posters, then cruise in on a Lynx heli-jet and greet the Lynx here like you're long-lost pals. That about straight?

Jet gripped Sorvashti's blanket and wondered how long Garrett had been watching. *It's not what it looks like. The two I know here are old war buddies of mine, and Zekk's had a change of—*

Garrett's jovial laughter skittered across his shields. *You think you can talk your way out of this? Just let Darien go and maybe I won't tell your family what a hunk of syn you are.*

Jet's breath tumbled out in a warm cloud. *They're alive?*

A belch-toad croaked in the quiet pause. *Maybe.*

Jet slammed a hand down on the roof railing and glared into the forest. *Garrett, please! Tell me where they are!*

"What does he say?" Sorvashti asked.

"He knows where everyone is!" Jet pulled his memory of being captured by Zekk and forced it through his shields, dangling it like a dog treat in front of him. *Can you see this?*

Another long moment passed. *Is that…?*

Jet gathered choice memories from the past several days: Zekk capturing them, Zekk stealing his memories, Zekk calling off his team and flying them back to Altair. He displayed them all in a sequence, one after the other.

You're an arbiter, Garrett thought. *You're making these up.*

Wouldn't you be able to sense it if they were fake, sifter?

I… I don't know. Garrett's surprise was apparent in his thoughts. *These can't be real. They're ridiculous!*

You're telling me. Jet turned his back to the wind, shielding Sorvashti from another gust. *Listen, Darien is not a captive, but I don't think he should know where everyone is right now. Take me to the Masters first, and we can figure out how to keep everyone safe.*

Offing Zekk would be a good start, Garrett muttered. *What's wrong with Darien?*

Jet glanced at the door that led down into the Lynx base. *It's not him; it's his mother.*

His mum?

Apparently she's Lynx. And it doesn't seem like he trusts her any more than I do. Jet looked down and pushed a windswept lock of hair from Sorvashti's searching eyes. "Would you get Fadahari for me?"

Sorvashti harrumphed. "Oh, I see. The *shlanga* kisses and then sends me to get another woman."

Jet choked. "Trust me, it's not—"

"Ha!" Sorvashti planted a kiss on him, then pulled her blankets away. "You owe to me."

Jet felt his cheeks flush, knowing Garrett was watching. Words failed him.

Hey, stop! I've got you in my sights!

Jet lurched forward and grabbed Sorvashti's arm, then swung around to place himself between her and the forest. *You're going to shoot us?* Jet yelled.

I don't trust the Lynx like you do! If you tell them about me—

Of course I won't, Jet snarled. *I just have to get the doctor. I can't go anywhere without her.*

You think I'll let you come with a Lynx doc on your heels?

Jet grimaced and glanced over his shoulder at Sorvashti, who blinked questioningly up at him. *I don't have a choice.*

I do, and the answer is no. Garrett's voice was firm. *I've seen your memories, so you're OK. But if Darien's mum's an issue, then you're the only one until we get this all straightened out.*

Jet pursed his lips. He slowly turned and looked down at Sorvashti. She tilted her head. "What?"

"He says I have to go alone," Jet muttered.

A snarl curled Sorvashti's lip over her teeth. "You tell Garrett, '*Yi hamul icreshna i barrut nyati. Und kerupf tus marinteiger?*'"

"Uh…" Jet glanced back at the woods. *Did you get that?*

The belch-toad croaked again before Garrett murmured, *She can come, too.*

36

Aleah flopped to the other side of the bed and pulled her sheets tight under her chin. She groaned at whatever had coaxed her out of sleep—maybe it was the fading dream with someone calling her name. Now she'd have to block out the cold again as it seeped through the walls and into her bones.

Yellow-orange light from the window flickered against Aleah's closed eyelids. *Is it morning yet?* She squinted through the glass. *Why's it so red...?*

Across the pasture, flames engulfed the barn and lit the countryside like a fallen star.

Aleah gasped and scrambled up, tossing her precious blankets to the ground. Her hands slammed onto the window as she stared out, begging the creator that her eyes had deceived her.

But the window's biting frost assured her that she was awake.

No!

Aleah scrambled for her shoes and grabbed her coat. She ran into the hall, threw the door open, and plunged into the darkness.

Snow clung to her fox-themed pajamas and melted into them, her socks, and shoes as she ran. She slipped on a patch of ice hidden beneath the snow, floundered for balance, and hit frigid earth on her knees. She looked up at the fire lapping over the tin roof.

Memories of fire and smoke and terror gnawed at her soul. She pushed them down, scrambled up, and kept going.

"Raydon!"

The Phoera element crackled in her blood, itching to compete with the roaring inferno. Aleah thrust her hand at the barn door, and the wood hissed from yellow to orange, then snuffed out to pitch black.

A man's indiscernible cry clawed through the flames.

Aleah covered her mouth with her elbow and ducked inside. Raw, wild heat buffeted her and tried to fling her right back out. Something fell from the rafters and crashed to the dirt at her feet in a flurry of cinders.

Aleah cried out to the element in her blood and thrust her hands outward, and the fire vanished. Not even smoke rose from the charred rafters and piles of soot. Darkness fell over her like a shroud.

She gasped for breath. "Raydon?"

"Aleah…"

She dashed in the direction of the broken voice and stumbled over a body on the ground. She buried her hand in a blackened bale, withdrew a handful of hay, and willed it to burst into flame as she tossed it to the dirt.

The light revealed Raydon lying on the floor, his wrists still bound by a thick, charred rope. He wheezed under a half-burned shirt and smears of ash. Bright red burns covered his face and arms, and a dead ember sat in his brown hair.

Aleah's blood froze. "Are you…?" She called for her gift and scanned him for further injury, but his anguished cry tore her focus away. He pulled against the rope and squeezed his eyes shut, sending tears over his angry burns.

"What happened?" Aleah fell to her knees beside Raydon and sent healing aether into the cracked flesh. Raydon screamed and jerked back, then panted and whimpered, holding himself against the pain.

Aleah's soul fractured. "It's OK." She looked over her shoulder and spotted the glass shards of an oil lamp on its side, blackened like the cattle trough it sat upon. *Maybe it was an accident—*

"Levi."

What? Levi wouldn't... Aleah turned back to Raydon, whose brown eyes had grown wide and wild.

"You have to stop him." Raydon's bloodshot gaze drifted to her. "You're the only one who can stop him."

Aleah jerked back as Raydon's aether pierced her mind—his agony and volatile rage. The barn blurred as Levi's words prowled through her head: *"Oh no, you won't freeze. I'll make it much more appropriate for your crimes."*

Hot tears watered her eyes. *He promised...*

But he'd also lied about the worldwide blackout to the students in Jade Glen. And ratted them out to the Lynx. And smiled for his mug shot on her parents' paperwork.

Aleah grabbed the rope that bound Raydon. The portion between her hands sparked and hissed and shriveled into a crisp.

She turned and walked out of the barn without a word. Snow melted and evaporated into steam around her as she strode toward the house, leaving dry, dead grass at her feet. She flung the front door open and didn't close it behind her.

The house lay quiet, as if the halls themselves were asleep. Either the people inside each room hadn't awoken because of the fire, or they didn't care.

Aleah passed the master bedroom and opened a door on her left. Soft snoring masked the creak of hinges.

A fluff of gray hair stuck out from a pile of blankets on the bed. Aleah rounded the dated bedpost, the dark lamp, and the moonlit curtains.

He started the fire and went to sleep? Tears streamed down Aleah's cheeks as she looked down at Levi. *He has no soul.*

Her pulse thrummed so loudly that she was sure it'd wake him. But he slept as peacefully as a toddler.

My parents, my brother, my boyfriend. You've done your best to take everything from me.

Her aether writhed in rage and terror, but she forced it to obey. It displayed Levi's arteries and veins, and the steady beat of valves in his heart. Such a beautiful, intricate, fragile system.

Aleah summoned her healing gift and lightly touched his chest. A burst of aether fused the valves shut.

Levi jerked awake. He blinked, found her face in the darkness, and stared at her with a confused grimace.

He opened his mouth, but no sound came out. Slowly he slid back onto his pillow, and the light in his silver eyes faded and snuffed out.

37

"That doesn't make any sense." Frozen weeds crunched under Jet's boots as he ducked under a cedar branch. He wished he could have flown—the hike had been long and the mountainside even more frigid since the sun had retired. "Raydon's been with us since Jade Glen. Is Levi sure?"

Garrett limped behind him, trudging through a furrow in the snow. "Sure enough to tie him up like a carcass in the barn." He held a branch out of the way for Sorvashti to duck under. "Said Raydon was looking for Darien for some... reason..."

Garrett trailed off and paused. "Do you smell that?"

Jet straightened and inhaled chilled air. *Is that smoke?*

He peered through the trees and realized that they were almost to the forest's edge. A pasture stretched up a hill to a house on one side and a dark barn on the other.

"The barn!" Garrett pushed past Jet and hobbled to the tree line.

Jet followed and squinted in the moonlit dusk. The barn wasn't just dark—it was charred a deeper black than the young night's embrace.

"Where is everyone?" Jet asked. "In that house?"

"No," Garrett whispered. His dark skin and clothes camouflaged him with the trees' shadows, but the whites of his eyes widened in horror.

Jet's pulse kick started. "What?"

"Master Willow." Garrett turned to him with a blank stare. "She says to be careful—Master Emberhawk was murdered."

The words hit Jet like a kick in the gut. *No, how can that... how could anyone murder a Grand Master?*

A small gasp stuttered from Sorvashti. "Who can do this?"

Jet clenched his fists. "Where's Raydon?"

Garrett's eyes glazed over. "He was in the..." He lifted a weak hand toward the barn.

Jet rounded on him. "Is he there now? Can you sense him?"

Garrett blinked and concentrated on the barn. After a moment, he said, "No, it's empty."

Jet gripped Garrett's shoulder. "Where is he?"

Garrett closed his eyes and took a deep breath. His arm raised and pointed northward, then his forefinger drifted up into the sky. "That way," he murmured. "Raydon and Aleah. Leaving... fast."

Aleah? Jet's stomach knotted. He grabbed his necklace and found his feather, then dashed through a snipped barbed wire fence and into the pasture. *Need more room—*

His arm snagged behind him, and he whipped back into Sorvashti's sharp stare. "Bring me with you," she said.

"They're flying, so I've got to be fast to catch them. My wings aren't built for speed." Jet kissed her quickly, then pulled away and summoned Kohesh's wings in a blinding flash. "I'll be right back." Snow exploded outward as he took off.

The forest appeared much brighter to his Serran eyes. White-capped cedars hung with shadows, but weren't as veiled as they had been. Jet shuddered against the biting wind and pushed higher above the mountainside. *Let me catch them!*

He reached out with his aether and felt a jade essence at the edge of his senses. *Aleah!* He dove forward with everything he had, ignoring his exhaustion and lightheadedness.

Two forms emerged below him, drifting over the a patch of aspens that spilled into the valley. Patterns on their broad sets of wings contrasted in the moonlight.

Jet gathered his aether and shouted. *Aleah!*

The smaller figure swayed and slowed. *Jet?* Silver hair glinted as she turned. *You're alive?*

Behind you! Land so we can talk!

The figures kept flying but slowed, hesitated, then dipped toward a frozen lake. Jet recognized the spot where Sorvashti had nearly killed Darien. *Victoria had better still be here.*

Aleah's soft white wings fluttered as she landed on the thick ice on the lake's edge with Raydon beside her. Jet frowned at the still water peeking through a small hole in the center of the lake. His feet threatened to slip under him as he landed near a patch of reeds on the shore.

"Where have you been?" Aleah stepped toward Jet, walking carefully. "I was certain your illness would have taken you by now!"

"Nearly did. I ran into Fadahari." Jet watched Raydon, who stood there, scrutinizing, like a snow leopard scanning its prey.

"Where are you going?" Jet murmured.

Aleah paused and looked back at Raydon.

"Just out for a late flight," Raydon said.

A dark feeling sloshed in Jet's gut. "Did you know Master Emberhawk was murdered?"

Aleah's face blanched as Raydon covered his lips with his fingertips. "Tragic."

Jet examined his sister, but she looked away from him. Her hands shook, but she didn't tuck them in her pockets.

He held a hand out to her. "Leah."

Aleah sucked in a breath and held it in. She pursed her lips as if holding back tears.

What's going on here? Jet reached out with his senses and did a double take when he sensed Raydon twice—once in his own body and once behind Aleah's eyes.

Jet's blood froze. He slowly turned to Raydon. "What have you done to her?"

Raydon shrugged. "I told her the truth."

Jet took a step toward her. "Leah, whatever he's said, he's lied to you. I can sense his aether in—"

Raydon snapped his fingers, and Aleah collapsed to the ice, unconscious.

Jet charged forward, slipped, and caught himself with his wings. He pumped them forward and slammed his shoulder into Raydon's middle. They hit the ice with a loud crack, and their wings vanished.

Raydon grunted and punched at Jet's face. Jet grabbed his wrist, wrenched it back, and twisted his shoulder. He flipped Raydon over and smashed his face into the spider webbed ice.

"What did you tell her?" Jet roared.

A shot of arbiter aether lanced up at Jet and sheared off a fragment of his shields. Jet twisted Raydon's arm until something popped. Raydon screamed.

"Did you kill Levi?" Jet demanded.

Raydon grew a smile over gritted teeth. He stared up at Jet through the corner of a livid brown eye surrounded by fresh burns. "No."

The word rang clear in Jet's head, but it swam on the blurred edge of half-truth.

Jet froze. *Then who...?*

Raydon struggled and Jet hit him in the jaw, ignoring the wave of dizziness. He grabbed his handgun.

Aether screeched and Jet's weapon skittered across the frozen lake. Jet cursed and pushed Raydon's arm even further.

Raydon hissed and grabbed something from his pocket with his other hand. It flashed toward Jet's leg.

Jet caught his wrist and recognized a Lynx-issue concealed blade. He released Raydon's other hand, wrested the knife from Raydon's grip, and stabbed him in the back.

Raydon howled in agony. "I'll kill her!"

Jet pulled the knife out and raised it for another strike.

"All I have to do is move my aether inside her brain! She'll be a bleeding invalid!"

Jet's arm twitched. He glanced at Aleah's form lying near the shore. He didn't move.

Spittle flew from Raydon's lips as he cursed. "Get off me."

Jet gritted his teeth and forced himself to stand. Blood dripped from the knife and spread along the cracks in the ice.

Raydon staggered to his feet and held his arm, which hung at an odd angle. Brown-spotted wings burst to life behind him. "You have nowhere to go," he spat. "When I get back you'll beg to be my slave."

Jet tossed Raydon's knife at him, and it clattered and slid across the ice. "M-kay. I'll just wait here and quiver in fear."

Raydon cursed at him and took off in a flurry of wind.

Jet watched him rise, then summoned his own wings and flew to the lake's far edge. Fresh snow piled in a flawless embankment, and Jet plowed into it. His fingers brushed cold steel.

Jet yanked Victoria free in a burst of white powder. He glanced up at the sky just as Raydon's figure vanished behind the trees.

Jet checked for a round in the chamber, then cycled the bolt with a satisfying clack. *Thank god she was built to withstand the elements!* He flew back to the opposite side of the lake, where the trees opened up his line of sight. Raydon's silhouette flapped for altitude over the northern aspens.

Jet splayed across the ice, flicked Victoria's stand open, and pressed icy steel to his cheek. He silently thanked Aeo for Serran form's night vision as he peered down the scope and found Raydon's figure.

A spotter would be nice. Jet gauged the wind direction and speed, then took a deep breath. The training sessions with Diamondback and Moccasin flashed through his mind.

He pulled the trigger. Victoria slammed into his shoulder and shattered the ice beneath her.

Raydon's figure spun and fell from the sky like a dove full of birdshot.

Jet released his breath and pulled the slide back. *Forty-two.*

Ice crackled as Jet carefully pushed himself up. He grabbed Victoria and flew to Aleah's side, landing lightly closer to the shore. He sat, laid Victoria down, and pulled his sister into his lap.

"Aleah." The side of her face was as cold as the ice she'd lain on. Her mind was infected with reddish-brown aether, so strong in some places that it seemed crystallized, while other spots oozed like a neglected wound. The weaker spots faded rapidly, confirming Jet's hope that Raydon was dead.

Maybe if the compacted spots take a while to fade, I could ask Zekk to pull this syn out. Could he do it without hurting her?

Jet shook her gently. "Leah."

Aleah took in a deep breath and her eyes fluttered open. She blinked at him with a furrowed brow, then jolted upright like she'd been pinched.

"Where...?" She glanced around the lake and squinted into the darkness. "Where's Raydon?"

"Easy, now." Jet curled his wings around them, sheltering them from the wind. "I bet you've got a world-record headache."

Aleah touched her forehead and swayed. "What happened?"

Jet steadied her. "It's OK. You're safe now."

Aleah stared at him, and her face flattened. "Where is he?"

Jet said nothing, but he didn't look away.

"You killed him?"

Jet looked at her forehead as if he could watch the slime dripping away. "Did you know that he brainwashed you?"

"No, I—" Aleah grimaced and rubbed her temples. A sob choked its way out. "You..."

"I'm sorry, but he was a Lynx," Jet whispered. "And he killed Levi."

Aleah froze. Color drained from her chestnut skin until it looked almond. She stared at a dead aspen leaf on the ice.

"Just rest now." Jet pulled her close, hoping his blood-drained body could offer some warmth. "His aether should dissipate within a few minutes. Some of it was pretty compact—"

Aleah shoved away from his arms. She crawled away, collapsed on the shore, and wept.

Jet's heart twisted. *I killed her boyfriend.*

He swallowed hard. "Hey, it's OK—"

"Where were you?"

Jet stared at the back of her fluffy coat in confusion. "I... We were in

Malaan. We were taken."

Aleah slowly turned and looked over her shoulder at him. Her silver eyes sparkled in the moonlight, glistening with overflowing tears.

Then she disappeared without a sound.

Jet blinked at the empty space. "Leah?"

A gust of wind engulfed him, and the lake fell silent and still.

She shouldn't be alone right now. Jet closed his eyes and reached out for her aether signature. It flickered at the edge of his range, moving fast in the northern sky.

Then it was gone.

38

Darien stared up at the ceiling of the room he and Garrett had shared last week. Same bed, same dresser and lamp, and that same weird orange painting, but it felt like a different universe.

Moccasin had assured Darien that he was safe, which he assumed Jet had something to do with. But then Jet and Sorvashti vanished, leaving Darien in the same base they'd once rescued him from.

Kerri wasn't exactly familiar company. Even Tera wasn't in the VIP suite—he'd checked. He'd never felt so alone. *This is pointless. I can't sleep here.*

Darien sat up in bed and glared at Zekk, who slept soundly in Garrett's bed on the other side of the room. *Cool, it's like an experimental victim slumber party.*

He threw the covers off and grabbed a coat from the closet, then crept through the dark halls to the front door. The goofy-looking one called Copperhead raised an eyebrow from his chair as Darien approached.

"Lookin' for some bubblegum, kid?"

"Just need some fresh air," Darien whispered back.

Copperhead shrugged, opened the door, and flourished his hand toward the blast of wind that howled in.

Darien zipped up his coat and pulled the hood over his head. He squinted over the moonlit skyline. The marketplace and government district lay dark, their streetlights long dead.

Where is everyone?

He refused to believe that everyone they'd left behind was gone. And he really didn't want to believe that Jet and Sorvashti had just abandoned him.

Darien glanced up the road to the residential sector. The smoke from Valinor Manor was hardly noticeable now. *Well, can't go there.*

He made for the main gate, choosing to walk on the crackling grass rather than risk his tailbone on the street. *A walk to the cliffs would keep me warm. And glory forbid there are any bleeding Lynx there.*

The hike took much longer since the land had frozen over, but Darien didn't mind—he had plenty of things to think about. Maybe Zekk really was sorry. Maybe Raydon taking his blood a few days ago meant that he was a Lynx—Kerri had mentioned that he'd been identified with a blood sample. But maybe Kerri was actually after Teravyn instead of him, just like everyone else.

Darien's breath clouded in a rapid pant by the time the tree line split on jagged slate. The cliffs bowed to the ocean beyond, and the full moon glinted off the silver hair of a young woman who sat on the edge.

Darien blinked in surprise. "Aleah?"

She didn't turn around. "I don't want to talk, Jet. Leave me be."

She's alive! Relief flooded Darien as he strode toward her, wary of ice patches on the rocks. "What did he do this time?"

Aleah looked over her shoulder and wiped her eyes. "Oh, Darien! What are you doing here?"

"Just wanted a quiet place to think." He noted the shimmering trails down her cheeks and put on a comforting smile. "It's good to see you alive and well."

Aleah returned his grin. "You, too. Jet said you were all taken."

"Yeah, that was fun." Darien sat down cross-legged behind her and made a point not to look over the cliff's edge. "Is everyone OK?"

"Not everyone." Aleah turned her back to him. "Raydon is dead."

Darien's breath tumbled out. "What..." His heart contracted and throbbed. *He can't really be... Did he die in the fire?* "What happened?"

"I'm not sure." Aleah's voice was barely audible over the wind. "Apparently he was a Lynx agent sent to look for you. But he joined Jade Glen before Teravyn tried to assassinate Whitlocke, so..." She gave him a sidelong look. "Are you wanted or something?"

Darien grimaced and looked down at the lichen beside his wet boots. "Something like that. Are you sure he was really Lynx? I thought he'd left them."

Aleah turned back to the ocean. She took a deep breath and wiped her eyes again. "He was more evil than I could have imagined. He manipulated me." Her voice warped, then steadied. "Maybe it was because of the connection between us. Or maybe he just wanted a pocket healer."

"Connection?" The fabric of Darien's hood shifted noisily as he tilted his head. "He wanted to manipulate you because you were going out?"

"No, I mean the connection between *us*." Aleah pointed a gloved finger at Darien, then at herself, then back at him again.

Darien's eyes widened. *What does she mean? There's never been anything but awkwardness between us!*

Aleah smirked faintly. "Don't think I forgot how we met."

Shame hit him like the tide pounding the rocks far below. *Great. I was really hoping that somehow she never realized I was ogling her like a creeper. Of course Jet told her.*

"Ugh, I'm sorry." Darien scratched his forehead with his glove, smearing cold water into his hair. "I was such an idiot."

She harrumphed. "You seem different now."

"Sure hope so," Darien grumbled. *Wait, if there's a connection, does she mean it goes both ways?*

He cleared his throat and shoved the thought aside. "I'm sorry about Raydon."

"I'm not." Aleah's voice warped and her shoulders shook. She turned back to the ocean. "There's something…" She crossed her arms over her stomach and took a steadying breath. "There's something else I have to tell you."

Darien tensed. He braced himself against the wind and waited.

Aleah sniffled and glanced back at him with watery eyes. "Master Emberhawk is dead," she whispered.

Darien stared at her for a long moment. "What?"

Aleah hunched over and sobbed.

Darien's mind blanked as he watched her. He wanted to ask again, but her cries confirmed what she'd said. *Levi can't be dead. He's a Grand Master!*

Agony tore through him. *No. This can't…* His body shook, and his knees hit cold slate. Hot tears blurred the night sky and fell unrestrained. *No!*

"I'm sorry!" Aleah screamed at the ocean. "Please, no! I'm so sorry!"

Darien tried to lift a hand to her back, but couldn't find the strength. He squeezed his eyes shut and fought to control his breathing. "What happened?"

Aleah buried her face in her hands. She sniffed and turned fully away from him. "I killed him," she whispered, "in his sleep."

Darien stared at her, motionless, waiting for her to say she was just kidding or this was all some big prank.

But she collapsed to the earth and wept.

Oh… my… Darien reeled from an onslaught of grief, confusion, and rage. He swallowed hard. "Why?"

"Raydon." Aleah panted for shuddering breaths. "He acted like he didn't know his gift, but he was a master arbiter. He"—she paused to gasp—"fed me false memories and controlled me over time. Like a brainless *tool!*" She grabbed a rock and threw it over the cliff. She watched it fall, and her voice quieted. "He used me as a weapon to kill Master Emberhawk. Guess he couldn't manage it himself."

Darien's jaw hung open. No words came.

"I came here to throw myself off the cliff." Aleah choked on her words and whisked her hand over the edge. "But every time I jump, my wings open and catch me. I guess I'm a coward."

She looked back at him with dripping emerald eyes. "I'm so sorry. Please..."

Darien's horror boiled into rage. "You said Raydon's dead?"

"Jet killed him." Aleah wiped a tear away. "Good riddance."

This can't be true. Darien gripped his legs until they hurt. *This is all so ridiculous!*

He glanced back into the forest. *Where's Jet now? He left to deal with this, then? Why didn't he bring me?* Anger wrestled with shocked sorrow inside him. *Levi!*

"Raydon's aether is dissipating from my mind." Aleah looked out over the ocean. "I feel like half of my brain is missing. And all of my soul."

Darien scooted closer and put an arm around her. Tears welled up again, and he let them fall. Time stretched into an abyss of sorrow.

Finally Aleah looked up at him with eyes as murky and deep as a pond. "I can't go back."

Darien's heart ached for her almost as much as it did for Levi. "Aleah," he murmured, "you have a family who loves you."

"Not anymore." Aleah sniffed and looked down at the waves below. "What's most terrifying to me is what has remained after Raydon's false memories disappeared. I think the Valinors just adopted me for the sake of their son. They only love me because I keep Jet alive."

"That's... that's definitely not true," Darien said. "I don't think Jet's that selfish."

Aleah raised her eyebrows as if he'd just told her that clouds were made of marshmallows.

Darien swallowed. "OK... I don't know. He's made it clear how much he cares about me. But I think he truly loves you."

"I have chosen not to be a part of that family anymore." Aleah's voice dropped into a whisper. "Being an orphan was lonely, but at least everything made sense."

Darien's pulse sent hot blood through his fingers. *What do I say? How can I...* He glanced over his shoulder. *Jet, you son of a d'hakka! Where are you?*

A memory drifted to the surface—Rigel telling him that his Serran oath was to protect orphans.

Darien's chest constricted. *No. She couldn't have meant it.*

He tightened his arm around Aleah's back. "Please don't try to hurt yourself. I know everything seems crazy right now, but it'll be OK."

"I don't deserve OK," Aleah murmured. "I should never use aether again."

"Everyone deserves a second chance," said a voice from the forest.

Darien whipped his head around and recognized his mother emerging from behind a cedar. *Great!*

Kerri bowed low. "I'm sorry for following you. I finally found you after all this time, and I didn't want to lose you again."

Aleah scurried out from under Darien's arm, eyes wide like a startled cat.

"It's OK!" Darien scrambled to his feet beside her and stepped away from the cliff. "Aleah, this is my mother, Kerri. Kerri, this is my friend, Aleah."

Soft wrinkles creased on Kerri's cheeks as she smiled. "A pleasure."

Aleah hesitated, then gave a curt bow.

"I couldn't help but overhear. You need a safe place to stay?" Kerri asked.

How much did you overhear? Darien took a step closer to Aleah.

Aleah cleared her throat. "You know of one?"

Kerri's thick red glove pointed north. "New Haelo—the city of Haevyn resurrected. They have security, beautiful lodgings, restaurants… even an elemental temple."

Darien furrowed his brow. "Is it Lynx controlled?"

"Everything is Lynx controlled, my dear." Kerri watched the shining rocks below her feet as she approached. "You would not be punished for your sister's crime. The only reason they want you is because of your power."

Something dark sloshed in Darien's gut. *Is that the only reason you want me, too?*

"But Haevyn is so far away," Aleah said.

"Moccasin could get us a transport. I'm not sure they'll want to keep the Altair base, anyway, considering the state of the city."

"No." Darien lowered his voice. "I am not going to live with the people who murdered Dad and butchered Jade Glen."

Hurt flashed across Kerri's face. "Trust me, rejoining them was the last thing I wanted to do." She reached out and touched his coat. "But the world is a different place now. This is the only way to be safe and live with basic necessities."

Darien stiffened. "At what cost?"

"Would they just let us live there?" Aleah asked. "Just like that?"

"Everyone pulls their weight." Kerri dropped her hand and squinted against a gust of wind. "They desperately need gifted people, but there are plenty of citizens who live everyday lives. There are teachers, architects, business owners—"

Aleah grabbed Kerri's arm. "Take me with you. Please."

Nausea sloshed through Darien. *How can she even consider it?*

Kerri grew a kind smile and nodded. "If this is what you want."

No! "Aleah…"

Her jaw was set as she looked at him. "If it's a city of butchers, it's where I belong."

Darien winced. Maybe she was right, but where did *he* belong? With the people who raised him like a lab rat and referred to him as 'property?'

"This isn't right," he murmured.

"Is it right to freeze or starve to death in the wilderness?" Aleah said.

Darien pursed his lips. Who was still alive to freeze?

He'd stayed with the group from Jade Glen because Teravyn had told him to. Now she was dead. His master was dead. And his mentor saw him as a burden.

Darien closed his eyes and felt the conflict tear at him like cat's claws. *I swore an oath to protect orphans. She says she's an orphan, so maybe I should go with her to look after her… and pay Jet back for rescuing me from the Lynx.* He grimaced. *The irony… it burns.*

He took a deep breath and slowly let it out. "Fine. I'll go with you."

"Leah!"

The beating of wings stirred the air. Darien turned just as Jet landed lightly on the rocks behind him.

39

Pain spiked through Jet's ankles as he landed a little too hard on the shale cliff. *Finally! Was she hiding here the whole time?* He shivered against the cold and straightened. Apparently, he hadn't just found Aleah, but Darien and his mother, as well.

"Feeling OK?" Jet tucked his wings behind him and hurried to Aleah.

"Yes, besides the most awful lockburn," Aleah said over the wind. "I think my brain is on fire."

Jet sensed that Raydon's aether was almost entirely gone. Relief flooded him. *She just needed some time.*

He reached out a hand toward Aleah, but she took a step back. He frowned and lowered his hand.

Something doesn't feel right. Jet glanced between the three of them. Darien looked at him sidelong, as if guarded. *Syn. I should have told him we'd be right back for him.*

"It's difficult to discern what's truth and what's not." Strands of Aleah's bright hair escaped from her hood and curled on the wind. "I remember recalling Raydon's false memories just as clearly, even if I can't remember the source memories now."

"I can help," Jet said, even though he didn't fully understand. "Ask me anything. I'll clear it up for you."

Aleah's eyes deepened into an expression he couldn't discern. "I'm leaving."

He blinked. "Where... Why?"

Tears swelled in Aleah's puffy eyes. "I don't belong here anymore."

"That's not true!" Jet grabbed her arms. "You just need some time to rest and think. I know you're hurting and confused, but don't make any snap decisions—"

"I know what I'm doing." Aleah pulled away from his grip. "Why don't you confirm for me what's real or not? If you change my mind, I'll come back with you. If not, you will let me go."

"Deal," Jet said instantly. *Just fix her confusion and everything will be fine.*

Aleah tucked a lock of wavy hair under her hood. "Is it true that Thracian and Marie adopted me right after you were discharged from the military for an incurable illness?"

Jet hesitated. "They'd put in an adoption request months before. It just took a long time to go through, so the timing doesn't mean—"

"But they knew at that point that you were sick, right?" Aleah asked.

"Yes, but—"

"Is it true that you would be long dead if I hadn't continuously healed you?"

Jet took a step back, wary not to slip on the icy slate. "Aleah, we didn't know you were a healer when we adopted you. And studying to heal me was your choice."

Her lips thinned. "Is it true?"

Jet released a cloudy breath on the breeze. "Yes, of course. I would be dead without you."

Darien shifted as Aleah asked, "Is it true that the Serran Grand Master Council had access to a sage who could have foreseen that I was a healer?"

What? That's... Jet furrowed his brow. "Yes... are you suggesting that the masters picked their own students by future-seeing their gifts?"

"Master Willow confirmed it," Aleah said curtly. "Is it true that there just happens to be one of each gift included in your group right now, including the rare gifts?"

Uh... how many rare gifts are there? Jet flicked through faces and numbers. "Maybe. Levi assembled this group to be well-rounded for survival when we left Jade Glen."

Aleah winced as if he'd cursed at her. She looked away as a tear fell.

Darien spoke up in a quiet voice. "Noruntalus told me he'd foreseen rare-gifted students before I killed him." He tapped his hand on his coat zipper. "He said that he told Levi to come and find me and Tera when we were stranded in the woods."

Jet snorted. "So you'd rather the Grand Masters have not taken you in, and let you die in the comet-pocalypse?"

"I have three more questions." Aleah stood up straight. "Were you the one who swayed me to believe in the creator, Aeo, instead of my family's deity, the elemental god Raisho, the spirit of the hearth?"

Jet narrowed his eyes at her. *What's she getting at?* "I told you the creator wasn't dead, and it was your choice to follow him."

"Is it true, then, that we are Aeo's people, and that he promised to care for his people?"

"Yes." Jet spread his hands. "We're alive after all this, aren't we?"

Aleah nodded upward, as if indicating the sky. "Is it true that Aeo's people are now homeless in the wilderness, without enough food at the beginning of winter?"

Jet looked up. Snow clouds loomed overhead, blotting out the stars and foretelling an oncoming blizzard from the dark ocean beyond the cliff. He bit back a curse and wracked his mind for an answer.

"Either the creator is dead, or he tortured us and left us all to die." Aleah took a step toward him, and her voice softened. "Come with us. I don't want you to die."

Jet threw his hands up. "You don't want me to die, but you just said I'll die without your healing!"

"You said you have Fadahari now. She taught me everything I know."

Panic wormed into Jet's chest. "Look, Aeo won't let us die out here. I met him in kai'lani. He'll come through." Jet looked to Darien. "Didn't you meet the human facet, Joshua?"

Darien pursed his lips and looked away.

"Then drop your shields," Aleah said, "so I can see your memories of *your* god."

"Yes," Kerri said. "That'll clear everything up. No need to be hostile." Her smile was sweet.

Jet's gaze snapped to Kerri. *This Lynx... it must have been her. She did this!*

He dropped his voice low. "I won't lower my defenses in front *her*. Someone murdered Master Emberhawk—if it wasn't Raydon, it must have been her."

"No," Aleah whispered. "I did."

Jet looked down at his little sister. His gift brightened around her words, confirming their truth.

His mouth fell open. *What...?*

"This is why I can't go back." Aleah's green eyes pleaded with him. "Do you understand now? I have to disappear."

Jet swallowed his shock. "We'll forgive," he forced out. "You were brainwashed. They'll understand."

Aleah shook her head. "I don't deserve it." She glanced out over the ocean. "This is what's best for everyone."

This can't be happening! Jet grabbed Darien's arm. "Darien, you know this is wrong!"

"My Serran oath is to protect orphans." Darien didn't meet his gaze. "I'll keep her safe for you."

Jet resisted the urge to physically knock sense into him. "She was adopted—she has a family. A family who loves her!"

"Not anymore." Aleah pushed up on her tip-toes and kissed Jet's cheek. Then she took a step back. "Your truth has not changed my mind."

Jet's heart fractured. "Leah... where will you go? Is this what you really want?"

Aleah turned and walked toward the tree line.

"I'm sorry," Darien whispered and turned to follow her.

Jet grabbed Darien's arm in a vise-like grip. "If you do this—"

"Don't fight." Darien's blue eyes were hard as glaciers. "You can't win."

Jet's blood simmered, and he growled through gritted teeth. "I won't forgive you!"

Darien ripped his arm away. "I'm not sure I care what you think anymore." He turned and followed Aleah.

Jet controlled his breathing and grasped for focus. *Stop them without hurting them.* But all of his training and weapons were meant for killing. *What do I do?*

His eyes flicked from Darien's back to Aleah's to Kerri's. *Take their feathers! No, just... share all of your memories—it worked with Zekk!*

"Wait!" Jet staggered forward, his wings steadying him as his footsteps slicked on stone. "I can—"

Darien caught his arm. "You made a deal and lost."

Jet ripped his arm away. "Get out of my way!" He shouldered around him.

Darien sidestepped and blocked Jet.

Jet's aether sizzled and exploded out at Darien, staggering him backward. Jet charged toward Aleah, who stood still with Kerri at the tree line, watching.

Blue energy slammed into Jet's shoulder. His foot landed on ice and slipped, and his knee met slate with a painful thud.

Jet growled and threw a wave of aether strong enough to send Darien tumbling over the cliff.

Darien sidestepped and held out his hand, and a collision screeched through the forest. He took his coat off and dropped it on the rocks.

Jet hesitated. *He countered that like he's been training for years.* Darien's shirt fluttered in the wind over a teenager's body, but a look glinted in his eye—one Jet had never seen before. Something calm and resolved and dangerous.

Jet pulled his wings in and formed a valnah spike to temper his disciple: fear and uncertainty and submissiveness. He shot it between Darien's eyes, where it deflected off his shields like a stone thrown at a tank.

Jet blinked in surprise. *Since when does he have decent shields?*

Light flashed as the wings of a bluejay appeared behind Darien. His palms turned upward on either side of him, as if he was holding twin cannonballs.

Syn. Jet glanced at Aleah to ensure she was still there, then readied a vanguard wall between him and Darien. *Maybe I shouldn't fight—*

Darien thrust a hand forward, and a sentinel strike crashed through Jet's wall and hit him square in the chest. It knocked him into the snow beyond the rocks and sent fresh pain blossoming in his lungs.

Jet gritted his teeth and regained his feet just in time for another blast to scream toward him. He curled his wings forward and filled them with aether, and a sound like clanging metal reverberated from the black feathers.

He doesn't have vanguard training. Jet kept his wings up like a shield and compressed an irresponsible amount of aether into a sentinel strike. The instant he opened his wings, he launched it at Darien at top speed.

Darien folded his wings and batted Jet's energy, reflecting it right back at him.

Shimmerwing— The world went black.

Jet blinked through wheezing agony as an aspen's fluttering leaves blurred into existence before him. He lay on something cold, and a shadow loomed over him. His necklace jingled.

"Wait..." Jet grabbed for the hand that tugged on the chain around his neck, but he missed. "Where are you going? To the Lynx? To be slaves or..." His voice sounded slurred in his ears. "Or slave masters?"

"I'm sure there are other options."

Jet's vision stabilized to find Darien standing over him and tucking Kohesh's feather into his shirt. "So you don't kill yourself trying to follow us. Get back to Fadahari."

"Wait!" Jet pushed himself up, but pain threatened to knock him right back out. "Don't do this!"

"I'll look after her." Darien turned and strode away, tugging his coat back on.

Jet screamed after him. He rolled onto his belly and pulled his arms and legs under him, but by the time his body allowed him to stand, the three were nowhere in sight.

Jet coughed and tasted coppery blood as he leaned against the aspen. *The backup...* He reached in his pocket for a thin notebook. He'd tucked the ancient Serran feather he'd taken from the ransacked temple at Jade Glen between its pages.

But the feather was gone. In its place was a thin, mint-flavored chocolate.

Aleah!

Jet flung his head back and roared at the heavens.

40

*R*aydon's feather!

Jet controlled his breathing and took a hesitant step forward, testing how much his body would punish him. His vision cleared, but the aching in his chest and shoulder remained.

I'd have to find his body... How far am I from the lake?

It wasn't the first time he'd staggered, alone and injured, across the Valinorian wilderness under the force of an oncoming blizzard. At least this time he didn't have a broken wrist, courtesy of Viper Unit.

He found the lake and tried to recall Victoria's trajectory and the angle at which Raydon had fallen. Victoria still laid propped on the ice, her scope and barrel dusted with flakes of snow. *Sorry, girl—you would have weighed me down. After this, I'll never leave you out again.*

Jet lost track of time as he searched for Raydon's body. He finally found the gruesome sight under broken cedar branches. Stained snow darkened the ground underneath the crumpled figure.

He found a white, brown-spotted feather inside a metal sheath—it looked to have been designed for protecting large feathers. *Nice.* It clicked open, and Jet took the feather out and held it tight against the wind's clutches.

It's too late. I have no idea where they went... Jet bit the inside of his lip as he stared at the feather. *This is probably not a good idea. Surely Raydon was bonded to a dark angel.*

He closed his eyes and sent a gentle wisp of aether toward the quill. *I have to try. Aeo, help me!*

A library flashed into existence around him, replacing the frigid forest with warmth and the smell of old paper. Ladders climbed level after level of books and scrolls, reaching up to a domed stained-glass ceiling. A single crystalline tree stood tall in the center of the room, surrounded by tables, couches, and plush chairs twice the size they should be.

Where am I?

A light brown gryphon with a barn owl's pattern looked at Jet from a massive ottoman across the room. It lounged in front of a scroll that sprawled across the floor.

"Ah, a new Serran already?" The gryphon's brown eyes looked Jet up and down. "I can't keep track of you all."

Jet didn't move. He didn't recognize this angel. *He has multiple Serrans?*

"Looks like you nearly lost in the arena." The beast straightened its long neck and shifted its wings tucked into its flanks. "What did they assign you?"

Syn! Jet's mind reeled. He cleared his throat and noted that his pain was a small fraction of what it had been. "I'm on a mission to find the sage girl." *That was Zekk's contract, right?*

The gryphon flicked a clawed hand dismissively. "And the keystone she stole, yes? You humans keep forgetting that."

"Right," Jet said. *How do I get out of here?*

"Scurrying like ants after the sage," the angel muttered. His hawk-like eyes stared at a bloodstain on Jet's shirt. "One more third-born won't help. I'm reassigning you."

If Jet's heart pounded any harder, he was sure it would pop out and flop on the glossy wood floor. "But the Lynx ordered—"

"The Lynx answer to us. Or did you not know that?" The gryphon reached to a table and pierced a green fruit with one long claw. "We need all four of the elemental *amos* stones to complete the summoning. The only one remaining is the Terruthian lord, Rosh." He popped the fruit into his open beak and swallowed it whole. "Go and find his stone and bring it to Alon."

Summoning? Jet tried not to look as terrified or bewildered as he felt. He forced himself to bow. "I will do as you say."

"Good. Don't make me motivate you, little Serran." The angel waved a hand at Jet, and the world snapped back to a Valinorian winter, complete with the full weight of his pain.

Jet gasped and collapsed to his knees. Raydon's feather nearly escaped on the wind, and he gripped it tight.

What in Zoth are they trying to summon?

He stared at the feather. *That was so stupid. Why did you do that, you idiot? He could have sensed I was lying and found out where Teravyn was!* He breathed evenly and steeled himself against the pain. *Did they bring her to the ranch house? Why do they want her so badly?*

Jet looked up through broken branches at the storm clouds heavy with eager snow. *I can still catch them...*

He closed his eyes and reached out with his senses, searching for his sister's gentle, mint-green signature. Then for Darien's vibrant, wild blue.

He couldn't feel any trace of either.

Jet gritted his teeth and snapped the quill of Raydon's feather in two. He opened his fist and let the wind steal it away.

Garrett, he called, having no idea if the sifter was listening.

Jet! What's going on? Garrett's thought was strained. *I can't sense Raydon anymore.*

He's dead. Jet let out a sigh of relief and grimaced when his lungs protested. *Please go back to Altair and ask Zekk and Doctor Fadahari to return to the ranch with you.*

A long silence passed. *He's straight-up Lynx, mate.*

Please. We're going to have to find a new place, anyway.

What?

Just please get Zekk. He wants to meet his grandmother, Ellie, so he'll come with you. Jet shuddered as the wind howled through the trees, tearing at his hair and clothes. *Fadahari won't go anywhere without him, and I'll die without her.*

Another pause, then Garrett's voice returned, strained. *Your girlfriend is going to kill me unless I let her talk to you somehow! I don't know how—*

Tell her where I am. Jet leaned on the trunk of a cedar with his back to the wind. He relaxed and closed his eyes. *Ask her to come to me. I need her.*

41

"**Y**ou want to do *what?*"

Zekk stared at Darien, his mother, Kerri, and Jet's sister, Aleah.

Aleah didn't look like she did in Jet's memories—her round face was drawn and ashen. And Darien's expression suggested he was actively being flogged.

"I want to live in New Haelo," Aleah repeated. "Sir."

They can't be serious. Zekk glanced at the office's reading nook, but Moccasin sat there with no reaction. *Good thing I'm here.* Zekk tried to catch Darien's gaze, but the sentinel looked anywhere except at him— the plush rug, the wires from the computer monitors, the Lynx crest on the wall.

"Does your brother know about this?" Zekk asked in a low tone.

Aleah winced. "Yes. He's not coming."

And he let you go? I highly doubt that. Zekk wished he was an arbiter at that moment, or that Jet was here to sort this out. Of course he'd left without telling anyone.

Zekk lowered his voice, carefully weighing his words. "Do you know what you're getting into?"

"I know they have food and shelter and security." Aleah pursed her lips. "I thought you were a recruiter."

Zekk barely hid his frown. He glanced at Moccasin, who apparently couldn't care less.

What can I do? His shoulders felt heavy as he looked between them. *If I try to prevent or dissuade them, I'll be branded a traitor.* And he knew what Alon did to traitors.

"You should stay where you belong," Zekk murmured.

"Didn't you tell me I was Lynx property?" Darien's blue eyes were sharp as a glint on a blade's edge. "Where does your allegiance lie, exactly?"

"With myself. And if you want to be a Lynx, you will never speak to your Confidant in such a manner again."

Darien looked down at his mud-clustered boots. "Sorry, sir."

"I spared you three only because I wanted to find my grandmother. Don't make me regret it." Zekk leaned back against the thick wood desk behind him and crossed his arms. *Well, if this is what they've decided on, at least I can keep them safe.*

"You are going to go to New Haelo and report that I captured and recruited you. Unless Alon has other needs, you will be a part of my team and will be transferred to Maqua."

Darien's gaze snapped back up to his. "We will not be anyone's slaves or own any slaves."

Zekk met his fire with cool rigidity. "Do you have any idea how difficult it is to be an independent agent?"

"I can handle it," Darien said.

"I don't want to be a Lynx," Aleah said, taking a step forward. "I'm an elementalist—I'll live in the temple."

You have no idea what you want. Zekk sighed, unfurled his arms, and rested his hands on the desk behind him. "Tell them I want you to start out at level three. You can requisition a thousand units from my account. Spend them wisely on equipment that will keep you on your feet in the arena."

"Sir," Kerri said. "May I have a word?"

Zekk examined her face for a moment. *Definitely Teravyn's mom.* He waved a hand toward the door, and Darien, Aleah, and Moccasin filed out.

Kerri cleared her throat and spoke quietly. "Thank you. I was..." She paused and stood up straighter. "My husband and I left the Lynx without permission many years ago. I rejoined after the meteor shower to find my children." She looked up at him with fear-filled eyes. "Sir, if I do not receive credit for bringing him in, I will be executed."

Pity and anger jumbled in Zekk's chest, and he fought to keep his face straight. *So you're giving up your son to save your own skin? Or do you actually think this is best for him?* But more so, he wanted to scream at Alon for overseeing the Titan Project and for killing those who'd tried to escape.

"Fine," Zekk said. *I have to maintain my cover, though...* "Bring them in on my behalf, and I'll give you half credit."

Relief bloomed in Kerri's face. "You're not returning, sir?"

"My purpose here was to recover the base and bring in three wild Serrans." Zekk gestured at the door. "There's one and two, but I still need the third."

"Was it a Valinorian?" Kerri asked. "Darien took his feather."

Zekk's heart seized. *Oh, no.*

He swallowed his shock. "Yes. Even without a Serran feather, he's a high-value target. Inform New Haelo that I was severely injured while MIA, and that I will recuperate here, then complete my mission by bringing him in."

Kerri bowed her head. "Yes, sir."

Oh, thank Lillian, Zekk thought as a ranch house emerged through the blizzard. Snow swallowed him up to his thighs and blanketed the darkness so thickly he could barely see ten feet ahead. But Garrett had guided him and Fadahari here as easily as if it were a clear, sunny day.

The Malo stone weighed heavy in Zekk's pocket as he thought of Lillian's name. *Uh, well… guess you don't deserve much thanks. Lazy bum.*

"I don't sense Jet here!" Fadahari yelled over the wind. "Is he somewhere else or already dead?"

Zekk grimaced. *If Darien took his feather… is he face-down in the snow somewhere?*

"He's coming in with Sorvashti," Garrett said. He turned around, holding up a gloved hand on one side of his hood to block the snow from his face. "They're almost to the barn."

"Bring me to him," Fadahari said. "Idiot's probably half-dead as usual. I'm gonna start charging him an arm and a leg."

Zekk let out a breath in relief. *Don't think that would change anything.*

Garrett turned away from the door, trudging a new path through the snow toward a dark barn Zekk could barely make out.

Zekk stood unmoving, wanting desperately to go inside the house just a stone's throw away. He felt like an ice pop despite his complete Lynx cold weather gear. "Should I go with you?" he asked.

Garrett paused and glanced over his shoulder with narrowed eyes. "Master Willow's inside the house. If you try anything, I promise you will not leave this place alive."

"Don't worry." Zekk forged toward the house as Garrett and Fadahari veered off to the barn.

The house blocked the wind's wrath, and Zekk thought his nose might not get frostbite after all. He hurried to the door, leaned away from an ice hornet nest hanging from an unlit sconce, and knocked on the wood.

There was no answer. *Maybe they can't hear because of the storm.* Zekk grabbed the doorknob and ducked inside, quickly shutting the door behind him.

A small entryway led to a living room beyond, but no one was in sight. A dusty lamp and bouquet of faded cloth flowers sat quietly on a thin table. The wood inside the walls groaned against the wind. Only a faint yellow light from the living room lit the small space.

"Hello?"

No one answered. Zekk took his hood down in a shower of snow, then removed his gloves. He almost unzipped his jacket, but aside from the lack of wind, it wasn't much warmer inside. *They'll freeze to death in here.*

He slunk toward the living room. As he rounded the corner, he saw three people huddled together beside a dark fireplace. Zekk recognized Jet's stepmother, Marie, from his memories, hiding with a redheaded girl behind Jet's father, who aimed a handgun right between Zekk's eyes.

"Whoa, I'm friendly!" Zekk put his hands up. "Friendly."

"On your knees," Thracian growled. "Who are you?"

The one who tried to stop your daughter from throwing her freedom away. Do you know she's gone?

Zekk sank to his knees behind a ragged pink couch. "I'm a friend of Jet's." *Well, that's kind of a lie. Maybe?* Jet's memories of his father assured Zekk that if he would have used the word 'frenemy,' he would've been shot.

"Zack!"

An elderly woman appeared from a hallway. Long gray hair, thick robes draping a plump frame, and bright aqua eyes—just like Eleanor Willow from Jet's memory.

Her face contorted, and she rushed at Zekk with surprising speed. Her hug nearly bowled him over and yanked him halfway back to his feet.

Zekk tried to keep his hands up as he looked at Thracian, but the man's gun now aimed at the ceiling.

Eleanor wailed against Zekk's coat and held him tight enough to strangle. "Uh…" Zekk slowly brought his hands down to pat her back. "It's Zekk…"

She looked up at him with eyes full of joyful tears. "What's that, sugar?" She grabbed his face, pulled him down, and kissed his cheeks.

Oh dear. Elderly people were rare on Lynx bases, so Zekk wasn't sure what to expect. "My name is… well… I'm known as Zekk Sorrowsong."

Eleanor's face wrinkled into an enormous frown. "That won't do. I'll call you Zack Happysong Willow if you want, but you're Bubbles to me, anyway!" She grinned and pulled back to examine his face. "Oh, I knew you'd be handsome! Your parents would be so proud!"

Embarrassment burned on Zekk's cheeks. He swallowed. "'Bubbles?'"

Eleanor's grin grew even wider. "You mastered the art of snot-bubble-blowing as a toddler and would entertain yourself for hours!"

Marie and the redhead giggled from the fireplace.

Zekk grimaced. *Seriously?*

Eleanor crushed him in another hug and trembled with gasping sobs. "Oh, thank you, Aeo!"

Shame lighted on Zekk's shoulders. *She wouldn't be like this if she knew I led the attack on Jade Glen.*

Eleanor stepped back and wiped at her eyes. "Come, sit!" She scurried to the dated couch and fluffed the cushions.

Zekk glanced at Thracian. The General looked just like Jet remembered him—cold and hard as an onyx slab, with eyes nearly as dangerous as his weapon. *Jet hates him, but he's exactly like him.*

Thracian didn't make any move to prevent Zekk from sitting next to Eleanor, but he didn't put his gun away, either. Marie and the redhead arranged twigs and woodcuts in the fireplace behind him, fiddling with matches.

Zekk slowly followed Eleanor to the couch, trying to be nonthreatening with his movements.

"What brought you here?" Eleanor sat on one side of the couch and patted the cushions on the opposite side with a little too much force. "Tell me everything. Where have you been? Did you eat well? You look a bit sick—are you injured? What are you doing now?"

Zekk sat lightly on the nasty couch not fit for a first-level suite. The stab wound in his gut pulled as he bent, and he couldn't mask a grimace. Fadahari had griped at him enough times for him to know that even with her healing, his body needed at least a couple of weeks to fully recover.

"I… Which question do you want me to answer first?" Zekk asked. *Does she know Darien and Aleah are gone? Should I tell her?*

Eleanor huffed a short laugh. "Oh, I'm sorry, honey. None of that really matters." She reached over and grasped his hand with soft fingers. Her eyes glistened. "What can I do for you?"

For me? Zekk blinked at her. *She doesn't even know me. Or, at least, the kid she knew is gone.*

"I think you're the one in need. It's freezing in here." Zekk glanced at the hearth, where Marie gently blew on a newborn flame in the kindling. "Does this place not have any power?"

"Just some trouble with the generator," Eleanor said. "Don't worry; Aeo will provide."

Zekk stared at her. *Is she joking? Without a heater, there's no way they'll survive the winter. Or it'd be miserable at the very least.*

But her wide eyes just drank him in with childlike awe and unquenchable joy.

She might be a little off her rocker… "Eleanor, do you have enough food—"

"Call me Meemaw. That's what you used to call me. Or Ellie is fine. Just not Eleanor." A flicker of sadness faltered her smile.

"OK… Ellie." Zekk shifted to minimize the pain in his gut. "I'm not sure what you remember about me, but I…" He hesitated as the unbridled happiness returned to her face. "I'm not that person anymore. I've done things no parent would be proud of."

Ellie waved a hand dismissively. "Haven't we all, pumpkin?" She phrased it more like a statement than a question.

Zekk examined her. "Do you know my position within the Lynx?"

Ellie chuckled. "I'm not sure there's a soul alive who doesn't, Bubbles! Your good-lookin' mug is all over the posters on every other building in Altair."

Great... Zekk forced an awkward chuckle. "Well... I'm not sure I'd pose for that shoot again."

"Why not?" Ellie blinked at him with huge, innocent eyes.

Zekk glanced at Thracian again as apprehension flopped in his gut. But the man just stood there, still as Alon's bodyguards, as Ellie waited for his response.

Well, I came all the way here to meet her, so I might as well...

He almost gave the answer he always did: the fame came with annoying side effects. People treated him differently. Women threw themselves at him. Men tried to schmooze him for their own gain, as if he'd just throw money from his balcony one day, and they wanted front row seats.

But no one had ever looked at him the way Ellie looked at him now.

So he decided to tell his grandmother everything, and she listened without judgement or chastisement or correction. He admitted that he'd been there at the fall of Jade Glen, and she nodded with a dim sadness, as if she'd known it all along. He told her he killed Headmaster Bondera by sucking his bulletproof vanguard wall away, but the love didn't fade from her eyes.

And by the time Marie coaxed a fire into nibbling at the stale wood, Zekk was certain that nothing he said would dissuade Ellie from forgiving him.

He got the feeling that he wasn't an exception—it wasn't just because he was her grandchild. She was like this with everyone: selfless and kind and peaceful as a songbird.

For the first time, Zekk realized what the Lynx had taken from him.

And he wanted it back.

42

Jet stared at the dusty fan in the living room ceiling of Rex's ranch house. He lay still, listening to the crackling fireplace and walls creaking against the night wind. Quiet, steady breathing surrounded him—Sorvashti's soft purring on the floor beside him, Ellie, Fadahari, and the redhead tangled on the couch, Garrett by the window, and Thracian and Marie near the fire. His father's snoring apparently didn't bother anyone except for him. Even Zekk had fallen asleep where he'd been sitting—slouched against the couch at Ellie's feet.

Jet relished the feeling of his own breathing—the pain had finally been replaced with a faint prickle and the numb aftershock of Fadahari's fresh healing energy. But still, sleep eluded him. Memories of Diamondback's scolding, Levi's smirk, Aleah's exhausted look of defeat, and that glint in Darien's eye ran circles in his head, mocking him. Haunting him.

He closed his eyes tight and focused on Sorvashti's warmth beneath their shared blanket, contrasting against the cold floor. *We're not safe—*

there's no time for mourning or even processing what happened. We can't stay here; someone will rat us out eventually. We'll have to get straight to work in the morning, so make a plan.

Jet took a shuddering breath and forced himself to focus on survival, like Diamondback had trained him. *Step one: get the generator to work. Two: take inventory of food and supplies. Three: find a place to bury Levi...*

Bile rose in his throat, and he nearly choked trying to swallow it. *I failed. I failed everyone.*

Levi wouldn't have died if Jet had seen through Raydon's deceit. He must have built two layers of mental shields, with a weaker, less assuming one concealing a master arbiter's defense. But that was no excuse.

I should have been able to convince Aleah. And Darien...

The thought of Jet's disciple sent shame gushing through him. Only with enough time to think had Jet been able to piece together Darien's actions on the island—and realize that he must have been in kai'lani for much longer than he let on. *He built good shields, learned how to fly to save us, and grew into a honed sentinel, and I didn't even notice.*

Jet finally identified that last puzzling piece of Darien's expression: dismay. And now he knew it came from what Darien thought was rejection.

I never rejected him. Jet watched the fire's light sway like living watercolor on the ceiling. *But I never really accepted him, either. And he grew up without me.* A different kind of pain lodged in Jet's chest, and he closed his eyes. *I have to find him.*

"Pssst."

Jet jolted and turned his head toward the voice. An arctic fox watched him from behind the sofa with pupil-less eyes that glowed vibrant green.

Jet blinked, certain he was seeing things. "Felix?" he whispered.

The fox tipped its head toward the hallway and trotted through an open door.

What's he doing here? Isn't he supposed to be with the other group of survivors from Jade Glen? Jet eased away from Sorvashti, tucking his blankets over her. The floor creaked as he sat up, and he paused, but no one stirred.

Jet slowly stood and tiptoed around the sleeping bodies, wishing he had a second pair of socks against the cold floor. A *clean* pair.

He ducked inside the room the fox had vanished into—the one beside Levi's. It appeared to be an office, with a roll top desk, filing cabinet, whiteboard and wall calendar opened to three months in the past. Snow-blurred moonlight filtered through the thin curtains on the lone window, under which the white fox sat.

"It's good to see you," Jet whispered, "but the orange fox form suits you better."

Felix snorted and his little mouth smirked. "A few years ago suits you better."

Jet couldn't stop a relieved smile. "How are the other Jade Glen survivors?"

"Flourishing. Good thing I found you when I did. Looks like you're not doing too hot." Felix raised a fluffy eyebrow. "Where is my vessel?"

Aleah. Jet's stomach dropped, and the ache of loss arose anew. "I don't know."

"What?" The curtains behind Felix spontaneously caught fire, dousing the room in buttery light, then snuffed out an instant later. "I left her in your care!"

Jet glanced at the open door behind him. "She left us to join the Lynx. My Serran feather was taken, so I couldn't follow."

The fox's lips curled up to reveal pure ivory fangs. "I should kill you, human—"

"Kill me, then." Jet watched him with nonchalance. *That would fix everything. Except I can't leave Sorva like this.*

Felix breathed out a long breath. "What happened? You let your Serran feather be taken?"

Do I have to repeat it? Jet glanced at the wall calendar. "My disciple got the better of me. He's accompanying Aleah, so she might be safe."

The fox tilted its head. "You got beat by your own disciple?"

Jet pursed his lips. "He had a sudden jump in skill—"

"So you weren't paying attention to him."

Jet gave Felix a warning glare. "We were in a survival situation, and I had amnesia, and—"

"And you're too arrogant to care about anyone but yourself."

Jet's mouth snapped shut. He lowered his voice. "Look, I'm sorry I lost Aleah. But you have no idea what I've sacrificed for my—"

"*Your* family? The woman *you* love?" Felix snorted, laid down on the carpet, and crossed his paws. "Even the Lynx love their own. If you want to follow the creator, you're going to have to do better than that."

Guilt smothered Jet's anger. He rubbed his eyes and sighed. "I'll get them back. Whatever it takes." He couldn't bring himself to look up at Felix. "But I don't know where they went. Can you sense her somehow?"

The room was quiet for a moment. "I can sense Phoera syn, but not her specifically."

Jet furrowed his brow. "Did you just cuss at me?"

Felix rolled his pure green eyes. "Syn was a metal long before it was a curse. It's the silver dust in human blood that lets you control your element."

Jet looked down at his hand. "You're telling me that syn is a metal in my blood?"

"Well, no, not *your* blood. You have hardly any at all, like most humans. And yours is Aris." Felix spat the last word as if it were a bite of rotten egg. "Aleah has an excess of Phoera syn because she's one of my vessels. But since most of the other Phoeran elementals are asleep, there's precious syn just lying all over the place. There's a large concentration in a museum in Altair, sediment at the bottom of the ocean, deposits underground, and some at elemental temples…"

Jet's tired mind strained to keep up. "So can you track her or not?"

"I can." Felix tilted his nose up. "Just might take a little while to sort through—"

The floor in the hall creaked. Jet glanced over his shoulder and found Sorvashti peeking around the doorframe. The whites of her wide eyes shone in the dim light. "*Shlanga…* are you talking to a *vulp?*"

"Uh…" Jet reached a hand out to her. "If that means 'fox,' then… kinda."

Felix tilted his head. "Who're you?"

She cautiously stepped forward and took Jet's hand. "I am Sorvashti of Ironhide. What *are* you?"

Felix lifted a furry brow. "I am a Phoeran elemental."

"A *lesser* Phoeran elemental," Jet murmured.

Felix snarled at him and hopped onto the desk, shifting its papers under his paws. "Is death so appetizing to you?"

Jet smirked and shrugged. "Sometimes."

Sorvashti whipped her head around to give Jet a chastising glare. "What is this lesser Phoeran elemental?"

The fox growled, but it sounded more adorable than menacing. "I'm not in the mood."

"Humor her," Jet said. "You just woke her up in the middle of the night."

"You humans and your sleep." Felix flopped down on the desk. "OK, short version: there are seven lesser *trai'yeth* and one greater *amos* of each element. I am Felix Kael Tae. Humans call me the deity of luck."

"Which is probably how you found us out here in the middle of nowhere," Jet said.

"There's nothing to that superstitious nonsense. I'm not in the stars, either. My constellation looks like a splotch of bird scat."

Jet chuckled. "Accurate."

Felix bared his teeth. "If anything has happens to my vessel, I really will kill you, human."

"Mmm." Jet put his other hand on Sorvashti's waist and delighted in the smooth curve. "You know, you're a lot scarier in dragon form."

Sorvashti glanced up at Jet with quizzical golden eyes. "Dragon?"

"Which reminds me," Jet said. "It seems the dark angels are looking for the Terruth *amos* stone and the keystone. They're trying to summon something. Any idea what?"

The fox's expression blanched. "Do they have the other three *amos* stones?" he asked in a deeper voice.

"Apparently," Jet said. Honestly, he couldn't even remember the names of all four primary elementals. They were a legend's legend.

Felix grumbled a word Jet didn't recognize. "They're trying to revive the *amos*."

Jet exchanged a clueless glance with Sorvashti. "And that's... bad?"

"The elemental facet sacrificed her life to lock them up. For several reasons." Felix jumped down from the desk, and his claws clacked against the floor. He trotted beside them and right out the door. "Come on. You fragile third-borns will catch your deaths out here."

Jet blinked after him. "Where are you going?"

"To a nearby mountain refuge older than both of our races. It's called Eremor."

Nearby? Jet turned into the hall and glanced over the piles of blankets as they passed. "I've never heard of that!" he whispered.

"That's because it's been hidden by deep magic since creation." Felix stopped at the front door and stared pointedly up at the doorknob. "It's one of the original Gardens."

Jet glanced at Sorvashti, who crept behind him, but she looked just as confused.

He opened the door and Felix slipped out. "Deep what?" Jet called after him, using his body to block snow from whipping through the crack.

"The creator's magic." The fox's form enlarged, its neck and tail lengthening as its fur melted into umber scales. Its front legs expanded into wide leathery wings. Serpentine eyes blinked sideways, watching Jet until he recognized the mythical form of a dragon-like wyvern crouching in the snow.

Felix lowered his neck toward the door. "Now stop asking questions and get on. I can only carry two at a time, so I'll have to make several trips." The glowing green eye slitted. "No fornicating on my back or I'll do a barrel roll."

Jet choked on his breath as Sorvashti peeked over his shoulder. "What is this 'fornicating?'"

"Nothing!" Jet grabbed a blanket from the living room, informed a half-asleep Garrett of where they were going, and threw the blanket around Sorvashti's shoulders. "Wanna ride a dragon?"

She was staring out the open door with eyes as wide as the moon. "By the earth…"

43

Jet held tight to Sorvashti's waist as she clung to Felix's neck. Riding on a wyvern wasn't at all what it was in the movies—he'd never been so cold in his life, the beating of wings almost gave him motion sickness, and he was terrified of falling off. He didn't have a pair of wings to catch him anymore.

Sorvashti shivered under him, and Jet leaned forward to cover more of her back. "We're gonna get frostbite!" he yelled over the wind.

"Oh." Felix twisted his neck to peer back at them, and the air around them was suddenly as pleasant as a spring afternoon. "Needy humans. Would you like a glass of champagne and a bubble bath while I'm at it?"

Jet exhaled in relief. He sat up and blinked through the haze of clouds they soared through. "No, let's fly through a volcano next and have you complain when we catch fire."

"Don't tempt me," Felix grumbled as his massive jaw flexed and faced forward again. "If you can't find my vessel, I just might."

Jet's stomach clenched as Sorvashti relaxed and carefully sat up, pushing off of Felix's thick brown scales. She gasped in awe. "Look!"

Jet looked to the side as the cloud layer opened, exchanging a blurred white atmosphere for a crystal-clear view of millions of stars flickering white, blue, and red. A thick swath of the galaxy's arm waved across the sky, accented by a crater-pocked full moon.

Wow... is this because we're above the cloud layer or there's no light pollution? He hadn't seen such a beautiful night sky since his deployment in the remote Kioan desert. Even the second and third moons were visible—a rare sight. One blotted out the stars with deep green, and the other glinted on the horizon like a swollen white star. *Tidal equinox must be coming soon.*

"I feel like I am in the dream," Sorvashti said. "I do not even know the dragons live any more."

"This is a wyvern—not a dragon," Felix corrected. "But both species went extinct a long time ago."

Sorvashti tilted her head, then looked over her shoulder at Jet. "Do I not know the Arisian, or does this not make the sense?"

"Both." Jet grinned. "I don't understand half the things he says."

"Oh." The bat-like wings stopped beating to enter a glide, and Sorvashti examined them. "How long do you know the Felix?"

"Few years. Turns out he was a package deal with Aleah." Jet loosened his grip on her waist and stretched his back. "I woke up one night to a green-eyed rat on my shoulder. Turned into a trace cat in my room and scared me half to death."

Sorvashti slipped a hand over his and squeezed it. "We will find her."

Jet swallowed and forced a smile. *Change the subject.*

He rested his chin on her shoulder. "How are you doing?" he asked, hoping Felix couldn't hear his lowered voice. It seemed like he and Sorvashti had slipped back into their old relationship, as if the past six years had never happened. He enjoyed the comfort, but it felt... surreal.

"I am good," Sorvashti said. She stared up at the moon.

Maybe I wasn't specific enough, Jet thought. "I mean regarding Noruntalus."

Sorvashti's face fell into a frown. "I am the fine until you speak of him."

Great. "I'm sorry." Jet wasn't sure if he should hug her tighter or pull away and try not to fall off of Felix's back. "Just tell me if I can do anything to help, OK?"

She twisted back again, and her guarded eyes found his. "I am scared of how much I love you so fast."

Jet froze, paralyzed in her gaze. "Do you want me to back off?"

"No!" She leaned into him. "Please, no."

His pulse thudded against hers, and he held her tighter. *I'm the luckiest man in—*

"Hey! Hey! I'm an elemental, not a pleasure cruise." Felix beat his wings hard enough to send them scrambling for grip. "Cut it out or I'll turn into a canary, and then you can find out how romantic falling to your deaths would be!"

"We didn't do anything!" Jet yelled, his knuckles turning white. "Are all elementals as crotchety as you?"

"Pray you never find out," Felix grumbled and dipped back into the clouds.

Mountains emerged, pale and solemn in the darkness. Felix veered toward a divot between three peaks, like a crater filled with a small patch of snow-laden forest. He reared back to land on a stone outcropping just outside of the trees.

He must be just taking a break. It's gotta be even colder up here than it was in the valley.

The muscles in Felix's back flexed as his feet hit the ground, sending a jolt through his spine. "Get off." He lowered his tail and neck to icy stone.

Sorvashti slipped down, and Jet hit the earth half as gracefully behind her. *If he leaves us here—*

"Hail."

A deep voice boomed from the trees, and Jet stared at a massive winged minotaur that emerged. The ironfeather angel looked down its bull-like nose at him. "New humans?"

"The other group of survivors from the Jade Glen Serran Academy," Felix said.

What's an angel doing here? Jet noticed that the snow sat only on the tops of the trees—the bottoms bore bright leaves of green, blue, and purple, and fruits of many more colors and shapes he didn't recognize. Beyond them, lights shone from structures and buildings he hadn't seen from the air.

What... the... Jet blinked, but the buildings were still there. Many of them made of living trees whose trunks and roots twisted together to form walls and roofs and opened for windows. Hot springs steamed on one side, and a pool in the center of the town square glowed with shifting waters.

Are we in kai'lani?

"Don't let your jaw fall off," Felix said behind him. "There are several old houses left. Take your pick—they'll need some sprucing up."

A wing shoved Jet's back, making him stumble forward. He turned and blinked back at Felix.

"Get it?" The wyvern bared its teeth in a sly grin. "Heh."

"How..." Words failed Jet, and apparently Sorvashti, too. She looked as dumbstruck as he felt.

"I told you it's one of the three Gardens from when Aeo created Alani. It's been preserved by angels since then." Felix stretched out a wing and pointed to the tops of the trees. "You can't see it, but there's a deep magic barrier. Only followers of Aeo can see it and enter."

Jet took a hesitant step forward, and the angel stepped aside to reveal a flagstone path leading through the trees. *A barrier... is that how it was kept hidden from humanity for all these years? So we had telescopes to see stars billions of lightyears away, but we couldn't see this in our own backyard?*

"I'll go back and get the others. I'm sure Ellie won't mind me relocating your hapless little group." Felix lumbered away and stretched his wings. "And when I get back, I'm going to wring you for every hint about where my vessel is hiding."

Jet found his voice and stood up straight. "Her name is Aleah, and I'm going to find her and bring her here."

44

Jet leaned against the trunk of the tree that composed his little house. The rickety porch was littered with what looked like pecans, but he didn't care, they tasted good—when he could crack them open. He took a long swig of the ale he'd found in barrels in the root cellar and savored the smooth bitter caress on his tongue.

This must have been a brewery at some point. Jet stared out over fields of tall purple grain—Marie had called it amaranth, whatever that was. He knew why this place hadn't been chosen by the former Serran Academy students—mostly teenagers—who lived in the small village at Eremor's center. It was far off the beaten path, huddled up against a mountain slope, whose snow ended halfway down its descent. *And to think this looked like a patch of snowy trees from the sky.*

Jet leaned his head back and soaked in the gentle leaf-splotched sunlight, then took a deep breath of sweet, earthy air. *Rest in peace, Levi.*

They'd buried him that morning in Eremor's ancient graveyard. The whole village had shown up, or at least what Jet had assumed was the whole village—something like forty students, graduates and masters. Levi had been well-loved at Jade Glen.

Jet took another drink. *And to you, Diamondback. I'll never forget you, brother.*

He sighed and set the mug down on the porch, then groaned as he sat up and stretched. Sleeping on the floor hadn't done him any favors, but somehow it had been a more restful slumber than he'd had in days. *I've got a lot of work to do.*

He glanced into the open window behind him, which was really just a curve in the branches that composed the walls. Dust coated the empty floor and bark peeled from the interior walls. *What am I going to do for a living? It's not like Eremor needs security.*

Someone hollered in the distance, and Jet squinted at the crumbling stone house on the other side of the field. Marie telling Thracian where she wanted to plant her new garden, no doubt. Or maybe they were arguing about how to fix the roof.

A rustling drew Jet's attention to the field. Sorvashti peeked her head out from the purple stalks with a wide grin. *"Ayah!"*

Jet chuckled. "Were you trying to scare me?"

"I was doing the test." Sorvashti frolicked up the flagstone path to his porch, swaggering to indicate her new half-skirt and tunic that looked to have been sewn from light fabric and deer hide. "Look what Ellie gets me! She says one of the students gives her this to do the welcome, but she is too fat to wear it."

Jet choked on a laugh. "I doubt she called herself 'fat.' You'd better not say that."

"Oh, is this rude?" Sorvashti skipped up the steps and hugged him tight, then drew back and wrinkled her nose. "You smell of the alcohol."

Jet grew a wide smile. "You've gotta try it."

Her eyes narrowed. "Where do you get this?"

"I'll never tell." Jet picked up his mug and offered it to her. "Come sit with me." He slumped back down on the porch, resolved to acquire patio furniture somehow, and patted a spot next to him.

Sorvashti plopped down beside him and sniffed the mug. Then she downed the entire thing.

Jet stared at her. "Uh, like it?"

She grinned mischievously. "You will tell me where you find this."

Jet chuckled and leaned his head back against the wall. "Ah, I wish we'd have just come here in the first place. Why did we split up after the attack on Jade Glen, again?"

"To get the keystone." The mug clacked on the porch in front of Sorvashti. "But Tera knows of this now, yes? And she sleeps in Ellie's house. Maybe she wakes up one day and tells us where this is."

Right. Now he knew why Ellie had been so adamant about retrieving the keystone—she must have known somehow that the dark angels and Lynx were after it. *Maybe it'll be safe under Eremor's barrier.*

"I like this house." Sorvashti crossed her legs. "It is small but good."

"Oh, really?" Jet said. "I thought you'd prefer the village over a beat-up place on the outskirts like this."

She snorted. "No! I always hate the city." She closed her eyes and took a deep breath.

Jet admired how her new outfit clung to her. "Have you decided on a place to live yet? That big treehouse on the far side would be nice. I can help you get that beehive out."

"I do not want the bees." She opened one eye just enough to peek at him. "I want to live here."

Jet blinked at her. "Oh. Well, I can move. This place needs a lot of fixing up, though."

Her eye closed. "Do not move. This will beat the point."

Jet stared as a breeze tousled Sorvashti's hair. *She doesn't mean...* "You want to live *with* me?"

She sighed. "How can you be so intelligent of some things and not of others?" She crawled around to sit in front of him. "I do not want to live alone, and I think you do not, too."

His heart thudded into a rapid pace. "Are you proposing?"

Sorvashti's brow furrowed. "What is this 'proposing?'"

"Are you asking to marry me?"

She pursed her lips. "No. In LaKota, the man asks the woman." She glanced to the side, then watched him out of the corner of her eye. "So you ask now, yes?"

Jet's breath tumbled out. "Sorva…" He took her hand and leaned closer. "I'm fine right now, but you know I'm sick. Fadahari can't keep me alive forever." He looked down at her smooth fingers, unable to meet her gaze. "You've already lost one husband. I don't want you to go through that again."

"I do not live forever, too. We are the humans." Sorvashti pulled her hand away, slipped it under his chin, and tilted his head up until he met her golden eyes. "I do not care if we live one day or the hundred or the thousand." A smile warmed her cheeks. "Why do we need to live the days alone?"

Jet drowned in her gaze and came up for air with more excitement than he could contain. "Let me find a ring!"

Sorvashti flicked her wrist. "I do not need the ring." She trailed a finger in a design on his shoulder. "Take the oath of my people."

His skin electrified at her touch. "Which one?"

"You choose." Her smile grew mischievous, as if she knew exactly how much she was torturing him. "There are seven—do you remember? I have the *fortlaben*," she said as she tapped her inked shoulder with her other hand, "which is the memory of the ancestors. There is the *mak'ret,* who do all kinds of work. And the *kiri,* who care of the needy ones. Oh! You must want the *han'tesh,* the military—"

"*Oba,*" Jet interrupted. "I choose *oba,* the male leader of a household. We'll start our own clan." He watched her expression, wondering if his suggestion was offensive.

Sorvashti raised her eyebrows, then nodded. "Then I will be of the *oma!*"

Jet couldn't stop a wide smile. "Is there a limit on how many oaths you can take? You already swore *la'avod,* too."

Her eyes narrowed. "Do not tell me what to do." She slid closer and slipped her hands behind his neck. His pulse peaked as she pressed her slender body into his, then kissed him until he burned for her.

Finally she pulled away long enough for him to pant for breath. "When?" He hardly recognized his own voice.

Sorvashti looked over her shoulder at the sun's angle. "It is hard to tell the hour of day in this place. But there is enough time before night, yes?"

God, yes!

"Uh oh!" said a voice below the porch. "We're interrupting something. Let's skedaddle!"

Jet recognized Ellie's voice and stopped breathing. *No. No. What did she...*

He peeked around Sorvashti to see Ellie's back as she hobbled away down the flagstone path, a redheaded girl's mortified expression, and Fadahari's intrigued smirk.

Wait—this is my house, and I can kiss my fiancée whenever I want!

Jet took Sorvashti's hips, picked her up, and sat her down beside him. He stood and hopped down from the porch, deciding to meet them no matter what color his face was. Without a distraction, he might not last until nightfall.

"What can I do for you?" he called after Ellie.

Ellie hesitantly looked back. "I think you should be askin' what I can do for you, buck. Looks like you need someone to officiate somethin'!"

Jet glanced back at Sorvashti, who nodded vigorously. Jet cleared his throat. "You busy this afternoon?"

Fadahari laughed out loud as the redhead hugged herself like she'd just watched a horror film. Ellie rejoined them and winked. "You bet, but we've got other plans for tonight, too, if you're not too busy."

Jet found no place for his hands, and had never stood more awkwardly in his life. "Depends."

"Have you met Cassie?" Ellie put a hand on the girl's shoulder, bouncing her red curls. "She's a weaver who's been with us since Jade Glen."

Jet swallowed and bowed to the girl, who looked away with olive skin blushing the color of a dusk rose.

"The doctor and I have come up with a solution for your illness that just might work," Ellie said. "Cassie can bind Fadahari's healing aether into your lungs, and my valnah energy to eliminate the pain."

Jet stared at her, dumbfounded. "Bind aether to living tissue?" His chest hurt just thinking about it. "Is that possible?"

A sparkle glinted in Ellie's eye. "Zekk's idea… It can work, if we're very careful. Of course Fadahari will still have to monitor you, but it should allow you to live a somewhat normal life—"

"Yes." Jet rushed forward and dropped to his knees in front of them. "Yes, please. I accept."

45

Zekk strained his wings for one last upward draft as he eased the ornate headboard to the ground. Sweat dripped in his eye, and he collapsed to his knees, panting.

Some wedding present, Confidant. You should have just found them a bottle of wine.

But Jet didn't have wings anymore, so he couldn't go scavenge to furnish their new home. And letting him borrow his own feather wasn't a good idea. The Guardian of Mortals would certainly ask questions if anyone but Zekk activated his feather.

Zekk straightened and released his wings, then put a hand on his stomach and hissed. *I'll have to go back for the mattress later or my middle will tear open.*

Life in Eremor would take quite a bit of getting used to. He had no skills that would be useful here, nor did Eremor require a man of his talents. He had no idea where to begin carving out a new, free life. Or even if that was really what he wanted.

But somehow, everything about this place seemed… *real*. No more fake smiles, no more silver platters. Just the dirt under his fingernails and the sun on his skin and the exotic fruits that tasted better than candy. And without having to pay taxes or rent or support a team under him, creating a decent place to live might not take too long.

But the best part about Eremor was that it was apparently hidden from the outside world. If Zekk could learn to trust that intangible magic barrier, maybe his mind would finally stop worrying about what Alon would do if he found out his Confidant was missing.

The only bad thing—aside from the lack of indoor plumbing—was not knowing anyone besides Fadahari. Well, he knew Jet, too, but that didn't really count. The newlywed was going to be his best friend; Jet just didn't know it yet.

"Oh, it's beautiful!"

Zekk turned to see Ellie hobbling toward him, avoiding a clucking red chicken that strutted on the path. She handed him a wooden cup filled with water.

She always knows just what I need. Zekk thanked her and downed the water, then wiped his forehead. "Think they'll like it?"

"They'll like it better than the floor." Ellie bent to examine the floral design carved into the headboard.

"How'd his… uh… procedure go?" Zekk asked, flapping the collar of his shirt to let air in. Despite the ice-capped mountains that rimmed the crater and pierced the sky, Eremor seemed to always be the perfect temperature.

"Just fine. He's happy as a clam's crazy uncle." Ellie picked up her robes and stepped over a sideboard. "So, I hid something from you." She grinned like a child caught with their hand in the cookie jar. "Don't be mad at me, OK, Bubbles?"

Does she have to call me that? Zekk raised an eyebrow at her. "Oh?"

"I wanted to see if you'd be able to pass through the barrier first." Ellie waved her hand toward the house. "This way."

Intrigued, Zekk followed and ducked under the low-hanging door frame. Their quaint log cabin appeared to be more recently built and decorated than the other empty houses, but it still reminded him of a historical exhibit.

Ellie opened the door to her room and beckoned Zekk in. "I've got a secret roommate." She walked around a dresser Zekk had found for her to a thin space between her bed and the wall. There, on a palette on the floor, slept Teravyn Aetherswift.

Zekk's eyes bulged. *She's... here? How did Ellie hide her from me?*

Hard lines shaped Teravyn's face, but her slender features glowed with femininity. Blonde hair swayed around her as if she were underwater, and she almost seemed to float off the floor.

What... the... Zekk couldn't tear his eyes from her. Aside from the eerie floating, Teravyn didn't look half as intimidating as the newscasters made her out to be. "What's wrong with her?"

"Good question," Ellie muttered. "She sacrificed herself so Jet could be resuscitated. They told me she had the keystone, but it vanished when she fell asleep." Ellie leaned over the bed and tugged on a portion of a blanket that had fallen from Teravyn's shoulders. "She's been like this for weeks, but she's still breathing. Apparently she doesn't have any needs. It's like she's lost in time."

The keystone... Zekk concentrated and sensed Teravyn's deep, rich aether—the signature that their best sifters had been sent sniffing after. It thrummed almost as intensely as Darien's.

But another energy flickered in her chest, like a gnat in a wine glass. Zekk took a step closer, but Ellie caught his arm.

"This was your mission," Ellie said, "wasn't it?"

"Not exactly." *But Alon would kill for her. The reward...*

Zekk severed the line of thought. *The reward wouldn't make my life in Maqua any better than it already was.* He stared at the freckles on Teravyn's nose. *Why does Alon want her so badly? What would he do with her?*

He'd never let himself think about what happened to his captives after he brought them in. But after seeing Sorvashti through Jet's eyes, the thought of what might have happened to her in Maqua struck him with disgust and shame.

Zekk knew Teravyn, too, even though she might only recognize him as a high-profile enemy. He'd lost count of the hours spent pouring over every public record of her, looking for any detail that might have led to her capture. He scrutinized hundreds of photos from the internet in which she smiled beside friends, coworkers, or her goofy little brother. He watched her videos and read her blog posts, searching for weaknesses and clues.

But all he found was a genuine, hardworking, beautiful young woman who only wanted to raise her brother right.

She can't be dead.

"Are you going to take her?" Ellie whispered.

"No."

Ellie released Zekk's arm, and he carefully stepped to Teravyn's side. She weighed half what he expected when he lifted her in his arms and laid her on Ellie's bed. Strands of her hair slowly waved over the pillow, like golden stratus clouds drifting on atmospheric wind.

Zekk rested a hand on Teravyn's stomach and concentrated harder. *There's something stuck in her core... What is that?* It was definitely an aether signature, but it tasted... inhuman.

He tugged at it, and the strange energy slid out of her skin and into his hand. He pulled harder.

Light warped and exploded outward, throwing Zekk back against the wall with a wave of force that rattled the cabin. He slid to his rump, and a fist-sized crystalline gem clattered to the floor beside the bed.

Teravyn shot up in bed with a gasp. Wide blue eyes darted around, then focused on him.

"Where am I?"

THE STORY CONTINUES
IN THE SENTINEL TRILOGY BOOK 3: SAGE

JAMIE FOLEY

"The Sentinel Trilogy... is brilliantly written."
—Reader's Favorite, ★★★★★

SAGE

THE SENTINEL TRILOGY BOOK THREE

Now available at a bookstore near you or at www.jamiesfoley.com

Ancient elementals awaken, fracturing a dying world to its core.

Teravyn Aetherswift returns to the land of the living, but everything seems unfamiliar... including her little brother. Zekk offers help, but can an alluring Lynx be trusted?

Sorvashti finally has everything she ever wanted, so the last thing she wants to do is run after traitors. But she won't leave Jet's side—unless the horrifying truth about his mother tears them apart.

Darien is sick of being used and lied to. But if he stands up for what's right, he'll pay the price with his life... or the lives of those he loves.

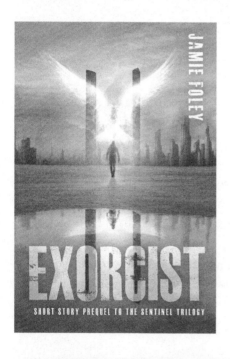
293

GLOSSARY

AEO The god who created the physical world of Alani, the spiritual realm of kai'lani, and all races therein.

AEO LEYWA AI SHEA A phrase used to say goodbye. Means 'Aeo be with you and protect you' in the Ancient language.

AETHRYN One who uses aether.

ALANI The planet on which the story takes place.

D'HAKKA A massive tree-spider native to Katrosi, thought to be extinct. Centuries ago, the bravest of the native Katrosi tribes hunted d'hakka for their scorpion-like tail blade as a rite of passage.

FACET The creator god Aeo made one facet of himself for each of the three races on Alani: angels, elementals, and humans. Facets, similar to demigods, have access to Aeo's deep magic on behalf of their race.

FOLLOWER Someone who follows the way of the creator god Aeo: love, justice, and forgiveness. Followers reject the legend that that Aeo was slain by the elementals and believe that he is still alive in the spiritual realm of kai'lani.

KAI'LANI The spiritual realm. Means 'sky of fire' in the Ancient language.

KEYSTONE An ancient crystal formed of the elemental facet when the *amos* were sealed into prisons of stone. Legends of the keystone's abilities abound, but one common belief is that it functions as a lens for aether, greatly magnifying one's power.

KO'HERZ A Terruthian word meaning 'blood oath.' If one's family member is murdered, they are traditionally bound to kill the murderer and avenge the victim.

LA'AVOD One of the seven LaKotan life-oaths in which a person may devote their life to the protection or service of another for reasons of honor or debt. The person offering *la'avod* becomes a member of the other's household and is protected from abuse under international law. Although the very meaning of the word is 'life bond,' most modern-day *la'avod* oaths last for seven years.

LILLIAN The Malo elemental *amos*, or ruler. Worshipped as a goddess in Malaan. Represented by a white fox with seven tails.

LOCKBURN A sharp pain, usually originating from the back of the skull, that is caused by an invasion of foreign aether into another's mind. The pain increases in severity depending on how long the foreign energy remains in one's mind.

OBA A Terruthian word referring to the male leader of one's household.

ORSO A deity in the form of a wind-serpent worshipped by some humans, who believe he absorbed the creator Aeo's power when the elementals slew him. Other humans believe Orso is an angelic facet of Aeo who rebelled and was cursed.

PERRUNT A Terruthian word meaning 'puppy.'

SERRAN A human who has accepted an angelic feather and undergone a physical transformation. Serrans may summon the wings of their bonded angel at will by placing their aether into their Serran feather.

SHLANGA A Terruthian word meaning 'snake.'

APPENDIX: THE AETHER GIFTS

Every human is born with a spiritual gift: a specialty fueled by the energy source inside their soul, called **aether**. It is regenerated by a human's soul—also called an aether core—and can be sensed by a trained individual called an **aethryn**. Depending on one's gift, aether may be detected in the form of a color, scent, taste, or otherwise.

Each aether gift is associated with a planet in Alani's solar system. There are four common gifts: sentinel, vanguard, arbiter, and valnah. There are four rare gifts: exorcist, healer, sifter, and weaver. The only exceedingly rare gift is sage.

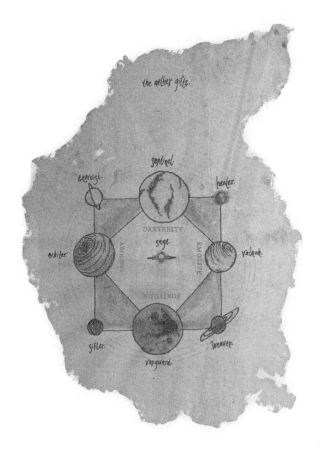

ARBITER

A common aether gift that can transfer thoughts and memories from one mind to another. Master arbiters can create elaborate visions and inflict them upon others.

VALNAH

A common gift that can influence the feelings and emotions of others. 'Valnah' means 'song of courage' in the Ancient language. Master valnah can manipulate many people simultaneously.

EXORCIST

A rare spiritual gift which can siphon another being's aether—whether human or angel. A slang term for an exorcist is 'vampire.' Master exorcists can house a far greater amount of aether than usual for a limited time.

SAGE

An extremely rare spiritual gift that allows the user to see possible futures. Master sages are called 'prophets,' but it's more common for sages to go mad than learn to control their visions.

SENTINEL

A common gift that releases aether in powerful waves or violent blasts. Master sentinels are very efficient and compress their energy into sharpened strikes.

VANGUARD

A common gift that can compact aether into solid walls, varying in toughness depending on the user's skill. Masters can create walls from a distance.

SIFTER

A rare spiritual gift that can sense aether from great distances and conceal one's own aether signature within their core.

HEALER

A rare spiritual gift that can detect injury and fuse torn flesh together with fiery aether. Master healers can learn to cure certain illnesses.

WEAVER

A rare spiritual gift that can bind aether into physical objects. Aether bound by a master weaver will not diminish for a very long time.

APPENDIX: THE ELEMENTS

Each element is associated with one of Alani's celestial objects. **Phoera**, the element of energy, is represented by Alani's sun: a yellow-orange main sequence star.

Aris is equated with Alani's smallest moon, which is covered in a silvery white dust, giving it a bright but blurred appearance in the night sky.

Terruth is represented by Alani's largest moon—the easiest to see with the naked eye.

Malo is equated with Alani's blue-green moon, whose greater mass is thought to have the strongest effect on the tides despite its size. Its dark hue makes it difficult to find.

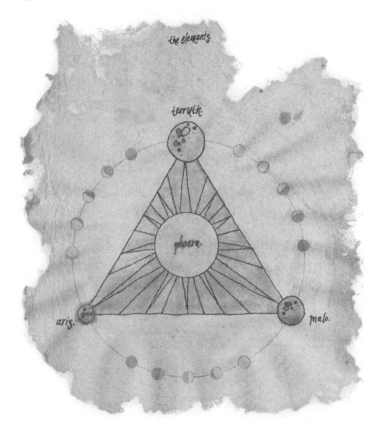

PHOERA

Phoera is the elemental power of energy. Phoeran elementalists can accelerate or decelerate molecules, forcing a state change within an object (heat ice to water and steam, or cool lava into stone).

Phoera can also manipulate electricity and light. Advanced elementalists can bend light around objects, making them invisible.

TERRUTH

Terruth is the elemental ability that allows its user to control anything in solid form. Solid matter such as stone or organic compounds like wood can be lifted, shaped and formed, or broken apart.

A skilled Terruth user could quickly fashion himself tools or weapons in a time of need.

ARIS

Aris is the elemental power to control anything in a gaseous state. The wind and weather obey the commands of an Arisian elementalist.

A masterful Aris user could control an airborne toxin, pull oxygen underwater to allow breathing beneath the surface, or remove the oxygen from a room.

MALO

Malo is the elemental power to control anything in liquid form. This includes water, poisons such as liquid mercury, and lava.

A skilled Malo elementalist is extremely dangerous—they can drown a victim with a surprisingly small amount of water held in the wrong place.

APPENDIX: THE FIRSTBORN

ANGELIC FACET OF THE CREATOR: ORSO

As the demigod of the angelic race, Orso was once renowned as the most beautiful and powerful angel. With access to the creator Aeo's deep magic, he thought himself equal with Aeo. Orso left Aeo's domain and claimed a region in the spiritual realm, kai'lani, for himself. This land is called Zoth.

Aeo rejected Orso for his rebellion, which turned thousands of angels--including two archangels--away from him and caused immeasurable chaos in the spiritual and physical realms. He cursed Orso to crawl on his belly by removing his hind legs.

Orso is depicted as a wind serpent, with the head, wings, and forelegs of a dragon, but the body and tail of a great snake.

ANGEL BREEDS & WING TYPES

Shimmerwing: Designed for high speeds and diving, the wings of these slender gryphon-like angels can reflect aether.

Ironfeather: Designed for soaring great heights, the massive wingspans of these minotaur-like angels can become impenetrable.

Quillsong: Designed for agility, the feathers of these cat-like angels can absorb large amounts of aether.

PRIME ARCHANGELS

Angel of Life: Ezrel, quillsong
Angel of Death: Rigel, shimmerwing
Angel of Song: Zimrah, ironfeather

ARCHANGELS

Guardian of the Chosen: Kohesh, ironfeather
Guardian of Portals: Chianti, shimmerwing
Guardian of the Land: Nephtai'el, ironfeather
Guardian of Knowledge: Sorrel, quillsong

APPENDIX: THE SECONDBORN

ELEMENTAL FACET OF THE CREATOR: KARYS

As the demigod of the elemental race, Karys bore all four elements with grace and dignity. But soon after the world's birth, humans began worshipping elementals instead of the creator. The amos—Nuri and Lillian in particular—entrenched themselves as rulers over humans of their elemental bloodline and waged war on any who did not submit.

The world became so evil and corrupt that Aeo regretted his creation and prepared to destroy it. But Karys sacrificed herself to imprison the four elemental *amos* in prisons of stone, causing herself to become the key—known as the keystone—that sealed them.

Although this occurred thousands of years ago, some humans still follow the religions of elemental polytheism. And some *trai'yeth,* whose prisons did not require the keystone to open, have been released by humans and walk free to this day.

AMOS

Meaning 'king' in the Ancient language, the *amos* serve as the central source of power for their element on Alani. There is only one *amos* per element.

Phoera: Nuri	**Terruth:** Roth	**Malo:** Lillian	**Aris:** Yvonne
The radiant dragon	*The wise owl*	*The seven-tailed fox*	*The gentle ram*
Honor & discipline	*Peace & patience*	*Fertility & generosity*	*Grace & joy*

TRAI'YETH

There are seven *trai'yeth* per element, who serve as stewards of the syn—the metallic substance that grants control of one's element for both elementals and humans. *Trai'yeth* means 'sealing vessel' in the Ancient language, hinting at their ability to store syn inside themselves. Their duty is to regulate the use of and return excess to the *amos.*

The *trai'yeth* are known for their ability to take the shape of any creature, so long as they have a sample of its DNA. If struck in center mass, they will revert to their prison of stone until reawakened—they are semi-mortal and bound to the physical realm.

PHOERAN TRAI'YETH

Felix Kael Tae, the green-eyed fox
Luck, stealth, & cunning

Brynn, the pale bear
Snow, winter, & loneliness

Neema, the flame salamander
Volcanoes & anger

Zamara, the emberhawk
Music, singing, & dreams

Solara, the trace cat
Combat & warfare

Anarys, the hydra
Festivals & humor

Raisho, the lazy hound
Family, the home, & the hearth

ARISIAN TRAI'YETH

Thrace, the white eagle
Storms & time

Regina, the regal crane
Royalty & lineage

Arianne, the noble stag
The breath of life & purity

Arielle, the mountain lion
Intellect & forethought

Brandon, the crow
Language & writing

Leander, the aether wyrm
Astronomy & light

Deirdre, the cricket
Dawn, dew, & the breeze

TERRUTHIAN TRAI'YETH

Equestus, the stallion
Exploration & commerce

Flint, the tusked boar
Crafting & forging

Sanger Terrúvyn, the longhorn
The harvest & animal husbandry

Zepphora, the ragged wolf
The hunt & caretaking of the environment

Esther, the gentle rabbit
Self-control & forgiveness

Ashena, the oliphant
Earthquakes, canyons, & rivers

Farrah, the blood hawk
Justice & law

MALO TRAI'YETH

Shayara, the seagull
Rain & mercy

Xavian, the d'hakka
Sickness, plague, & poison

Serene, the leviathan
Oceans & death

Tahiri, the xavi
Art & beauty

Tameru, the peacock
Gardens, herbalism, & medicine

Jasper, the laughing dolphin
Creatures of the sea, fishing, & luck

Koryn, the giant sea turtle
The seasons & the afterlife

FAYETTE
══ PRESS ══

If you enjoy *The Sentinel Trilogy*,
you'll probably love these other clean fantasy series:

THE
STONES OF TERRENE

THE
THREE ROYAL CHILDREN
AND THE **BATTY AUNT**

THE
UNDERWORLD MYTHOS

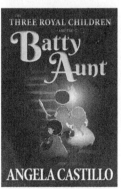

Welcome to Terrene—where dragons exist, the past haunts, and magic is no myth. Welcome aboard the Sapphire.

When Prince Torrin sees a light in a forgotten palace tower, he meets a mysterious aunt who unlocks a world of adventure he and his siblings will never forget.

Josh stumbled into the Underworld—rife with backstabbing fae and ancient powers—and he can't get out.

Made in the USA
Coppell, TX
14 November 2020

41380934R00184